Maybe This Time

Maybe This Time

JENNIFER CRUSIE

ST. MARTIN'S PRESS

NEW YORK

This is a work of fiction. All of the characters, organizations, and events portrayed in this novel are either products of the author's imagination or are used fictitiously.

MAYBE THIS TIME. Copyright © 2010 by Argh Ink, LLC. All rights reserved. Printed in the United States of America. For information, address St. Martin's Press, 175 Fifth Avenue, New York, N.Y. 10010.

www.stmartins.com

ISBN 978-0-312-30378-5

First Edition: September 2010

10 9 8 7 6 5 4 3 2 1

This book is for

Sarah and Cecilia

who want cereal for breakfast every day
and who fill those days with joy.

My Thanks To

THE GLINDAS and the ARGH PEOPLE,
who suffered through this book with me

GAIL HOGAN,
who helped me with the TV research
and who is *nothing* like Kelly O'Keefe

HEIDI and DAN CULLINAN,
who suggested the salvia

BROOKE BRANNON, SUE DANIC, MOLLY HASELHORST,
LANI DIANE RICH, ROXANNE RICHARDSON, and
ANNE STUART,
who beta read brilliantly

RACHEL PLACHCINSKI,
who gave me the original house that became Archer House,
a picture of herself as a small child that became Alice,
a translation of American English into British English for
one character,
and constant support throughout the writing of this
(as in, "Hurry up and finish the [British expletive deleted]
book, Crusie")

JODI REAMER and AMY BERKOWER,
who went above and beyond the call of agenthood . . . again

JENNIFER ENDERLIN,
the finest editor an author can have

and
HENRY JAMES and TRUMAN CAPOTE,
who were here first.

Maybe This Time

This book takes place in 1992.
Because.

One

*A*ndie Miller sat in the reception room of her ex-husband's law office, holding on to ten years of uncashed alimony checks and a lot of unresolved rage. *This is why I never came back here,* she thought. *Nothing wrong with repressed anger as long as it stays repressed.*

"Miss Miller?"

Andie jerked her head up and a lock of hair fell out of her chignon. She stuffed it back into the clip on the back of her head as North's neat, efficient secretary smiled at her, surrounded by the propriety of his Victorian architecture. If that secretary had a chignon, nothing would escape from it. North was probably crazy about her.

"Mr. Archer will see you now," the secretary said.

"Well, good for him." Andie stood up, yanked on the hem of the only suit jacket she owned, and then wondered if she'd sounded hostile.

"He's really very nice," the secretary said.

"No, he isn't." Andie strode across the ancient rug to the door of North's office, opened it before the secretary could get in ahead of her, and then stopped.

North sat behind his walnut desk, his cropped blond hair almost white in the sunlight from the window behind him. His wire-rimmed glasses had slid too far down his nose again, and his shirtsleeves were rolled up over his forearms—*Still playing racquetball,* Andie thought—and his shoulders were as straight as ever as he studied the papers spread out across the polished top of the desk. He looked exactly the way he had ten years ago when she'd bumped her suitcase on the door frame on her way out of town—

"Miss Miller is here," his secretary said from behind her, and he looked up at her over his glasses, and the years fell away, and she was right back where she'd begun, staring into those blue-gray eyes, her heart pounding.

After what seemed like forever, he stood up. "Andromeda. Thank you for coming."

She crossed the office, smiled tightly at him over the massive desk, decided that shaking his hand would be weird, and sat down. "I called you, remember? Thank you for seeing me."

North sat down, saying, "Thank you, Kristin," to his secretary, who left.

"So the reason I called—" Andie began, just as he said, "How is your mother?"

Oh, we're going to be polite. "Still crazy. How's yours?"

"Lydia is fine, thank you." He straightened the papers on his desk into one stack.

A lot of really big trees had died to make that desk. His mother had probably gnawed them down, used her nails to saw the boards, and finished the decorative cutwork with her tongue.

"I'll tell her you asked after her."

"She'll be thrilled. Say hi to Southie for me, too." Andie opened her purse, took out the stack of alimony checks, and put them on the desk. "I came to give these back to you."

North looked at the checks for a moment, the strong, sharp planes of his face shadowed by the back light from the window.

Say something, she thought, and when he didn't, she said, "They're all there, one hundred and nineteen of them. November nineteen eighty-two to last month."

His face was as expressionless as ever. "Why?"

"Because they're a link between us. We haven't talked in ten years but every month you send me a check even though you know I don't want alimony. Which means every month I get an envelope in the mail that says I used to be married to you. And every month I don't cash them, and it's like we're nodding in the street or something. We're still *communicating.*"

"Not very well." North looked at the stack. "Why now?"

"I'm getting married."

She watched him go still, the pause stretching out until she said, "North?"

"Congratulations. Who's the lucky man?"

"Will Spenser," Andie said, pretty sure North wouldn't know him.

"The writer?"

"He's a great guy." She thought about Will, tall, blond, and genial. The anti-North: He never forgot she existed. "I'm ready to settle down, so I'm drawing a line under my old life." She nodded at the checks. "That's why I came to give you those back. Don't send any more. Please."

After a moment, he nodded. "Of course. Congratulations. The family will want to send a gift." He pulled his legal pad toward him. "Are you registered?"

"No, I'm not registered," Andie said, exasperated. "Technically, I'm not even engaged yet. He asked me, but I needed to give you the checks back before I said yes." She didn't know why she'd expected him to have a reaction to the news. It wasn't as if he still cared. She wasn't sure he'd cared when she'd left.

"I see. Thank you for returning the checks."

North straightened the papers on his desk again, and then looked down at the top paper for a long moment, as if he were reading it. He'd probably forgotten she was there again because his work was—

He looked up. "Perhaps, since you haven't said yes yet, you could postpone your new life."

"What?"

"I have a problem you could help with. It would only take you a few months, maybe less—"

"North, did you even hear what I said?"

"—and we'd pay you ten thousand dollars a month, plus expenses, room, and board."

She started to protest and then thought, *Ten thousand dollars a month?*

He straightened the folder on his desk again. "Theodore Archer, a distant cousin, died two years ago and made me the guardian of his two children."

Ten thousand a month. There had to be a catch. Then the rest of what he'd said hit her. "Children?"

"I went down to see them at the family home where their aunt was taking care of them. They'd been living there with their father, their grandmother, and their aunt since the little girl was born eight years ago, but the grandmother had died before Theodore."

"Down? They're not here in Ohio?"

"The house is in a remote area in the south of the state. The place is isolated, but the children seemed fine with their aunt, so we agreed it was best that they'd stay there with her in order to disrupt their lives as little as possible."

And to disrupt yours as little as possible, Andie thought.

North waited, as if he expected her to say it out loud. When she didn't, he went on. "Unfortunately, the aunt died in June. Since then I've hired three nannies, but none have stayed."

"Lot of death in the family," Andie said.

"The children's mother died in childbirth with the little girl.

The grandmother died in her seventies of a heart attack. Theodore was killed in a car accident. The aunt fell from a tower on the house—"

"Wait, the house has *towers*?"

"It's a very old house," North said, his tone making it clear that he didn't want to discuss towers. "The battlements are crumbling, and she evidently leaned on the wrong stone and fell into the moat."

"The moat," Andie said. "Is this a joke?"

"No. Theodore's great-great-grandfather had the house brought over from England in the 1850s. I don't know why he dug a moat. The point is, these children have nobody, and they're alone down there in the middle of nowhere with only the housekeeper taking care of them. If you will go down there, I will pay you ten thousand a month to . . . fix them."

"Fix them," Andie said. Ten thousand a month was ridiculous, but it would pay off her credit card bills and her car. In one month. Ten thousand dollars would mean she could get married without debt. Not that Will cared, but it would be better to go to him free and clear. "What do you mean, fix them?"

"The children are . . . odd. We wanted to bring them here in June after their aunt's death, but the little girl had a psychotic break when the nanny tried to take her away from the house. The boy was sent away to boarding school at the beginning of August, but he's been expelled for setting fires. I need someone to go down there and stabilize the children, bring their education up to standard for their grade level so they can go to public school, and then move them up here with us."

Andie shook her head and another chunk of hair slipped out of her chignon. "Psychotic breaks and setting fires," she said, as she stuffed it back. "North, I teach high school English. I have no idea how to help kids like this. You need—"

"I need somebody who doesn't care about the way things are supposed to be," he said, his eyes sliding to her neck. "I think that's where the nannies are going wrong. I need somebody who will do the unconventional thing without blinking. Somebody who will get things done." He met her eyes. "Even if she doesn't stay for the long haul."

"Hey," Andie said.

"I would take it as a personal favor. I've never asked you for anything—"

"You asked for a divorce." As soon as she said it, she knew it was a mistake.

He looked at her over the tops of his glasses, exasperated. "I did not ask you for a divorce."

"Yes you did," Andie said, in too far to stop now. "You told me that I seemed unhappy, and if that was true, you would understand if I divorced you."

"You were playing 'Any Day Now' every time I came up to the attic. As hints go, it was pretty broad."

He looked annoyed, so that was something, but it didn't do anything for her anger. "There are people who, if their spouses are unhappy, try to do something about it."

"I did. I gave you a divorce. You had one foot out the door anyway. Do we need to review that again?"

"No. The divorce is a dead subject." *And the ghost of it is sitting right here with us.* Although maybe only with her. North didn't looked haunted at all.

"I realize you're getting ready to start a new life," he went on. "But if you haven't made plans yet, there's no reason you couldn't wait a few months. You could use the money for the wedding."

"I don't want a wedding, I want to get married. Why are you offering me ten thousand dollars a month for babysitting? You didn't pay the nannies that. It's ridiculous. For ten thousand a month, you should not only get child care, you should get your house cleaned, your laundry done, your tires rotated, and if I were you, I'd insist on nightly blow jobs. Did you think I wouldn't notice that you're still trying to keep your thumb on me?" She shook her head, and the lock of hair fell out of her chignon again. Well, the hell with that, too.

He sat very still, and then he said, "Why do you have your hair yanked back like that?" sounding as annoyed as she was.

"Because it's *professional*."

"Not if it keeps falling down."

"Thank you," Andie said. "Now butt out. Ten thousand is too much money. You're still trying to pay me off—"

"Andromeda, I'm asking for a favor, a big one, and I don't think the money is out of line. We didn't leave our marriage enemies, so I don't see why you're hostile now."

"I'm not hostile," Andie said, and then added fairly, "well, okay, I am hostile. You didn't do anything to save our marriage ten years ago, but every month you send a check so I'll think of you again. It's passive aggressive. Or something. You know the strongest memory I have of you? Sitting right there, behind that desk. You'd think I'd remember you naked with all the mattress time we clocked in that year together, but no, it's you, staring at me from behind all that walnut as if you weren't quite sure who I was. You have no idea how many times I wanted to take an ax to that damn desk just to see if you'd *notice me*."

North looked down at his desk, perplexed.

"You hide behind it," Andie said, sitting back now that she wasn't repressing anything anymore. "You use it to keep from getting emotionally involved."

"I use it to write on."

"You know what I mean. It gives you distance."

"It gives me storage. Have you lost your mind?"

Andie looked at him for a moment, sitting there rigid and polite and completely inaccessible. "Yes. It was a bad idea coming back here. I should go now." She stood up.

"She said the house is haunted," North said.

"Excuse me?"

"The last nanny. She said there were ghosts in the house. I asked the local police to look into things to see if somebody was playing tricks, but they found nothing. I think it's the kids, but if I send another nanny down there like the previous ones, she's going to quit, too. I need somebody different, somebody who's tough, somebody who can handle the unexpected. Somebody like you. And you're the only person like you that I know." Suddenly he was the old North again, warm and real with that light in his eyes as he looked at her. "They're little kids, Andie. I can't get them out of there, and I can't leave them there, and with Mother in France, I can't leave the practice long enough to find out what's going on, and even if I could, I don't know anything about kids. I need you."

Ouch. "I don't—"

"Everybody they've ever been close to has died," North said quietly. "Everybody they've ever loved has left them."

Bastard, Andie thought. "I can't give you months. That's ridiculous."

North nodded, looking calm, but she'd been married to him for a year so she knew: He was going in for the kill. "Give them one month then. You can draw your line under us, we don't need to talk, you can send reports to Kristin, hell, take your fiancé down there with you."

"I'm the least maternal person I know," Andie said, thinking, *Ten thousand dollars.* And more than that, two helpless kids who'd lost everyone they loved, going crazy in the middle of nowhere.

"I don't think they need maternal," he said. "I think they need you."

"A psychotic little girl and a boy who's growing up to be a serial killer. He didn't push his aunt off that tower, did he?"

"They're growing up alone, Andie," North said, and Andie thought, *Oh, hell.*

The problem was, he sounded sincere. Well, he always did, he was good at that, but now that she really looked at him, he had changed.

She could see the stress in his face, the lines that hadn't been there ten years ago, the tightening of the skin over his bones, the age in the hollows under his eyes. His brother Southie probably still looked as smooth as a boiled egg, but North was still trapped behind that damn desk, taking care of everyone in the family. And now there were two more in the family, and he was handling it alone.

And two little kids were even more alone in a big house somewhere in the wilds of southern Ohio.

"Please," North said, those gray-blue eyes fixed on her.

"Yes," Andie said.

He drew a deep breath. "Thank you." Then he put his glasses back on, professional again. "There's a household account you can draw on for any expenses, and a credit card. The housekeeper will clean and cook for you. If you come by tomorrow, Kristin will give you a copy of this folder with everything you need in it and your first check, of course."

Andie sat there for a moment, a little stunned that she'd said yes. She'd felt the same way after he'd proposed.

"I'd appreciate it if you could go down as soon as possible."

"Right." She shoved her hair back, picked up her purse, and stood up again. "I'll drive down tomorrow and see what I can do. You have a good winter terrorizing the opposing counsel."

She headed for the door, refusing to look back. This was good. She'd given back the checks and cut the connection, so she could spare a month to save two orphans. Will was in New York for the next two weeks anyway, and he'd come home to a fiancée with no debt, and then—

"Andie," North said, and she turned back in the doorway.

"Thank you," he said, standing now behind his desk, tall and lean and beautiful and looking at her the way he'd used to.

Get out of here. "You're welcome."

Then she turned and walked out before he could say or do anything else that made her forget she was done with him.

. . .

After Andie left, North sat for a moment considering the possibility that he'd lost his mind. He'd had the résumés of several excellent nannies on his desk, and he'd hired his ex-wife instead. *Fuck,* he thought, and deliberately put her out of his mind, which was difficult since she'd mentioned blow jobs. Which were irrelevant because he and Andie were over, had been for ten years. *Blow jobs.* No, she was right: Draw a line under it. He went back to work, making notes on his newest case as the shadows grew longer and Kristin left for the night, definitely not thinking about Andie, his black capital letters spaced evenly in straight rows, as firm and as clear as his thinking—

He stopped and frowned at the page. Instead of "Indiana" he'd written "Andiana." He marked an *I* over the *A* but the word sat there on the page, misspelled and blotted, a dark spot on the clear pattern of his day.

There was a knock on the door at the same time it opened.

"North!" his brother Sullivan said as he came in, his tie loosened and his face as genial as ever under his flop of brown hair.

Say hi to Southie for me, Andie had said. It had been ten years since anybody had called Sullivan "Southie."

"You look like hell." Sullivan lounged into the same chair Andie had taken and put his feet on the desk. "You can't work round the clock. It's not healthy."

Your whole life isn't the damn law firm, North, Andie had said a month before she'd left him. *You have a life. And you have me although not for much longer if you don't knock off this I-live-for-my-work crap.*

"I like my work," he said to his brother now. "How's Mother?"

"Now that's health. That woman was built for distance."

North pictured their elegant, platinum-haired mother running a marathon in her pearls, kicking any upstarts out of the way with the pointed end of her heels as she crossed the finish line. She'd been thrilled when Andie left.

"It's you I'm worried about," Sullivan was saying. "You're working too hard, too much on your plate, trying to run the whole practice with Mother gone—"

"My plate is fine. However, I am in the middle of—"

"No, no, it's time I helped out." Sullivan smiled at him. "I've been thinking about what I could do, but I figure you'd fall on your number two pencil before you'd let me help with the practice."

North looked down at the black pen mark that made "Andiana" such a blot. A number two pencil would be a good idea if he was going to start making mistakes.

"So I was thinking of something a little more in my area and out of yours," Sullivan said. "People. You're not a people person, North. I am."

"People." North turned the top sheet on his legal pad over so he didn't have to look at the blot. *Andiana. What the hell?*

"You remember those two kids that second cousin left you a while back?"

"Yes," North said, fairly sure that had been a rhetorical question, although with Sullivan, you never knew.

"I thought I might drop in, check on things for you, see how they're doing."

North looked up at that. "You want to 'drop in' to the wilds of southern Ohio to visit two children you've never met."

"Yes."

"Why?"

Sullivan grinned at him. "I want to see the house."

"The house isn't worth anything. It's in the middle of nowhere."

"It's haunted."

"Sullivan, there are no such things as ghosts," North said, and for a moment he was twelve again and Sullivan was six, staring wide-eyed into the room where their father was laid out in his coffin. *He's not going to sit up, Southie,* North had said then. *He's dead. There's no such thing as ghosts.*

"I know that," Sullivan said now. "But I want to see a house that everybody thinks is haunted."

"'Everybody' being a nanny who got bored and wanted out."

"Other people have thought so, lots of rumors. So I thought I'd go down there and talk to some of the people. See what's going on."

"And how did you find out about these rumors?"

"I did some research for a friend of mine. She's interested in hauntings, and she looked me up at a party and talked to me about the house and, you know, it *is* interesting."

"She," North said, Sullivan's motives becoming much clearer now. The combination of a shiny new hobby and a shiny new girlfriend must have been irresistible.

"Kelly O'Keefe. The ghost thing is fascinating. I've talked to—"

"Kelly O'Keefe?" North thought of the tiny, sharp-faced, sharp-tongued newscaster he'd avoided after one viewing. "The little blonde with the teeth on Channel Twelve?"

"They're very good teeth," Sullivan said, going for indignant and missing.

"They look like they were very expensive," North said, and re-membered Andie the first time he'd seen her, her big eyes dancing, her curly hair wild, her wide smile flashing her overlapped front teeth. She'd never had her teeth fixed.

"Well, you need good teeth for TV."

"True." That had been the first thing his mother had said about her. *For God's sake, North, get her teeth fixed.*

"The close-ups are murder," Sullivan said.

And he'd said, *I like her teeth. I like everything about her. And now you do, too, Mother.*

Sullivan was looking at him oddly. "Are you okay?"

"I'm fine," North said.

"Okay. Well, then, I'd like to take Kelly down there and look into the ghosts. I can check on the kids for you while I'm there."

"I'd prefer you didn't," North said bluntly. "I don't see Kelly O'Keefe being a good experience for them."

"No, no, she's not interested in reporting on kids anymore, she's on to ghosts now. She found out that the house was originally a haunted house in England and she's very excited about it. Did you know they brought the house over here in pieces and rebuilt it? Kelly could be really grateful if I took her down there. Plus, I'd get to investigate a haunted house. I've talked to two highly regarded ghost experts and there's something behind this stuff. I told the experts that there's a haunted house in the family, and one of them would like to see it. Kelly would like to see it. *I'd* like to see it. We won't talk to the kids."

"The children own the house, so it's not in our immediate family," North said, picking up his pencil again. "And you're not going to disrupt their lives because you think you might like to be a Ghostbuster."

"No, no, I told you, we won't bother the kids. My plan is that I take Kelly and Dennis, the expert, down there, we talk to people—not the kids, adults only—I see what's going on and report back to you, you get to know the kids are safe, Dennis gets more research, Kelly gets her video whatsis . . ." Sullivan shrugged. "We all win. Plus, I get away from Columbus before Mother gets back from Paris. She doesn't like Kelly. Says she's all teeth and hair."

North looked at his little brother with an exasperation he hadn't felt in years. *Southie's permanently thirteen,* Andie had said. *Thirty-four hobbies and a hard-on.* But she'd been laughing when she'd said it . . . "Southie, when are you going to stand up to Mother?"

"Southie?" Sullivan said.

"What?"

"You called me 'Southie.' You haven't called me that in years."

"Well, grow up and I'll never call you that again. You're running down there because you don't want to face Mother with your latest career plan or girlfriend. It's not much of a rebellion if you keep running away."

"I'm not rebelling. I don't have anything to rebel against. I have a great life. And to keep my life great, I'd like to avoid unpleasantness while learning about something that interests me and makes my girlfriend happy. Plus the last nanny quit last week so the kids are there alone. That's not—"

"The children are not alone."

"You hired another nanny?" Sullivan shook his head. "She won't last. Better I should go—"

"This one will last." North hesitated and then said, "I sent Andromeda."

"*Andie?*" Sullivan whistled and then grinned. "Ghosts versus Andie. The supernatural is going to get its ass kicked. I didn't even know she was back in town. When did you talk to her?"

"Today. She's going down there tomorrow."

Sullivan smiled. "Called me 'Southie,' did she?"

"What?"

"That's why you called me 'Southie.' Andie did it first."

"Yes," North said, realizing it was true. Half an hour with Andie and ten years were yesterday. "She sent her regards."

"She changed much?"

"Her hair's . . . different," North said, remembering her sitting in that chair, bundled up in an awful suit jacket, all those crazy curls yanked back, her face scowling as she argued with him. And then that one lock of hair, sliding down her neck—

"Her *hair's* different?" Southie said. "You see your ex-wife for the first time in ten years and that's all you got?"

"She looked . . ." Serious. Tense. Her old smile gone. ". . . quiet. She looked tired." He shook that thought out of his head. "She was only here for twenty minutes. I didn't pay that much attention."

"Twenty minutes in the old days, and she'd have had you on your knees."

"Southie," North said repressively.

"I remember the first time I saw her," Southie went on, ignoring him. "I was supposed to talk you into an annulment, and her old clunker of a car pulled up, and you said, 'There she is,' and she got out and came walking toward us, and I knew there wasn't going to be an annulment. I told you she looked like there was music playing in her head, and you said, 'Yeah, it's—'"

"'Layla,'" North said, seeing her again, moving across the lawn that bright summer day, the bounce in her step translating to the bounce in her hips, everything about her electric and alive and smiling at him . . .

"So does she still move to 'Layla'?"

"Yes," North said, remembering her walking across the carpet to him. "Except now it's the acoustic version."

Southie grinned. "I can't wait to see her again. So we'll go down this weekend—"

North thought of Andie opening the door and finding Southie and his toothy, microphone-wielding girlfriend on the step with some charlatan ghost expert. "No."

"Maybe she could use your help," Southie said. "The two of you used to—"

"She's getting married again. Now if we're finished here . . ." North looked back to his notes as a hint, but when Southie didn't say anything, he looked up.

"I'm sorry," Southie said, his face kind. "I really am."

The twinge North had felt when she'd told him stabbed at him again and he put a lid on it again. "Why? We've been divorced for ten years. It's not as if I thought she was coming back."

"Yeah, but it's still a shock. At least it is to me. Maybe I thought she was coming back."

"Well, she's not," North said, more sharply than he'd intended.

"So, who's the guy? What do we know about him?"

Southie looked serious now, which was always a bad sign.

"Will Spenser. The writer."

"The true crime guy?" Southie said, raising his eyebrows.

"I think he writes mystery fiction, too."

"Probably not much difference. What did the McKennas find out about him?"

North gathered his patience. "I did not put a private detective on my ex-wife's fiancé."

"Right, she was just here, you haven't had time. Want me to call Gabe for you?"

"No."

Southie shook his head. "You know, she used to be family. As far as I'm concerned she still is. We need to look out for her. This guy could have anything in his past. He's a writer, for Christ's sake."

"No," North said.

"And I should go down and check on her in that house," Southie went on as if North hadn't spoken. "I can't believe you sent her down there without backup. God knows what's down there."

"Two kids and a housekeeper. You're not going."

Southie sighed. "Kelly's not going to be happy."

"Such is life."

Southie hesitated and the silence stretched out. "All right then," he said, standing up. "You going to see Andie again?"

"No. You have a good evening." North flipped the page back to where it had been as a signal for Southie to leave and saw the "Andiana" in the middle of the page again. "Damn."

"What's wrong?" Southie said.

"I made a mistake." North flipped the pad shut, annoyed with himself.

"Sending Andie down there?"

"What?" he said, looking up.

"You think you made a mistake sending Andie down there?"

"No," North said, and then thought about Andie, down in the wilds of southern Ohio. She might like it. She'd been wandering around ever since they'd divorced, moving someplace new every year, teaching in some really godforsaken places. Maybe that had been his mistake, keeping her in the city. Trying to keep her at all He shook his head. "No, it wasn't a mistake. She'll handle things."

"Yeah, she will," Southie said, his voice odd, and when North looked up, he saw Southie regarding him sympathetically. "Maybe you should go down there. Get out of the office, check to make sure she's all right. Spend a night in the place so you know what it's like."

"She's fine."

Southie waited a moment and then said quietly, "You could have gone after her, you know."

North looked at him blankly. "Why would I go after her? She'll be fine down there."

"Not now. *Then*. When she left. You could have gone—"

"No."

"You ever think maybe that divorce was a mistake?"

"No," North said, putting as much "you-should-leave-now" in his voice as possible.

"Because I always thought it was," Southie said. "If you'd gone after her, you could have gotten her back. That's all she wanted, she was just lonely—"

"Was there anything else?" North said coldly. "Because unlike you, I have work to do."

"Right. Well, you have a good time with your work," Southie said, and left, shaking his head.

Damn it. The divorce hadn't been a mistake. She'd been miserable. He'd been miserable because she was miserable. Going after her wouldn't have changed that. They were both happier now. He had work to do.

She'd looked so good, warm and round; sounded so good, the old huskiness of her voice brushing down his spine; moved so good, her step still in that old rocking rhythm—

And now she was getting married again. Good for her. Moving on . . .

He pulled his notebook back in front of him and then thought,

Maybe good for her. Because Southie was right, he didn't know any-thing about this yahoo she was getting engaged to. She probably didn't, either. She'd married him after twelve hours of phenomenal sex, she could be lunging into another mistake. And she hadn't smiled. She'd smiled all the time when they were married. In the beginning.

He picked up the phone and called the detective agency the firm used and ordered a background check on Will Spenser.

Then he flipped open the notebook to go back to work and saw the "Andiana" blot.

No, he thought, and ripped out the page and copied the whole thing over again. With no mistakes.

By late afternoon the next day, Andie had finished packing and tying off the loose ends of her life. There weren't many loose ends since she'd been moving around the country for ten years, which tended to limit most ends, loose or otherwise, but she did call Will in New York to tell him the good news. "Ten thousand dollars, Will. It'll pay off all my debts with some left over. I'm being prac-tical and mature here."

"I don't care about your debts," he said, sounding exasperated, and she pictured his handsome boyish face, scowling at her for the two seconds he could hold a scowl before he started to grin again. "I'll pay your debts. What I'd really like to hear is that you're going to marry me."

Of course, Andie thought, and said, "Maybe." She heard a thunk-ing sound on the other end of the phone. "What's that?"

"That's me beating my head against the wall."

Andie grinned. "That's you beating the phone against your mouse pad."

"Same difference. Do you take this long to answer all your mar-riage proposals?"

It took me five seconds to say yes to North. "Yes. I ponder them, and the guys get bored and wander off. Will, I want to do this, it really is important to me to be free and clear financially before I start a new life. I've been spinning my wheels for ten years. I want a new start with nothing left over from before."

"Okay," he said in that easygoing voice she loved. He was so Not-North. "Call me often. Tell me you love working with kids and want to have twenty."

"Twenty?" Andie said, alarmed. "I don't want any."

"Well, maybe you'll change your mind." Will hesitated and then he said, "You won't be seeing North, will you?"

Andie frowned at the phone. "Are you jealous? Because, trust me, he'd forgotten I existed until I showed up in his office. And no, I won't be seeing him."

"Nobody has ever forgotten you," Will said with feeling. "Just remember who you're potentially engaged to."

"How could I forget?" Andie said, and moved on to the I-love-yous before North became a permanent part of their conversation. Then she picked up the last of her three suitcases and her CD player and went out to deal with her mother, who was standing on the sidewalk in front of her little brick German Village cottage in her jeans and faded Iron Maiden T-shirt, looking worried as she stared at Andie's ten-year-old bright yellow Mustang.

"I don't like this," Flo said, for the fortieth time, her long, curly, graying hair bobbing as she shook her head. "I dreamed about you last night. You fell into a well."

"Thank you, Flo." Andie opened the hatchback. "That's encouraging."

"It means your subconscious is calling to you. You've been repressing something. That's what the water means anyway. The falling part is probably about being out of control, or since it's you, maybe it's about running away. You know what a bolter you are."

"I am not a bolter," Andie said to her mother, not for the first time. "I go toward things, not away from them."

"I think you got the bolting thing from your father," Flo said. "You're very like him."

"I wouldn't know," Andie said coldly. "Except that I don't desert children, so no, I'm not like him."

"Don't go," Flo said.

"Because you had a dream? No." Andie put the suitcase in the car next to the sewing machine she'd already stashed there.

"There was so much negative energy in your marriage," Flo fretted.

That wasn't negative energy, that was raging lust. "I'm not revisiting my marriage. I'm taking care of two orphaned kids for a month—"

"This is a terrible time astrologically," Flo went on as if she hadn't spoken. "Your Venus is in North's Capricorn—"

Andie slammed the hatchback closed. "Flo, my Venus isn't anywhere near North. If his Capricorn was in my Venus, I could see your point, but it's staying here in Columbus while I go south." She went around and opened the back door of the car and shoved over the boxes of school supplies that Kristin had given her to make room for her stereo while her mother obsessed about her life.

"North is a powerful man, and you're still connected to him." Flo frowned. "Probably sexual memory, those Capricorns are insatiable. Well, you know, Sea Goat. And of course, you're a Fish. You'll end up back in bed with him."

Andie slammed the car door. "You know what I'd like for Christmas, Flo? Boundaries. You can gift me early if you'd like."

"If you keep seeing North, he's going to get you again, and you were so miserable with him—"

"I'm not seeing North. I'm going to have a stable, secure relationship with a good man who loves me and won't desert me for his career. Which reminds me. I left that stupid suit jacket on the bed, so the next time you're at Goodwill, drop it off, will you? I don't know why I kept it. I'm never going to be near anybody who'll want me to wear a suit again."

Flo folded her arms. "Will's a Gemini. Volatile. Well, he's a writer. You're not sexually compatible, you're both so scattered. You must be all over the place in bed."

"*Boundaries,* Flo," Andie said, thinking, *The sex is just fine.* Not wall-banging, earth-shattering, oh-my-god sex, but fun and energetic and damn satisfying just the same. Wall-banging, earth-shattering, oh-my-god sex was probably for people in their twenties. At least that was the last time she'd had it. "Will and I are good. And I don't believe in astrology. Or dreams." She looked sternly at Flo.

"Of course you don't, dear. Did you get the birth signs for the children?"

"The boy is a Taurus and the girl is a Scorpio. And yes, even if it turns out that means they're going to kill me in my sleep, I'm still going."

"Well, the boy will be all right. You can always count on a Taurus. Steady as they come. Strong. The Bull." She looked thoughtful. "They like *things,* you know? Good food, comfort, they're very materialistic. If you need to win him over, that could help."

"I'd think good food and comfort would win anybody over," Andie said, and Flo looked at her curiously.

"Now why would you think that? The little girl's going to be completely different. Intense. Secretive. You won't buy her with comfort. And you won't be able to bamboozle her, either. Scorpios. They'll kill you as soon as look at you. They like sparkly things, though. You might get her with sequins."

"Flo, she's a little girl."

"Although I've always liked Scorpios. They're *interesting.* And they're survivors. Taurus, too, those are both survivor signs. Tough kids. They'll make it without you." Flo bit her lip. "Andie, don't go."

"I'm going." Andie opened the driver's side door to escape before her mother started on rising signs. "I'll be back in a month, and everything will be fine."

"No it won't." Flo took a deep breath. "It's not just the dreams and the stars. I read your cards last night. The Emperor was crossing you. That's power and passion, so it has to be North. It was a bad, bad reading. You're going down a path that's all conflict and struggle. There's no peace there. Will can't help you, he's not strong enough for you. North's too strong."

"*Mother*—"

"Leave both of them," Flo said, serious as death. "I'm scared for you, Andie."

"Well, stop it," Andie said, and got in the car. Then she got out again and hugged Flo, who hugged her back, hard. "Sorry, Mom. I love you much. Don't worry. In a month, I'll be back and living here in town and you can run the cards for me every day if you like."

"You don't understand," Flo said. "You're not a mother. When you have a child, you can't let her go into danger, you have to be there for her—"

"Flo, I'm thirty-four. The child part is over."

"*It's never over,*" Flo said, and Andie shook her head at her obtuseness and got back in her car.

"I'll call you while I'm there," she said, and put the Mustang in gear, and then waved at her mother in her rearview mirror as she drove away.

Sea goat, she thought.

A little Flo went a long way.

Andie headed south on I-71 and then turned off onto a winding two-lane highway and then from there onto another narrower road that moved into a heavily wooded area, making the drive dark in the middle of the day. The general air of desolation was not helped by the fact that she saw only two other cars once she passed the last sign of civilization—a shopping center—before she hit New Essex, the depressed little town that marked the turnoff to the long dead-end road the house was supposed to be on. By then the sun was going down, so fifteen miles later, when she saw the battered sign that said AR- CHER HOUSE in the middle of some weeds, she pulled off to the side of the road in the deepening twilight and got out to investigate.

There had been a drive next to the sign, but it seemed to have collapsed. What was left was a steep slope, not anything she'd want to drive down if she had a choice.

She got back in the car and drove slowly over the edge, her wheels crunching on sparse gravel.

The road dipped down sharply, scraping the Mustang's front fender, which made her shudder, and then leveled off into the pothole- laced lane that wound through the trees for about a quarter of a mile and came out into meadow gone to seed. Beyond that an an- cient three-story stone house rose up, flaunting two rose windows, a crumbling tower, and a moat, all its windows dark in the twilight and beyond that more clustered trees over which crows circled and cawed. "The House of Archer," Andie said to herself as she slowed to take it all in. Well, it was a dull, dark, and soundless day in the autumn of the year.

She followed the drive around to the side where a little bridge crossed the moat onto an untended stretch of pavement that split, the right going to the front of the house and its weathered, stone- arched entrance and the left to the back and a large, weedy flagstoned yard beside a row of garages that had probably once been stables.

She pulled the Mustang up in front of the garages and got out, looking around the deserted yard as she slammed the door, the sound echoing in the gloom. The place wasn't just neglected, it was slov- enly: weeds everywhere, the flagstone broken, the steps to the back door crumbling. The house was plainer in back, with just a single column of porch topped by bay windows, one to each floor, the window frames peeling and the gutters rusting, and everything oppressed by the bleak gray stone.

And all of it was really wrong. North wouldn't leave property looking like this. Not for two years. And he'd have made sure there was somebody there to greet her when she pulled up.

She shook her head and got one of her suitcases and headed for the house, now really wary of what she was going to find. She pushed the back door open, banging the case on the frame, and then went through a small mudroom and into a big, cold, gloomy, sitting room filled with heavily carved Victorian furniture including an ornate couch covered in green-striped silk, green-striped bolsters against each arm, and several side chairs covered in threadbare needlepoint.

She opened a side door into another cold room, this one all mahogany and brass, with a long, heavy dining table surrounded by equally heavy, ornate chairs.

There was another door in the opposite wall, and she opened that one, feeling more and more like Alice through the Looking Glass, but this time, light hit her as she walked in. It was a huge, white kitchen, but a less welcoming heart-of-the-house would be hard to imagine, nothing like the kitchen full of color North had given her in Columbus. Every surface was scrubbed and empty except for the long wood farmhouse table in the center.

A boy sat at the end, all shoulder blades and elbows, hunched over a bowl of something orange, his brown hair falling into his eyes as he looked up at her from under his thick lashes, his mouth set in a tight, hard line. Sitting close to him was a thin little girl cupping her hands around her own bowl of orange, her pale gray-blue eyes narrowed under her long, tangled white-blond hair, her T-shirt almost covered by all the stuff she had strung around her neck: an old strand of discolored purplish plastic pearls, an ancient locket on a pink ribbon, a string of tiny blue shells, a blue Walkman on a black cord, and a glittery bat on a black chain.

Wonderful, Andie thought, and said, "Hi."

Two

"You're late," a voice snapped from behind Andie, and she turned and saw a plump, overly powdered, elderly woman, her pale, watery, protruding eyes hostile under her improbably red-orange updo, her large white arms folded.

"Yes," Andie said, putting her suitcase down on the floor. "You must be Mrs. Crumb. I'm—"

"Andromeda Miller. Mr. Archer told me." Mrs. Crumb nodded, her arms folded over the aggressively flowered apron that covered her equally aggressive bosom. "He tells me everything. He trusts me like I was his own mother."

The enormity of the lies in that short speech left Andie stunned, not just at the thought of North telling the old lady everything— North didn't tell *anybody* everything—but also at him somehow collating Lydia and Mrs. Crumb.

"I know what's best, so you do as I say, and we'll all get along fine." She smiled at Andie, but her eyes were cold. "That's Carter," she went on, jerking her head toward the boy without looking at him, "and that's Alice, and they're your students. Everything else,

I take care of." She transferred her reptile smile to the little girl. "I'm the one who stays with the little lambs. They know I'm the one they can count on."

The girl ignored her, but the boy looked back at her, his eyes like stone.

If that kid is a lamb, the wolves are toast, Andie thought.

"So now that you understand how things work," Mrs. Crumb went on, "I'll take you to your room." She took a step closer and Andie caught a whiff of peppermint and booze. "But don't you get any ideas about me working for you."

Andie looked at her, exasperated. She might just be feeling threatened—

Mrs. Crumb made a short nod toward Andie's suitcase. "You'll have to carry that. I'm not your servant. And I'll be needing some help around the house, so don't think you're too good to pick up a broom." She sniffed. "I know your kind."

"I'm afraid there's been a mistake," Andie said, stepping on her temper. "I'm not a nanny. And for the next month, I'm the one in charge."

"Oh?" Mrs. Crumb smiled again, false pity in the tilt of her head. "Mr. Archer put somebody he doesn't even know over me?" She chuckled without humor. "I don't think so. You'll do as I say or I'll tell Mr. Archer. And then we'll just see what happens."

The little girl continued scooping orange whatever, but the boy was watching now.

"Miller is my professional name," Andie said. "My married name is Archer."

Mrs. Crumb's smile froze in place.

Andie shoved her ringless left hand in her coat pocket. "Mrs. North Archer. My husband sent me here for a month to fix whatever's wrong." She walked over to the table and looked into the bowls, since meeting Mrs. Crumb's eyes after that lie was not easy. "After we make our assessment, we'll decide on the children's future."

"Your *husband*?" Mrs. Crumb said, sounding torn between outrage and fear.

Andie pointed to the kids' bowls. "Mrs. Crumb, what are the lambs having for dinner?"

"Macaroni and cheese." Mrs. Crumb put her chin up. "That's good for them."

"And . . . ?"

"And what?"

"Where are the vegetables? Fruit? Protein? Grains? Dairy? You have fat, starch, and yellow dye number two covered, now let's try fiber and vitamins."

"I don't need to listen to this," Mrs. Crumb said, her smile gone now.

"Actually, you do." Andie went over to the cupboard and opened it to see boxes of mac and cheese and jars of pasta in some kind of toxic orange sauce. "Oh, my God."

"You fancy city people," Mrs. Crumb said as Andie opened the refrigerator.

There was a jar of jam, a loaf of white bread, a gallon jug of milk that was almost empty, and two squares of American cheese.

She turned back to the table. "You're going to have to do better than this."

"That's what they *eat,*" Mrs. Crumb said. "That's *kid food.*"

The children were both watching her now, the little girl scooping more mac and cheese, the boy with his head ducked low, two pairs of Archer blue eyes boring into her over Archer cheekbones. They were thin, pale, and hostile, but nothing about either one of them said "victim."

Andie smiled at the little girl. "So you're Alice."

The little girl put on the headphones to her Walkman and turned up the volume.

Andie transferred her smile to the boy. "And you must be Carter."

He ignored her.

"Yeah, I'm thrilled to be here, too," Andie said. "But since we're stuck with each other—"

"Now you listen here," Mrs. Crumb blustered. "You can't come in here and change things all around. I don't believe you're married to Mr. Archer." She lifted her chin again. "You are not a lady."

"And you are not a cook." Andie turned her attention back to Carter. "Things will get better," she told him.

He ignored her and ate more mac and cheese.

Andie took a deep breath. "Okay, look, it's my job to make you safe and healthy and I'm going to do that. For the next month, you'll have decent meals . . ."

"Well, I *never*," Mrs. Crumb said.

". . . and I'll see to your education and maybe we can get you both back to school in your regular grade levels, and when I leave, there'll be good people taking care of you, I promise."

Carter stared at her with his flat eyes, unimpressed.

"Not military school. We'll put you in public school. In Columbus. There are very good schools there." She looked at Alice.

Alice kept eating, her headphones blocking all other sound.

"She won't go," Mrs. Crumb said, her voice fat with satisfaction. "You don't understand—"

"Mrs. Crumb, do you want to remain employed?" Andie said. "Because right now, it's not looking good for you."

The housekeeper glared at her, and Andie stared back, unimpressed.

After a moment, Mrs. Crumb pursed her painted lips and sat down across the table from where Andie stood, forcing a smile. "We got off to a bad start."

"Yes," Andie said, waiting to see what her next move was.

"There are things about this house you don't know," Mrs. Crumb said, leaning forward, and Carter stopped eating to watch her. "It's a big house, there's *history* in this house. I've been here all my life, since I was sixteen, I *know* this house. You need me."

Carter went back to his mac and cheese and Andie thought, *That's not what he was expecting.* "The history of the house isn't important to me. The kids are."

"It ain't just the history," Mrs. Crumb said, her eyes dark. "There's things here you can't understand."

"Ghosts?" *How dumb do you think I am?* "I don't believe in ghosts. I do believe in nutrition and basic curriculum skills, so that's what I'll be concentrating on."

Mrs. Crumb dropped her voice. "Some things you can't believe are real."

"Like this stuff you're feeding the children." Andie looked at the orange smears left in Alice's bowl as she polished off the last of her pasta. "I've never seen macaroni and cheese that color before. Does it glow in the dark?"

Mrs. Crumb got up and took the children's bowls. "We should get along, you and me. You're going to need me."

Andie looked at the old woman's cold little eyes. *Jesus, I hope not.* "I'd like to see my bedroom, please."

"I'll show you everything," Mrs. Crumb said, her defiance back. "I'll just show you."

"Just my bedroom," Andie said, but Mrs. Crumb had already headed for a door in the far wall, so she smiled one last time at the kids, picked up her suitcase, and followed the housekeeper.

It was going to be a long month.

Andie followed Mrs. Crumb into a short dismal hallway with faded wallpaper and a worn wood floor. The housekeeper turned to go up a narrow flight of equally worn wooden stairs that were probably the servant stairs, and then she stopped on the first step, her watery, protruding eyes even with Andie's now.

"I hope you didn't get the wrong idea," she began. "I'm sure Mr. Archer just forgot to tell me—" She looked past Andie and scowled.

"Now what are you doing out here?" she snapped, and Andie turned and saw Alice standing behind her, looking even smaller and thinner than she had in the kitchen, her neck festooned with all that jewelry, the headphones from her Walkman still over her ears.

"Hello, Alice," Andie said.

The deep shadows under Alice's eyes and cheekbones made her little face almost skull-like. She stared at Andie for a minute and then pushed past her and Mrs. Crumb and began to climb the stairs, something stuffed under her arm.

Andie reached out and touched her sleeve and Alice jerked away and kept going.

"Is that a doll?" Andie asked, and Alice stopped a couple of steps above her and took her headphones off.

She held up a stuffed doll with a bluish-white head, its three-tiered sepia-toned skirt flaring out from a faded gold ribbon belt around its lumpy waist. The thing looked like it had been left to mold before Alice had found it, the face and dress mottled with age. "It's Jessica," Alice said and went on up the stairs.

It's dead, Andie thought.

"She won't give that up," Mrs. Crumb said, in her idea of a whisper. "I've tried giving her other dolls but she just wants that one. It's not right. We should do something about that, you and me."

Andie watched Alice's straight little back climb the stairs without wavering even though she must have heard the housekeeper's voice. "If that's the doll Alice wants, that's the doll she gets."

Mrs. Crumb sucked in her breath and shook her head and then continued up the stairs.

They reached another short hall on the second floor, and Mrs. Crumb walked around the stairwell and started up another flight. "Nursery's on the third floor. Keeps the noise down."

"Noise?" Andie said, following an entirely silent Alice, but Mrs. Crumb didn't speak again until they were on the third-floor landing in another cramped little hall.

"This is the bathroom," she said proudly, opening a door opposite the stairs that led to a large vintage washroom with a freestanding brass-and-frosted-glass shower in the middle of the hardwood floor. "You're sharing this with me. My room's on the other side"—she nodded toward the front of the house—"but I know you won't mind since we're going to be such good friends." Then she moved toward the back of the house to a door that was ajar because Alice had walked through it moments before.

"This is your bedroom," Mrs. Crumb said, pushing the door open wider.

Andie followed her into a large, high-ceilinged paneled room, dominated by a four-poster bed and a stone mantel surrounding a gas fireplace. The long stone-lined windows looked out over the old woods behind the house, and Andie could hear the last calls of the crows in the flushed sky.

"And that's the nursery through there." Mrs. Crumb jerked her thumb at a door to the right that was also ajar, probably from Alice walking through it, too. "I'm going to go make you a nice hot toddy now. Just the thing to help you drop off to sleep." She smiled again, and again it didn't reach her eyes, and then she went back out through the hall door.

"Hot toddy," Andie said, not even sure what that was, and walked over to the open door and looked through it.

The nursery was huge, maybe thirty feet across, with a bank of barred windows across the back including a little bay-windowed alcove with a window seat full of books spilling onto the floor. There were two narrow twin beds, their mattresses naked, an ancient rocker with chipped white paint, a rump-sprung old sofa, a battered table with paper and pencils on it and several mismatched chairs scattered around it, and an old TV in the middle of the room with an ancient boom box on top of it. At the far end was a cold gas fireplace with a small, modern fire extinguisher on the mantel. It was about as cozy as an abandoned mental hospital.

Andie crossed the room and opened a door on the other side and found herself in another short hall. In front of her the door was open to a small bathroom, to the right was a stone archway to another hall, and to the left was a closed door.

Jesus, she thought. *This place is Little Gormenghast. I'm going to get lost here and never be found.*

She opened the door to the left and found Alice sitting on a twin bed, leaning toward an old white rocker at the foot of the bed. The walls were pink, her bedside table had a pink lamp, and her bedspread was pink and covered with daisies.

"This is my room!" Alice said, straightening as she clutched her blue Jessica doll to all the jewelry on her thin little chest. "You have to knock before you come in!"

Andie surveyed the little room, puzzled. "Do you like pink?"

"No!"

"I didn't think so. Sorry about not knocking."

Andie closed the door and then crossed the small hall into the larger one and found another staircase on her left, this one stone and much grander, and to her right a massive stone archway. On the wall in front of her was another door, so she opened it.

Carter jerked back against his headboard, his eyes wide, almost dropping the comic book he'd been reading. Then he saw her and scowled. "You ever hear of knocking?"

"Sorry," Andie said. "I can't tell which doors are rooms and which ones are halls."

"This one's a room," Carter said, and went back to his comic.

Andie looked around the room and saw ancient heavy furniture and a bed covered with old blankets in various shades of drab. The only interesting things in the whole room were the stacks of comic books, papers, and pencils on the bedside tables that said Carter did something besides glare and eat, and the carpet at the end of the bed that was riddled with scorch marks. *Pyro,* she thought, and was grateful the house was mostly stone. She looked up to see Carter watching her, his face stolid, so she nodded and began to close the door only to stop when she took a second look at his bedside table.

There was a lighter on it, a cheap plastic job. She opened the door wider and saw two more on the other table.

He was still staring at her, and she thought about saying, "What in the name of God do you need three lighters for?" But it was her first night and Carter already didn't like her and she was too damn tired.

"Don't set anything on fire," she told him, and closed the door.

Then she walked through the stone arch on her right and almost ran into an ancient wood railing that ran around three sides of an open space. The railing rocked a little as she put her hands on it, so she looked over the edge carefully.

The opening dropped two stories down to a stone floor, empty in the growing darkness.

Okay, then, Andie thought, and made a circuit of the gallery, discovering doors that led into the nursery and into the servants' stairwell. Then she went back to the little hall and to Alice's room, where she knocked.

"Go away," Alice said.

Andie went in and saw that Alice had changed into a too-large jersey T-shirt that hung down past her knees, clearly a hand-me-down from some adult. She looked both pathetic—poor little Alice had to get ready for bed on her own—and eerie—poor little Alice's shirt said BAD WITCH on it in glowing green letters. She looked oddly defenseless without her armor of necklaces—they were hanging over her lampshade now—but with her white-blond hair standing out every which way, she also looked demented. *We'll comb that tomorrow,* Andie thought.

"Sorry," she told Alice. "I just wanted to say that if you need me, I'm on the other side of the nursery."

"I won't need you." Alice got into bed and pulled her covers over her head.

"Right." Andie noticed that Jessica had fallen to the floor. "You dropped something." She bent and picked up the old doll and poked Alice under the covers.

"Hey!" Alice said, and then Andie pulled back the covers and handed her the doll.

"Good night," Andie said, and Alice pulled her covers up over her head again.

"Yes, we're going to be great pals," Andie said, and headed back across the nursery to her own room, thinking that it was no surprise the nannies had cracked. They'd probably expected to be put living in the tomb at any moment, probably by Carter and Alice.

She heard something from the hallway by Alice's room and went back to check. Alice's door had come partly open, and inside Alice was talking.

"She's not staying," Alice was saying. "She's just going to be here a month. She's not even a nanny. It's okay. We're staying right here."

Andie pushed open the door a little more, expecting to see Carter, and Alice looked around, alone in her room.

"I *told you,*" she began.

"Who were you talking to?"

"Nobody," Alice said, turning her head toward the wall.

Imaginary friend, Andie thought, and said, "Okay."

Then she turned to go and saw the white rocker at the end of the bed.

It was rocking.

She looked back at Alice, who met her eyes defiantly.

"What?" Alice said.

She did that, Andie thought, and said, "Nothing. Good night," and closed the door, now in complete sympathy with the nannies who'd bolted.

Anybody with sense would.

. . .

Andie put the weirdness that was Alice and Carter out of her mind and spent the next hour unpacking and settling into her new room. It was surprisingly charming: white paneled walls and high, sculpted ceilings and long stone-lined windows covered with full, patterned draperies that clashed with the incongruously cheap silver-patterned black comforter that somebody with a lot of romance in her soul and no money in her checking account had bought to cover the large walnut four-poster bed. The rest of the furniture in the room was a mixture of styles probably inherited from different parts of the house as hand-me-downs, and the crowning touch was a cheap metal plaque over the bed that said ALWAYS KISS ME GOOD NIGHT. There was something a little obsessive about that which, given Andie's surroundings, leaked over into creepiness. She put her pajamas on, brushed her teeth in the bathroom, put Kristin's folder about the kids on the bed, and then, looking at the "Archer Legal Group" label on the folder, went to find her jewelry box. Buried at the bottom in a small manila envelope was her wedding ring, pretty and cheap, now painted and varnished to keep it from tarnishing again, the last thing she had left from her marriage. She should have thrown it out since it was worthless, but . . .

She slid the ring on her left hand and smiled in spite of herself, remembering North going crazy trying to replace it with a real gold ring that wouldn't turn her finger green. Then she put the jewelry box away and was pulling back the covers when she heard a knock at the hall door and opened it to see Mrs. Crumb with a small tray. "A little cuppa before bed," the housekeeper trilled, her red cupid's-bow mouth smiling tightly, as she put the tray on the table next to the bed. "I got no problem bringing you up a cuppa every night since it's only going to be a month?" She let her voice rise at the end, part question, part hope.

"Uh, thank you." Andie eyed the tray doubtfully, but the yellow-striped teapot smelled richly of peppermint and there were violets painted on the big striped cup.

Mrs. Crumb nodded. "I put in a little liquor, too. You sleep good now." She glanced down at the foot of the bed. "Sweet dreams."

She retreated back through Andie's door, and Andie closed it behind her and sniffed the pot. Minty. Very minty. She sat down on the bed and poured tea into the cup and then took a sip and got a full blast of at least two shots of peppermint schnapps. *Whoa,* she thought. The tea was good and peppermint was always nice, but unless Mrs. Crumb was trying to put her into a schnapps-induced stupor, the housekeeper had an exaggerated idea of "a little liquor."

Maybe she should make her own tea.

She began to read Kristin's notes, sipping cautiously. The kids' mother had died giving birth to Alice, she read, their father had died in a car accident two years ago, and their aunt had died in a fall four months ago in June. *And now,* Andie thought, *they're alone with Crumb. And me.* That thought was so harrowing that she forgave them the weirdness of their first meeting. Things would get better.

Poor kids.

She sipped more tea and read more notes. The three nannies had all said the same thing: the kids were smart, the kids were undisciplined, the kids were strange, there was something wrong, and they were leaving. Only the last one had tried to take the kids with her, and Alice had gone into such a screaming fit that she'd lost consciousness and the nanny had had to detour to a hospital. After that, the nanny took the kids back to Archer House and left them there. "These children need professional psychological help," she'd written, and Andie thought, *So North sent me.*

That was so unlike him, not to send a professional, not to get a team of experts down there, and she thought, *He's not taking it seriously.* Either that or he wanted her buried in southern Ohio for some reason.

She tilted her head back to think about that and saw the curtain of the window nearest the bed move, a flutter, as if from a draft. She watched, and when it didn't move again, she shook her head and went through the rest of the folder, sipping the liqueur-spiked tea until the combination of that and the dry curriculum reports from the nannies made her so sleepy, she gave up. She turned off the bedside lamp, and the moonlight seeped into the room—*full moon,* she thought— and it was lovely to be so deeply drowsy on such a soft bed in such soft blue light that she let herself doze, thinking, *I should have called Flo to tell her I arrived, I should have called Will, I should have . . .*

Something moved in her peripheral vision, maybe the curtain again, she was pretty sure nothing had moved. Exhaustion or maybe the liqueur in the tea. She looked sleepily around the room, but it was just gloomy and jumbled, a gothic kind of normal, although it seemed colder than it had been, so she let her head fall back and snuggled down into the covers and drifted off to sleep, and then into dreams where there was shadowy laughter and whispering, and someone dancing in the moonlight, and as she fell deeper into sleep, the whispering in her ear grew hot and low—*Who do you love? Who do you want? Who kisses you good night?*—and she saw Will, smiling at her, genial and easygoing with his blond frat-boy good looks, and then she fell deeper and darker, and North was there, his eyes hot, reaching for her the way he used to, demanding and possessive and out of control in love with her, and she sighed in relief from wanting him, and somebody whispered, *Who is HE?,* and she went to him the way she always had—impossible to ever say no to North—and lost herself in him and her dreams.

Andie woke at dawn with a headache, which she blamed on Mrs. Crumb's hot tea along with the hot dreams about North, probably evoked because she'd taken his name again. *Guilt will always get you,* she thought and resolved to stop lying, even if it was the only way to defeat Crumb. She took an aspirin and went down and moved the rest of her things from her car to her room, and then drove fifteen miles into the little town at the end of the road and hit the IGA there for decent breakfast food. Then she headed back to the house, determined to Make a Difference in the kid's lives, but once there, she hit the wall. Alice was in the kitchen demanding breakfast, but she didn't want eggs or toast or orange juice. Alice wanted cereal. She'd had cereal the day before and the day before that and the day before that and today wasn't going to be any damn different. Andie looked into Alice's gray-blue eyes and saw the same stubbornness that had defeated her in her short marriage.

"You're an Archer, all right," she said and gave Alice her cereal.

Then she made ham and eggs for Carter on the stubborn old stove, thinking of the kitchen North had remodeled for her when she'd moved into his old Victorian in Columbus, of the shining blue quartz counters and soft yellow cabinets and the open shelves filled with her Fiesta ware. It'd been her favorite place in the world, next to their bedroom in the attic. This kitchen was like a meat locker. Very sanitary but . . .

"That is not good," Alice said, looking into the pan, but when Andie dished it up for Carter, he ate everything. He kept his eyes on his comic book the whole time and then shoved the plate away and left, still reading, but he ate it all. Progress.

"You're welcome," Andie called to his retreating back, and turned around to see Mrs. Crumb smiling at her, her powdery, jowly face triumphant over Alice's empty cereal bowl as Alice deserted them, too.

Andie ignored her and tried to call Flo using the kitchen phone, staring at the battered white bulletin board that held only a list of faded phone numbers and an even more faded church collection envelope, which probably summed up Mrs. Crumb's life. When she couldn't get a dial tone, she said, "No phone?" and Mrs. Crumb said, "It goes out sometimes." *Terrific,* Andie thought and went to scope out Archer House before she made a trip to the shopping center she'd passed on the two-lane highway the day before.

The layout of the house was, for all its size, fairly simple. The center of the house, as Mrs. Crumb told her, was the Great Hall, more than twenty feet square with a stone fireplace large enough to party in. The hall rose three stories to a raftered ceiling that dated back to the original house, sometime in the sixteen hundreds, each level ringed by a gallery with that ancient wood railing that Andie had almost fallen through the night before. *Impossible to heat,* Andie thought. *And those railings are not safe.* There were six rooms on each floor: one room on each side of the hall at the front of the house, and four rooms across the back. The first floor had empty rooms in front, and the kitchen, dining room, sitting room, and library across the back; the second floor had two bedrooms in front and four in back, all with four-posters and naked mattresses; and the third floor had Mrs. Crumb's bedroom on the front left and Carter's on the front right, and then Andie's room, the doublewide nursery, and Alice's room across the back. In between the front rooms and the back were staircases—the narrow servant's flight behind a discreet door on the left and the massive formal stone staircase through an equally massive stone arch on the right. A long, white-paneled, red-carpeted entrance hall separated the rooms on the right from the Great Hall, but otherwise it was pretty much two rooms in front and four in back all the way up. Every room in the place was covered in dust, the paintings on the walls looking muddy and faded in the gloom and the bedrooms on the second floor doing a nice business in cobwebs and the occasional dead mouse. Jessica the ancient blue-faced doll would have fit right in there. Still, Andie was cheered by her ability to navigate the stone barn she was living in, so when she had the scope of the place, she went back to the library where Carter had folded his gangling body into a deep, red-cushioned window seat.

Tauruses like things, Flo had said, and even though astrology was a crock, Andie thought, *Books.*

"I'm going out to shop," she told him. "Want to come along? There's a bookstore."

"There's no bookstore in New Essex," he said without looking up.

"Is that the little town at the end of this road? There was a shopping center I passed on the highway about half an hour before I got to New Essex. It had a bookstore."

He stopped reading. "Grandville?"

"Yes."

He nodded and went back to his book, and Andie took that for assent and went upstairs to find Alice, wondering what sequined promise would lure a little Scorpio out of the house.

Alice was in the nursery with her Walkman, dancing and singing "Gloria" at the top of her voice. She caught Andie watching and stopped, her colorless skin and straight white-blond hair making her look like a little ghost herself, almost translucent in the morning sun.

"I'm going to town to shop," Andie said. "If you come along, I'll get you a new bedspread. With sequins."

"No," Alice said automatically.

"Carter's coming."

"No he's not. We don't leave here."

Andie came into the nursery and sat down on the ancient rocker near the TV. "Why?"

"We belong here."

"Alice, it's just for the day. We'll be back for dinner."

"That's what *she* said," Alice snapped, her stolid little face growing grimmer.

"She who?"

"Nanny Joy. She said we'd just go for the day and then she kept driving and driving and driving, and when Carter said where are we going, she said we were going to a new home." Alice's hands were curled into fists now, her face even whiter than before. "I'm not going. *I'm not going! I'm NOT GOING! NO NO NO NO NO NO—*"

Andie said calmly, "Alice, all my stuff is here. I wouldn't leave my stuff."

"NO NO NO NO NO NO—"

"All my clothes are in my room," Andie went on. "Boxes of your school supplies. My sewing stuff. I didn't bring all of that here yesterday to leave it today."

Alice closed her mouth and regarded Andie darkly.

"Do you want to see the boxes?"

Alice thought about it and nodded.

"Okay then." Andie stood up and held out her hand to the little girl who ignored it to march toward the door to Andie's room. She wrenched open the door and stalked in, and Andie followed her in and opened the closet door. Alice came closer to stare inside, suspicion in every cell of her body. "I'm unpacked," Andie told her. "Why would I do that if I was going to take you away?"

Alice ignored her to kick the sewing box.

"So do you want to come with Carter and me to go shopping?"

Alice set her lower teeth in her upper lip, thinking hard. Then she turned and marched back into the nursery.

Andie grabbed her purse and keys and followed her into the nursery in time to see Alice go out of the nursery and slam the door. "Wonderful," she said, and was trying to think of something else to bribe the girl with when Alice came out with her blue Jessica doll under her arm.

"I want a blue bedspread with sparkles," she said, "and it should flutter. Like butterflies. Or dancing." She headed for the door out of the nursery and onto the gallery and beyond that, presumably, the stairs and Carter.

"Hold it," Andie said, and Alice turned around, a dark look on her face. "We have to comb your hair."

If possible, untangling Alice's hair was worse than Andie had anticipated since Alice screamed through the whole thing, loud enough that Carter came up to see what Andie was doing to her. "You're next," Andie told him over a shrieking Alice, and he left and came back five minutes later with his hair combed, in time to see Andie pull Alice's hair up into a topknot and tie it with one of her scrunchies.

Andie sat back to survey her work. Except for the fact that Alice was still screaming, tears streaking down her contorted, red face, she looked pretty good. "Alice, I'm not doing anything to you. Stop screaming and go look at yourself. You look cute."

Alice screamed louder, directing the volume directly at Andie, so Andie went into her room and got a hand mirror and brought it out to her. "Look."

Alice stopped in mid-scream, possibly because she realized she looked god-awful with her mouth open like that, possibly because it had been so long since she'd seen her face without hair sticking out all around it. "I hate it," she said, but she said it instead of screaming it, so Andie counted it as progress.

"That's my girl," she said, standing up.

"I'm not your girl," Alice said, and stalked out the door past Carter, clearly fed up with Andie and life in general, although she gave grudging approval to Andie's yellow Mustang when she saw it.

The ride to Grandville was uneventful except for the one bad moment when Andie drove through New Essex and turned onto the highway, and Alice thought she was being kidnapped again. She screamed until Carter, sitting beside her in the back seat, said, "Chill, it's the next town," without taking his eyes off his comic book. Alice stopped. Evidently if Carter said it, it was fact.

"Thank you," Andie said to him, looking in the rearview mirror to see his face.

He ignored her.

When they got to the mall in Grandville, he got out of the car and headed for the bookstore. Andie and a silent, glowering Alice went to a bedding store for a blue comforter for Alice and a red-striped one for Carter. When Alice objected to hers, saying, "It doesn't have sparkles," they went to a fabric store for some blue sequined chiffon and thread, and after that an office supply store where Alice picked out a sketchbook for Carter, and a set of markers, a big pad of quarter-inch grid paper, some pencils with skulls on them, and a pencil sharpener, all without interacting with Andie in any way until Andie offered her a set of Hello Kitty pencils. The scorn on Alice's face was searing.

They moved on and bought T-shirts and black-and-white-striped leggings and a stretchy black jersey flounced skirt for Alice who made gagging sounds, but once they began on Carter's clothes, the little girl got serious, meticulously choosing what he needed. *Shopping therapy,* Andie thought, and dragged her to a home store where she bought white paint to take the pink out of Alice's room. "I want *black,"* Alice said, the first thing she'd said since they'd left the car, and Andie said, "You can draw on the white with your markers," and watched Alice almost smile. It was a little ghoulish. Then they went to the bookstore.

"Is that your kid?" the store clerk said, when she walked in. He was pointing at Carter, so she said, "Yes." "And you're going to buy all these books?" the clerk said, pointing to the stacks on the counter. Andie sorted through them and saw comics and books on drawing and books on drawing comics. "Yes, I'm going to buy all these books," Andie said, flashing North's plastic, and a few minutes later Alice came up with two books on butterflies, and Andie added them to the pile.

When they were done and had everything loaded into the car, Andie said, "Groceries," and Alice started to scream, "No, no, no, NO, NO, NO," until Carter said, "Chill. We have to eat." Any illusion Andie had of them picking out meals together was dashed when Carter got in the car, and Alice followed him. Andie moved up and down the grocery aisles with speed and precision and was back in the car in half an hour.

"Now," she said when she got in the car. "Home."

She turned on the car and the tape player kicked in, startling her. She recognized the song and turned to the back seat as "Somebody's Baby" bounced out of the speakers. "Did you put this tape in?"

Carter shrugged.

"There's a whole thing of them," Alice said, scowling. "Right here. Nobody was using them. I didn't hurt anything. It's *your* tape."

Andie craned her neck and saw an old box under Alice's feet, the tape case she'd shoved under the driver's seat on a road trip a couple of years before and then forgotten about in favor of her CD player. Alice kicked it and then stared at her defiantly, and Andie hit eject and caught the tape as it slid into her hand. It had "Andie's Music" written on it in North's strong block caps.

Mix tapes. They really had been young. Then it came back to her, he hadn't given it to her, just slid it into his car player one night. "You made me a mix tape?" she'd said, and he said, "No, this is just songs you like." She shook her head but Alice said, "Put that back in," so she did, and Jackson Browne sang about the guys on the corner as Andie pulled out of the parking lot. He'd been singing about the guys on the corner when she'd first met North. *Our song,* she thought, and almost ejected it again. Avoiding old memories warred with avoiding Alice's screams, and Alice won.

"Why does he try to shut his eyes?" Alice asked.

"Who?" Andie said.

"Because she's so pretty," Carter said, deep in a book again, and Andie realized they were talking about Jackson Browne, singing his troubles on the tape.

"Why wouldn't he want to look at her if she's pretty?" Alice said.

"Because she's going to make him feel like a dork and then dump him," Carter said, still in his book.

Whoa, Andie thought. That was pretty cynical for twelve.

"She's not nice," Alice said.

"He doesn't know that," Andie said. "He hasn't asked her yet. If he asks her, maybe she'll dance with him." *And maybe go home with him and marry him the next day. It happens.*

"He should ask her," Alice said, and moved on to another topic.

Andie listened to them, Alice asking questions and Carter answering them even though he was trying to read, talking to each other as they ignored her completely. They were a family of two, screwed up maybe, but not screwed up in their relationship with each other. Maybe that's why they were still moderately sane in that creepy house with that wack-job housekeeper. They must have been miserable when Carter was sent away to school. A school that immediately turfed him . . .

She looked at Carter in the rearview mirror. Carter was quiet but not quiescent. If the only way he could get back to Alice was to set fires . . . "Carter," she said, and waited until he looked up, his brown hair flopping in his eyes. "I'll make sure you're not sent away from Alice again."

His blue eyes stayed as flat as ever, and then he went back to his book.

Maybe she didn't need them to like her. Maybe she just needed them to trust her for the next month. If she got them books and clothing and whatever else they needed, maybe they'd trust her enough to let her take them away from the hellhole they were living in. One step at a time.

When they got to New Essex, she pulled into the Dairy Queen. "Hamburgers and ice cream for lunch," she said, and when they were surrounded by food, she went to the pay phone and dialed.

If she got Carter cable, he might even speak to her.

North looked up as Kristin came into the office. "I'll see Mrs. Nash now."

Kristin closed the door. "Miss Miller is on the phone. I know she's supposed to talk to me, but she insists on speaking with you."

Andie. Well, if he was going to act on stupid impulses, he was going to pay the price. "I'll take the call. You stall Mrs. Nash."

Kristin nodded and faded out the door, and North thought, *Make it quick and hang up fast,* and picked up the phone. "Hello?"

"You weren't kidding about rural," Andie said, her voice low, the laugh that was always there underneath making it richer. "I had to leave the house to make a phone call."

"Where are you?" North said, trying not to be seduced into prolonging things just to listen to her.

"The Dairy Queen in New Essex. The kids are inhaling food at a picnic table over by the car, so I can talk. Have you been to that house? It's like something out of Dickens."

"Because you had to leave to make this call?"

"Because it's bleak as hell. We need cable TV, North. I can't believe Carter is surviving without it."

"Fine. Call the cable company." *Get off the phone,* he told himself.

"I just called them and they were unhelpful. The house is too far out. I need somebody with clout."

"I don't know anybody at a cable company." *Get off the phone.*

"Well, you undoubtedly know somebody who does know somebody at a cable company. Put Kristin on it. She looks like she'd enjoy a challenge."

"I will do that," North said. *For Christ's sake, get off the phone.*

"Also, have you been here lately?"

"No. Is there a problem?"

"The place is falling apart. The stone's crumbling, there are weeds everywhere, anything that's metal has rusted and run down the outside of the house, and the drive is a real hazard."

"Damn it," North said. "I sent funds to fix all of that two years ago."

"To Mrs. Crumb?"

North pictured the housekeeper. Elderly. Dyed red hair. Smelled like peppermint and rubbing alcohol. "Yes, I sent a check to Mrs. Crumb."

"Well, the funds stayed with Mrs. Crumb. I suggest you hire people directly this time."

"I'll have a contractor come out and look at the place."

"Tell him to talk to me, not Mrs. Crumb. And to look at the inside, too. The kitchen is awful. I can't even bake here."

He closed his eyes and remembered late afternoons, Andie home from teaching and doing the Four O'Clock Bake, the smell of banana bread or chocolate chip cookies or cinnamon rolls, dozens of different smells telling him the day was almost done—

"North?"

"Right," North said. "Contractor. I'll put Kristin on it."

"Also, if anybody calls from this end of the world, we're still married."

North stopped looking at his watch. "What?"

"It's the only thing that gives me clout. They're very impressed with you here. I figured, what could it hurt? You're never coming down here. Will's never coming down here. Nobody in Columbus will ever know. So I took back my married name."

"You didn't take my name when we were married," North said, trying to find his footing again.

"I was going through an independent phase. Now I'm going through a practical phase. It's a good thing to be an Archer down here. Come to think of it, it was probably a good thing to be an Archer up there. I should have taken your name just for the power. As your mother so often told me, I was an idiot."

So was I, North thought, and then shook his head before regret could set in. The past was gone and the present had Mrs. Nash in the waiting room. "I'll get Kristin on the cable—"

"That'll be a help," Andie said over him. "Because frankly I could use a bargaining chip with the kids, too. I made a hot breakfast this morning and Alice refused to eat it and went for the damn cereal anyway. Mrs. Crumb thinks she's winning. According to her, the two of you are very close. You think of her as a mother."

"Is she delusional?"

"Everybody here is delusional, including your nannies. Carter didn't set fires because he's crazy, he set them so he'd get kicked out of school and could come home to take care of Alice. He needs to be in a good public school where he can make friends and then see Alice every night. They're really close, North. If you don't separate them, I think he'd go to school without a fight."

"Damn." North leaned back. "I knew boarding school was a bad idea. My mother tried to send me away when Southie was six, and I wouldn't go. Kids need each other. But the last nanny kept telling me he needed discipline, so—"

"He has discipline. He's so self-disciplined he's barely breathing. Alice, on the other hand, has no discipline at all. If something's going on that she doesn't like, she screams. But it's not like a normal temper tantrum, there's something else going on there. Carter I can eventually reach, I think. Alice . . . I don't know."

She sounded worried, and North tried to think of a way to make her feel better and then realized that was ridiculous. She was doing a job for him, she hadn't called for comfort, they weren't married anymore no matter what lies she was telling down there, he had Mrs. Nash waiting, and there was nothing he could do anyway . . . "Do you need me to come down there?"

"No, I can handle this," she said, her voice as confident as ever. "It's the kids I'm worried about. I don't know if I can make things normal for them. I think I can make things better."

"You always make things better."

The silence stretched out at the other end of the phone as he thought, *Dumb thing to say,* and then she said, "Thank you." Her voice was softer than it had been, and it brought the past rushing back again.

"You're welcome," he said, thinking, *Get off the damn phone.* "I'll get you your cable and your contractor and somebody to fix the phones."

"I know you will. You always come through."

Jesus. "Call me if there's anything else," he said briskly, trying to find his way back to normal.

"I thought we weren't supposed to talk to each other."

"I was going through an independent phase," North said, and then closed his eyes as her laugh bubbled through the phone.

"That was a helluva long phase. I'll call if there's anything else. You have a good day."

She hung up, and he sat there with the phone in his hand for a minute, trying to find his way back to normal, until Kristin came in.

"She needs cable down there," he told her, hanging up the phone. "Get it for her, please."

"That's going to cost you," Kristin said.

It's the only thing she's asked for in the entire time I've known her. "Get it for her. Also find a good contractor down there and have him go out to talk to her, not to Mrs. Crumb. And call the phone company and find out why they lose service and if there's anything we can do about it. Bills to come here."

Kristin nodded. "And Mrs. Nash in the waiting room?"

"Give me a couple of minutes," North said, and Kristin nodded again and went out.

Andie had never asked for anything. He'd kept waiting for her to, it was crazy of her not to, to ask for a house instead of his apartment in the attic of the family's Victorian—he'd heard her bitching at the stove once and sent in people to redo the kitchen for her—for a car instead of public transportation—he'd surprised her with a bright yellow Mustang and she'd loved it—hell, for an engagement ring and a decent wedding ring—he'd tried to give her a good ring once and she'd insisted on keeping that damn green band—but she'd just gone on with her life, tromping around in those crazy skirts and tight tank tops, her hair wild no matter how much she fought it, arguing with him, laughing with him, falling into bed with him . . .

He closed his eyes and thought, *I really was an idiot.*

He just wasn't sure if he'd been an idiot for marrying her or for letting her go.

Not that it mattered anymore. She was gone, and he had a client to interview. He punched a button on the intercom and said, "I'll see Mrs. Nash now," and went back to work.

Three

After North hung up, Andie put more coins in the phone and called Flo and told her everything was fine, and then called Will and said the same thing, but he wasn't as easily put off.

"Have you talked to North?" he said.

"Yes," she said. "I asked him to get us cable."

"I wish you weren't talking to him."

"I'd talk to Satan to get cable," Andie said, and changed the subject, giving him half her attention while she watched Alice lean against Carter's arm, sitting as close to him as possible. "I have to go," she said when they'd finished their ice cream, and then realized she'd interrupted him in mid-sentence. "Sorry, the kids . . . I have to go." She hung up and went back to collect the kids, taking a phone number tab from a flyer for the Happy Housekeepers cleaning service she found on the Dairy Queen's bulletin board. She lost the kids again as soon as she stopped the car on the flagstones behind the house, Carter taking the bookstore bags and Alice dragging the bags of clothes and office supplies. Andie took everything else into the kitchen and put the food away, taking a surprised satisfaction in seeing the fridge and cupboards fill up. Then she took the rest of the bags upstairs, dropped Carter's striped comforter off in his room without getting so much as a glance from him, and took Alice's blue comforter into the nursery where she set up her sewing machine, tore the sequined chiffon into strips, and sewed the strips all over the comforter.

Then she went to Alice's room, knocked on the door, and said, "Alice, I have your comforter."

"Come in," Alice said, suspicion heavy in her voice, and Andie opened the door and went in.

Alice watched critically as Andie pulled the old pink bedspread off and shook the glittery blue comforter out, snapping it over her bed and making the chiffon strips flutter and gleam as it settled. Alice looked closer at it. "It should have swirls," she told Andie.

"Swirls."

"Like dancing. I'll do it with my marker." Alice narrowed her eyes. *"Okay?"*

"Okay," Andie said. "You do that, and I'll go make dinner."

Alice got the blue marker out of her new set, put the headphones to her Walkman back on, and began to draw swirls on the chiffon.

Half an hour later, Andie came back with two bowls of tomato soup, two grilled cheese sandwiches, and two glasses of milk, and put half on Alice's bedside table. Alice ignored her and kept making swirls. Then Andie took the rest of the tray in to Carter, who ignored her knock and glared when she came in, closing the new sketchbook he'd been drawing in.

"Dinner," she said, and put the tray on the table beside his bed.

He looked over at it, picked up a wedge of cheese sandwich, bit into it, and opened the sketchbook again, careful to shield it so she couldn't see what he was doing.

"You're welcome," she said, and went back to her bedroom to work on the curriculum since she was going to start beating education into them the next day.

At eight o'clock, she went to collect their dishes and call bedtime.

Alice was sitting on her bedspread, her dinner gone, staring at the sequins and the swirls she'd marked all over the chiffon. "It's bee-you-tee-ful," she was saying when Andie walked in.

"Yes, it is," Andie said, and Alice looked up surprised, as if she hadn't noticed she was there.

"Brush your teeth," Andie said, prepared for a fight, but Alice went off to the little bathroom on her own. When she came out, changed into her too-big Bad Witch T-shirt, Andie said, "Bedtime," and Alice picked up her Jessica doll, got into bed, and smoothed the comforter under her hands after Andie pulled it up over her knees. "Let me get the scrunchie out of your hair."

"NOOOOOOOOOOOO," Alice began, and Andie said, "We'll put another one in tomorrow," and pulled the scrunchie out while Alice was taking a breath to scream again.

Her white-blond hair dropped around her ears, smooth and silky now. Alice scratched the top of her head and said, "Okay," in a normal voice and slid down under the covers.

So far, so good, Andie thought, blessing her mother for the tip on the sequins.

Now maybe if they started a bedtime ritual, Alice would start talking to her.

"So this bedtime thing," she told Alice. "Is there anything I should be doing for you?"

Alice looked down at the rocker at the end of the bed.

"Get you a glass of water?" Andie said. "Read you a story?"

"*Tell* me a story," Alice said, and Andie thought, *Oh, hell,* and sat down in the rocker.

Alice froze.

"What's wrong?" Andie said, looking around.

"Don't sit there," Alice said, and Andie moved over to the foot of the bed, and Alice relaxed. "Okay. Tell me the story."

"Okay." Andie thought fast. "Once upon a time, there was a princess named Alice who lived in a big stone castle."

"Was there a dungeon?"

"No, but there was a moat," Andie said, thinking of the ugly water that surrounded the place. Their very own mosquito breeding ground.

"Okay," Alice said.

"She lived there with her brother and her nanny and a cook," Andie went on, thinking, *This story sucks.*

"The nanny was a Bad Witch," Alice said, ignoring the message on her nightgown.

"And everybody," Andie went on, ignoring Alice, "loved Alice."

"That's right." Alice sat back against her pillows, still clutching Jessica. "Because Alice was very beautiful."

Andie looked at the plain little girl in front of her, white-blond hair and skin as pale as her pillows. "Yes."

"What did she look like?"

"She had beautiful blond hair," Andie said, almost reaching out to smooth the wisps away from Alice's face, but stopping just in time. Alice would not like it. "And big blue eyes."

"Blue?" Alice said, frowning again.

"Gray-blue. Like a stormy sky."

"And did she have lips as red as blood and skin as white as snow?"

Andie looked at Alice's pale little face. "She had skin as white as snow because she didn't eat a good breakfast. If she'd had a hot breakfast instead of sugary cereal—"

"Princesses don't eat hot breakfasts," Alice said, looking stormy again.

"They do if they want rosy cheeks."

"*This* princess doesn't want rosy cheeks."

"Fine. She had skin as white as snow."

"And she wears a beautiful blue gown that flutters when she walks," Alice said, kicking her comforter so the chiffon fluttered again. "Like wings or cobwebs or butterflies."

"Sure," Andie said, losing her place in the story.

"And she is very strong," Alice went on, "and nobody can make her do anything, not even her Bad Uncle who tries to kidnap her."

"*Hell*-o," Andie said, pulling back a little.

"He does," Alice said, very sure. "He is tall and he has white hair and he frowns and he says, 'You must leave!' but Alice *shoves* him out the door"—Alice pushed her palms out in front of her—"and he has to let her stay in the castle."

"Alice met her uncle?" Andie said, taken aback, and then remembered that North had said he'd gone to see the kids right after his cousin had died.

Alice nodded. "Nanny Joy said that Bad Uncle said they had to go away."

"Nanny Joy, huh?" *Rotten bitch of a nanny.* Although it was possible North had said that. He wouldn't have known how upset they'd be since he'd have kept his distance.

"Nanny Joy was a bad fairy," Alice was saying, warming now to her story. "She wasn't like the other princess."

"There was another princess?"

"Yes. A blue princess. And she would dance all the time. Like this." Alice pushed the Jessica doll away and slipped out of bed before Andie could stop her, her feet hitting the floor with a thunk, and began to dance, a kind of hoochie-coochie Kabuki glide that involved twitching hips and swaying hands, stopping for moments of tai chi. She hummed something as she moved, completely absorbed in herself, and then finished with a twirl, spreading her arms as she turned in a moment of absolute grace. "She was a very good dancer," Alice said as she climbed back into bed. "Then what happened?"

"Uh," Andie said, trying to figure out where Bad Uncle and the dancing princess fit with Alice in the castle. "Well. Alice lived in the castle with her brother and the cook and the, uh, dancing princess, and she was very happy except for one thing."

Alice folded her arms, but it seemed to be more of a concentration thing than resistance.

"She was very lonely," Andie ventured.

Alice frowned.

"She had her brother and the cook and the dancing princess," Andie went on hastily, "but she wanted somebody her own age to . . . dance with."

Alice frowned harder.

"So she decided to go on a quest."

"What's a quest?"

"A trip to find something. Like to school, to find other children to play with. She went out to look for a school—"

"No she didn't."

"Okay, what did she do?"

"I don't know," Alice said, exasperated. "*You're* telling the story."

"If I'm telling the story, why doesn't Princess Alice eat her hot breakfast and go on a quest for a school?"

"Because that's *wrong.*"

"Okay." Andie gave up. "I have to think about this story for a while and then tell you more tomorrow."

Alice sighed. "All right. But there should be more dancing."

"More dancing. Got it. Anything else?"

Alice grew still, and her eyes seemed sadder suddenly, the shadows underneath them growing darker. "No," she said, and rolled over, away from Andie, scooting down under the covers as she turned.

"Okay." Andie got up, picked up the Jessica doll from where it had fallen to the floor, tucked it in beside Alice, and turned off her bedside light. "I'll be right across the nursery if you need me."

"I won't," Alice said, her voice muffled by the covers.

"Right." Andie hesitated and then bent and kissed the top of Alice's head, and Alice batted her away. "Sleep tight, baby," Andie said, and went across the hall to check on Carter.

He said, "Come in," when she knocked, which she considered progress, and when she said, "Don't stay up too late, we have to start schoolwork tomorrow," he nodded without looking up from his book. Since saying "Stop reading so you can learn something to-morrow" seemed contradictory, Andie picked up his empty tray, said, "Good night," and left the room, closing the door behind her.

Dancing princess, she thought, and wondered which one of the nannies that had been.

Andie put the dishes in the sink and then used the phone in the kitchen, now complete with dial tone, to call the Happy Housekeepers number she'd found at the Dairy Queen to set up a cleaning crew. Surprisingly, they said they'd come the next day. Something moved behind her as she hung up, and she turned around expecting to see Mrs. Crumb, but she was alone. *Weird,* she thought, but that was the least of her problems. She was making a difference with the kids, a small difference, but a start, but there was something just out of her reach, something about the place that she couldn't put her finger on yet. Mrs. Crumb might be up to something, the kids were probably always up to something, but there was something else.

Frustrated because she couldn't puzzle it out, she got out a bowl and cookie sheets and the baking supplies she'd stocked up on and made chocolate chip cookies. The oven was ancient, but chocolate chip cookies were hard to screw up. She hesitated before adding the almonds and cashews, pretty sure Alice would turn her nose up at nuts, and then decided that if Alice wanted cookies, she could damn well eat nuts. The measuring and the mixing always smoothed out her thinking processes—nothing was as calming as creaming butter— and when the kitchen was warm from the oven overheating and the smell of baking chocolate, she took final stock of where she'd been and where she was going. Everything was fine. There was no reason to be uneasy. She was in a transition phase and so were the kids. In a month, the kids would go to Columbus together, where they'd start their life with North and she'd start hers with Will . . .

She went on planning, keeping a close eye on the cookies and turning down the heat as they browned too fast. She pulled out the first tray of cookies and slid in the next unbaked tray, and by the time the whole batch was done—the oven really was a sadistic bastard, doing its damnedest to scorch everything she put in it—she was back to normal. Everything was fine. The former nannies had been idiots. It was going to be okay.

She left the cookies to cool and went back upstairs and got ready for bed. Then she climbed into the big four-poster with the third- and seventh-grade curriculums, along with a box of workbooks for grades one through ten since the nannies hadn't been able to pinpoint exactly where the kids were in their education. At ten, she heard somebody outside her door, but by the time she opened it, the only thing in the hall was a tray with a pot of liquor-laced tea and a striped cup, with two of her cookies on a plate beside it.

She crawled back into bed and sipped her tea—Mrs. Crumb still with the heavy hand with the schnapps—and ate her cookies, which were exceptional, as always. *God, I'm good at this,* she thought, and then put her mind back on the trouble at hand: Mrs. Crumb. They were going to talk about housekeeping and when that was over they were going to talk about ghosts. It was one thing for the housekeeper to have a few screws loose after living in the House of Usher for sixty years, another thing entirely to drive nannies away with ghost stories, especially when there were two kids who so desperately needed their help. Not that the kids looked like they wanted any help. In fact, they were downright hostile. *Maybe I shouldn't have come,* she thought, feeling the old urge to break and run to someplace better, but Alice and Carter needed her, North had been right about that, and she could last the month, get them back to Columbus where North could get them professional help. It was only a month.

She put her empty cup back on the bedside table, punched her pillow, slid down into bed, and turned out the light, her thoughts still racing even though the tea had made her groggy. She was going to have to tell Mrs. Crumb to knock it off with the tea, she was going to have to tell Mrs. Crumb a lot of things. Mrs. Crumb was . . .

Who do you love? She heard the whisper as the night grew chill and she drifted off. *Who do you want?*

Not Mrs. Crumb, she thought, but the whisper was insistent. *Who do you love?* And then North was there in her dreams again, turning toward her with his rare, slow smile—

Who is HE?

Andie roused and looked around, disoriented. That had been a real whisper, not a dream, and the room was cold, much colder than it had been when she'd turned out the light, it was always cold in her dreams—

The window across from her bed rattled, and she thought, *That's what I heard, the window's got a leak and it's letting in the cold air,* and got up to stick a piece of paper into it to stop the noise and pull the drapes against the cold. There were too many noises at night in this house, walls sighing and floors creaking and now this damn window . . .

She tried to shake the top pane but it was tight, stuck, not rattling at all, so she dropped her hand to the lower pane and then froze, looking down at the ground two stories below.

North stood there, his hair white in the moonlight, staring up at her.

Andie caught her breath, blindsided by the fact of him, looking at her with the same intensity of their first night, the night they'd made love until dawn, starving for each other, and he was down there now, she couldn't believe it, *he was down there now.* He'd asked her if she wanted him to come, and she had, but she'd said no, but maybe he'd known, maybe he'd come for her, the way he'd crossed the bar all those years ago to meet her, maybe—

A cloud scudded across the moon and everything went dark, and when the moonlight lit the lawn again, he was gone.

This is still a dream, she thought. She was losing her mind. She was almost engaged to another man. She didn't even want North. It was because she'd taken this job, with these two kids who didn't want her. She should get out of there, she should run—

Tell him to come to you.

She closed her eyes and thought about rolling in his arms again, the weight of him bearing her down, the push of his hips and the surge of him sliding hard into her—

Call him!

Andie jerked back from the window and looked around. Somebody had said that, somebody must have said that, but there was no one in the room but her. *This is a dream.*

Yes, it's a dream, you're dreaming of him. Call him. He's the one. Bring him here.

Andie shook her head to clear it, dizzier than ever now. And cold, so cold that she climbed back into bed shivering. She pulled the comforter up over her, and thought, *No more dreams,* and then sank down into the pillows and eventually into a fretful sleep, ignoring the voice that whispered, *Who do you love?,* and then dreamed of making love with North.

North had been sitting at his desk, working late to figure out a way to keep the next day's jury from noticing his client was a total waste of space and air, when his mother opened his office door without knocking and walked in, elegant and annoyed, and said, "We need to talk."

Oh, hell, not now. North stood up. "Hello, Mother. How was Paris?"

"Loud." Lydia sat down, every platinum wave in place, the pearls around her throat in regimented rows.

North sat down. "The little people talking in the streets again?"

Lydia ignored that. "I assume Sullivan has been in." She sat with her back straight and her arms along the arms of the chair, symmetrical and unbending.

"Yes," North said and waited to cut to the chase so he could get rid of her.

"And?" Lydia said and waited.

"He's looking well."

"He always looks well. He's my son. What did he say?"

"He said you were in good health."

Lydia smiled, her lips curving in the tight little half circle that had sent opposing lawyers scurrying to offer settlements for forty years. "This is amusing, North, but I don't have the time. What did Sullivan tell you?"

North leaned back. "That's privileged. I'm his lawyer."

"North—"

"What do you want, Mother?"

Lydia drew in air through her nose, her patrician nostrils flaring like a Derby winner's. "He's found another woman."

North nodded. "He does that."

"Or should I say, she's found him."

North nodded. "They do that."

Lydia's brows snapped together. "You are not being helpful."

"I don't want to be helpful."

"He's your brother—"

"Which is why I don't want to be helpful." North straightened. "Mother, he's thirty-four. And although you may not have noticed, he has a cheerful cunning that has kept him single and solvent through adulthood."

"Only because we were watching him," Lydia snapped.

"I never watched him."

"Well, you should have."

North smiled back at her, the same tight smile she'd given him, the one Andie had called "the crocodile smile." *Has the same sincerity as crocodile tears,* she'd told him once in the middle of an argument. *Just less emotion.*

He twitched his lips to get rid of it now. "Southie's fine, he always has been. Leave him be."

"Southie?" Lydia said, suddenly alert.

"Sullivan."

"You haven't called him Southie in years." Lydia narrowed her eyes. "What's going on?"

North sighed. "Mother, go away."

"He's seeing that woman from Channel Twelve. The one obsessed with children in jeopardy who browbeats the people she interviews."

"Imagine that," North said, meeting her eyes.

"I do not browbeat people."

"Mother, you've made a career out of browbeating people."

"Witnesses," Lydia said. *"Lawyers.* Not *people."*

"Thank God you have standards."

Lydia glared at him. "Are you telling me that that woman is like me?"

North pictured Kelly O'Keefe in the last interview he'd seen her do, the one where the woman she was haranguing cried so hard she threw up on camera. "No."

Lydia sat very still for a few moments and then said, "I have heard it said that men either marry their mothers or their mothers' opposites."

"Well, they'll say anything." North smiled at her, a real smile this time. "Mother, you are not like Kelly O'Keefe. Sullivan is not interested in her because he thinks she's you. Neither of us is Oedipal."

"Oh, please," Lydia said. "Andromeda was exactly like me."

North lost his smile. "I beg your pardon."

Lydia frowned at him again. "Aside from her teeth and those damn peasant skirts, she was practically my twin." She thought for a moment. "Except for the baking. I don't bake. I haven't had decent banana bread since she left."

"No," North said, showing what he thought was remarkable restraint. "I never looked at Andie and saw you."

"Not consciously, but a weak, silly woman would have bored you to tears." She nodded once at him. "You picked a ballbuster, just like me."

"Excuse me," North said. "I'd like to continue this conversation but I find myself in need of a therapist."

"Kelly O'Keefe is a stupid woman. She thinks bullying people will make her look tough. Instead, she just looks like a sociopath." Lydia stared angrily into space. "I think she is a sociopath. They're often very successful, you know."

"I know. I've defended several. Well, this has been—"

"I'm going to call the McKennas, have them look into her. She's hiding something. And of course, she's using him."

North was tempted to argue the "of course, she's using him," but of course, she was. And of course, Southie was using her, too. It seemed fair. "No, you will not put a private detective on Kelly O'Keefe."

"Then I'll have to meet her." Lydia narrowed her eyes at him. "You should meet her, too. Your judgment is very good."

"I don't even like watching her on television. Was there anything else?"

"Yes," Lydia said, exasperated. "I want you to stop Sullivan from seeing that woman. I don't want teeth like that on my grandchildren."

"I doubt very much that Kelly O'Keefe will give birth."

"Which is another problem," Lydia said. "Sullivan is my only hope for grandchildren. I don't want all my genes in Kelly O'Keefe's egg basket, especially if she's not going to use them."

North raised his eyebrows. "Leaving aside Kelly's . . . basket, Sullivan is your only hope?"

"Well, you're not going to give me any. You'll never stop working long enough to procreate."

North opened his mouth to disagree and Lydia ran right over him.

"We have to stop this, North."

"Mother, leave Sullivan to his dentally challenged newscaster. He won't marry her. If he does, it's his life and his choice. The umbilical cord was cut thirty-four years ago, stop trying to haul him back by it. You don't do that with me, give Sullivan the same respect."

"I can't do that with you. You bit through yours at birth."

"And now I'll be canceling dinner."

"I have heard that she's asking about Archer House. She's asking about the children and the house."

North considered how much to tell her. "She's interested in the ghost stories."

"She's not asking about ghosts. She's asking about you and the children. That's her specialty, stirring up outrage about children. I don't like it. I especially don't like it with all the trouble we've had keeping nannies. How's the new one doing?"

"She quit. I don't see how Kelly O'Keefe can use the kids. They're not being starved or beaten. What's her hook going to be?"

"That they're down there alone in a haunted house?" Lydia snapped. "I think if she got hold of that last demented nanny, she could make a story out of that. You've got to get somebody else down there—"

"Already did," North said, seeing danger ahead. "Very competent. Not a problem. You're looking tired, Mother. I'd make it an early night if I were you."

Lydia narrowed her eyes. "Would you? That's very thoughtful. Where did you get this nanny? From the same service?"

"No." North picked up his pen. "Anything else?"

Lydia's icy blue eyes met his. "Are you going to tell me what's going on now, or do I have to sit here all night and stare at you until you break?"

North put the pen down. "I sent Andie."

Lydia's face went slack with surprise, which was some reward, North thought. It took a lot to surprise Lydia.

"Andromeda?"

"Yes," North said. "You remember her. Dark eyes, curly hair, smart mouth, about this tall"—he held his hand out at about ear height—"used to be married to me."

"Andromeda is back?"

"She called and asked to see me two days after the last nanny quit. She was free, and I asked her to go down there and straighten things out, and she said yes."

"Are you going to resume the relationship?"

"No. Now I have work to get back to—"

"It wouldn't hurt you to see her again. It's been ten years, she's probably dressing like an adult now—"

"She's engaged," North said flatly.

Lydia lost her smile. "Why?"

"I assume because she'd like to be married again."

"Who could she find that would be better than you?" Lydia said, outraged.

"I think 'better' is subjective." North picked up his pen and tapped it on his legal pad. "And now I really have to work."

Lydia looked at him, exasperation plain. "I gave birth to idiots. My oldest son can't keep his wife, and my youngest son is chasing a woman that's mostly teeth and hair."

"We blame you," North said.

"Are you going to see Andromeda again?"

"No."

"Are you going to keep that harpy away from your brother?"

"No."

Lydia lifted her chin. "Fine, I will handle things myself." She stood up and tucked her purse under her arm. "But if the future face of the Archer line is ninety-nine percent tooth enamel, it'll be your fault."

Of course, North thought as she walked out.

He tried to go back to work, but his mother had broken his concentration. *She's probably dressing like an adult now,* Lydia had said, and Andie had sat there in an awful suit jacket, acting like an adult. If they got back together, he was burning that damn jacket—

They weren't getting back together. She was marrying somebody else.

She's a bolter. Even if she marries this other guy, she won't stick.

Unless she'd really changed. Unless she'd found somebody she wanted to stick to.

That was the worst thought he'd had in a long time, so he shoved it out of his mind and went back to work.

The next morning Andie went downstairs, made breakfast, and put French toast in front of Alice and Carter.

"Cereal," Alice said, clutching her pearls, her locket, her shells, her Walkman, and her bat as if the French toast was going to contaminate them. She'd put her hair up in a topknot on her own, and it was sliding down the side of her head, but Andie was willing to let that go if Alice was going to be proactive about grooming.

"Try the French toast," Andie said while Mrs. Crumb sniffed.

Alice shrank back. "No, no, *no,* NO, *NO—*"

"It's good," Carter said without looking up from his book.

Alice stopped shrinking, leaned forward, and took a tiny, cautious bite. *"AAAAAAAAAAAAGH."*

"Fine," Andie said, and took the plate away.

Alice pushed her chair back and went and got her cereal and ate a big bowl of it. She was scraping the bottom loudly when they heard a loud, sharp rapping echo through the open door to the hall.

"That's the front door," Mrs. Crumb said, surprised.

"Right," Andie said, remembering. "That might be a cable company, and there's also a team of housecleaners coming in to clean—"

"What?" Mrs. Crumb said, her eyes protruding even more in her shock.

"I'll get the door," Andie said, and went out into the small hall, through another door, across the Great Hall, through the stone arch into the entrance hall, and finally arrived at the heavy front door. "Sorry," she said as she opened it. "It's a real trek to get here." Then she stopped.

There was a crowd on the doorstep.

"We're the Happy Housekeepers," the woman in front said cheerfully. "Where do you want us?"

"The whole house is filthy," Andie said. "Go nuts everyplace but the kitchen. Mrs. Crumb is in there with knives."

"That's a good one," the woman said. "We'll start at the top and work down."

They all piled in, one of them stopping to say, "That driveway of yours is awful."

"I know, I know, I'm getting it fixed," Andie said.

"It's all right," the woman said. "We'd have *climbed* down that bank to get to see into this house."

"Oh. Uh, good," Andie said, and went back to the kitchen where Mrs. Crumb was hyperventilating. "Look," she said when she was facing the old woman, "you can't keep this place clean. No one person could keep this place clean."

"This is *my house*," Mrs. Crumb snapped, shaking with rage, even her teased red updo quivering now.

"No," Andie said, when she heard the doorknocker again and went to let the cable guy in.

"That driveway," he said, and she said, "I know, let me know if you need anything," and then she went back to the kitchen to deal with the red-faced housekeeper again, only to be pulled back to the front door by a FedEx guy, who handed over a big box.

"I had to walk that down your driveway," he said as she signed for the package. "You need to get that fixed."

"Yeah," Andie said, and then met Carter at the bottom of the stairs as he headed for the library. "Here," she said, handing him the package. "This is addressed to you, and I have to deal with Mrs. Crumb before she knifes one of the cleaning people."

She turned back to the kitchen but the knocker went again, this time a guy named Bruce who said he'd been sent to look over the house for repairs. "I walked around it," he said slowly. "You gotta lotta work here."

"Driveway first," Andie said, "and then—"

Upstairs, Alice began to scream, "NO NO NO *NO NO NO*," and Andie said, "Just make a list," and ran for the stairs.

Once she'd gotten Alice's comforter away from the poor woman who was trying to put it in the laundry—"It's new," she said, "it's okay"—and Alice and the comforter and Jessica-the-dead-blue-doll back down to the kitchen with some cocoa as an apology, she confronted Mrs. Crumb again.

Mrs. Crumb turned on her and spat, *"I'm not going to put up with this!"*

"You're quitting?" Andie said, hope rising, but Mrs. Crumb saw the abyss and stepped back.

"You brought those women into *my house*," she said, and pressed her lips together until her small mouth almost disappeared. "You had *no right*—"

"It's not your house," Andie said calmly. "It's Carter and Alice's house. And they deserve to live someplace clean."

Alice looked up at that, a cocoa mustache making a pinky-brown slash on her colorless face. Her topknot was now over her ear, and Jessica had a new brown splotch on her blue-white face.

"You are the house*keeper,*" Andie went on as she pulled out Alice's scrunchie and moved her topknot to the center of her head again, "which means you're supposed to keep the house in good condition, which you have not done because it's impossible for one person to do so." *And because you haven't tried.* "Therefore I have brought in people who will. You can assist them, you can ignore them, or you can leave. It's your choice." She picked up the doll and wiped the cocoa off and part of the discolored paint came with it. "Sorry," she said to Alice and handed the doll back to her.

Alice put the doll under her arm and drank more cocoa, watching as Mrs. Crumb turned an interesting shade of puce.

"I've been here for *sixty years*," Mrs. Crumb said, and Andie started to slap her down and realized that it wasn't just rage, it was fear.

The woman had been at Archer House since her teens and she was in her seventies now. She wasn't going to get another job and the chances that she had much retirement were slim. *Oh, hell,* Andie thought. Torturing old ladies was not in her job description even if the old ladies were hags from hell. "I suggest that we have the Happy Housekeepers come in every week, and you supervise. After all, no one knows the house like you do."

"Well," Mrs. Crumb said, her breath slowing slightly.

"Somebody named Bruce is going to be doing some repairs, too," Andie said, not adding, *And Mr. Archer would like to know where the money he gave you for that went.* Let North fight that battle.

"I don't know," Mrs. Crumb said, but it was all bluster now.

"Is it lunch yet?" Alice said from behind them. "Because I would like a cheese sandwich. But no tomato soup."

"How about chicken noodle?" Andie asked her.

"No. NO NO NO *NO NO*—"

"Oh, for crying out loud, Alice, it's soup, not poison."

Alice looked at her darkly. "Maybe."

"I'll make it, you try it."

"No."

"I made cookies last night. Try the soup, you can have a cookie."

"No."

"I said *try* it. One spoonful."

"NO."

"Fine." Andie turned back to Mrs. Crumb, who seemed distracted now, her eyes darting like a cornered rat's, falling finally on Alice, slopping her cocoa onto the table.

"You be careful," she snapped at Alice, her eyes cold on the little girl. "You're making a mess on my nice clean table."

"It's not your table," Alice said calmly. "It's mine. Andie said so."

"We'll clean it up later," Andie said, taken aback by Alice's use of her name.

"This ain't right," Mrs. Crumb said, and Andie realized she was near tears. "I been here for sixty years. None of you was born yet but I was here. You don't know this house. You're *stirring things up*. You—"

"Which brings us to my next point," Andie said. "You will stop talking about ghosts. I have no idea why you thought that was a good idea, but from now on the official position in this house is that there are no ghosts."

Alice drained her cocoa cup. "I want my sandwich *now*."

Andie got out the whole wheat bread as Mrs. Crumb said, "I never said there were no ghosts."

"Yes you did," Alice said, and Mrs. Crumb glared at her with absolutely no effect.

"Even if there were," Andie said, "I don't see why a good housecleaning would upset them. They don't live in the dust."

"Oh, they care," Mrs. Crumb said to Andie, folding her arms over her orange-flowered apron. "You'll see they care."

"For the last time, I do not believe in ghosts—" Andie began, and then Carter came into the kitchen with the box opened.

"It's computers," he said, more confused than defiant, and Andie looked inside and saw two sleek Apple boxes holding Mac Power-Book 145s. She took the boxes out and put them on the table and found a note from Kristin that said, "Mr. Archer wanted to make sure the children had computers."

"Those are from your Uncle North," Andie said, showing him the note, thinking, *Thank you*. North never missed on the details.

"Who?" Alice said.

"Bad Uncle," Andie told her. "They come with a graphics program," she told Carter.

"What is it?" Alice said poking at her box. "Is it candy?"

"Better," Carter said, and left with his Mac, undoubtedly heading for the library.

"You think you're so smart, but you're not," Mrs. Crumb said. "All this change, all this stuff. It's bad."

Andie gave up on the pity. "Mrs. Crumb, I do not want to have to fire you, but I will if you cause any more problems. You will keep the kitchen clean and you can supervise the Happy Whosis, but you will not tell any more stories about ghosts, and you will not make any more veiled threats, and you will either assist me with the cooking or get out of my way, and you will answer any questions I have without muttering. Is that clear?"

Mrs. Crumb's nostrils flared, but she said, "Yes."

"Good," Andie said, and finished making Alice's lunch.

When she was done, she put the sandwich in front of Alice.

"I think I'll have cookies," Alice said.

"I think you won't," Andie said.

Alice glared at her, and Andie glared back, and Alice put her headphones on and ate her sandwich, swathed in her pearls and her shells and her locket and her bat, pretending Andie didn't exist.

It's only a month, Andie thought, *and no matter what North thinks, I can make it a month easy.*

"It's mean not to give me a cookie," Alice said.

Not that it mattered what North thought. He'd forgotten her already. He—

The doorknocker thudded again.

I'm going to get a scooter, she thought, as she race-walked across the Great Hall and opened the door.

A deliveryman with a clipboard stood there. "We got a stove for a Mrs. Andromeda Archer."

"A stove," Andie said.

North had sent her a new stove.

"This the place?" the guy said.

"Yeah, this is the place," she said, and silently apologized to North as they wheeled in her new stove, the latest model of the stove he'd bought her ten years ago. She hadn't asked then, but he knew. She hadn't asked now, but—

So he's good with stoves, she thought, trying to dismiss the whole thing.

But he hadn't forgotten her.

"It means nothing," she said to nobody, and went back to the kitchen to feed Carter.

Four

That afternoon, while the cleaning crew worked around them, Andie sat the kids down in the library and explained their educational goals to them: They had to be up to their grade levels by January, and the only way she'd know that was if they took the achievement tests. Carter looked at his PowerBook with longing, and Andie handed him the curriculum. "Here's what you need to know. The notes from your last nanny said you had all your textbooks. I can go over this with you, or you can look it up and ask me for help when you hit a snag." *Unless it's math; then we're both screwed.* She went over everything with him and then said, "Can you do this on your own?" He nodded. "Yell if you need me," she told him, and turned to Alice.

"I'm not gonna do it," Alice said, folding her arms.

"Too hard, huh?" Andie said. "Poor baby. Here, you can start with the kindergarten workbook."

"I'm not in kindergarten!" Alice said, outraged.

"Oh, sorry." Andie handed her the first-grade workbook.

"I'm not in first grade, either!"

"Prove it. Do the final test at the back of the book. I bet you can't."

Alice grabbed the book and started working, bitching the entire time. Andie went to see how the cleaners were doing on the second floor—"You're going to need new linens everywhere," one of the women told her, "this stuff is rotted through"—and checked to make sure the cable guy hadn't fallen in the moat—"You're ready to go," he told her, "but it wasn't easy, all this stone, and some of it's loose"—and gave a glowering Mrs. Crumb instructions for dinner, and then went back to Alice and Carter.

"You've got cable TV," she told Carter, who said, "Cool," the first positive word she'd had from him, and then she turned to Alice.

Alice was working on the fourth-grade final test. Andie went back and checked the first-, second-, and third-grade tests. Perfect scores on first and second and near perfect on the third.

"How is this possible?" she asked Carter, showing him.

"The nannies weren't dumb and neither is Alice." He held up the curriculum. "You got a test for this?"

"I can make one up," she said, just as Alice pushed the fourth-grade final across to her.

"Can I have candy now?" she said.

"Candy?" Andie said, and Carter said, "They bribed her to work." Andie shook her head at Alice. "No, no candy. Here's what you missed on the third-grade test." She shoved the workbook back to Alice who looked outraged again. Alice was looking outraged a lot today. *Suck it up, Alice.* "We'll go over the questions you missed in a minute." She looked back at Carter. "I'll make up the test for you to see if you've got the curriculum down, and then we'll figure out independent studies for you. I'm telling you now, I'm terrible at math, so we'll have to get you outside help there, but I'm a whiz at language skills, so there I've got you covered." He gave her his usual blank stare, so she said, "I'll give you something to read, and we can talk about it—or not—and then you'll write a short paper on it. I'll show you.

It's easy. You just think about what you read, organize your thoughts, and write it down. As long as your arguments are clear and make sense, you're good. Math, of course, will still be math."

He went back to the computer.

"These questions were wrong," Alice announced, looking at the ones she'd missed.

Andie sighed and sat down with her and went through everything, including the fourth-grade test, which Alice had done pretty well on, considering she was a third-grader. "This is what we're going to be studying," she told Alice. "Candy," Alice said, and Andie worked out a series of rewards for her, including the right to pick out bedding for each of the ten bedrooms in the house and a dinner at Dairy Queen for every completed unit.

"The stove is exactly right," she told North when she called him to thank him after the kids were in bed. "I'm making banana bread tonight in celebration. And the computer for Carter was a genius move."

"Banana bread," North said. "Send some of that up here, would you?"

"Sure," Andie said, surprised he was asking for something. He never asked for anything. "I'm going to teach Alice to make cookies tomorrow. You want some of those, too?"

"Chocolate chip?" North said, sounding like a kid.

"Yes."

"Yes, please." There was a pause, and when he spoke again, he was back to business. "So everything is going well there?"

"Sort of. The kids have been through a lot, and this place is Amityville, the House of Usher, and Hill House combined, so their environment isn't working in their favor, but they're very bright and very tough and they've had each other. The worst mistake was sending Carter away to school. But if I can keep bribing Alice, and Carter will do the work, they'll be ready to go back to school by January. The nannies did a good job educating them. From what

I can tell, they were sensible, competent women except for the last one. Nanny Joy. Telling her to kidnap them and take them to Columbus was not a good idea. Alice calls you 'Bad Uncle.'"

"I did not tell her to kidnap them," North said, sounding exasperated. "I told her to bring them to Columbus if she possibly could."

"Sorry. I wasn't sure. You are sort of a hand-of-God, forget-the-feelings, don't-bother-me-while-I'm-working kind of guy. And in your defense, it was a good idea, her execution of it just sucked. We have to find a way to get them to agree to go, not trick them into it."

"Well, you have a month," North said, his voice suddenly cold, and she reacted to the undercurrent more than to the words.

"What's that supposed to mean?"

"That was our deal, a month."

"And what's wrong with that?"

"Nothing, assuming you don't bolt before then."

"I beg your pardon."

"Never mind. Is there anything else you need?"

Andie scowled at the phone. "Yeah, I need you to back off that bolting thing." *Or no cookies, you jackass.*

"Tell me you haven't thought about it."

"I just *got* here," Andie said, ignoring the sympathy she'd felt for the nannies who'd left. "What's wrong with you?"

"Hand-of-God guy?" North said.

"Well, you do like your distance. You like to do your caring from another room."

"Whereas you do limited engagements and then head for another state."

"Hey, I'm not the one taking care of Damian and the Bad Seed from a hundred miles away. I'm *here*."

"And at the end of the month, you won't be taking care of them at all. You don't stay."

"*You don't care,* you don't even *see them.*" There was a long silence, and Andie thought, *This is stupid.* "I'm sorry. I don't want to have this dumb argument. Of course you care, you sent me down here."

"Fair enough," North said, as distant as ever. "Is there anything else you need from me?"

Not anymore, Andie thought. "No, we're fine. Unless you're willing to come out here and burn the place down for me so we have to leave."

There was a sharp intake of breath on the phone.

Andie thought, *That wasn't North, somebody is listening in.*

It had to be Crumb; Carter wasn't interested in anything but his books and his drawing, and Alice would have contributed to the conversation by now. "Well," she said brightly. "I can't wait to get home to you, baby. I really miss you."

"What?"

"I know how hard this separation is on our *marriage,* but it's worth it to see that the kids are safe."

"What?"

"But I'll be home in a couple of weeks," Andie said. "I'll send the cookies and banana bread tomorrow. Can't wait to see you. Love you. Bye."

"Uh, good-bye," North said, and Andie thought, *Jesus, you suck at improv,* as he hung up.

She went downstairs and told Mrs. Crumb to stop eavesdropping—"I never!"—and that she'd be making her own tea from now on. She went into the pantry, a dark narrow little room off the back of the kitchen, and found a row of old glass decanters in a cabinet, most of the bottles empty except for one with peppermint schnapps and another that smelled like musty Amaretto and a third that was some kind of brandy. She made a cup of tea with a shot of Amaretto in it—one shot—and took the cup upstairs and sipped it in the warmth of her bed while looking over the kids' schoolwork, which was really very good. When she was done, she put the empty cup on her bedside table, and slid down into the sheets, thinking about the kids. They had such potential if only they weren't so . . .

Her thoughts clouded, and she slipped into a deep tea-and-liquor-aided sleep. The whispers began again—*Who do you love? Who do you want?*—and she thought, *Yeah, yeah, yeah,* and when North showed up in her dreams, she thought, *Bad Uncle,* and refused to have anything to do with him.

After the first week, Andie kept pushing and the changes came fast. Alice worked her way through the third-grade workbooks, her tongue stuck between her teeth, her pearls, shells, locket, and bat swinging forward as she bent over her papers, her Walkman cast forlornly to one side so she could concentrate. It really was a miracle she hadn't become hunchbacked from the weight around her neck. She'd decided she liked the black-and-white-striped leggings Andie had bought her, but they were too small, so when Andie went back and bought her the larger size, Alice cut the pants off the too-small ones and tied her topknot with one of the legs. She liked it so much she began ordering Andie to do her hair every morning, which was an annoying improvement. It took Andie a while to realize who Alice looked like: a very short Madonna in *Desperately Seeking Susan,* except Alice hadn't discovered earrings and eye shadow yet. Well, it was only a matter of time.

Alice cooperated with everything once she was bribed, earning many trips to the shopping center, which resulted in each of the bedrooms sporting different treatments: red and black paisleys, pumpkin-orange stripes, purple checks, a violent green leaf pattern, a multicolored dot extravaganza that made Andie dizzy when she looked at it, and a green *Sesame Street* comforter with Bert and Ernie waving on the top. "Bee-you-tee-ful," Alice said with each one, and since Andie didn't have to sleep in any of them, she said, "Yep," and moved on. Alice and Andie painted Alice's bedroom walls white, and Alice spent the ensuing days drawing pictures on her wall in marker. The black got quite a workout since that's what she drew everything in, and the red was almost as bad since there was a lot of blood in Alice's imagination, but the blue ran out first, used for many butterflies and a woman in a long blue dress. "Who is that?" Andie asked, and Alice said, "Dancing princess," and drew on. She also badgered Andie to tell her the princess story every night and then critiqued it mercilessly as it evolved into a story about a brave princess in a black ruffled skirt and striped stockings, and the Bad Witch who lived with her and tried to make her eat soup.

But it wasn't all Bad Witch. Alice also began to follow Andie around after school time, asking, "Whatcha doing?" and then criticizing whatever it was with great interest and enthusiasm, which evolved into the Three O'Clock Bake, when Andie would turn on the radio and they'd listen to the only station they could get—"All the Hits All the Time"—while Andie mixed up whatever she was making in time to the music, and Alice helped a little and danced around the kitchen a lot, belting out the hits with fervor if not technical accuracy.

Alice was singing "I'm too sexy for my shirt" one afternoon as Andie began to make banana bread. "This is my specialty," she told Alice as she got out her mixing bowl. "Do you want me to show you how to make it?"

Alice said, "My specialty is *dancing*," and kept hoochie-coochie-ing to Right Said Fred.

My specialty used to be dancing, too, Andie thought, and began to peel bananas for banana bread.

Alice stopped and peered over the bowl. "The bananas are yucky," she said. "They are spotted and brown and *dead*."

"They're supposed to be spotted and brown for banana bread," Andie said, smooshing them up in the bowl with her fork. "That's how you know they're ready to make into banana bread. If they're yellow, they're no good for bread. Everything has a time, Alice, and it is time to make these bananas into bread. It's very good."

"I do not like nuts," Alice said, frowning at the bag of walnuts on the counter.

"Then don't eat the banana bread," Andie said, and beat the banana bread in time to the music, bouncing while she stood at the counter and Alice danced around singing, "I don't like nuts" to "Achy Breaky Heart" ("I do not like nuts, I really don't like nuts"). Then Andie put the bread in the oven, and Alice went back to singing with the music.

When the banana bread came out, Alice ate it.

The next day she danced to "Everything Changes" while Andie made chocolate chip cookies with nuts—"I do not like nuts." "Then don't eat the cookies"—and ate the cookies. The day after that, she belted out "I Will Always Love You" as cupcakes came out of the oven—"I will eat these because there are no nuts"—and after the first two weeks and many Hits All the Time, she added waffles and pancakes and lasagna and spaghetti and whole wheat rolls to her menu— "I do not like whole wheat." "Then don't eat the rolls"—and began to put on ounces and bounce just from consuming Andie's quality calories as she danced around the kitchen. After a while, Andie danced, too, which Alice, surprisingly, approved of. She was still pale as a little ghost, but she was a healthy little ghost. By the time the first three weeks were up, the only problems Alice still had were intractable stubbornness, occasional screaming, and nightmares.

Andie didn't realize Alice was having nightmares until she used the kids' bathroom one night and heard her crying as she came out. She knocked on the door and went in, and found Alice weeping helplessly in her sleep. She woke her and then picked her up and carried her to the rocker and began to rock her, saying, "What happened, baby, what did you dream?" and Alice sobbed, "They had teeth." "What had teeth, baby?" Andie said, and Alice said, "The *butterflies*." Andie kissed her forehead and said, "Butterflies don't have teeth, it was just a bad, bad dream," and rocked and rocked as Alice cried, quietly now. *I need a lullaby,* she thought, but the only one she could think of was from a Disney cartoon Alice played over and over. She began to hum "Baby Mine," and when Alice quieted down a little, she sang, "so precious to me," holding her close. Alice sighed and in a little while fell back asleep, and Andie held her for a while longer, just for the chance to hold her and in case she dreamed again, and then she put her back to bed and tucked her in. The next day she asked Alice about the butterflies, but Alice said, "I don't remember," and turned away, stubborn as ever in the daylight. After that, Andie put a baby monitor in Alice's room so that when the little girl had bad dreams, she could go to her.

Meanwhile, Carter aced the tests Andie wrote based on the curriculum, listened patiently to her explanation of whatever lesson was next, and wrote his critical thinking papers. Whenever possible he wrote on comic books, but his arguments were clear and concise and that's all Andie was looking for. After one particularly good paper on the way comics were drawn, she took the kids to an art supply store on their way to the shopping center and saw him smile for the first time. *Okay,* she thought, *I'm getting the hang of this,* and loaded him up with quality drawing supplies. Other than that, nothing changed: Carter did his work silently, read silently, drew in his sketchbook silently, worked on his computer silently, and ate everything Andie put in front of him, although he was now growing at such an alarming rate that she thought there was something wrong. "I swear, he's grown two inches in three weeks," she told Flo when she called her for help. "I expected him to grow out with all the food I'm shoving at him, but not *up.* And he walks like his legs hurt. I want to call a doctor but he won't go." "He's twelve," Flo said. "It's a growth spurt. Keep feeding him, he'll be fine." So Andie bought him new pants that would cover his newly exposed ankles and gave him aspirin when he winced, and kept feeding him, and Flo was right, he was fine. Silent, but fine.

And during it all, Andie tried to figure out what the hell was wrong in Archer House.

Because once the routines were settled—schoolwork in the morning, grilled cheese and tomato soup for lunch, reading and drawing and baking in the afternoon, reluctant eating of new food for dinner, Go Fish after dinner (there was a routine Andie regretted immediately since Alice seized on it and refused to give up, snarling, *"Go fish!"* with venom whenever possible), and then bedtime and reading comics for Carter, and bedtime and the princess story for Alice—once all that routine was in place and the house was clean, and at least the illusion of stability had been established, Andie still felt that whatever was wrong was as strong as ever, waiting out there for her. And she was pretty sure the kids felt it, too: Carter seemed to be always looking over his shoulder, waiting for something, and Alice's screaming seemed to be tied to more than just being crossed, erupting when anything threatened her routine. There was more fear in those screams than Andie had realized at first, mostly rage, true, but definitely fear underneath. *It's the house,* Andie thought, and tried to find a way to break through their resistance to comfort them with no success.

"They're just tolerating me," she told North when she called him at the end of the third week to give him the update on their education. She was on the pay phone at the Dairy Queen, which wasn't the best place to have long conversations but had the advantage that Mrs. Crumb would not be listening in. Add to that it was a sunny day in late October, and she was wearing her favorite skirt—greeny-blue chiffon with turquoise sequins—and Alice hadn't screamed at all so far that day, and things seemed more doable than usual. It helped that she and North were being polite again after sniping at each other for a couple of weeks. The politeness was cold, but it wasn't annoying.

"You're getting the job done," North said, his voice brisk and detached. "Everything is back to normal there."

Andie thought about Alice sobbing the night before in another nightmare. "I think normal is still a long way off. I can hear Alice over the baby monitor talking to an imaginary friend at night after she's supposed to be asleep, and she's still having terrible butterfly nightmares."

"Butterfly nightmares?"

"She cried last night because the butterflies were mad because we hadn't mulched their garden. She said she and Aunt May put in a butterfly garden here and we needed to get it ready for winter. We just got mulch, so we can do that tomorrow, but in a day or so, there'll be another nightmare. She has a lot of angry butterflies in her dreams. And she loves butterflies, North. I just don't get it."

"Poor kid," North said. "I don't know what a butterfly garden is, but we'll put one in. How's Carter?"

"Still silent as the grave. The only things he cares about are comics, drawing, and Alice. He won't let me see his drawings but he works hard on them. I took him to an art supply store, and he looked like he'd died and gone to heaven. There was a drawing table there he kept looking at, but I didn't want to buy it and put it in at the house since I'm trying to get him to move to Columbus."

"Let me know which one it was and we'll put it in his room here. Mother's getting the bedrooms on the second floor cleared out now. She asked if there was anything the kids wanted."

"Alice likes blue. And sequins. And butterflies. The butterfly garden will be important for that."

"I'll call a landscaper in the spring. That way Alice can plan whatever she wants with him."

"Oh," Andie said, taken aback by how careful he was being. Somebody else would have just socked in a butterfly garden, but North wanted Alice to be a part of it. "That's a great idea, it really is. Carter will just want bookshelves and art stuff. He loves that computer, too. He's a really quiet kid"—*completely silent, actually*—"so books and drawing supplies and the computer are probably all he needs."

"What kind of books?"

"Comic books, drawing books, books on drawing comics . . ." Andie thought back to what he'd been reading, what he'd written about. "He likes . . . justice, so maybe some novels like that?"

"Justice?"

"He's big on fairness, on lousy people getting what they deserve. His school papers are about that a lot. And his favorite TV is old *Equalizer* reruns. So any stories like that . . ."

"His dad was a lawyer. You think he's interested in law?"

"As a career? Maybe. He's twelve, he's probably more interested in the hot cars and the cool spy gadgets."

"And the cool babes," North said, which was so out of character for him that Andie laughed.

"He's *twelve*," she said.

"Southie chased girls in kindergarten."

"That's Southie. When did you start?"

"I didn't."

"Excuse me?"

"Girls were always around, but I wouldn't have passed up hot cars and cool spy gadgets for them."

"So they chased you based on your limitless charm and devastating good looks," Andie said, only half kidding.

"Well, the money helped."

"It wasn't the money," Andie said, remembering the first time she'd seen him, leaning against the bar talking to some blonde in a black dress and looking like something out of an old movie. Cary Grant. Paul Newman. "It definitely was not the money. But still, you never chased girls?"

"Just you," he said.

"Oh."

"And you met me halfway. It's hard to chase somebody who's coming right at you."

"I couldn't help myself," Andie said. "I'd never seen anybody like you before. It was like meeting a giraffe."

"Well, thanks for coming to the zoo," North said. "Although I'd have gone after you, if you hadn't."

"Next time I'll play hard to get," Andie said, and then realized what she said. "You know, in the next life. Or whatever. So the drawing table for Carter would be great, and the butterfly garden for Alice, but I'm still not getting anywhere in convincing them to leave. And you'd think they'd want to. This place is creepy." *Please don't ask me what I meant by "next time." Because I have no idea.*

"You still think the house is creepy?" North said, moving on, to her relief. "I figured you'd be past that by now."

"No, North, I'm not past it because you can't get past it, it's *creepy.* And then there's Mrs. Crumb. She has some very odd habits. Like she plays gin by herself."

"What?"

"Gin rummy. She deals herself a hand and sticks another hand in a card rack across the table, and then she plays both hands. It makes no sense but she does it most nights with a cup of spiked tea beside her. Several cups." *I have tea,* Andie thought, trying to separate herself from the crazy woman. *But I don't drink peppermint schnapps. I have standards. I hit the Amaretto.* "I think the house has made her insane. I swear, sometimes she's two different people. One of them is grumpy and dumb and hates me, and the other is a lot sharper and thinks I'm an idiot. It's like her mind comes and goes. We'll be talking and she'll just . . . change."

"Is she dangerous?"

"No. She's not that proactive. Hell, she usually loses to the other hand. She's just . . . cantankerous and strange. Like everything else here."

"Well, your month is almost over," North said briskly. "Congratulations for sticking it out for three weeks."

"Thank you," Andie said coldly, prepared to bitch if he said "bolter" again.

"If the place is getting to you and you want to leave early, you can. I've found another nanny. She seems very—"

"What?" Andie said, jerked out of her annoyance.

"The next nanny. She's coming out the first of next week to meet the kids, so if you want to leave early, I'll tell her that's when she starts."

He went on, explaining the nanny's educational background, all her sterling qualifications, and Andie watched Alice and Carter talk over their hamburgers, and thought about telling them that there'd be somebody new moving in to teach them, that she'd be leaving them alone again in all that weirdness.

Get out, every instinct she had said. *Get out now. You hate it here, and the kids don't like you, and the new nanny is more qualified than you are anyway. She does math.*

"So she'll be there Monday afternoon—"

"I'm staying," Andie said, and there was a long silence before North spoke.

"For how long?"

"Until I can figure out a way to get them to Columbus. I'll stay until they move in with you, and then Will and I will be in Columbus, and I can still see them and . . . help with the butterfly garden. Or whatever." The instinct in her that was saying *Run away* was still there, just not so loud. She'd only been there three weeks. It hadn't been that bad. It wouldn't take that long to figure out what was going on and get them to Columbus. She'd have them out by Thanksgiving. Christmas at the latest. "Lose the nanny. I'm staying."

After a long minute, North said, "All right. Thank you."

"You're welcome," Andie said, and then hung up, thinking, *I'm sure Will won't mind. Much.* Especially if she never mentioned that she'd told North there might be a next time for them. Because there wasn't going to be. She loved Will.

Then she called him to give him the news that she was staying, and he minded. A lot. "I'm coming down there," he said when she told him she'd be there for at least another month. "I miss you, and I can write anywhere."

"No."

"Why?"

Oh, hell. "Because the people here think I'm still married to North. If you show up, I'm going to have some explaining to do."

"Did he tell them that?"

"No, I did. He was as surprised as you are."

"I don't think 'surprised' really describes how I feel. What the hell, Andie?"

"Look, I'm starting to make progress with the kids, it's just another month—"

"Is he there? Is he there pretending to be married, too?"

"No, of course not. He has a law practice, he's not going to come down here and play house. Especially in this place. It's creepy."

"Can't you bring the kids up here?"

"That's what I'm working on. I'm hoping I can do it before Thanksgiving, definitely by Christmas."

"Christmas?"

Andie felt a tug on her skirt and looked down to see Alice standing in front of her, ketchup on her chin. She pulled the chiffon out of Alice's hands before any tomato got transferred and said, "What?"

"Can I have two ice creams?"

"No. That's greedy. You can have one cone."

"Andie," Will said.

"Just a minute," she told him as Alice said, "I want a big cone," her usual calculating gleam in her eye.

"The last time you got a big cone, the top fell off. Wouldn't you rather have a medium and keep the ice cream?"

"It won't fall off this time. That one was a *bad* cone."

"Okay, fine, big cone. You've got ketchup on your chin. Hold still." Andie licked her thumb and wiped the ketchup smear off Alice. "I'll be over in a minute to pay for your cone. Tell Carter he can have one, too."

"Okay," Alice said, and went back to Carter, yelling, "Andie says we can have cones. *Big* ones."

"Okay, sorry about that," Andie said to Will, licking the ketchup off her thumb.

"You sound just like a mother," Will said, his voice softer now.

"More like a wrangler," Andie said, looking after Alice's straight little back.

"Ready to have some kids of our own?"

"What?" Andie looked at the phone. "I don't want kids. Didn't we have this conversation?"

"Yeah, but you're a natural, Andie. I can hear it in your voice."

"That's exhaustion, which is probably about the only thing I have in common with real mothers. I'm not sleeping well here."

"That's because you're sleeping alone. I'll come down and—"

"And have sex with me? Somebody's gonna notice that, Will. I will not be committing fake adultery. I'll be back in a month. We'll have an orgy then."

Will sighed. "I don't like any of this. You were supposed to be home next week. I miss you."

Andie kept her eye on Alice, standing on tiptoe in front of the Dairy Queen window. "I have to go now."

"I love you," Will said.

"I love you, too," Andie said, frowning as Alice took a towering cone from the counter girl. "I'll—oh, for crying out loud."

Alice began to scream.

"What?"

"Alice dropped her ice cream. I *told* her—"

Alice screamed louder.

"I'm *coming,* knock it off, Alice! Will, I have to go."

"Call me—" Will began as she hung up the phone to go rescue Alice.

"Stop it," she said to the little girl. "Stop crying and I will fix it. Keep crying and we're going to the car. You cannot shriek every time something goes wrong, you have to *fix* it, Alice. Screaming doesn't do any good." Alice kept screaming, and Andie looked up at the counter girl. "Give us another large cone, please. And a cup." When the girl handed the ice cream over, Andie paid her and took the cone, upended it into the cup, and stuck a spoon in it. "Here," she said to Alice, "try not to wear most of it, please."

Alice stopped screaming and took the cup. "Thank you."

"You're welcome," Andie said, and Alice began to demolish her ice cream. "Alice, next time there's a problem, just *ask,* okay? If you can't fix it, I will."

Alice licked her spoon, transferring chocolate ice cream to her nose, narrowly avoiding dragging the end of the stocking that drooped down from her topknot through the cup. Andie tied the stocking up higher as Alice said, "You're not gonna be here."

"Yes I am." Andie gave the stocking a last tug. "You have chocolate on your nose."

"Carter says you're leaving on Halloween."

Andie looked back at Carter who met her eyes without expression. "No, I'm staying with you. The only way I leave is if you leave."

Alice licked up more ice cream from her cup. "How long are you staying?"

"As long as it takes," Andie said.

"Uh-huh." The little girl stabbed her ice cream with her spoon, looking mutinous again.

"Okay, how about this," Andie said. "I will bet you one of your necklaces that I will stay with you until you don't need me anymore." That seemed safe; she was pretty sure that Alice thought she didn't need her now.

Alice tilted her head. "What if that's forever?"

"Then I'll stay forever," Andie said, feeling a clutch of panic in her stomach. *Forever.*

"What do I get if you don't stay?"

"What do you want?"

Alice thought about it. "Ice cream."

"You'll get that anyway, Alice. Think of something big."

Alice tilted her head again, thinking hard as her ice cream melted, the striped stocking on her topknot sliding to the side of her head. "That skirt," she said finally, nodding at Andie.

"My skirt?" Andie swished the blue-green chiffon, watching the turquoise sequins sparkle in the sunlight. *Flo gets it right again,* she thought, and said, "You're on. What do I get? One of your necklaces?"

Alice frowned, looking down.

"Pearls?" Andie said, looking at the dingy lavender beads.

"They were my mom's."

"Oh," Andie said, remembering that Alice's mom had died giving birth to her. The pearls suddenly looked a lot more important. "The shells?"

"My daddy gave me those."

"The locket?"

"No, I found that. It's a treasure."

"You're going to need the Walkman."

"It was my mom's," Alice said, nodding.

"So that leaves the bat," Andie said, looking at the dubious piece of cheap metal and glittery stones.

"Aunt May gave that to me."

"So we'll think of something else."

Alice frowned in thought. "No," she said after some length. "You can have the bat if you stay." She licked up more ice cream. "But you won't stay. Carter is never wrong." She looked at Andie again, frowning. "Are you really going to give me that skirt when you leave?"

"I'm not leaving," Andie said. "Not without you anyway. But if something happens and I lose the bet, you get the skirt. Pinky swear."

Alice nodded and went back to her ice cream, still evidently a nonbeliever but now in line to get a sequined skirt, and Andie turned to see Carter regarding her over his own cone, his expression as flat as ever.

"You want to bet?" she said.

"You don't have anything I want," he said, and went back to his ice cream.

"Fair enough," Andie said.

One day at a time, she thought, *one day at a time.*

One day at a time may have been the plan, but it was the nights that were wearing Andie down. Alice was still having nightmares although not as often, and even when Alice slept through the night, Andie had her own dreams, carnal dreams about North that were so vivid that she woke up shaking, wanting him so much she ached. And she still heard whispers in her sleep asking, *Who do you love?* She'd told Mrs. Crumb she didn't want her to bring a tray up to her bedroom anymore, sticking with the spiked tea she made herself, but the dreams persisted. Finally one night she bypassed the tea completely, so exhausted that she was half asleep already, and slid down under the covers to shut out the chill—it was always cold as hell in her room at night—and dozed off, only to sit up again to punch her pillow into shape, and see something at the foot of her bed.

She froze as the vague shadow grew clearer and she could see a young woman, a girl, really, big-eyed and pretty with masses of curly hair, her form translucent and shifting in what looked like a party dress.

Hello, the girl said, swishing her full skirt as she pirouetted, blue in the moonlight.

"Who are you?" Andie said, and her voice seemed dreamlike, as if it were coming from very far away.

Oh, I'm you. The girl laughed. *I'm you when you were nineteen.* She leaned forward, the illusion of her shadow shifting a few seconds behind her movement so that she disassembled and reassembled as she moved. *Don't we look alike?*

"Don't do that," Andie said, feeling nauseous now. She didn't have dreams about past lives, that was entirely too twee, or maybe too Flo. Her mother would be all over this if it were happening to her. She struggled to wake up, but the girl only moved again and disoriented her, and another wave of cold nausea hit, so she stopped.

What happens to me after nineteen? the girl said. *Do I have wonderful adventures?*

"What?" Andie sank back on the pillows, sick to her stomach.

I want to know what happens next, the girl said. *I want to know the future. Do I fall in love? Is it wonderful?*

Andie thought of North, and then guiltily of Will. "Yes."

The girl drifted closer and the room grew colder and Andie shut her eyes to block out the sickening vertigo.

Tell me about him.

"He's a writer." Andie kept her eyes shut, picturing Will, laughing and warm.

Is he exciting? Does he make me crazy for him? Do I want him all the time?

"No." Andie tried to roll over, away from her. "I'm thirty-four. I grew out of that."

Terrible. That's terrible. You never get exciting?

"The first one. Go away."

Tell me about him.

"I'm freezing. Go away."

The girl moved back to the window, and the air around the bed grew marginally warmer.

Tell me about the other one.

"I want to sleep now."

Is he the one you dream about? The hot one?

She thought of North, of the muscle hidden by his suits, the passion behind that calm beautiful face, all of it focused on her in the first months of her marriage, those memories on perpetual replay in her dreams every night. "Yes. But then his uncle Merrill dies, and he works sixteen-hour days at the family firm, and he forgets I . . . we . . . exist, and I leave."

You left that guy? You should have done *something. You should have seduced him again. You should have—*

"Hey," Andie said, struggling to sit up. "I had therapy for this. Sometimes things end. The bastard broke my heart, and I got over it and moved on."

The girl drew back, alarmed. *All right.* Andie lay back down, and the girl said, *Tell me how you met. How do we meet him?*

Andie closed her eyes. It was weird to be harassed in a dream. But she remembered . . . "We're twenty-four, after too much to drink, we look across the bar and see a man watching us."

What does he look like? He's the blond guy in the dream?

"Yes. Almost white hair, cropped short. Tall. Great shoulders." She yawned again. "Wire-rimmed glasses."

This guy gave you the head-banging sex you've been dreaming about? The shadow sounded doubtful.

"Bluest eyes you've ever seen. Classic nose. Beautiful mouth. Women stop to stare at him and he doesn't notice because he's looking at me. Us. Are you sure you're me?"

Yes, the girl said. *Although I like guys who are built.*

"No you don't," Andie said, confused. "You go for musicians and art majors. And your mother tells you to stop chasing water signs and find an earth."

What?

"Flo. Our mother. You're not me." She struggled to sit up again, and the girl moved, and the vertigo sent Andie back to her pillows. She squinted at the shifting shape. "I think my hair was bigger then. Who are you?"

I'm you. You saw him. Then what happened? Did you smile at him?

"I was already smiling," Andie said, sinking deeper into the bed, trying to get from dream to sleep. "I stopped smiling when he walked toward me."

And you waited until he came to you. You made him come to you.

"No, I met him halfway. The band was playing 'Somebody's Baby.' It's hard to stand still when you hear 'Somebody's Baby.'"

The girl swished her skirt again. *It would have been better to wait.*

"I don't wait for anybody." Andie pulled the covers up over her head, feeling like Alice.

The girl was quiet for so long that Andie was almost asleep when she said, *That's better.*

Andie pulled the covers off her face. "What?"

Not waiting for anybody. That's better. Then what happens?

Andie shifted against the pillows. "We dance, and I'm so turned on I can't talk."

Dancing is good.

"And he says, 'Come with me,' and I do, and he kisses me in the street and it's the best kiss of my entire life. I want to go to sleep now."

Then what happens?

"We go to his apartment and have head-banging sex, and twelve hours later, he proposes, and I think he's crazy, but we go to Kentucky." Talking about it brought it all back, how crazy happy she'd been, how crazy happy *he'd* been. Not like himself at all. "He remembered to put Jackson Browne in the tape player, but he forgot a ring and we stopped in an antiques store and got this old gold band that I loved." Andie pulled her hand out of the covers and looked at

it. "A week later, it turned my finger green, and he went crazy because he wanted to get a real one, but I said no."

You're wearing a green ring? the girl said, disapproval strong in her
voice.

"I cleaned it up and painted and varnished it so the green didn't
happen again. I should get rid of it." Andie closed her hand so the
ring wouldn't slip off and put her hand under the covers again.

Then what?

"Then we got married. Because I can't say no to him. Couldn't
say no to him for a whole year. From the minute he said, 'I'm North
Archer and I think we should leave,' I was done."

The shadow shifted quickly, moving closer. *You were married to*
North Archer?

Andie woke up at that.

The girl was much more solid now, still translucent but clearer,
stronger, beautiful, big dark eyes and mad curling hair, and when
she moved, all the parts of her moved together so the vertigo was
almost gone. *You were married to North Archer and you divorced him?*
WHY?

"Because the guy I married disappeared into his law office and
came out a walking suit." Andie sat up. "What kind of dream is this?
You're not me. I was never beautiful."

The room was very clear now, the moonlight almost like sunlight, edges sharp and entirely non-dreamlike, and the place was
freezing.

"This isn't a dream," Andie said. "You're a ghost."

Don't be silly, the girl said. *There's no such things as ghosts.*

She moved toward Andie again, but this time Andie stayed sitting up, staring into the eye sockets of a dead woman.

"*No,*" she said, and the girl flowed over her, freezing her to the
bone, saying, *You should get him here. You should bring him here. He*
should be here to kiss you goodnight, and the nausea swept over her again,

a disorientation so fierce that she fell back onto the bed, spiraling down into the dark again.

When she woke up, her windows were full of sun and the room was perfectly normal.

The girl had been so real. *I don't believe in ghosts,* Andie thought, especially ghosts in dreams. She shook her head and went to get dressed and deal with Alice and Carter, reminding herself that it was just a dream.

Five

Andie was distracted during breakfast, and Alice took full advantage, scoring cookies with her cereal as she listed all the things she was *not* going to do that morning. Andie answered her automatically, thinking about the dream, until Alice said, "I should have *four* cookies," and she said, "No, you should not," and took the cookie plate away from her.

There were dreams and there was reality, and reality was stopping Alice before she made herself sick.

"You are *mean*," Alice said, scowling at her.

"Yeah, yeah, yeah. Alice, do you know a woman who has lots of curly dark hair?"

"You," Alice said, and drank the last of her milk.

"Not me. Really pretty. Wearing a party dress. A blue party dress."

"No," Alice said, her nose in her glass.

"Huh."

"I need another cookie."

"No. You have to do your reading now. You can have a snack

later. And then we'll mulch your butterfly garden." She wiped the chocolate from the cookies off Alice's face, still thinking about the blue girl in the moonlight.

Blue girl. Blue dancing princess.

"Alice, who's the blue dancing princess?"

"I want to read outside." Alice got up and left the room, and Andie thought, *This is not good.*

Alice must be dreaming about the same girl. That brought up all kinds of things that Andie didn't want to think about and Alice obviously didn't want to talk about. And when Alice didn't want to talk . . .

"Come on," Alice said from the doorway into the dining room. "I've got my book."

"Get your hoodie," Andie told her. "It's chilly out." When Alice came back with her black hoodie zipped up, they headed out toward the pond, a large, green, stagnant surface that looked more like a massive leak in the moat than a planned water feature, which made sense since the moat was equally green and disgusting. Alice walked in front, her black-and-white-striped legs kicking through the fallen leaves and making her black flounced jersey skirt bounce. *Cute,* Andie thought, and considered telling Alice how good she looked. The last time she'd tried it, Alice had made gagging sounds, but she'd worn the skirt and leggings every day since then.

"Looking good, Alice," Andie called.

Alice made gagging sounds.

When they got to the pond, Andie shook out the old quilt they used to picnic, and Alice threw her book down and announced, "This is the Sea of Azof. It is the world's shallowest sea."

Andie looked at the turgid, green pond. "Okay."

Alice nodded. "We should go look at the butterfly garden."

"Now?" Andie said, but Alice was already marching around to the far side of the house, so she dropped her things on the blanket and followed her around.

The garden was pretty bleak in October, most of it dead or dying with only the spiky purple asters still giving it their all.

Alice looked sad. "It's dead."

"We'll put the mulch down after lunch, and that will keep it warm, and then it'll all come back again in the spring."

"I know. But that means the butterflies are gone."

"They'll be back in the spring, too." Andie watched her, trying to see what she saw. "Did you plant this garden?"

"Aunt May did," Alice said, sadly. "But I helped. A lot. She said it was my garden, too."

Andie almost said, "In the spring, we'll clean it all up," and then she remembered that in the spring, God willing, they'd be in Columbus. "We can plant a garden like this in Columbus." She tried to remember how much sun the backyard of North's Victorian got.

"Last year, Aunt May collected seed. From the black-eyed Susans and the coneflowers and I forget what else." Alice kicked at a bushy serrated-edged plant. "And this stuff takes over *everywhere* so we have to get rid of some of it." She sounded like an exasperated adult, and Andie thought, *Aunt May said that.*

She kicked it again, and a lemony smell floated up to Andie. "What is it?"

"Lemon balm," Alice pronounced, and Andie pictured a kindly, older woman bending down and saying, "Lemon balm," to Alice in that same tsking voice, Alice nodding wisely beside her.

"Aunt May really knew her plants," Andie said.

"These are what butterflies like." Alice pointed to a stalky-looking plant that looked like giant dead daisies. "Coneflower." She pointed to another. "Black-eyed Susan. Parsley. Columbine. Joe Pye. Zinnia. Salvia. Milkweed. Bergamot. Aster. Butterfly bush."

She pointed to each of them, naming them lovingly, with a softness Andie hadn't seen in her before, and then she stooped and plucked a big, ugly withered plant with a fuzzy stem. "Weed," she said, disgusted, and threw it away.

"They must be very beautiful in the summer," Andie said. Now, it looked like a garden of death except for the plucky asters.

"The butterflies are bee-you-tee-ful," Alice said. "Swallowtails and monarchs and skippers. I'm going to be a lepidopterist when I grow up."

"That's very cool," Andie said, meaning it.

Alice nodded, accepting the approval as her right. "And sometimes we get hummingbirds, which are also very cool. Aunt May said we could plant hummingbird plants next summer . . ."

Her voice trailed off, and Andie thought, *Ouch,* and then Alice turned her back on the garden, her face blank, and marched back to the blanket, where she plunked herself down, put her Walkman headphones on, and picked up her book.

Andie sat down beside her. "We'll make a hummingbird garden, Alice. Either here or in Columbus, wherever we are, we'll have a butterfly and hummingbird garden. And we'll put the mulch down to keep these plants warm all winter."

Alice shrugged and opened her book.

Andie thought, *Tell North we need a hummingbird garden, too,* and then went back to considering the thing that had been haunting her since the night before: the blue girl. Maybe Alice had inspired the dream. They were telling the Princess Alice story every night now, Alice correcting her and shaping it as they went, but the blue dancing princess was always in there. Maybe she was just dreaming Alice's story . . .

She smelled something horrible and looked over to see Alice poking at something with a stick. When she looked closer, it was a dead frog, bloated in extinction.

"Alice, don't do that, it's dead."

Alice pulled her headphones off, and Andie repeated herself.

"It only looks dead," Alice said. "It'll be okay."

She poked it again, and Andie took the stick away before she broke it open and released God knew what. "It's dead," Andie told her firmly. "Leave it alone."

Alice looked up at her, her eyes flat. "You don't know so much."

"Probably not. But that frog is dead."

"No, *it isn't*," Alice said, her face screwed up to yell. "No, no, *no, no—*"

She turned away as her voice rose, and then she stopped, staring across the pond.

"What?" Andie said, and looked, too.

There was a woman there, dressed in old-fashioned black, her flounced skirt motionless in the October wind, her body half-bowed.

"Who is that?" Andie said.

Alice jerked around and stared at Andie for a moment, her eyes wide with surprise.

"Alice, who is that woman over there?"

"There's nobody," Alice said, and sat down with her book.

Andie looked back at the woman, thick-waisted and clumsy as she moved closer to the edge of the trees. "Alice?"

"I don't see *anybody*." Alice stared at her book, and for the next minute the pages didn't turn while she stared down. Then she stole another look across the pond and closed her book. "Tell me the Princess Alice story again."

Andie looked back at the woman. Maybe just a neighbor. Alice wasn't the neighborly sort, maybe she didn't like people watching her. Andie didn't like people watching her, either.

"Princess Alice," Alice said. "Tell me."

"Right." Andie started the never-ending Princess Alice story again, beginning with how brave the princess was and how her brother was the best artist in the kingdom, and how the mean witch was defeated once again—

"And Princess Alice got all the cookies she wanted," Alice said, evidently still brooding on her lack of a fourth cookie.

—and how the dancing princess danced through the halls with her curly hair flying—

"And the Bad Uncle did not come because he was afraid of Princess Alice," Alice said for the umpteenth time.

"No, he didn't come because he was busy working. The dancing princess has curly hair?"

"She dances," Alice said impatiently. "And Bad Uncle is so afraid—"

"Bad Uncle isn't afraid of anything. He just *forgets* people. Alice, who is the dancing princess?"

"She dances. She has a glittery skirt like yours and she dances. And Princess Alice isn't afraid of anything, either. Now tell me new stuff."

"Alice, did you know the dancing princess?"

Alice looked at her warily. "It's just a story, Andie." She stole a glance across the pond.

Andie looked, too. The woman was still there, watching. "Who is she, Alice?"

"Princess Alice goes to the shopping center," Alice said, "and she buys beautiful material and makes a beautiful cover for her bed, and then she goes to the bookstore and gets a book on butterflies because butterflies never die." Alice stopped and looked back out over the pond quickly. "And then she comes home," she said, jerking her face back to Andie. "To the Bad Witch. The Bad Witch is not so bad but she should let Princess Alice have many cookies."

"Are there neighbors back there?" Andie said, shading her eyes to see the woman better.

"No," Alice said. "And then what does Princess Alice do?"

The woman stepped out of the trees onto the shore, clumsy in her long, heavy clothes. She was wearing a long three-tiered skirt, and her hair was pulled back tightly in a bun. She moved stiffly, no grace at all, and she looked oddly old-fashioned, almost sepia toned.

Andie said, "There, do you see her now?"

"No. *I want my story!*"

"Okay," Andie said, still watching across the pond. "After Princess Alice went shopping, she went to the Dairy Queen and she met a friend there."

"Okay," Alice said, keeping her head turned away from the pond.

There was something very wrong about that woman, wrong enough that Alice had forgotten her dead frog to pretend she wanted a story instead of yelling her head off at being thwarted. "Are you afraid of her, Alice?"

"Who?"

"The woman on the other side of the pond."

"I don't see anybody."

"Alice," Andie said, staring at her. "What the hell is going on here?"

"I don't see anybody. I want my STORY!"

Alice stared back, wild-eyed and, Andie realized, afraid. "Okay," she said soothingly. "The friend told Princess Alice about the school she went to, and Princess Alice said she wanted to go to that school, too, even though she'd have to leave the castle and go to Columbus—"

"I'm tired of that story," Alice said, and picked up her head-phones again.

Andie looked back at the woman who still stood there staring at them. Whoever she was, she was creepy. "Let's go in."

Alice shoved her book into Andie's hands without a word of protest, stood up, and headed for the house at a good clip even for her. Andie got up and shook the quilt out, and then picked up their things and turned to go and caught sight of somebody up on the tower of the house. She shaded her eyes again but the sun was behind him so all she could see was a tall man up there, his shoulders oddly box-like, as if he were wearing an old-fashioned coat, standing very straight, both hands on the ledge as if he owned the place.

It might be Bruce the contractor. If Bruce had started dressing funny and dyed his hair red and grown a beard and started showing up for work.

"I want a snack *now*," Alice said from twenty feet away, and Andie pointed up to the tower.

"Who's that?" she said, and Alice jerked her head up to the tower.

"I don't see anybody," she said, and kept moving toward the door, yelling back, "We have to mulch the butterfly garden today!" and Andie watched the figure on the tower watching her, and then looked back to see the woman in the trees, also watching her.

Okay, now I'm getting some answers, she thought, and followed Alice in to find Mrs. Crumb.

When Alice was curled up in the library with her book on butterflies, her Jessica doll, a cup of milk, a peanut butter and jelly sandwich, and two cookies, Andie went back to the kitchen to find Mrs. Crumb sitting at the table in another of her faded flowered aprons, hunched over a cup of heavily pepperminted tea, holding a hand of cards and facing the card rack across the table.

"There was a woman out by the pond," Andie said to her.

"Woman?" Mrs. Crumb said, suddenly cautious.

"In a long, old-fashioned dress. Alice saw her. I think she knew her."

Crumb looked startled. "Alice told you that?"

"No. She pretended not to see her, but Alice is not that good an actress."

"On the other side of the pond?"

"Are there neighbors over there?"

Mrs. Crumb shrugged and went back to studying her gin hand.

Andie sat down across from her and shoved the card holder to one side, and Mrs. Crumb looked up, startled.

"You know, I'm getting really tired of mysteries," Andie said. "Is there some weird-ass neighbor wandering around?"

"Language." Mrs. Crumb looked more offended by the "weird-ass" than she was alarmed at the idea of a stranger wandering the grounds.

"Who was that woman? Because Alice doesn't want me to know so it's no good asking her."

"You won't believe me."

"Try me."

Crumb hesitated and then put down her cards and leaned closer. "It's *her*. She watches Alice. She wants a child to look after. She won't hurt Alice. She *protects* her."

"Tell me you're talking about a fired nanny. I'll get a restraining order—"

"She was the governess in this house once," Crumb said, warming to her tale. "A long time ago. A hundred years ago. More. In England. Miss J, Alice calls her. She was a lady, but a bad man dragged her down. Peter. She died. And now she *walks*."

Andie looked at the light in the old woman's eyes and thought, *She really believes that.* Or maybe she just wanted Andie to believe so she'd run away screaming. Maybe she'd hired somebody to stand on the other side of the pond. The woman in the dream would be harder to fake, but—

"It was that Peter's fault." Mrs. Crumb was positively animated now. "He was a hound, an *evil* man. There were lots of women. She was just the last. And the poor woman paid for it!"

"Mrs. Crumb—"

"Pregnant, you know." Crumb shook her head sadly, playing to the balcony. "I'm not sure how she died. She doesn't speak of it."

"She talks to you."

"No, but she'd sit with me. Before Alice came. Alice's mother died when she was born, so they brought the poor babe here and that's when she stopped sitting with me. She just takes care of Alice now. That's all she wants, to look after Alice. She thinks Alice is her baby. Now Peter, he wants the house. Peter and Carter, they're *close*." She said the last with contempt.

Oh, dear God, Andie thought. Either Mrs. Crumb was completely nuts or there were ghosts stalking Alice and Carter. Andie wasn't sure at this point which she'd prefer. "How do you know all this?"

"I know things," Mrs. Crumb said, her eyes shifting away.

"Who told you this?"

Mrs. Crumb got up. "It you don't want to believe me, fine."

"Look." Andie regrouped. "You believe this ghost exists. That . . . disturbs me."

"*You've* seen them." Crumb looked arch. "And Alice likes Miss J!"

"I think even Alice would draw the line at the undead."

"That little girl has seen a lot of death. She knows there's Something Else out there."

Andie rubbed her forehead. "Okay. Forget Miss J and . . . uh, Peter. Did a nineteen-year-old girl ever die here? Beautiful, curly hair, liked to dance?"

Mrs. Crumb shivered for a moment and then leaned back looking calmer, saner. "A lot of people have died here. This house is over four hundred years old."

"I keep dreaming about a nineteen-year-old-girl. At least she says she's nineteen. She talked to me last night in a dream. I know she's not real. Look, there's something going on here, and I'm going to find out what it is, and if it turns out that this is some scam you've cooked up—"

Mrs. Crumb laughed, a much gayer sound than Andie had expected. "How would I give you bad dreams? Or make you see a woman at the pond?"

"Or the guy on the tower?" Andie said. "I thought it might be Bruce finally come to start work, but he was dressed funny."

Mrs. Crumb smiled, the curve of her lips almost youthful. "Tower? Oh, that's Peter. He thinks the house is his. He's just looking out for his property—"

A loud screeching sound made Andie jump, and she looked around to see a teakettle on the stove, blowing steam.

Get a grip on yourself. The damn house is getting to you. "Mrs. Crumb, I don't believe in ghosts."

"Well, you're the one who's seeing them," Mrs. Crumb said, and got up to take the kettle off the stove, moving with an oddly youthful grace. "You should have Mr. Archer come down here." Mrs. Crumb took down a teacup and saucer. "He should be here if you're worried. Can I make you some tea?"

"No, thank you," Andie said, and thought, *I need real information.* The Grandville library wasn't that far away. They might have a history of the house. Or a book on faking hauntings. Or exorcisms.

She left Mrs. Crumb smiling to herself and stirring her Earl-Grey-with-schnapps in the kitchen and went to get the kids.

They were talking in the library when she opened the door, their heads close together, both of them open and unguarded until they saw her. Then their faces shut down again.

"Come on. We're going to spread the mulch on Alice's butterfly garden and then go to the Grandville library," she told them, and they looked at each other and then got up without argument and went to get their coats.

Alice's Jessica doll had fallen when she'd stood up, and Andie went to pick it up and put it on the window seat. Its hair was disarranged as usual, and Andie tried to pat it back into its bun, straightening the three-tiered skirt gathered into the ribbon band—

Three tiers. The woman on the other side of the lake had been wearing a dress like that. And her hair had been like the doll's, too.

I'm hallucinating, she thought. *There wasn't a woman over there, I hallucinated Alice's doll. Alice was acting weird because I was trying to make her see a hallucination.*

Except Alice had seen it first.

There are no such things as ghosts, she told herself, put the doll on the window seat, and went to help with the mulch.

Two hours in the Grandville library looking for "Archer House," "Faked Hauntings," and "Parapsychologists, Ohio" gave Andie nothing except a book called *Ghostbusting: The Story of One Man's Battle Against the Undead* and a very old newspaper article about the insane

Archer who'd brought the house back from England. She copied the article and checked out the book, and then took the kids home. She tried asking them a few general questions—"So, ghosts. What do you think?"—and they ignored her, so she tucked them into bed and then went to bed herself with the book. The author's name was Boston Ulrich and he was from Cincinnati, which meant he was in the general vicinity, which was a plus, but two chapters in, she knew it was going to be no help because it was more about how smart Boston Ulrich was than it was about ghosts.

That made sense, she decided, because there were no such things as ghosts, so he hadn't had anything else to write about. The woman across the lake was probably just looking at the house, and the man in the tower was probably checking the cable, and Mrs. Crumb hadn't told her he was there so she could push the whole this-house-is-haunted bit. Or something. There were no ghosts. She put the book away and turned out the light and let herself drift to sleep. Maybe she'd dream about Will tonight. That would alleviate some guilt about all the hot North dreams. *C'mon, Will,* she thought but it was the ghost girl who showed up, smiling at her from the foot of the bed.

"Who are you?" Andie said, and the girl said, *I'm you,* and sat down on the edge of the bed.

She seemed more solid this time, as if she'd been eating better, whatever ghosts ate. More fleshed out and, although she still had a disconcerting translucency, the vertigo wasn't nearly as bad. Andie frowned at her, trying to place what buried memory she'd dredged her up from.

Oh, stop it, the girl said, and settled in at the foot of the bed. *Can't you accept that I'm you? Everybody's prettier and more interesting when they're younger.*

"Thank you. But no. You're some weird memory. After my divorce, I used to dream about my husband all the time. One of my therapists said it was because I was trying to say a better good-bye. But I have absolutely no recollection of anybody like you."

That's because there's nobody like me.

They need somebody like you, North had said. *And there's nobody else like you.*

Tell me about the guy we marry, the girl said. *North Archer.*

"He's a good man," Andie said. "Just distant. The thing is, if you're some buried memory, why would you be haunting my dreams now?" She stopped. "Haunting. Are you somebody else's memory?"

Tell me three things about North Archer, and I'll go away.

"I'll trade," Andie said. "Tell me three things about you, and I will."

You go first.

"Okay." Andie took the first thought that came to mind. "The one Valentine's Day we were together, he brought me a heart-shaped Valentine's Day box full of potstickers because he knew I liked those better than candy." She remembered him handing her roses and the box with a completely straight face and then breaking into one of his rare smiles when she opened the box and said, *"Potstickers!",* delighted beyond measure. And they'd finished them off that night in bed, and she'd licked some spilled dipping sauce off his chest and—

Potstickers?

"Chinese dumplings." Okay, they'd had some good moments, but it was over and done with. "Your turn."

I've never had Chinese dumplings.

"That's too bad, they're great. It's your turn."

I took my turn. I've never had Chinese dumplings. The girl slid off the bed and did a pirouette in front of the window, her skirt moving in multiple dimensions, but not bothering Andie nearly as much this time.

"Fine," Andie said. "I've never had squid."

The girl stopped twirling. *That's not fair. Three things about North Archer.*

"Okay. I'm fairly sure he has had squid." North tried everything. He'd certainly tried everything with her anyway.

The girl put her hands on her hips. *I want to know things about him, real things.*

"Well, I want to know those about you, too."

Okay, the girl said, not happy at all. *Your turn.*

"I took my turn. The second one is that he's had squid. Your turn."

We could not count that one.

She sounded like Alice, bargaining for more cookies.

"Then we're back to you. I gave you a Valentine's Day memory."

Okay. The girl chewed on her lip. *My favorite Valentine's Day gift was a heart-shaped necklace set with little diamond chips that my boyfriend gave me.*

"Boyfriend," Andie said. "I do not remember this necklace, so again, you're not me. Anybody I know?"

Your turn. She swished her skirt again, impatient.

"You're not me."

The girl pouted and somehow was even lovelier pouting, even transparent.

"Who are you?"

It's your turn to tell me something.

"Okay." Andie watched her move in the moonlight, seeing her skirt swish with her. "Is that a prom dress?"

Your turn.

"Okay." Andie sat back a little to think. "We had to go to this big fancy party and I didn't want to go because I was going to have to get dressed up in this little black dress his mother had bought for me and act like a wife, and the day of the party he came home and said, "Here's your dress," and when I opened the bag it was a long greeny-blue chiffon skirt with sequins on it and a turquoise sequined stretchy tank top. He said he saw it in a window on his way to a meeting and stopped to get it because it looked like me. And then I found out he was late to the meeting because of it. That was a big deal." And she'd been really grateful, and they'd been late to the party—

I don't get it. What's wrong with a black dress? I think they're sexy.

"North understood it. Is that a prom dress you're wearing?"

Yes. The girl swished the skirt again. *I was trying it on again when . . .*

"When?" Andie prompted.

That was my turn. Yes, this was my prom dress. Your turn. And tell me something besides what he bought you. Unless it was diamonds.

"Okay. The one birthday I had during the year we were together, he forgot. No gift at all."

Not even later?

"Yes, but later doesn't count." Now *she* sounded like Alice.

What did he get you later?

"Diamond earrings. Very tasteful." She was pretty sure his secretary had picked them out, which made it so much worse. He'd never have bought those for her; if there was one thing she knew about North, it was that he knew her. Until he forgot her.

See, that's better, diamonds.

"No. Better was his brother Southie who remembered and showed up on the day with a cake and these big green hoop earrings with bluebirds sitting in them. I still have those earrings." She smiled to herself, remember Southie handing her the box and saying, "Bluebirds of happiness, Andie. They called your name." Maybe he'd bought them because he'd known she wasn't happy.

Well, you still have the diamonds, too.

"No." Andie folded her arms over her chest. "I left them behind when I left. Your turn. Something about you."

I would never leave behind diamonds, the girl said, and pirouetted once and was gone.

"Hello?" Andie said to the empty room, and waited a minute but the girl didn't come back. "Damn."

She lay back on her pillows and tried to figure out what the hell was happening.

You could have hallucinations about things you didn't know about. Maybe the girl was a hallucination.

I'm hallucinating, Andie thought. *I have a brain tumor or something.*

No she didn't. She just needed an explanation.

It's a ghost.

No, that wasn't it, either. It was probably her subconscious.

If it was, her subconscious had a thing for her ex-husband.

"That's not it, either," she said out loud. She was completely over North. Done.

And now she was hallucinating ghosts.

I need help, she thought, and was making plans when she fell asleep.

The next morning, Andie told Mrs. Crumb to watch the kids and went to Columbus to the Ohio State library, calling Will when she got into town to tell him she was there and could have dinner with him if he was available.

"If I'm available?" he said, laughing. "I haven't seen you in three weeks. I'll meet you at Max and Erma's whenever you say."

Max and Erma's in German Village. That was two blocks from Flo's place. She should stop and see Flo. Or not.

"Andie?"

"How about six? That'll give me all afternoon at the library." *And put me on the road in time to get back to the kids.* If they ate at six and she left at seven, she could be home by ten-thirty, too late to put them to bed, but—

"Can't wait to see you, babe," Will said.

"Me, too." But it would be early enough she could get some sleep before Alice started demanding cereal—

"So are you going to see North?"

"What?"

"Are you going to see North while you're in town?"

"No. Why would I see North?"

"Well, you're in Columbus. So is North."

"So is Flo, two blocks from Max and Erma's, but I have to get back to the kids. I have time to see one person. You."

"You're not staying the night?"

"No. *I have to get back to the kids.*"

"Andie, it's been almost a month," Will said.

"What's been . . . oh."

"I'm a patient man, but—"

"Yes, you are, and I appreciate it," Andie said. *But I have to get back to the kids.*

"—my patience is running out here. You won't let me come down to see you and you won't stay up here—"

"I know, I know. Look, we should talk about this because for a while here, the kids are going to come first. I know that's not fair to you—"

"I haven't even met the kids yet, give me a chance."

"Honey, I'll give you all the chances you want once I get them back to Columbus and settled in."

"How much longer do you think it'll be?"

"I don't know. I'm hoping to get some help at the library. Can we talk about this at dinner? Because I really have to go."

"Sure," he said, but he didn't sound happy, which was understandable. It had been almost a month for her, too.

Except it hadn't. She hadn't even thought about sleeping with Will. Maybe it was age. Except women were supposed to hit their peaks in their thirties.

Or maybe it was because she'd dreamt of making love with North almost every night since she'd gone south, that it was North she wanted even though she knew that the North she wanted was a fantasy.

Maybe it was time to break it off with Will until she got her head back in the right place. He was a great guy and he deserved better. And she really wasn't missing him, which wasn't a good sign.

Later for that, she thought and went out to the university.

At the OSU library, she found a newspaper article on a panel discussion on ghosts. The big name there was the professor from

Cincinnati named Boston Ulrich, the guy who'd written the book she'd found at the Grandville library, who'd evidently wowed the crowd with his assertions that ghosts did exist, although not in the ridiculous portrayals in movie and fiction. "They're like us," the article quoted him as saying, "except dead." The buzzkill in the group was another professor, this one named Dennis Graff from Cleveland, who'd sourly asserted that there was no proof of actual hauntings. He was not popular. Andie wrote down his name and found his contact information by digging deeper. Boston Ulrich wasn't the only writer on ghosts; Dennis Graff had written many dry papers on paranormal phenomena, two of which Andie found in the library, but evidently all of which had the same theme: No Such Thing As Ghosts. It took a lot to make the supernatural dry, but Dennis Graff had managed it. There were also a host of "ghost experts" that Andie was pretty sure would be of no use at all. The best of that bunch, a medium named Isolde Hammersmith, charged nosebleed prices, so somebody must have thought she was good, but the last thing Andie needed was somebody who thought she could talk to ghosts. What she needed was somebody who could explain why ghosts didn't exist and how somebody was faking them or Andie was hallucinating them or whatever.

She left the library and drove slowly down High Street, trying to avoid hitting any jaywalking students while preoccupied with her options. Maybe a psychiatrist, maybe her mind was playing tricks. Or maybe a detective, the Archers had an agency right there in Columbus they used, so maybe somebody just needed to investigate and find out . . . Something. There had to be *something* . . .

She looked up and realized she'd automatically turned off High and onto Fifth Street, force of habit from when she'd been married to North and made that drive every day, so when she reached Neil Avenue, she turned left, heading south again. But when she neared the big blue Victorian that said ARCHER LEGAL GROUP on the tastefully painted sign out front, she slowed and then pulled over when the car behind her honked.

The light was on back in North's office. It was almost six but he was in there, she could see the glow from his window. He'd be in there for hours yet probably. The second floor of the house was dark, Lydia must be out, and of course the attic apartment wasn't lit up; North wasn't there. *I'm not there.*

So he was working late behind that damn desk. She hadn't always hated that desk. There'd been many an evening when she'd gone downstairs from their apartment at six and said, *Hey, you have a wife,* and shoved his papers on the floor, and he'd kissed her and they'd ended up on that desk, breathing hard. That was a sturdy piece of furniture, which had been a good thing, until the day she'd gone down to see him, and he'd snapped, Not now, *I have to finish this . . .*

The door to the house next door opened and Southie came out with the usual bounce in his step, off to have dinner with whatever woman he was chasing or drinks with some pal or something else that would make him happy. *Maybe I should have married Southie,* she thought, and then realized how awful that would have been. Southie was a sweetheart but she'd have killed him before the year was out just from sheer exasperation at his inability to focus on anything for longer than a month. And he didn't work. It really was hard to respect a man who didn't work seriously at *something . . .*

Wow, she thought. *That came out of nowhere.* Maybe that had been part of North's pull, that he was such a hard worker. There was irony for you.

Southie got in his car and drove away.

She looked back at the light in North's office. She could go in there and talk to him. She could tell him that they should look into art schools for Carter, she could tell him that Alice would love to meet a lepidopterist although she wouldn't act like it, she could tell him she thought somebody was playing tricks on her, that she was having weird dreams . . .

No, she couldn't tell him about the dreams. And she couldn't go in there, either. He was working.

She looked at the clock and saw it was almost six-thirty and started the car. She was late, and there was no reason in the world for her to walk through that door again, walking through that door just made her angry.

She made two turns and got back on High Street, irrationally upset, and angry with herself for being irrationally upset.

She had bigger problems than being discarded ten years ago. *Focus,* she told herself, and turned the car down Frankfort and into German Village and her future husband.

Andie found a parking spot not far from Flo's house and ran the block and a half to the restaurant. Will was sitting next to the window in the narrow side bay, and his face lit up when he saw her and he waved as she ran by, so when she kissed him and then sat down across from him, breathless, he said, "Easy there, kid."

"I'm sorry I'm late," she said, leaning back to catch her breath.

"I'm just glad to see you," he said, laid-back as ever, the soft overhead light shining on his blond hair, and she thought again what an extremely nice guy he was.

Oh, hell, she thought. *I haven't seen him for over three weeks. I should be thinking of something besides "nice guy."*

"What's wrong?" he said, his smile fading.

"I'm not sure." She shook her head. "Nothing."

"Did you see North? Did he upset you?"

"No, I didn't see him." *I thought about him, though.* She looked at Will and realized that she'd never once felt the same way about him that she felt now for North, even now when it was over and she was never going to be with him again, she'd still been parked outside his house thinking, *I could go in there.*

"Well, then, let me get you a beer," Will began.

"No, I have to drive tonight," Andie said, remembering that long trip home in the dark. "Diet Coke would be great, though."

Will caught the waitress and asked for a Diet Coke, and Andie picked up the menu. The year they'd been married, North had just ordered a Diet Coke and ice water with whatever he ordered. So if she was late, the drinks were on the table when she got there. It wasn't important, in fact, it was kind of controlling of him, really a black mark against him . . .

It had been nice. To have the little stuff like that just . . . *handled.*

"Andie?"

If she told Will that she'd like him to order the Diet Coke and water before she got there, he would. He wasn't a mind reader, for Christ's sake.

"Andie?"

"What? Oh, sorry. Distracted." Andie looked at her menu without seeing it. Something was really, really wrong, and it wasn't ghosts. She put the menu down again and looked at Will, really looked at him.

He was a good guy. Sweet, thoughtful, charming, smart, a really hard worker, she'd fallen for him because he was all those things and because he'd never break her heart the way North had because she didn't love him that way, that hopeless, helpless, all-consuming passion for somebody that wrecked your life . . .

"Now I'm getting nervous," Will said.

She didn't want that kind of love again. But maybe Will did. Maybe he deserved somebody who loved him that way.

"Andie?"

"It's just strange coming back here," she told him.

"To Max and Erma's?"

"To Columbus."

"You've only been gone three weeks."

"It's been an intense three weeks."

"All the more reason for you to spend the night," Will said, smiling, easy. "Give yourself some time to decompress."

"I've been compressed since I walked into North's office."

"I love hearing about how he makes you feel crappy," Will said. "Does that make me a bad person?"

He was grinning at her, trying to get her into their usual laughing conversation, but she shook her head.

"You're one of the best people I know," she told him.

"Well, thank you very much. So what's wrong?"

"I'm just really tired. It's me, not you." Well, it was a little him, but mostly it was the kids. She looked at her watch. It was almost their bedtime now, but Crumb probably wouldn't put them to bed, and she definitely wouldn't tell Alice a story and—

"Andie?" Will said, and she jerked her attention back to him.

"Sorry. It's the kids' bedtime. I'm thinking about tooth brushing and storytelling. Not very romantic."

"See? I knew you'd want to be a mother after you had some time with kids."

"I don't want to be a mother," Andie said, really sick of saying that to him. "I want to take care of Alice and Carter."

"I can't wait to meet them," Will said, trying to placate her.

He was being nice. She was being bitchy. "Oh, hell, I'm sorry again. I don't know what's wrong with me."

"Maybe you're sexually frustrated," Will said. "Come back to the apartment and I'll take care of that. You can go back tomorrow."

I don't want to. "That's very generous. But if I leave now, I can be home by midnight. I don't like leaving the kids alone." Andie leaned back as the waitress put her Diet Coke in front of her. "Thank you." Would she have said no to North? She never had, not until the end, when she was on her way out the door, trying to save herself—

"There's a housekeeper."

"Yeah, well, you haven't met the housekeeper."

"I'd *like* to," Will said, his smile gone. "But you won't let me—"

"Will, can we just . . ." She looked at him then, at the great guy he was, and thought, *Great guy but the wrong guy. Goddammit.*

"Can we just what?"

"You're a great guy, Will."

"Thank you." He smiled at her again.

"You're sweet and you're kind and you're smart and you're hard-working, you're everything I admire in a man."

"If you're trying to make me feel better, you're doing a great job." He saluted her with his beer.

"And you're very good in bed."

"So about tonight," Will began.

"And those are all the reasons I wanted to be with you."

Will's smile disappeared. "Wanted?"

"I chose you because you really are an amazing man, somebody I could have fun with for the rest of my life, somebody I could trust, somebody who would always be there for me." The words were pouring out of her now, she couldn't stop if she tried—

"These are good things," Will said, looking confused.

"And I really do love you," Andie said.

"Good," Will said, even more confused.

"When I left North, I left him. I never went back. I didn't see him for ten years. And then when I went to give him the checks back, I sat in his reception room just simmering with anger, I was still so angry with him, Will, I was irrational."

"Hey, if he makes you that unhappy, stay away from him."

"If he makes me that unhappy, I'm not done with him," Andie said, and there it was, right there out loud.

Will nodded. "I know. I think it's good you're talking to him again. I mean, I don't like it, but I can see where you need to sever that connection—"

"That's not it," Andie said. "I love you, I think you're a great guy, and I'm not going back to North, I can't go back to him, but . . . I'm still *tied to him,* and until I work that out . . . I'm so sorry, Will. I'm so, so sorry."

"So I'll wait until you work it out."

"No," Andie said, and then the waitress came back to take their order and she shook her head. "No," she said, and the waitress left again, and she said, "No, I need to stop this. I can't see you anymore."

Will sat back, looking stunned. "Just like that?"

"It's not just like that, it's been like that since I saw North again and met the kids." She frowned, trying to think of how to explain it. "I've been running ever since I left North ten years ago. Well, before that, if I'm going to be honest. But now I've got something I can't run from." She leaned forward, trying to make him see. "The kids need me. They don't want anything from me, they'd be delighted if I left, but they need me. And things are so much better—"

"I don't care about the kids," Will said. "I care about you. I—"

"I need to be without North and you," Andie said. "Until I get the kids safe, until I figure out what the hell I want, I need to just be . . . me."

"When have I ever asked you to be anything else?" he said, clearly annoyed now.

"You haven't. I put that badly." Andie rubbed her forehead. "Okay, I'll make this simple. I can't give you what you deserve, and I'm not going to feel guilty about it anymore, so we're finished."

"Don't you think I should decide what I deserve?"

"I think I should decide what—"

"Because 'I need to take care of two kids I barely know' is not a good enough reason."

"I still want North."

As soon as she said it, she slumped, as if the tension of denial had been keeping her upright. *God, that felt good,* she thought. *The truth really does set you free.* Then she looked across the table at Will as the silence stretched out and thought, *Oh, hell.*

"I'm sorry," she began, and then somebody rapped on the window and Andie jerked around.

Flo was outside, waving.

"Wonderful," Andie said, and got up.

"Wait a minute," Will said, looking furious.

"No," Andie said. "I am so sorry I did this to you, I am so sorry I'm doing this now, but . . . no."

She turned and walked away, out of the restaurant and around to Frankfort Street where Flo was waiting.

"I saw your car," she said. "You look awful. What's going on?"

"I just broke it off with Will."

"Good." Flo patted her arm.

The sympathy was almost too much. "I think I might still be in love with North."

"I know, honey." Flo put her arm around her. "Come on back to the house and I'll make some cocoa."

That sounded so good that Andie almost said yes, just to be able to go back home with her mother, put her head down on the old wood kitchen table, and cry like a baby from all the released tension while Flo made soothing noises and put marshmallows in her hot chocolate.

"I can't," she said. "I have to get back to the kids."

"Then I'll walk you to the car," Flo said, and made soothing noises for a block and a half.

"Thank you for not saying 'I told you so,'" Andie told her when they reached her car.

"Like I would." Flo stretched up and kissed her cheek. "If you need me, you call."

"Right," Andie said. "I will. I really will. Thank you, Mom."

She kissed her mother good-bye and then made good time heading south, turning off onto the ever-more-deserted roads and then finally onto the narrow lane to the house, taking that insane drop to the driveway that Bruce still had not gotten around to fixing—"I'll probably be out in a couple of days or so," he said whenever she called—all the while thinking about North. Not Will, the nice guy she'd just dumped who would have been a good, steady, loving husband who'd never neglect her, but the rat bastard who'd deserted her for his career, just left her upstairs in their attic apartment to rot . . .

I have to stop thinking about this, she told herself, and drove out of the trees and started around the curve to the house and then hit the brakes, her heart pounding.

The girl from her dreams was dancing on the lawn, translucent and glowing faintly blue in the dark night, her skirt flowing around her.

Alice's blue princess who danced.

Andie drove on slowly, trying to see better, but as she rounded the curve, the headlights hit the dancing girl for a second and she wasn't there anymore, and when Andie drove on, the lawn was empty, even after the headlights had passed.

"I'm not asleep," Andie said out loud, her heart pounding, "and that was a ghost."

More than that, it was a ghost Alice knew. Just like Alice knew the woman across the pond and the man on the tower. If she was hallucinating, she was hallucinating with Alice.

"This can't be happening," Andie said, trying to jar herself back to reality with the sound of her own voice. It was late, she was tired, she was upset, she was . . .

That was a ghost.

She drove on around the house automatically, thinking furiously. Tomorrow she was calling the experts. And talking to Alice. And . . .

"Oh, *Christ,*" Andie said, and parked the car, looking for ghosts everywhere before she bolted for the house.

Six

Andie spent a sleepless night expecting to see the blue girl at any moment and fighting the urge to call North—*There are ghosts!*—and when the sun came up, she wasn't sure if she was grateful she'd spent the night without a visit from the girl or not. She was awake so the girl must have been a dream, but she hadn't been asleep at the wheel so had that been a hallucination?

We have to get out of here, Andie thought, and went down to the kitchen to begin talking Carter and Alice into a move to Columbus, but they didn't come down for breakfast, and when she looked in their rooms, they weren't there, either. She finally tracked them down in the library.

"Hey," she said. "Breakfast."

Alice stared at Andie, an odd look on her face, something between anger and relief.

"We thought you left," Carter said.

"I did, I went to the university library in Columbus." Andie came into the room and sat down on a chair closer to them. "I was home by midnight last night."

"Mrs. Crumb said you weren't coming back," Carter said.

"And you didn't tuck me in," Alice said, wounded. "*Nobody* tucked me in."

"Well, that's the last time Mrs. Crumb babysits," Andie said, feeling the now-familiar urge to kick the old lady. "Of *course* I was coming back. I told you I was coming back when I left. Want some breakfast?"

Alice looked outraged. "And you didn't leave me your skirt with the sequins and you *promised*."

"*I came back,*" Andie said. "That was only if I left for good. What is it with you guys?"

Alice stood up and went for the door, but Carter hung back. "What were you looking up in the library?"

"Ghosts," Andie said, watching for his reaction.

Carter nodded and headed for the kitchen, too.

"See, I thought you'd be more surprised," Andie called after him, and went to fix them pancakes, which Alice smothered in butter and syrup and slurped down. Andie brought up moving to Columbus as artfully as possible, but Alice said, "No," and went on eating and Carter ignored her, so she regrouped. When the kids were done and back in the library working, she called the two numbers in her notes. For Boston Ulrich in Cincinnati, the author of the not-much-use ghostbuster book, she got an answering machine and left a message. For Dennis Graff in Cleveland, the there's-no-such-thing-as-ghosts guy, the phone just rang until she finally gave up. "Damn it," she said to nobody, and checked that Carter and Alice were doing their morning work. "I should get a cookie for this," Alice said. "Let's see how it all works out," Andie told her, and went upstairs to find Mrs. Crumb. The whole idea of ghosts seemed ludicrous in the daylight, but it was going to be night again and when it hit, she was going to be prepared.

Andie found the housekeeper in the upstairs hall, dumping Carter's wastebasket into a trash bag. "I need to talk to you," she said, and startled the old lady so that she dropped the basket, spilling papers to the floor.

Andie bent to pick them up. "Why did you tell the kids I wasn't coming back?" she said, and then stopped to look at the drawings Carter had thrown out.

Mixed in with the copies of comic book characters were amazing rough portraits, capturing Alice laughing, something Andie had never seen, and Mrs. Crumb looking surly, and . . .

Andie straightened.

And the blue girl who'd visited her every night and danced on the lawn.

"Who is this?" she said, holding up the page for Mrs. Crumb to see, the blue girl with her wildly curling hair and big eyes and that generous laughing mouth . . .

"That's nobody," Mrs. Crumb said, and picked up the garbage bag and walked away, leaving the mess on the floor behind her.

"Right," Andie said, and went downstairs to the library to find Carter, but the only one there was Alice, reading a butterfly book in the window seat. Andie held up the drawing. "Alice, who is this?"

"That's Aunt May," Alice said. "Carter is very good at drawing."

"Yes, he is," Andie said automatically, and looked at the drawing again, a little breathless. "This is the aunt who took care of you?"

"Yes," Alice said. "She died."

"Right." Andie sat down next to the window seat.

The woman she'd been talking to in her dreams was a ghost, that's all there was to it. Ghost. She'd never seen her before, never seen a picture of her before and yet . . .

"Are you okay?" Alice said. "You look weird."

"I'm fine. Thank you for asking."

"Can I have that?" Alice said. "The picture of Aunt May. Can I have it?"

"Of course," Andie said, and handed it over. "Alice, I'm sorry your aunt died."

Alice nodded, not looking at her.

"Do you talk to her?"

"She's dead, Andie," Alice said, sounding very adult.

"Because she talks to me at night."

Alice blinked at her. "Maybe you're dreaming."

"And I saw her on the lawn last night as I drove home."

"You were very, very tired." Alice looked back at her butterfly book. "I'd like to read now, please."

Andie sat back, frustrated. Pushing Alice to admit there were ghosts was wrong, even if Alice was talking to her dead aunt every night. That's who had to be sitting in that damn rocking chair. Alice didn't have an imaginary friend, she had a dead aunt.

"She was really young," Andie said, remembering how she'd danced. May. How May had danced.

Alice nodded but didn't look up.

I need to know more, Andie thought, but not from Alice, not if she didn't want to talk. "Is there a family photo album?"

"In the cabinet by the fireplace." Alice dropped her butterfly book and picked up Carter's drawing. "You don't need to see a picture. This is what she looked like."

"She was very pretty."

"She was bee-you-tee-ful," Alice said, looking sadly at the drawing. "And she laughed and she danced. She said when you stop dancing, you're dead." Alice touched the drawing.

"She must have been fun to live with."

"Sometimes." Alice put the drawing inside her butterfly book and closed it. "I did my work. Can I go to the kitchen and get a cookie?"

"Yes," Andie said, not interested in fighting a sugar battle while her head was exploding and Alice was coping with death.

It took her a while to find the photo album, stuck in the back of a cabinet with books piled in front of it. But when she pulled it out and turned to the last filled pages, there was her ghost girl, vibrantly alive, laughing at the camera as she hugged Alice and Carter close, both of them smiling, which made Andie's heart hurt, that they'd lost those smiles. She flipped to the earlier pages, Carter as a young boy standing next to his dad, leaning on his leg, Alice in her father's arms. Their father looked kind and more than that, he looked like he loved them, cuddling Alice close, his arm draped comfortably across Carter's shoulders. They'd gotten a good start before he'd died. And then Aunt May had done her best, too, because they'd smiled again.

She flipped back to another earlier page and found Alice's baby pictures. Several other pages before that there was a photo of the kids' dad with a pregnant blond woman who looked much like Andie thought Alice would look someday, attractive in an offbeat way, interesting beauty as opposed to classic. Another one of the woman, still very pregnant, holding a four-year-old Carter close. And then earlier than that, wedding pictures with Aunt May as a very young bridesmaid, about Alice's age. She must have been a late baby to be that much younger than her sister. In fact, given her brunette curls in comparison to her older sister's straight blond hair, she might have been from a second marriage. And then still earlier, sister pictures, and more family Andie couldn't recognize, and she closed the album and thought, *Their aunt May is still here for a reason.* It was getting easier to believe in ghosts the more she thought about it, but it was still . . .

Maybe this was the reason the kids wouldn't leave the house. They didn't want to leave their aunt alone, haunting a cold stone house with only Mrs. Crumb for company. Maybe if she found a way to get Aunt May to . . . to go toward the light or something, maybe she could get the kids out of there, get them to Columbus and a normal life.

"Experts," she said, and tried calling Ulrich and Graff again and got nothing.

Lunch and lessons and supper took up the rest of the afternoon, along with a sharp chat with Mrs. Crumb who was still denying that May was May and was defensive about telling the kids that Andie wasn't coming back—"How was I to know?"—so it was almost six before Andie tried calling for a third time, starting with Boston Ulrich again.

This time, a man answered the phone, and Andie said, "Professor Ulrich?" and when he said, "Yes," she said, "I'm Andie Miller, no," looking around for Mrs. Crumb, "Andie Archer, I left you a message earlier. I have a ghost problem." He didn't laugh or hang up, so she said, "I see a dancing blue woman. I think I know who she is, and I need to know how to . . . send her on. Or whatever."

"You say you're at a house in southern Ohio," he said.

"Yes. Archer House."

"I see."

"Is that significant?" Andie said, praying they weren't on a list of the most haunted places in the Buckeye State.

"Someone else was asking about that house. It has quite a reputation, right?"

"Someone else? Is there something I should know?"

"Tell me what's happening."

"This woman talks to me at night," Andie said, and then remembered the woman at the pond and the man on the tower. "And there may be . . . others. I don't drink and I don't take drugs but I see . . . ghosts. I need help."

"Of course," he said, and then talked on for a good half hour, mostly about his research and the success he'd had, without giving her anything of use at all, much like his book.

"Who was it that asked about the house?" Andie said, interrupting him when she couldn't take it anymore.

"I can't tell you that, of course. However, I could come to you the first of November," he finished. "Only for the day. My fee is five thousand dollars—"

"I'll get back to you on that," Andie said, pretty sure that Boston Ulrich knew less about ghosts than she did. She hung up and tried the other expert, Professor Dennis Graff up in Cleveland, and still got no answer even though she let it ring for a long time.

That left her with only one expert to turn to.

"Flo, I need help," she said when her mother answered the phone.

"Andie! What's wrong?" Her voice dropped. "Is it North?"

"I don't believe in ghosts," Andie said, realizing that she was crossing over into Flo territory with the conversation she was about to have.

"Of course not, dear. You have ghosts?"

"I could be losing my mind. Hallucinating. Brain tumor."

"No, honey, lots of people see ghosts."

"Yes, but they're crazy."

"Forty-eight percent of Americans believe in ghosts."

Flo using statistics was almost as unsettling as the statistic itself. "Where do you get these numbers?" Andie said. "Who takes polls on this stuff?"

"CBS before Halloween. It was on the news. And really, Andie, if forty-eight percent believe, don't you think that some of them must actually have seen one?"

"No." *Except I have.* Maybe. "Let's assume for the moment that there are ghosts. Tell me how to get one out of here."

"Well, the surefire way is to dig up the body and burn it," Flo said, as if she were saying, "Use soda water to get wine out of silk."

"Okay," Andie said, thinking, *You had to call Flo, didn't you?* "And Plan B would be . . ."

"Well, there are all kinds of *superstitions,*" Flo said, dismissively. "You could hold a séance and ask them to leave, but I never think that works. Why would they go polite on you all of a sudden? But if you burn their bodies, there's nothing holding them to this plane. Where is this ghost buried?"

"I don't know," Andie said. "Also, this is an insane plan. Plus, illegal. I'll bet anything it's illegal."

"Andie, if you have ghosts, you're going to have to think outside the box. Call North. He can get you anything."

"Right." Andie rubbed her forehead again at the thought of telling North to burn a body. Not that he couldn't get it done, he could get anything done, it would just be explaining it to him that would be difficult. "Let me get back to you on this."

"Do you want me to come down there?" Flo said. "I'm very sensitive. I might be able to help. For instance, water and fire bar ghosts, they can't cross running water and they abhor fire."

"Really," Andie said, thinking, *My mother is a nutjob.* Except she was sitting in the only house in southern Ohio that had its own moat. And a fireplace in every room.

"I should come down there," Flo said. "I can *help.*"

Andie thought of her mother, wandering through the house, trying to find ghosts so she could ask them where they were buried. And what their signs were. "Just wait. I'll get back to you. I promise. Thank you."

Then she hung up and called her very last resort.

Southie knocked and came into North's office a little before seven that night. "Your secretary's not out there," he said, looking back into the empty anteroom. "You know, she's a cute little thing."

"You can't have her," North said automatically as he scanned down his neatly printed notes. "She's intelligent and efficient and I don't want her quitting because you seduced and abandoned her."

"Not my type," Southie said. "Which is what I came to talk to you about. Kelly wants to go down to that house. Somebody else is calling the experts and asking questions, and she's afraid she's going to get scooped. I don't see why she shouldn't go."

"Because it's private property and she's not invited."

"Yes, but she would like to be invited. She would like me to invite her. I would like me to invite her. There's no reason for me not to invite her."

Outside the office, a phone rang.

"Yes there is," North said, ignoring the blinking light on his phone. "You're not invited."

"Shouldn't I be able to go see my third cousins without your permission?"

"In a better world, possibly. In this one, no."

Southie sat down. "Let's discuss this rationally."

"Let's not," North said, pointedly staring at the case notes he was working on.

The phone rang again.

"I have a parapsychologist, a pro at debunking fake ghosts. We could take him down there, he could find out how they're faking the hauntings, clear everything up. That would be a big help to Andie."

North looked up. "There are no ghosts."

"*I* know that," Southie said reasonably. "*You* know that. But a lot of people don't know that. If Dennis can show how it's being done—"

"Dennis."

"Professor Graff. He's the real deal, North. Teaches at the university."

"Which one?" North said automatically.

"I don't know, one of the ones in Cleveland. You should meet this guy."

"No, thank you. I have work to do—"

The phone had not stopped ringing, Kristin had evidently forgot to send it to voice mail before she left, so when it rang again, he picked it up and said, "Yes?"

"I need help," Andie said, and she sounded upset, which wasn't like her.

"Go away, Southie," North said to his brother, and then spoke into the phone. "What now? Bats in the belfry?"

Across the desk, Southie said, "Is that Andie? I should go down there. She might need help."

North covered the receiver. "The help will not be you." Then he went back to Andie. "What do you need?"

"Can you find out where the kids' Aunt May is buried. And maybe who used to live in this house a long time ago? And where they're buried? In England? And where the kids' aunt is buried?"

"Where they're buried?"

"Just for the hell of it," Andie said, trying for breezy and missing. "Because we may have to dig up their bodies and burn them."

Jesus, she's lost it.

"Buried?" Southie said. "Does she need help with a body?"

"No," North said to him.

"No on the finding the bodies or no on the burning them?" Andie asked.

"Not you," North said. "The 'no' was for Southie. I'll find out what you need. Why?"

"We may have a ghost," Andie said. "Maybe more than one."

Southie leaned toward the desk. "You know, North, I have all my research on the house. It probably has the information in it that she needs. Let me go down there and help."

"Andie has enough on her hands." North spoke into the phone. "That seems, uh, far-fetched."

"I thought so, too, until I started seeing her. Is it illegal to burn a corpse? If it's already been buried and everything?"

This is not good, North thought. "What's going on?"

"Has she seen a ghost?" Southie said.

North glared at him. "Leave."

"North, I can help," Southie said.

"Leave."

Southie sighed, clearly disappointed in his brother's shortsightedness. "You let me know if she needs help. I'll be right there. I'm staying in tonight, so if you want a nightcap, come on over."

"She doesn't need—" North began, but Southie was already heading for the door. "—your help," he finished as the door closed behind his brother, and then he went back to the phone. "Yes, generally speaking, it's illegal to burn a corpse. I'll call a friend in England tomorrow, it's after midnight there now."

"He won't think you're crazy?" Andie said, and North thought, *Well, at least she knows it's crazy.*

"Simon's not a run-of-the-mill guy," he told her. "He won't bat an eye. I'll put Kristin on finding May Younger's grave tomorrow. Are you all right?"

"Yes, thank you. Sorry to sound hysterical."

"You don't sound hysterical. The corpse burning is over the top, but otherwise you're pretty calm."

"Ignore that part. Because mostly we're normal." Her voice brightened, and he thought, *Somebody else came into the room.* "And thank you again for the computers. The kids love them."

"Was it too much for Alice?"

"No. Alice uses it to play Frogger. What? No, you can't play Frogger now, it's almost bedtime. Go brush your teeth and then I'll come up and tell you the story. Yes, *now*. It's Bad Uncle."

Who? North thought.

"Alice wants to talk to you," Andie said.

"Okay," North said cautiously.

"Hello?" Alice bellowed into the phone.

North held the phone farther from his ear. "Hello, Alice."

"We're not leaving here!"

"That's fine," North said.

He heard the phone clunk and then Andie came back on and said, "Sorry about that."

"No problem," North said.

"No, you can't tell him anything else. You're just stalling. Go brush your teeth. He doesn't want to talk to you again, you were rude. Yes, yelling at people is rude. Now go upstairs and brush your teeth. No. *Upstairs now, Alice.*"

He leaned back, listening to her argue with Alice, partly intrigued by this new bossy, maternal side of her and partly still dealing with the whole body-burning thing. She'd sounded as if she really believed there was a ghost. A nanny with a vivid imagination, he could dismiss. Andie saying it was different. If somebody was playing tricks, trying to drive outsiders away—

A wail rose up on the other side of the phone, and Andie said, "I have to go beat up a kid. The information would be gratefully appreciated."

"Of course," North said, and then the wail in the background was cut off by the dial tone. He put the phone back in the cradle and thought, *Maybe I should go down there.*

Except he was swamped with work. And Andie could take care of herself, the body-burning thing notwithstanding. She always had taken care of herself. She didn't need him.

The memory of her turning to him with that glorious smile, opening her arms to him . . .

Don't go down there.

That Andie was gone, she was marrying somebody else, she was having a really bad time and she did not need him down there, trying to get her into bed—

The memory of her rolling hot in his arms hit him again, one he'd been trying to forget for ten years. Andie, tangled in the sheets, clinging to him, shuddering under him, her mouth hot on him—

"Jesus!" he said, and got up from the desk and began to pace.

He needed to see her again. They had unfinished business. He wanted to finish it. Or start it again.

She was going to marry somebody else, so that was a problem. And she was still mad as hell about him neglecting her ten years ago. Neither of those were insurmountable obstacles unless she really loved this other guy. Plus there was the ghost thing.

He should go down there, see for himself what was going on. Find out about the ghost. Find out about Andie. If it was over, it was over. Of course it was over, it had been over for ten years.

But if it wasn't . . .

Andie, hot in his arms again.

Oh, fuck, he thought, and went to get that drink from Southie.

Andie had gone up to the nursery after forcing Alice to brush her teeth—"Because they'll rot out of your head if you don't, and you'll be ugly, and you won't be able to eat cereal because you'll have *no teeth!*"—her mind back on her own problems. If good old Aunt May showed up in her dreams that night, they were going to have a talk. In fact—

Alice came in to the nursery, her Bad Witch T-shirt-nightgown slipping down over one shoulder, her face washed and her teeth scrubbed. "I want my story."

"Let's try something new," Andie said, determined to get more information before Aunt May showed up to play Three Questions again. "How about tonight you tell me a story about the dancing princess."

"I would like to dance." Alice went back in her bedroom and came out with her Walkman, popping it open in front of the boom box on the TV. "Put this in, please."

Andie took the tape and read "Andie's Music" on the label. "This is mine."

"I know," Alice said, sounding exasperated. "Put it in."

Andie put the tape in the player and punched play, heard Cyndi Lauper start "She Bop," and prayed that Alice wouldn't ask what "She Bop" meant.

"I like this," Alice said. "I dance to it."

She began to bounce around the room singing while Andie thought about Aunt May.

The thing was, May didn't seem malevolent. Young, pushy, a little spoiled, but not . . . horrible.

The song ended and Alice said, "Aren't you going to dance?"

"What kind of music does the dancing princess dance to?" Andie said, and then "Somebody's Baby" started, and Andie thought, *Oh, hell.*

"Did you used to dance to this?" Alice said, and Andie closed her eyes and remembered North walking across the floor of that dark bar to her the night they met, pulling her close, whispering in her ear as he moved against her, and all the nights they'd danced to it after that, in their attic bedroom.

"Yes," she said. "I danced to this. I danced to this a lot."

"Show me," Alice said, holding out her arms, "show me a *real* dance," and Andie was so surprised that Alice was reaching for her that she went.

Alice's little hand was cool in hers, and there was a moment when Andie first took it that Alice went still, and then she said, *"Show me!"* and Andie showed her the basic box step, figuring that Alice would like the symmetry of that. Alice added a hip bounce which improved it tremendously, and then Andie showed her how to twirl under somebody's arm which Alice loved, and then they just danced around the room while Alice sang, "Somebody's baby," over and over because she didn't know the words yet.

"Play that again," Alice said when it was done, and Andie thought, *Jeez, twist the knife, kid,* but she rewound the tape, and they danced again, Alice demanding many twirls, breaking off to bop by herself for a while but always coming back and holding up her arms for more, which charmed the hell out of Andie, singing, "Gonna shine tonight," with fervor.

"Again," Alice said, but Andie let it go to "I've Got a Rock 'n' Roll Heart," which had its own memories since North had been a huge Clapton fan. She and Alice danced wildly around the nursery, the box step and May forgotten for the moment, Alice singing like mad, completely happy since the first time Andie had met her.

She looks relaxed, Andie thought, holding on to Alice's hand as she flailed happily, doing what was basically the Snoopy dance. She'd been so tense and unhappy at the beginning of the month, but now she was laughing. Maybe things were getting better, maybe—

Carter opened the door, and Alice said, "Come in. We're *dancing.*" He shook his head and Andie said on impulse, "Someday there will be girls in your life and they like to dance. Get in here."

He rolled his eyes, but before he could leave, Alice ran forward and grabbed his hand. "Come *on,* you *need* to dance."

He let her pull him in, clearly in hell but also clearly unable to say no to Alice.

"It's easy," Andie said, hitting the pause button on the boom box as the song ended. "Look. This is the box step. You move in a square . . ."

She stood beside him and made him take the four steps—"Don't move on the diagonal, trace the box"—and Alice did it with him, saying, "See? *See?*" He frowned, concentrating, clearly out of his element, but once Carter understood something, Andie had learned, he didn't stop until he mastered it. Once he had it, she said, "Okay, now with a partner, and you lead." She put his hand on her waist and he stiffened, and she realized that was the first time she'd ever touched him. *Gotta spend more time with Carter,* she thought, and took his other hand. "Lead with your left," she said, and as he stepped forward, she stepped back, following him, and they walked through the step until Alice hit play and "Man in Love" came on, and Andie remembered North barreling down I-71, singing it at the top of his lungs. It seemed impossible now that he had ever done that, North Archer did not sing, but he had, and she'd just laughed and loved him. She'd been with him all that time, and she hadn't even realized what it had meant back then, that he'd sing like that.

"This is too fast," Carter said, and Andie shook herself out of the past and said, "No it isn't. Just follow the beat," and to her surprise, he did, finding the music almost immediately.

"That's it," she said, "that's great!" She leaned into his arm, and he automatically led. "You're a good dancer," she told him, "you're a natural," and he shook his head, but she saw him start to smile, not broadly but a real smile. Alice danced around them, finally yelling, "Me! Me!" Carter let go as Andie twirled under his arm, and Alice grabbed Carter's hand to finish out the song, and Andie watched them and remembered North singing, "I want the whole world to know," at the top of his lungs. They'd danced to this in the attic, too. The man had hips, she remembered, closing her eyes and seeing him again with one hand on his longneck beer and the other on her ass, laughing off the workday . . .

I'd give anything to have that back, she thought, and then the song stopped and she kicked herself because it wasn't coming back. Keep the good memories but let the past go, that was the key.

Maybe that was the key to May, too. If May could let the past go and move on—

Alice said, "Wait a minute," and hit rewind on the boom box, and Jackson Browne began to sing again. Alice grabbed Carter's hand and said, "I like *this* one," and he smiled back, amazingly, he really smiled, and they started their own kind of box step, as Alice belted out, "Gonna shine tonight!"

And Andie leaned against the wall and replayed that first night again, how gorgeous North had been with his tie loosened, looking at her like she was the only woman in the room, sliding his arm around her waist when she met him halfway, rocking her to the music while he looked in her eyes, twirling her, then pulling her back to all his heat, and she'd laughed, completely free, warmed by the music and the movement and the light in his eyes even though she didn't know who he was.

And when the music stopped, he'd said, "I'm North Archer, and

I think we should leave," and she'd thought if he didn't kiss her right there, she'd die, and he'd pulled her out into the dark street—

"Are you okay?" Carter said, looking concerned.

"Yes," Andie said, straightening, and thought, *No, I haven't been okay since I saw him again,* and all the pent-up need for the only man she'd ever loved swept over her. She was in a haunted house with two lonely kids who needed her and she wanted him there with her, to help her save them and to hold her and to make love to her until they were themselves again, until they'd found everything they'd lost again. *Maybe this time we could make it work,* she thought, but even as she thought it, she knew she'd go crazy again when he forgot she existed. She was high maintenance, that's all there was to it.

Move on, she thought. *May and I have to move on.*

She watched Alice boss Carter through the box step again, but when "Man in Love" came back on, they deserted the box step and just danced, and Andie went to join them because she couldn't help it, they were so happy. It wouldn't last, but for right now, they were dancing. *At least I got this part right,* she thought, and raised her arms above her head to do a hip bop, and Alice saw her and raised her arms, too, then "Layla" came on, the old hard-rock version, and Andie shut off the treacherous tape and said, "Bedtime," over Alice's wail, shutting off, too, all the memories that had come with it.

She had a ghost to talk to.

Andie sat up in her bed until past midnight waiting for May, but she never came. There were no voices on Alice's baby monitor, either, so evidently the undead were taking the night off. Or she'd hallucinated everything. That theory appealed to her, and the next day was normal, too, or as normal as anything ever was at Archer House. It was spoiled only by a heaviness in the air and early darkness from thick cloud cover, a big storm brewing up, the radio said. *Just what I need,* Andie thought, *a dark and stormy night.* Still, the ghost was delightfully unpresent, so when the doorknocker sounded at close to five that evening, she made the trek down the long, dim stone entry hall without foreboding. Ghosts didn't knock on doors.

Outside, thunder rolled, and she thought, *Cut me a break here,* and opened the door.

Southie's handsome face beamed at her. "*Andie! Wonderful* to see you again."

"Southie," she said, glad to see him because he was Southie, but also suspicious because he was Southie. "What are you doing here?"

"We've come to help!"

"We?" Andie said, looking around for North, but there were strangers coming up the path instead: a bespectacled, worried-looking, middle-aged man in a green argyle cardigan, his basset-hound eyes darting to take in the bleak landscape as it began to rain; a much younger, surly guy in jeans striding past him with a long silver bag, and then pushing past the young guy as if she were speed-walking, a pixieish blonde with the eyes of a hawk, her face set in killer determination . . .

"Kelly O'Keefe?" Andie said to Southie.

"Yes," Southie said, and then she was on them, talking over him.

"My *God,* this place is *remote,*" she said, stopping in front of Andie. She barely came up to Andie's shoulder, which may have contributed to her hectic enthusiasm. "*Tell me* you have indoor plumbing."

"We have indoor plumbing," Andie told her. "Would you like to use it before you go back where you came from?"

"This is Andie," Southie said to Kelly, and the little blonde blinked as if recalculating, and then smiled, all white teeth. Hundreds of them.

"*Hello,* Andie!"

"Hello." Andie looked back at Southie. "Why?"

"I was with North when he got your phone call," Southie said, "and I knew you were out here alone with two kids and could use some help—"

"North sent you?" *Why didn't he come?*

"He didn't exactly *send* me," Southie said. "I just got the feeling you needed me."

"So you brought me a TV reporter?"

"Broadcast journalist," Kelly said crisply, and followed it up with another blinding smile. "It's *raining*. Could we come *in*?"

Andie looked at the younger guy with the silver bag. "And you are?"

"Cameraman," he said, bored by the conversation already. "Bill. I drove the truck."

Andie craned her neck to see a red Miata that had to be Kelly O'Keefe's parked just this side of the bridge beside a huge satellite truck that said NEWS4 on the side. She spared a moment to wonder how the hell they'd gotten that truck down the drive and how the hell they were going to get it back up again now that the rain was turning dirt to mud, and then she looked at Southie. "A TV reporter, a cameraman, and a . . ." She smiled at the baggy-eyed man, not sure what he was, but he was glancing around again, his face practically twitching with suspicion over his truly ugly argyle cardigan.

"Professor," Southie said. "Professor Dennis Graff."

Andie nodded at the professor and then turned back to Southie. "And again, why?"

"He's bringing you . . . *the chance of a lifetime,*" Kelly said, practically singing the words.

"No, thank you." Andie stared at Southie, still waiting for an explanation.

Southie tried another smile. "Let's go inside and—"

"You are not filming anything here," Andie told him. "Especially not my ki . . . these kids. Forget it."

Dennis looked from Andie to Southie and back again. "Weren't we invited? I thought we were expected."

"*Honestly,* Sullivan," Kelly said, giving him a playful little push. "You mean you didn't *call*? You didn't ask about the *séance*?"

"Séance?" Andie said.

"It'll be *wonderful*," Kelly enthused. "I've hired *the best* medium in Ohio—Isolde Hammersmith, she's coming later—and Dennis is here to provide the counterpoint! Could we come *in*? It's *raining*."

"Counterpoint?" Andie said. "What counterpoint? What the hell, Southie?"

"We can talk about all that later," Southie said hastily. "But now we should go inside because you want to hear everything Dennis has to say." He clapped the professor on the back and made him stumble forward a little bit. "Sorry, Dennis."

"Wait a minute—" Andie said.

"Who are they?" Alice said from behind her.

Andie sighed. "Hello, Alice. This is your uncle Southie."

"Hi, Alice," Southie said, with that smile that had charmed thousands of females. "What's new?"

Alice considered it. "I like nuts now."

"So do I," Southie said, evidently willing to bond over damn near anything.

"*Hey,* there, honey." Kelly crouched down in front of Alice in faux-equality. "I'm *Kelly*."

"You have a lot of teeth," Alice said.

"Aren't you just *precious*?" Kelly said, her smile fixed in place.

"No," Alice said, and looked past her. "Who are they?"

"This is *Bill*," Kelly said, gesturing to the younger guy as she stood up again, still in that too bright voice. "He's a *cameraman*!"

Alice and Bill looked at each other with an equal lack of enthusiasm.

"I'll get the pizzas," Bill said, and went back to the truck, ignoring the rain.

"Pizza?" Alice said, perking up.

"And this is *Dennis*. He knows about *ghosts*!"

Alice froze.

"Hello," Dennis said to Alice, politely but with no enthusiasm.

Alice moved closer to Andie. "Why is he here?"

"I don't know," Andie said, looking at Southie, now really alert. "Why is he here?"

"Because he's an *expert*," Southie said, leaning on the last word so hard it almost broke. "Tell her, Dennis."

"I'm a parapsychologist." Dennis frowned as Bill came back up the walk with four pizzas. "I'm sorry, Mrs. Archer, I thought we were expected here."

"Wait, you actually, academically, know about ghosts?" Andie said to him, and then the name finally registered. "You're Dennis Graff? From Cleveland? Professor Dennis Graff?" *The buzzkill from the panel who doesn't believe in ghosts?*

He nodded, taken aback.

Thunder rolled again and Andie opened the door wide.

"Come on in, Dennis," she said. "We need to talk."

Seven

They'd filed into the entrance hall and then into the Great Hall—"This is *amazing*," Kelly had said, beaming at Andie as she shook the rain off her coat; "Terrible light," Bill groused, shaking his head at the mullioned windows in front; "Early seventeenth century," the professor said, gazing at the gallery—and Andie led them into the dining room, directed them to chairs, called on a hostile Mrs. Crumb to leave her gin rummy game and bring paper plates and sodas. She put the professor at one end of the long dining room table and Kelly at the other end, while Kelly tried to give Andie forty reasons why it was her duty to invite the undead to dinner or at least to a séance the next day.

"Not now," Andie said to her, and when Southie called the little blonde back down to the other end of the table, Andie sat the professor down on her right and Alice on her left, put pizza in front of both of them, made sure Alice's was cut into smaller pieces, that her jewelry and the front of her already grubby black T-shirt were covered with a paper napkin, and that her stocking-tied hair wasn't flopping in her face or her dinner, checked to make sure that Carter had pizza and wasn't sitting next to Kelly-the-child-interviewer, and sat down beside her ticket to enlightenment.

"So, Dr. Graff," she said. "You're a parapsychologist."

"Uh, yes. Yes. I am." He raised the pizza to his mouth and then stopped and said, "You can call me Dennis. It's, well, you know. No classroom." He laughed for a second—a reserved little *heh-heh* sound that was almost spooky in its weirdness—and then frowned and bit into his pizza, dripping tomato sauce onto his green argyle cardigan.

"Right," Andie said, thinking, *Well, the normal ones probably don't go into parapsychology.* She resisted the urge to wipe the sauce off him as if he were Alice and bit into her pizza, savoring the spices and the crunch of the crust, but keeping her eyes on the prize. "I've read about you. You're a ghost expert."

Dennis shook his head, trying to chew the gluey cheese and wipe the tomato sauce from his mouth at the same time. "No," he said, when he'd swallowed. "I study ESP, telepathy, remote viewing, that kind of thing, which is how I got into poltergeists. Well, not into . . ." He shook his head, did that little insane laugh thing, and bit into his pizza again.

"So you don't do ghosts," Andie said. *Damn.*

"I'm well versed in general psychic phenomena." Dennis reached for his Coke and noticed the sauce on his sweater. He dabbed at it with a napkin, making the spot bigger and the sweater uglier. "I have not, however, personally seen any kind of supernatural apparition, nor have I seen any irrefutable documentation."

"That must be disappointing. I—"

"Not really. It stands to reason. Dr. Gertrude Schmeidler showed that skepticism suppresses psychic abilities." Dennis gave up on the tomato sauce spot and went back to his pizza. "The very fact that I'm a scientist makes it impossible for me to see that which I most wish to study."

"So you don't think they exist," Andie said. "The thing is—"

"I would doubt they exist except for one thing: Every culture has ghosts." Dennis took another bite of pizza.

Andie frowned. "I don't see—"

"Every culture in every millennium has had people from all social classes, all age groups, all degrees of education and intelligence see ghosts. Unless you're a believer in an ongoing worldwide, millennium-spanning mass hallucination"—he did his weird little *heh-heh* laugh, which ended this time in an asthmatic cough— "ghosts exist."

"Yeah," Andie said. "I know."

Dennis bit into his slice again, but this time instead of concentrating on the pizza, he was concentrating on her. He swallowed and said, "You strike me as a skeptical kind of person. Not somebody who believes in the paranormal."

"And a week ago, you'd have been right," Andie said.

"But now you think you have a ghost," Dennis said.

At the other end of the long table, Kelly jerked her head toward them, away from her conference with Southie. "What?"

"All we have for breakfast is toast," Andie said, and caught Alice watching her, looking interested.

"We have cereal," Alice said. "And French toast, which I will not eat."

"And cereal," Andie called down to Kelly, and then she looked at Alice. "Are you finished with your pizza?"

Alice shook her head.

"Then keep eating." Andie turned back to Dennis. "So you don't think ghosts exist."

"Oh, they exist," Dennis said. "We just don't know what all of them are."

"All of them?"

"There four kinds. Like the Beatles." He heh-hehed again, but Andie was getting used to it now.

"Of course there are," Andie said, thinking, *I had to get an academic who thinks he's a comedian.*

"The most common is the crisis apparition. It appears once within twelve hours of a death or coma or whatever the crisis is."

"Appears. Like . . ."

"Like a ghost." Dennis smiled a tight little professorial smile. "Usually it's someone who's just died and needs to say good-bye, more telepathy than apparition. Crisis can activate that kind of skill."

"Telepathy. For real," Andie said.

"As real as we can test for, but yes, for real. Crisis apparitions are well documented with anecdotal evidence and fit with what we know of telepathy. They're often just voices, not really an apparition at all."

Andie was pretty sure they hadn't lost anybody in the last twelve hours, so she said, "We don't have those here."

"Then there's the haunting," Dennis went on. "The apparitions show up in the same place, at the same time, doing the same thing. More like a voice-over." *Heh heh.*

Andie thought of May, dancing at the foot of her bed every night. "That kind. Are they dangerous?"

"They're not even a 'they.' The theory is that it's just leftover energy from some cataclysmic event like a murder. The way you can smell perfume in a room after somebody has left, you can see the energy in the room after the catastrophe has passed." Dennis kept plowing through the pizza as he spoke, his mind clearly divided between Food and Lecture, which Andie had a feeling was probably the majority of his life.

"Catastrophe," she said. Archer House was definitely the kind of place that had catastrophes. Still . . . "I don't think it's that kind. At least one of them is more than perfume. We have conversations."

"Then there are apparitions of the living," Dennis said as if she hadn't spoken. "Also called astral projection. The doppelgänger."

"No," Andie said. "This one is dead. Let's go back to that second one again. I think that's the one we have."

"Really," Dennis said. "I would have assumed that you have the fourth one, a poltergeist. A noisy ghost. Throws things, breaks things—"

"It's really pretty calm here," Andie said. *Aside from the ghost.*

"—because you have an angry teenager," Dennis went on, and then picked up his next piece of pizza. "Poltergeists are caused by telekinesis awakened by puberty."

"Carter?" Andie said, looking down the table at him.

Carter caught her staring and rolled his eyes, probably at how uncool she was, but possibly about what a pain in the ass Kelly was being since she was trying to talk to him across the table.

Andie turned back to Dennis. "Carter's not a teenager, he's twelve. And if he wanted to throw something, he'd just throw it. Carter does not need an intermediary."

Dennis shook his head as he chewed. "The children don't even know they're doing it. Completely involuntary."

"Carter doesn't do involuntary. We don't have a poltergeist. So, the haunting. Is that common?"

"Oh, yes," Dennis said. "Very common. Borley Rectory in England is probably the most famous, but there are many." He picked up the last piece of pizza from the box.

"Okay," Andie said. "How did they get rid of their ghost?"

Dennis looked at her over his glasses. "They discovered that the lady of the house was having an affair with a lodger and faked the haunting to fool her husband."

"Oh. Well, nobody's having an affair here." Andie thought of May. "Although the ghost I talk to is all in favor of it."

Dennis stopped chewing. "You talk to it?"

"Yes," Andie said, taking the plunge into crazy. "Either that or I've dreamed it. I think Alice's aunt talks with me. I think she sits with Alice at night in the rocking chair at the foot of her bed. Or it might be the woman out at the pond who was looking at Alice. I'm not sure. This is all really new to me."

"Alice?" Dennis looked across the table at Alice, now plastered with tomato sauce, strings of cheese on the napkin at her neck.

Alice looked up when she heard her name and stared back long enough that Dennis looked away.

Andie nodded, keeping her voice low. "The housekeeper thinks the ghost that sits with her is somebody who died a hundred years ago. I've only seen that one once by the pond, and really, she could have been anybody, a real person in fancy dress. Although why anybody would dress up and hang around a pond is beyond me."

Dennis put down his pizza. "*You've* seen this."

"The one by the pond, yes. And the one in my room."

Dennis pushed his plate away. "No offense intended, but had you been drinking or taking sleeping pills or—"

"No," Andie said. "Sometimes I have a cup of tea at night with a shot of brandy, but I hadn't been drinking when I saw the woman at the pond. Look, you just said there are hauntings—"

"I said that was a classification," Dennis said, serious now. "I said there were stories. I didn't say they existed."

"But you said poltergeists—"

"The other three kinds of ghosts aren't ghosts at all in the popular sense of the word. They're projections, telepathy or telekinesis, from living people or from people who have just died and are making the transition from one life to the next. They're ephemeral. The kind of haunting you're talking about lasts. On anecdotal evidence it can last for centuries, but it's completely unsubstantiated. The others all have been shown to be real and explainable, but the haunting is folklore or fraud."

"Not here it isn't," Andie said, annoyed that he'd led her on.

"You've only seen this woman once," Dennis said.

"I thought I saw a ghost across the pond, and I think Alice saw her, too, but she wouldn't say so. In fact, she refused to look that way at all, which is what made me think she saw her, too." She looked over at Alice who was chomping into her pizza again, ignoring them with great purpose. "I've talked with her dead aunt several times. I thought I was dreaming, but now I don't know. I'm new to all of this, I'm still getting it sorted out."

"I thought you said the ghost was at the foot of Alice's bed."

"There's a rocking chair there that Alice talks to. It rocks on its own. Mrs. Crumb thinks it's the really old ghost that I saw at the pond, but I think it's the ghost of Alice's aunt who died this June. A new ghost." *She has that new-ghost smell . . .*

"Uh huh. Well, Miss, uh . . ."

"Mrs. Archer," Andie said, looking around for Mrs. Crumb. "But you can call me Andie."

"Andie," Dennis said awkwardly. "It could be a projection of, uh, repressed needs. Say if you had issues with an uncaring mother and wanted to see someone watching over Alice—"

"No," Andie said. "My mother is not uncaring." *My father was, but my mother is just odd.*

"—or possibly not," Dennis went on smoothly. "But sometimes our own needs—"

"Look, I'm not a believe-in-ghosts kind of woman."

Dennis looked at her appraisingly, his pale eyes surprisingly shrewd. "No, I don't think you are."

"So we'll just leave my mother out of it."

Dennis nodded, and Andie turned to wipe down Alice, torn between being glad she had a ghost expert and thinking she was insane for being glad she had a ghost expert. At least he was nice, a little pompous but sympathetic, and he was treating her seriously, which was a relief.

"I'm done now," Alice said, as Andie wiped pizza sauce off her bat necklace, and she slid off the chair and went upstairs to get ready for bed, Carter close behind her.

At the end of the long table, Kelly waved to her. "We need to talk about the séance," she called.

"The séance?" Andie said, looking at Dennis.

He rolled his eyes.

"So you don't believe in séances."

"I'm here to provide skepticism," he said.

"Oh, that's why you're the counterpoint. And Kelly's the believer?"

"No, I believe that's Mrs. Hammersmith, the medium. She's due to arrive tomorrow. She apparently had an engagement with the Other Side tonight."

"Would a séance do any good?"

Dennis looked at her with great patience. "Since ghosts only exist in folklore, fiction, and fraud, no."

"You are not much help," Andie said, exasperated. "You and Boston Ulrich—"

"Don't put me in the same sentence with that man," Dennis snapped, the first lively thing he'd done since he'd arrived.

"Really," Andie said, impressed. "I read you were on a panel together—"

"Complete charlatan. Advertises himself as an academic and a . . . *ghostbuster.*" Dennis said the last word with such loathing that Andie was taken aback. "He's everything that's wrong in the academic paranormal world. He wants to be *popular.*" He looked off into the distance, practically grinding his teeth. "And he just got another book deal."

Okay, don't mention Boston Ulrich again. "Dennis, I *need* a ghostbuster."

Dennis said, "No you don't, there are no such things as ghosts." He bit into the last slice of pizza. "I could write a book on ghosts, too, you know. But I'd have to point out that they don't exist. Nobody wants to hear that."

"Okay, then," Andie said, ignoring Kelly's call for a chat and Dennis's obvious disapproval as she stood up. "Thank you for explaining all of that. Enjoy your pizza."

So much for an expert opinion, she thought, and went to help Mrs. Crumb handle four overnight guests.

An hour later, after a scowling Mrs. Crumb had taken Southie, Kelly, Dennis, and Bill to four of the six bedrooms on the second floor and then put out the house's meager supply of decantered booze for after-dinner drinks; after Andie had cleaned up the pizza and checked that Alice was ready for bed and told Carter he had to shut down his computer and go to bed, too; after Southie had come up to give Carter a book on the history of comics and Alice a book on butterflies and then told Andie how good it was to see her again and made her feel he meant it; after all of that normal stuff, Andie was almost back to believing she'd imagined everything. Going downstairs to endure Kelly O'Keefe in the sitting room didn't do anything to improve her day, but at least it was something that normal, non-haunted people did.

Kelly was relentlessly cheerful and clearly up to something.

"*There* you are." She swept up to Andie as she came in, her sharp little face avid under her feathered blond hair. "Where *have* you been?"

"Putting the kids to bed," Andie said, as Southie followed her into the room. "So what is it that you're doing here exactly?"

"Let me get you a drink," Southie said to Andie. "You deserve one." He went over to the table behind the sofa where Mrs. Crumb had arranged the decanters, and Andie watched him, ignoring Kelly so she could see his face when he realized all they had was peppermint schnapps, Amaretto, and the bastard brandy that Mrs. Crumb was so fond of. He came back and said, "My God."

"I know," Andie said sympathetically. "But it's alcohol."

"Plus it's been decanted," Southie said gloomily. "God knows what label that stuff was."

"Is there a top-shelf peppermint schnapps?" Andie said, and he grinned at her, like old times.

"On the bright side," he told her, "I have a Bert and Ernie bedspread in my room. Let me guess: Alice is your decorator."

"It made her happy," Andie said, laughing at the thought of Bert and Ernie and Southie sleeping together.

"It makes me happy, too," Southie said.

"Just get me *something to drink,*" Kelly said.

"I'll make a run to a liquor store tomorrow," Southie told her. "Assuming the road doesn't wash out in this storm." He looked at the decanters again. "No, even if the road is washed out. I can walk it for decent booze. For tonight, I'll make you a . . . something."

"Aren't you leaving tomorrow?" Andie said, but he had already headed back to the booze, leaving Kelly to smile fixedly at Andie. The smile didn't reach her eyes.

"You asked what am I *doing* here?" Kelly said. "I'm researching *ghosts.* Do you have any?"

"No," Andie said, not planning on sharing anything with Kelly. "Also don't talk to the kids."

"I've been *interviewing* your Mrs. Crumb," Kelly went on, and Andie thought, *Oh, hell.* "She tells me the house has been haunted for *centuries.*"

"She's often wrong."

"She says the house was brought over from *England,* and the ghosts *came with it.*"

"Yeah, how would that work, exactly?" Andie said. "I'm not up on my ghost rules, but wouldn't they be sort of stuck in the old country?"

Kelly leaned closer. "Evidently," she said, a thrill in her voice, "they're *tied to the house.*"

"Kelly, there are no ghosts," Andie said, and thought about

siccing May on her. Let Kelly get quizzed about her lovers for a change. It was bound to be a longer conversation than she'd had with Andie.

"You know how we'll be *sure*?" Kelly said, light in her eyes. "When we hold the *séance*. Isolde was booked today, but she's *driving down tomorrow—*"

"No."

"Well, let's keep an open mind." Kelly looked across the room to where Southie was talking with Dennis as he poured brandy from one of the old cut-glass decanters. "So, you and North Archer are *back together*!"

"I beg your pardon?"

"You and *North*," Kelly said, impervious to chill. "I understand you're *together* again? That's why you're down here taking care of *his children*?"

"That would be private," Andie said. *Why would you want to know that?*

"Well, yes, but since Sullivan and I are, well, *you know*, then you and I *must—*"

"No," Andie said. *Southie and Kelly? Lydia must be having a coronary somewhere.* "We mustn't."

"After all, you're here taking care of *his children*," Kelly said again, watching her closely.

"Wards. He's their guardian, not their father."

"So he's *distant*," Kelly said sympathetically.

"Not at all," Andie said, thinking, *Hell, yes, he's distant, have you met the man?* "After all, he sent me."

"After *three nannies*." Kelly smiled as if to soften what she said. "That's *pretty distant*."

How do you know about the three nannies? "And as soon as I was available, he sent me," Andie said.

"And what were you doing *before* this?" Kelly was wide-eyed with interest now.

"None of your business," Andie said. "I thought you were interested in ghosts."

"Oh, I *am*. That's why the séance tomorrow is going to be so
important—"

"There is no séance tomorrow."

"—and you'll be glad to know that Isolde Hammersmith is the
absolute *best* medium in the tristate—"

"I'm thrilled, but there's still no séance."

"—so we'll get *wonderful* results, guaranteed."

"She guarantees results?" Andie said.

"No, I guarantee results," Kelly said, the grimness in her voice
holding a ring of truth. "Mrs. Crumb showed me the Great Hall,
and I think that would be *perfect* for—"

"Here we go." Southie interrupted them with two glasses, one
of which he gave to Andie, the other of which he shoved in Kelly's
face. "Here you are, darling. I promise you a better selection tomorrow." He took Kelly's elbow. "Come over here and talk to Dennis.
He seems a little confused about what his role here is." He turned
her in the direction of the couch, mouthing "Sorry" to Andie over
Kelly's head.

Kelly craned her head back. "But Andie and I were just—"

"Oh, you go on ahead," Andie said. "I'll just stand here and . . .
drink."

Southie steered the little blonde across the room, but it didn't last.
Kelly patted Dennis's shoulder and left him and Southie to go to Bill,
who was going through his camera bag. Bill looked surly, and she
looked like she was trying to do something about it, so Andie joined
Dennis and Southie on the green-striped sofa to watch.

"Bill does not look happy," she said to Southie.

Dennis looked at his drink with caution. "I hadn't noticed. This
brandy is interesting. Did you say they make it in the basement?"

"That was a joke," Southie said, and then sipped his brandy again.
"I think it was a joke."

Andie leaned closer to Dennis. "So what is Kelly up to?"

"I don't know." Dennis sipped his brandy, made a face, and sipped again. "She was very interested in hauntings, but now . . ."

"I'm beginning to wonder, too," Southie said. "She hasn't been asking about the ghosts, she's been asking about the kids."

Andie drank her brandy, tasting an odd but not unpleasant woodsy undernote that the tea must have muted, and watched Kelly as she bent close to Bill, whispering to him between belts of her own brandy. Kelly was socking it right down, woodsy undernote be damned. "Well, her specialty has always been children."

"Child ghosts?" Dennis said. "That's a narrow specialty."

"No, live children. In peril. And as it happens, I have two of those. I don't trust her." She glanced up at Southie. "And you brought her."

"She brought Dennis," Southie pointed out. "It's a package deal. The kids-in-peril thing, though, that's bad."

"Well, the peril is . . ."—Dennis heh-hehed—"not true. There are no ghosts. Ghosts don't exist. People are very good at faking them, but in the end, that's all they are: fakes."

Andie knocked back the rest of her drink and put her glass on the table beside Dennis's. "If I take you upstairs, show you where I saw Alice's rocker move, can you tell me how those things could be faked?"

"Of course."

"Then come with me." Andie stood up, and the brandy rushed to her head and made her blink.

"Now where are *you* going?" Kelly said gaily from across the room, and Andie said, "Away," and waited until Dennis refilled his glass and then took him out through the Great Hall while Southie blocked Kelly from following by handing her another glass of brandy and asking her about the séance.

There is no séance, Andie thought, and took Dennis upstairs.

. . .

"It was here," she told Dennis when they were standing in Alice's room while Alice propped herself up by her elbows in bed. Dennis was sipping his drink and looking at the drawings she'd done on her walls with a mixture of academic interest and paternal disapproval. "The rocking chair, right there."

Dennis stared skeptically at the chair at the foot of Alice's bed. "That chair."

"Yes."

"Well, it's not surprising that it rocks. It's a rocking chair."

"I know."

"Is she there now? Your, uh, ghost?"

"I can't see her." Andie looked at Alice. "Alice, is the woman in the old-fashioned dress there now? Or your aunt May?"

"What woman?" Alice said, pretending to yawn.

"The woman in the long dress with the tiers, the flounces, that we saw out by the pond. Is she the one who makes the rocker move?"

Alice slid down under the covers and ignored her.

"You said she was wearing a long dress with flounces," Dennis said. "Was her hair in a bun?"

"Yes," Andie said. "How did you know?"

Dennis pointed to the Jessica doll on Alice's bedside table, her age-mottled dress in three tiers and her hair in a bun.

"Yeah," Andie said. "I noticed that, too, but I can't figure out what it means."

Dennis nodded, and Andie wanted to kick him. Then he said, "Could I see you in the hall, Andie?"

Andie picked up the Jessica doll and put it beside Alice. Then she leaned over and kissed the little girl on the top of the head. "Good night, baby."

"Good night, Andie," Alice said, her voice muffled in the covers.

Andie followed Dennis into the hall and closed the door.

"I think Alice is a telepath," Dennis said.

"What?"

"Oh, she doesn't know it. She's had a most unusual childhood and she's highly emotional and those probably combined to awaken latent talent. She's probably a natural. Add to that the fact that she's been alone so much, and that she probably wants to see somebody sitting at the end of her bed taking care of her, and it's not surprising that she imagines there's somebody there. That's very common, the imaginary friend." He smiled at her reassuringly. "It's not at all dangerous. She'll be fine."

"Imaginary friend?" Andie said. "But *I* saw the woman by the pond."

"You saw the telepathic image that Alice projected, based on the doll." His tone was kind, he wasn't patronizing her at all, but he was very definitely in the there's-no-ghost-here camp.

"Okay, Alice is telepathic," Andie said. "But the chair *rocked*."

"Telekinesis. Making a rocking chair rock would not be a problem for somebody with the psychic energy Alice has probably accumulated."

Psychic energy. "There is no ghost."

"I'd say almost certainly."

"Almost."

"There is no ghost."

Andie tried to wrap her mind around it, wanting to feel relieved and yet . . . "What about May, the kids' aunt? I thought I was dreaming but I don't think so anymore, I think she was real. The room was really cold."

"But you'd had a drink," Dennis said, swirling what was left of his brandy in his glass.

"Tea with Amaretto," Andie said. "One cup of spiked Earl Grey. I don't think—"

"But it was at night, you were half asleep, and this house has a very definite mood to it."

"Creepy."

"Exactly. It wouldn't be surprising if late at night, on the edge of sleep, you thought you saw something."

"I didn't just see her, I had *conversations* with her."

Dennis shook his head. "Did she talk about something that had been bothering you?"

North. "Yes."

"The subconscious finds ways to work out its problems. A dream state is as good a way as any."

It was so plausible, it was demoralizing. "I feel like a fool," Andie said. "I was really starting to think there were ghosts."

"I'm worse," Dennis said morosely over his glass. "I was hoping there were. Just once, I'd like to see one. It's like studying the dodo. No matter how much you know, you can never get primary evidence." He sighed. "If they were real, I could write a groundbreaking paper on them. It could revolutionize the field. I could be . . . ." He met her eyes, his face flushed now. "Because, unlike Boston Ulrich, *I am respected in my field.*"

"Of course you are," Andie said, startled. Then he took another sip of his drink and she realized the brandy was doing its good work. But even tipsy, Dennis made sense. There were no ghosts, of course there were no ghosts. "Listen, I am very grateful. And I will make you a huge breakfast in the morning before you go back as a thank-you. If you give me your sweater, I'll even get the pizza sauce out for you."

He smiled at her, his face relaxed now. "That's very kind of you." He handed her his glass, and then took off his ugly green sweater and handed it to her. Then he patted her arm as he took back his drink, his basset-hound eyes sympathetic. "You get some sleep now."

"All right, thank you," Andie said, and watched him toddle down the big stone staircase, weaving a little. The guy could not hold his after-dinner drinks. But still he'd been patient. And he knew about ghosts. *Good guy,* she thought, and took his sweater into the bathroom and washed the tomato sauce out of it and hung it to dry, patting it a little in sympathy with its owner who'd been kind without making her feel like she was crazy. All that angst over nothing.

I really did believe in ghosts there for a while, she thought and went back to Alice's room to make sure she wasn't upset about the whole ghost conversation, cracking the door just an inch to make sure she was asleep.

The woman in the tiered dress was standing at the end of Alice's bed, pale and dreadful, watching Alice. Andie clutched the doorknob, and opened the door farther, and the chill in the room hit her as the woman looked up. Andie saw two black, blank eyes staring at her, empty and implacable, as the cold went into her bones.

Not a woman. Not telepathy. A ghost.

"Oh, my God," Andie whispered, staring at the thing, and Alice sighed in her bed, fast asleep, unaware that the temperature in the room had dropped by thirty degrees.

Alice. I have to get Alice out of here.

She stepped into the room and the ghost wafted toward her, sepia toned and translucent, like old tea. "I have to take Alice," she whispered to the thing, trying to keep from screaming. "It's too cold in here for her. She'll get sick."

The thing grew darker, the form stronger, and then Andie heard a whisper from behind her.

I wouldn't do that.

She turned around and saw Aunt May in the little hallway, swishing her long skirt that became translucent as it moved.

She'll kill you as soon as look at you, May said. *She killed me.*

Eight

Andie could see the stone floor flickering through May's skirt as she swished it, and the old vertigo came back with a new surge of terror that this was real, that she wasn't hallucinating, that there were ghosts and one of them was talking to her *right now* and the other was at the foot of Alice's bed, that Alice was there, *she had to get Alice out of there—*

If I were you, May said, *I'd call North. He ought to be here. He ought to help.*

"May," Andie said, making one last grab for sanity. "You're a dream."

No, May said, flipping her skirt again, like a teenager trying to be cool. *That was really me, talking to you. I wanted to see if you were a keeper.*

"A keeper," Andie said, her heart pounding as she looked back at the thing at the foot of the bed, terrible in its immobility, more terrible when it moved. *Gotta get Alice out of here, gotta find out if I'm losing my mind, gotta talk to Dennis, gotta get Alice out of here—*

The other nannies were boring, May said. *You're different. And you're married to North Archer.*

Andie kept her eye on the thing. "Listen, if it's all right with you, I'll just move Alice into my bedroom—"

My bedroom. That's my bedroom. You're just sleeping there.

"The nursery," Andie said. The thing at the foot of Alice's bed drifted a little as she watched it, like a sheer drapery caught by a draft, but mostly it just stood and stared at Alice. "We'll both sleep in the nursery and you can have your bedroom back—"

She won't let you take Alice. May left the doorway and came closer, and Andie backed up a step as more cold hit her. *That wack job'll kill you dead if you try to move Alice. I tried to get the kids out of here, I knew they'd have a better life in Columbus if we went to live with North Archer, and that bitch put me over the gallery railing. Alice saw her do it. You'd think she'd have thought of Alice, wouldn't you? What kind of thing is that for a kid to see, her aunt murdered? But no, she put me over right in front of her.* May swished her skirt again. *Of course, she has no brain, so thinking was probably not part of the picture.*

"Jesus," Andie said, looking at the thing at the foot of Alice's bed with even more horror than before. "Does Alice know she's there? Can Alice see her?"

Of course. She's always been there for Alice.

Andie thought of the little girl, living with that horror her entire life. "Oh, God."

That's nothing. You know why Carter's sleeping in that room at the front of the house? Crumb thinks he killed me and he might do her next, so she keeps him as far away from her as possible, locks her door at night, and drinks herself unconscious. She dragged my body out to the moat so he wouldn't be suspected because she doesn't want anybody shutting this house down, but she won't talk to him because she thinks he did me in. And he thinks Alice did it because I'd kind of yelled at her right before that. You know Alice, she has a temper.

Andie tore her eyes from the thing to face May. "You didn't tell Mrs. Crumb the truth? You didn't tell Carter?"

She doesn't trust me, May said, her beautiful lips curving in a beautiful dead smile. *She doesn't like me.*

Andie swallowed, trying to process it all. She was having another conversation with a ghost. With May, who was practically a pal at this point, especially in comparison with the horror at the foot of Alice's bed. "The . . . thing at the foot of the bed. The one who watches Alice. What . . . who is that?"

An old governess, May said, drifting up to stand beside Andie, bringing icy cold with her. *Alice calls her "Miss J." There's not much left of her. It's been over two hundred years. The humanity kind of evaporates after a while and all that's left is the need, the thing they didn't get while they were alive. For her, it's Alice. All she wants it Alice. Try to take Alice from her, hurt Alice, and she'll get rid of you, but she won't talk. She doesn't have anything to say. She's just . . . a need. A thing. A thing that holds on to Alice.*

"She won't hurt Alice," Andie said, zeroing in on the important part.

Her whole existence is Alice. She's still here because Alice is here. She loves her, as much as a thing like that can love.

"Okay," Andie said, not really reassured but taking what she could get. Her left side was icy cold because May was standing there, but it seemed rude to move away, and until she had a grasp on what the hell was going on, she wasn't doing anything rude. She looked back at the thing. It was still drifting at the foot of Alice's bed, its hands folded at its waist, watching her. "So, listen, I need to go see a friend of mine."

You need to call North. Things are going to get a lot worse now that all these people are here.

"People."

There's a lot of energy here now, May said, stretching like a cat. *Lots of emotion. You know that little blonde who came here with your friend? She's sleeping with the other guy, the one with the camera. And he's jealous of your friend. He had a fight with her earlier tonight. It was fabulous, all that emotion. Perked us all right up.*

"Oh, hell," Andie said, believing every word of it.

No, no, it's good. Makes us stronger. She's probably gonna sleep with your friend tonight, that'll be good for a recharge because the other guy's really jealous. And then when your friend finds out he's being cheated on, we'll really be cooking. May smiled at Andie. *It was harder when it was just you. You were too calm with the kids, the other nannies went crazy, but you just kept plugging away. We got stronger whenever you talked to North, though. I can't believe you left him. You should call him now, have him come here.*

"I'm marrying somebody else," Andie lied.

May laughed. *Nobody believes that. Even* she *doesn't believe that—* she nodded to the thing at the end of Alice's bed—*and she doesn't have a brain anymore. It's North who makes you hot. Bring him here and we'll all be happy.*

"I'm having a hard time with this," Andie said, holding onto the raveling edges of her sanity while she stared at the thing. It was a ghost. It was definitely a ghost. She was talking to a ghost. They were both ghosts. There were ghosts. *We have ghosts.*

May nodded. *Hey, I understand. I didn't even know there were ghosts when I was alive. You're ahead of the game.*

"Yay," Andie said.

Call North. Alice is safe here. Go.

"Right." Andie looked once more at Alice, wrapped in her comforter and sound asleep, and at the hollow-eyed thing at the end of her bed.

Alice is safe, May said again. *That thing has been with her since she was born. Go call North.*

"Okay," Andie said. "I'll be back. Don't . . . do anything."

Then she escaped into the warmth of the hall and ran for Dennis.

Half an hour later, after a visit to Alice's room where Dennis failed to see or feel anything out of the ordinary even though the thing was right there at the foot of the bed, Andie stood in the hall just outside

Alice's door listening to him give several non-ghostly explanations for what she'd seen while she kept her eye on the thing. He could talk as long as he liked, but she'd passed from wavering on the ghost question to being a true believer. "There are *ghosts* here," she told Dennis. "I can't leave Alice alone in there with that thing." She looked through the door to where Alice slept peacefully under the dead gaze of a dead governess. "I should be in there with her. *She's* in there with her."

"Okay." Dennis smiled at her as if she were a stubborn under-graduate. "Let's assume there are ghosts."

"Yes, *let's.*"

He gave her a stern look. "Hysteria will not help. You're starting to sound like Kelly. Has this ghost ever hurt Alice before?"

"The one at the foot of the bed? No. The other ghost, May, says Alice is safe."

"Then she is," Dennis said.

"Dennis, you don't know that, you don't even believe in her. I can't leave my baby in there with her."

"Alice is not a baby. Alice is an extremely intelligent, extremely adept little girl. Leave her be and go to bed. You're exhausted and hallucinating."

"Go to bed? *There are ghosts in this house.* I have to do something about this. The séance. My mother said you can ask ghosts to leave in a séance. Is that true?"

"Well, you can ask, but séances are superstition and chicanery," Dennis said, his basset-hound eyes practically rolling. "You'll just be fueling a charlatan's ego and reputation."

"Good, we'll do that," Andie said, and went out into the main hall and headed down the stairs to the second floor to find where Kelly was sleeping.

But Kelly wasn't in her room, and it wasn't until Andie looked over the gallery railing that she found her in the darkened Great Hall, talking in low tones to Bill, the cameraman.

"The séance tomorrow," Andie called to her over the rickety railing. "Bring on your medium, I'm all for it."

"Wonderful!" Kelly called back. "Oh, Andie . . . honey . . . that's *wonderful*. Bill and I were just *talking* about that . . . hoping you'd change your mind, and *we're so glad*." She treated Andie to a flash of teeth in the dim light and then went on, her voice a little unsteady, as if she were drunk. "I'll call Isolde to confirm now that *you're on board*." Her smile morphed into manufactured sympathy. "You look really wiped out . . . all these *unexpected* guests. You go back up to bed and *get some rest* now."

"Right," Andie said, and went back up to Alice's room, sparing a thought about warning Southie that Kelly was two-timing him. And when he asked why, she could tell him that a ghost told her. One crisis at a time.

When Andie went in, the old ghost was still standing at the end of the bed, her hands folded in the flounces of her skirt, her eyes still empty pits, and Alice was still fast asleep. May had been waltzing around in the hall by the bathroom, but she came back in when Andie went in.

Did you call North?

"No," Andie said, as she felt Alice's forehead for fever or any other signs of distress.

Alice smiled in her sleep and then rolled over.

Alice is fine. I told you, that nightmare has been watching her since birth.

Andie turned on May. "She's a nightmare? What does that make you?"

Hey, May said. *All I ever did was ask you questions.* She swished her skirts again. *You were sleeping in my bedroom. You owed me that much. When are you going to call North?*

"Tomorrow," Andie lied, sitting down on the floor next to Alice's bed. "It's too late, he'll be in bed now."

He won't care if it's you.

"No." Andie leaned her head against Alice's mattress. She wasn't calling North, that was the last thing she needed, North here feeding May's fantasies, not to mention her own. No, she was going to have a séance, tell the ghosts to leave, and then get the kids the hell out of Dodge and back to Columbus. There might be ghosts in Columbus, too, but she was damn sure they weren't in North's house. If they fed on emotion, they'd starve to death there.

Call him tomorrow then, May said and left, and Andie wrapped her arms around herself against the cold from the thing at the end of the bed and settled down to watch through the night until Alice woke up.

When Alice woke up the next morning, she looked at Andie, half asleep with her head on the side of the bed, and said, "What are you doing?"

Andie straightened to get the crick out of her neck and checked out the foot of the bed. Nothing there. "I was worried."

Alice looked down at her, perplexed. "Why?"

"Because there was a ghost at the end of your bed."

"There aren't any such things as ghosts."

"I saw her, Alice," Andie said, pretty sure it was the right thing to say. "Your aunt May told me all about her. I can see them just like you can."

Alice stared at her for a long moment, and Andie thought, *She doesn't see ghosts, she thinks I'm crazy, she thinks she's trapped with a crazy person,* and then Alice said, "That's just Miss J. She doesn't hurt me."

"Miss J." Andie was torn between relief that Alice saw the ghosts, too, and horror that Alice saw the ghosts, too. "Good to know. We're moving into the nursery anyway." Andie got up slowly as her muscles screamed. "You and me. There are two beds in there. We'll be roommates."

Alice shrugged. "Miss J can go in there, too."

"Yeah, but in there I have a bed," Andie said, and went to take a shower and face her day.

It began with cornering Carter in the library where he was reading in the window seat, ignoring the storm that still raged outside.

"I talked to your aunt May last night," she said to him, and watched his eyes freeze on the page. "She said Mrs. Crumb thinks you killed her, but it was the ghost at the foot of Alice's bed who pushed her through the railing because she was going to take Alice away. I don't know how ghosts can push humans, but May says that's what happened."

He kept his eyes on his book.

"She thinks you think Alice did it."

He was still for a long time, and she was about to turn away when he said, "Alice wouldn't hurt anybody."

"Okay, then," Andie said, filing that under "May doesn't know as much as she thinks she does." "I need you to know that I am going to get you out of here."

He ignored her, his eyes on his book, but he didn't turn the page. He was listening.

"It's going to be okay. But first, I'm going to make you breakfast."

"French toast?" he said, looking up.

"If that's what you want, that's what you get."

He nodded and went back to reading.

Dear God, she thought as she went to make breakfast, *he listens to me talk about ghosts and still asks for French toast.*

When everybody except Alice was eating, she went to get Alice's cereal, pulling Crumb into the kitchen with her.

"Carter didn't kill his aunt," she said as she got the Cheerios box from the shelf.

Crumb frowned. "What?"

"Also, you're fired."

Crumb drew back, shocked. "You can't fire me. You didn't hire me. I've been with this house for sixty years and—"

"And you moved a body in a violent death and left two kids un-cared for after the trauma. I'm calling Mr. Archer, and then you're gone."

"I did it to save that boy," Crumb said, panic making her voice rise, her watery blue eyes protruding even more. "I *saved him.*"

"He didn't kill May. The thing at the foot of Alice's bed did that." She went to the fridge and got out the milk.

Crumb snorted. "He told you that? Well, how? That's what I want to know. You think ghosts have hands? *He did it.*"

"He didn't tell me anything. May told me. She said you dumped her body in the moat, and then instead of getting him help, you stuck him away in a corner of the house." Andie gripped the milk carton harder on that one, and then she got a cup down from the shelf. "You just abandoned him."

"Well, I wasn't going to turn him in to the police," Crumb said virtuously.

"He didn't kill her." Andie poured Alice's milk. "You hung a little boy out to dry for no reason."

The phone rang, and Andie went to pick it up, telling her, "Pack your things. You're done."

"That's not fair," Crumb said, and Andie said, "I don't care, you're done here."

When she picked up the phone, it was Will. "It's me," he said. "I've been thinking about us."

"Not *now,* Will, I have problems here." She stuck the phone be-tween her chin and her shoulder and opened the Cheerios.

"We can make it work," Will said. "The kids can come live with us."

"I'm going to call Mr. Archer," Crumb said, her powdery white face even paler now. "That's what I'm going to do."

"Make sure you tell him what you did to Carter," Andie said as she dumped Cheerios into the bowl. Then she spoke into the phone. "I appreciate the offer, Will, but no." She put the milk back in the fridge. "Look, my plate's a little full today." *I've got a TV reporter, a ghost expert, a wack-job housekeeper, two disturbed children, homicidal ghosts, and a séance this afternoon.* "I have to go."

"I think I should come down there."

Andie clutched the Cheerios box. "Jesus, *no,* that's all I'd need, more tension. I have to take care of these kids, I can't handle anybody else."

"That's right," Crumb said. "You *need me.*"

"Maybe you wouldn't be handling me," Will said, annoyed. "Maybe I'd be helping you."

Sure, right after you have me committed for believing in ghosts. "No," she said, shoving the cereal back in the cupboard. "I absolutely cannot take one more person here. I have to go."

She hung up, feeling annoyed, and then Crumb said, "Now you listen here," just as Andie heard Alice scream, "No, no, NO!"

She went into the dining room, saw the plate of French toast Southie had just put in front of Alice, and said, "Chill, I have your cereal," swapping out the toast for the bowl of Cheerios and cup of milk. "You'll get the hang of this," she told Southie, deciding to give him the bad news about Kelly and the cameraman later. No point in bulking up the ghosts on emotion before the séance.

Then she pulled Alice's bat necklace out of her cereal bowl, picked up a fork, and started to eat Alice's rejected toast.

Outside, thunder rumbled.

It was going to be a long day.

Late that afternoon, North was on the phone when he heard his door open and looked up to see his mother striding toward his desk, tailored and furious in black.

"He took that woman and went to that damn house," she said, biting the words off. "Did you know he was going?"

North held up his hand to finish his phone call. "Thank you, Gabe. I'll get back to you on that." He hung up and said to his mother, "I told him not to, but today was not my day to watch him."

"Very funny. We're going down there." Lydia went over to the cabinets on the wall opposite his desk and opened the one that held his TV.

"No we're not. The worst that can happen to Sullivan is that he'll have sex with a television reporter."

"He's not the only one she's threatening." Lydia took a VHS box out of her purse, opened it, and slid the tape inside it into the player. "This was on the news this morning. I made them send me a copy."

A newscaster popped up in mid-sentence. ". . . Kelly O'Keefe with a breaking report from the south of the state," he said, and then Kelly O'Keefe appeared, her face pale in some kind of dark paneled hall, her lips blazing red in her white face.

"I'm here . . . at a country house . . . in southern Ohio," she whispered, leaning closer to the camera as if afraid of being overheard, "where one . . . of the *leading lawyers* . . . of our great city . . . keeps his *secrets*." Her nostrils flared. *"Two young children . . .* left *alone . . .* to face . . . what *some* say . . . are *ghosts."*

North frowned at the screen. He'd only seen Kelly O'Keefe's broadcasts a couple of times, but she seemed odder than usual. Drunk, maybe.

The picture shifted to Kelly in a studio talking with the last nanny who'd quit.

"The place was haunted," the girl said, her eyes huge.

Enjoying herself, North thought from long experience with witnesses.

"And those two *little babies,"* Kelly went on, "left there *alone* with no one to *protect* them . . . Their guardian was *no help!"*

"He told me not to contact him unless it was an emergency," the nanny said, looking equal parts outraged and thrilled to be there. "When I told him there was something in the house, he sent the *police* to investigate. Of course they couldn't find anything. The place is *haunted*."

The picture shifted back to Kelly, standing in what North now recognized as the Great Hall at Archer House.

"Something . . ." Kelly whispered, her eyes glassy, "is *very wrong* . . . in this old house . . . These children . . . are in *danger* . . . and their guardian . . . a man of immense wealth and *stature* . . . *does not care!*" Her face grew larger as she stepped closer to the camera, her pupils dilated so that her eyes looked black. "Are you watching . . . *North Archer?*"

She lifted her chin, defiant, and North said, "Look at her eyes. She's stoned."

Kelly stepped back. "Tune in tomorrow, Columbus . . . I'll have *interviews* . . . with *the children* . . . and proof of their *neglect* . . . at the hands of their *newest nanny* . . ."

North got up and went around to sit on the desk, his arms folded.

". . . North Archer's *ex-wife*."

You're done, O'Keefe, North thought grimly.

". . . much more about . . . the *Orphans of Archer House!*"

Lydia clicked off the TV with the remote. "I'm having her killed, of course." She turned back to North. "I know you can take care of yourself, but that kind of thing does us no good."

North picked up the phone and punched in the number for Archer House.

"What are you doing?" Lydia snapped.

The phone rang and he got a recording claiming a disruption of service. Was O'Keefe crazy enough to cut the phone lines?

"North, pay attention. If you don't care about what she's doing to you, think about your brother. She's got him alone down there, duping him because I'm damn sure he'd never let her say that about you."

North put the phone down. "First, Sullivan is not stupid so you can stop treating him as if he's ten. Second, she doesn't have him alone down there. I sent Andie, remember."

Lydia turned back to the TV, punched the eject button, and took out the tape. "Get your coat. I don't know the way to the house, so you'll have to come with me."

"No." *I can do more damage to her up here.*

"North, your brother and a predatory news reporter are in a house in the middle of nowhere with two disturbed orphans and your ex-wife who is not a patient woman." Lydia put the tape in her purse. "Imagine the possibilities."

North imagined them. The best was Andie strangling Kelly O'Keefe with videotape. The worst was O'Keefe finding out that Andie thought the house was haunted and was sending him after bodies in Britain.

"Why are you smiling?" Lydia snapped.

"Andie and Kelly O'Keefe in a smackdown."

"She's probably a biter," Lydia said.

"She is."

"I meant Kelly O'Keefe," Lydia said, her voice frosty.

"Right," North said. "Leave Andie to handle it."

"You're an idiot," Lydia said and walked out.

In the ensuing quiet, North sat on the edge of his desk and considered his options. Some were fair—calling the station to point out libel could be expensive—and some were not—calling the McKennas to find out what string he could pull that would shut Kelly O'Keefe up about the Archers for good. If there was anything, the McKennas would find it, although they'd looked into Will Spenser and found nothing wrong with him, which was disappointing. "Well, he's a writer," Gabe had said when he called. "You know those guys. But no debt, no police record, people like him. He's clean."

Kelly O'Keefe was not going to be clean. And she was down there sticking a knife into Andie right now.

But if he showed up out of the blue, O'Keefe would think she was on to something. He needed a reason to go. Checking on his wards? He could have done that anytime, probably should have done that. He needed a reason to go back, something like Andie's alimony checks. "I had to bring this down . . ."

Yeah, because FedEx was broken. He didn't have to take anything anywhere. Unless it was something he had to deliver . . .

He got up and went over and opened the farthest cabinet on the end of the wall, and then reached in, far to the back, and pulled out the box that Andie had left behind, forgotten under their bed, an old cheap wood thing that she'd glued shells to in junior high or something. Really ugly. She'd loved it, and he'd put in it all the odds and ends she'd left behind, thinking he could give it back when he saw her again because he couldn't imagine not seeing her again. And then he hadn't seen her again.

He took it back to his desk and put it in the middle of his blotter and then opened it to see what thing he could announce was crucial to deliver in person.

Junk. Ticket stubs from concerts—why hadn't he thrown those away? he thought even as he remembered each one, Andie close beside him in the night—and a single earring—she must have taken the other half of the pair with her—and the diamond earrings he'd given her for her birthday—late, he remembered, but he couldn't remember why he'd bought such boring diamonds, she wouldn't have wanted diamonds anyway, it must have been his secretary who'd bought them, he'd been too busy—and finally Polaroids, losing color with age. He pulled the photos out and went through them, seeing Andie with Southie, Andie with her first-period English class, Andie laughing with him, and then he turned over the last two, the oldest, the ones he'd taken of her the morning after they'd gotten married. She'd been tangled naked in the sheets, half awake, and he'd gone out to the car for his evidence camera and snapped the pictures, and she'd yawned and said, "What are you doing?" and then she'd smiled and he'd snapped another one . . .

He didn't need a reason. He could just go down there because it was his house and his wards.

And his ex-wife.

He put everything back in the box and closed the lid, left a note on Kristin's desk to cancel his appointments for the next two days, and went upstairs to pack an overnight bag.

He was fairly sure he knew what he was doing.

The storm knocked out the phone lines—"They must be made of tissue paper," Andie told Southie, "they go out every fifteen minutes"—and then knocked out the sun, too, the heavy cloud cover making it dark when Andie moved Alice's things into the nursery. "I don't like it here," Alice said as Andie began to move her own things in. "I like my wall drawings."

"You can draw them again in here," Andie said, and Alice looked at the vast expanses of white wall available to her and went to get her markers.

Andie looked around and saw no ghosts and went downstairs to help Southie get ready for the séance, feeling ahead of the game. He'd gone out earlier for groceries and liquor, but he was back now, having fully stocked the pantry and the bar.

"I don't see why we can't do this in the dining room," Andie told him as they shoved an old round table into the middle of the Great Hall.

"Kelly wants it here." Southie looked around the room. "It's probably a good place for it. Hard to fake results in here. Not impossible, but not as easy as in a smaller room with lots of furniture."

"I thought this Isolde woman was the best medium in Ohio." Andie frowned. "Which, come to think of it, probably isn't that great a distinction. How many mediums does Ohio have, anyway?"

"I think Kelly wants it in here for the filming," Southie said.

"She's interested in ratings." He smiled at Andie. "I, on the other hand, am interested in ghosts."

Andie raised her eyebrows. "Don't tell me. Your newest hobby is séances?"

"Hauntings," Southie said. "I don't know if there's anything in it, but researching it has been interesting."

"There's something in it," Andie said, and waited for him to laugh.

"Really." He sat on the edge of the table. "You've seen them?"

"Yes. So if you've seen anything weird here, it's not you. It's real."

"I had weird sex last night."

"You had sex with Kelly?"

"She showed up in my room, acting strangely. It wasn't because of the Bert and Ernie bedspread. The lights were off."

"So of course you slept with her." *And now the cameraman is furious.* Andie shook her head, picturing May sucking up power like a milkshake, making that scraping noise with the straw when she got to the bottom.

"She was naked," Southie said, as if that explained everything. Then he frowned. "So, you really think there are ghosts here."

"Yes, and I want them out, which is why I let you and Dennis in. It's a shame we had to let Kelly in, too, but as you said, package deal." She watched him, wondering if it was kinder not to tell him that Kelly was also sleeping with the cameraman or better to clue him in. May was probably already glutted from last night, maybe now was the time.

He smiled at her cheerfully: happy, uncomplicated Southie.

"Southie," she began, and then Kelly came in looking hungover and said, "So, are we *ready?*"

"For what?" Andie said, looking at her with distaste.

Kelly frowned at the table. "We need *candles,*" she told Southie. "Go find *a lot* of them."

He nodded and ambled off, and Kelly smiled brightly at Andie. "Now we'll be *filming* this, and I think it would be really *interesting* if the *children* were here."

"Over my dead body," Andie said.

"Okay then," Kelly said brightly. "I'll just *interview* them before—"

"You will not go near my kids."

"*Your* kids?" Kelly arched her eyebrows. "So you and North are *adopting* them?"

"Stay away from the children," Andie said, and the note of dead seriousness must have soaked in through Kelly's big hair because she lost her smile.

"Well, really, Andie, I'm just trying to give as *unbiased* a report on the ghosts as *possible*. The children have lived in this house longer than anyone except *Mrs. Crumb*. They'll have *many* insights." She flashed her toothy smile again. "So you *see*—"

"Suppose I give you a choice," Andie said, watching her. "You can film the séance or you can interview the kids."

"Oh." Kelly brightened. "Well, I'd prefer *both*, of course, but if I had to *choose*, interviews are *always* better, *human interest* and all, and the kids are so *bright* that I'm *sure* my viewers will prefer that." She patted Andie's arm. "I'll take the kids."

Andie bit back the urge to snarl. "That's what I thought. You don't give a rat's ass about ghosts, you're here to get at those kids. I don't know why, but trust me, if I find you anywhere near them, I'll have your ass out on the driveway faster than Southie had you in bed last night."

Kelly drew back, outraged, and Andie plunged on.

"You cannot talk to them, you cannot approach them, hell, I don't want you waving to them across the Great Hall. They are forever off limits to you."

Kelly stared at her for a long minute and then said, "I would have thought a *woman* would have more *sympathy* for me."

"What?"

"I'm trying to *rebuild my career*," Kelly said, stepping closer. "You make one mistake and it's *gone*—"

"You made a woman throw up on television."

"—but all I need is *one great story* and I could be *back* again. I just want to do a *little ghost story*, Andie, is that *so much* to ask?" She put her hand on Andie's arm. *"One woman to another?"*

"You go near my kids and I promise you, *you'll* throw up on TV."

Kelly pulled her hand back. "So that offer of the kids or the séance wasn't an *offer* at all. I took your offer as a *contract*, and a verbal contract is *binding*, you know."

"So is my foot up your ass," Andie said, as Southie came back into the Great Hall with a box of candles.

"Mrs. Crumb gave me these," he said. "We're all set."

"Would you like to discuss legally binding verbal contracts with my lawyer?" Andie said to Kelly, gesturing to Southie. "Or would you like to quit now?"

Kelly glared at them both and left the room.

"You want to catch me up?" Southie said to Andie.

"I won't let her near the kids," Andie said.

"Of course not. She'd probably suck their souls out." Southie started to take pillar candles out of the box.

"Isn't this the woman you're sleeping with?"

"Yes. She sucked my soul out last night."

"That I didn't need to know," Andie said, feeling nauseated.

"Oh, no, I meant the weird, cold sex, not that she . . . although she did that, too."

"Southie, I'm having a bad day—"

"Mother kept talking about her teeth but I never really thought about them until she was—"

"Southie!"

"Now I can't stop thinking about them."

"Southie, please stop."

"I'm just saying, that's a scary woman." He pulled out a Precious Moments candle and looked at it, frowning, and then put it on the table.

"So you're not going to sleep with her anymore," Andie said, thinking, *Good, I don't have to tell him she was doing the cameraman, too. That'll cool May's jets.*

"Of course I'll sleep with her again," Southie said. "I'll keep the lights off. Can't see her teeth then."

Andie shook her head and helped him unload the last of the candle assortment onto the table, and when they were done, he hesitated, and then he said, "You know North still loves you, right?"

Andie stepped back. "What?"

"I'm not going to tell you there haven't been other women because there have been. Quite a few, to tell you the truth."

"Good for him," Andie said, frowning at him while she ignored the little leap her heart had taken when he'd said "still loves you." "Although not information I really wanted. I have other problems right now—"

"But it's always going to be you for him," Southie said, sounding mystified. "I do not understand this one-woman-for-life thing, but then we're different, North and me."

"Really? I never noticed." Andie jerked her head toward the dining room, pretending she didn't care. "I have to get the chairs. Want to help?"

"I'm trying to help," Southie said, sounding exasperated. "If you and North would stop being so damn civilized and just have that knock-down-drag-out fight you've been spoiling for for ten years—"

"We've been fighting."

"You've been bitching at each other. You need to just let it all out. And then everything will be fine."

"You're delusional," Andie said, and went to get the chairs.

"The makeup sex would be phenomenal," Southie called after her.

The sex was always phenomenal, Andie thought. *But now there are ghosts, so no, thanks.*

She picked up the first dining room chair and carried it into the Great Hall as Southie went in to get another one, trying really hard not to feel good about the idea that North still loved her. Southie was such a romantic, it was probably all in his head. Where it should have stayed.

When he came back, she said, "You annoy me."

"Good. I'll stop when you and North get back together."

"Never gonna happen," Andie said.

"Then why are you wearing his ring?"

Andie looked down at the ring she'd forgotten she was wearing. "Because I'm pretending to be married to him."

"And why are you doing that?"

"Because . . ." She glared at Southie. "Hey, this is none of your business." She didn't have to explain anything to Southie, especially now, when she was trying to evict ghosts.

She went back to the dining room for more seating.

"Okay, fine, tell me about the ghosts," Southie said, following her, and grateful for the change in subject, she told him everything as they set up the séance.

The medium arrived at six, just after Andie settled the kids in the library with Coke, cheese sandwiches, carrots and ranch dressing, potato chips, and strict instructions not to come into the Great Hall for any reason. Then she heard the doorknocker and went to get it, but Kelly beat her to it, letting in a lot of the storm along with her hired ghost wrangler.

"This is *Isolde Hammersmith,*" Kelly said, as if she'd just invented her and they should applaud.

Andie wasn't sure what she'd been expecting a medium to look like—probably something between Madame Arcati and Miss

Havisham. Kelly's medium was somewhere between forty and death with a face like a hatchet: high forehead, high cheekbones, long nose, long chin, the verticality broken only by Cleopatra eyes, narrow green leopard-print glasses, and lips so huge and red they practically ran from ear to ear even though Isolde was not smiling. "Fucking Motel Six," she said to Kelly, pulling a wildly patterned scarf from her explosion of black, teased Farrah hair and shaking the rain from it. "Fucking storm."

"You should stay here for the night," Andie said, hanging up Isolde's coat. Putting one more person to bed on the second floor wasn't going to cause a blip in her life at this point.

"Oh, yeah, I'll stay *here*." Isolde snorted, her blouse glittering as she turned to survey the place. She was wearing an orange, red, and yellow Picasso-print silk shirt dotted with sequins and tiny glittery beads over skintight black pants and black stilettos.

Alice was going to shriek with envy when she saw the blouse.

Isolde jerked her head in the direction of the front of the house, making her big gold bangle earrings swing. "Fucking driveway. Almost took my bumper off. And your phone is out. Harold doesn't like it."

Andie looked around for Harold, but Kelly said, "Harold's her *spirit guide*."

"Of course he is." Andie tried smiling at the medium, who was surveying the stone corridor with suspicion. "Kelly thought you'd want to hold the séance in the Great Hall. We have smaller rooms if you'd rather."

Kelly beamed at Isolde. "Oh, I'm *sure* the Great Hall will be *perfect*."

"We'll see," Isolde said flatly. "Who's this?"

Andie turned to see Dennis coming toward them, argyle-covered once more, probably trying to maintain a façade of polite neutrality but just looking academically snotty behind his glasses instead. At least his sweater wasn't tomato-stained anymore.

"This is Professor Dennis Graff," Andie told Isolde. "He's a para-psychologist."

Isolde snorted.

"Very pleased to meet you," Dennis said, but inside, Andie was sure, he was snorting back.

"And this is Sullivan Archer," Andie went on as Southie came out of the Great Hall to join them.

Southie stuck out his hand, flashing that charming smile.

"Very glad to have you here, Ms. Hammersmith."

"Mrs." Isolde ignored the smile and the hand. "So this is the full bunch?" She surveyed them all. "I don't know." She looked at Dennis. "Harold says you don't believe. You should go."

"No," Dennis said, managing to sound polite and pig-stubborn at the same time, and Andie looked at him again and realized he was angry.

Doesn't like charlatans, she remembered. *Boston Ulrich and Mrs. Hammersmith, enemies to the death.* Of course, death wasn't what it used to be in her world . . .

Isolde looked at Southie. "You don't know what you believe."

"Open mind," he said genially.

Isolde nodded and looked at Kelly. "You don't believe, either. Jesus, what a mess."

"No, no, *open mind,*" Kelly said brightly, but Isolde was already looking at Andie.

"And, finally we have a winner."

"Just get rid of them," Andie said.

"We'll see what Harold can do," Isolde said. "How many of them are there?"

Andie opened her mouth, but Dennis said, "You tell us."

"Oh, sure," Isolde said, looking unsurprised and unimpressed by Dennis. "No problem." She paused. "Harold says you're a putz."

"Well, *come on,*" Kelly said, "Dr. Graff is our *expert*—"

"And Harold says you're up to no good," Isolde said to her. "He says you try anything funny, you'll get your head handed to you. The spirit world is nothing to fuck around with."

Andie began to wish for a Harold of her own.

"You got a bathroom?" Isolde said to Andie, shoving her big black leather sling bag over her shoulder.

"Right this way." Andie led her down the hall and through the door to the little hall by the library, but Isolde stopped her as soon as they were out of earshot.

"Kelly O'Keefe," she said.

"Hag from hell," Andie said.

"She believes in séances about as much as I believe in TV psychics."

"I picked that up."

Isolde looked at her, exasperated. "Then why are you letting her do this?"

"Because we really do have ghosts," Andie said.

Isolde stared at her for a moment, and then nodded. "Okay, then. Fuck Kelly O'Keefe, let's find out about your ghosts."

"Thank you," Andie said, feeling some hope for the first time. "The Great Hall is this way—"

"After I go to the bathroom," Isolde said.

"Whenever you're ready," Andie said, pointing the way, and then she went to check on the kids, thinking, *I love this woman.*

Especially if she was going to get rid of the goddamned ghosts.

Nine

Isolde's eyebrows climbed up her considerable forehead as she took in the three stories of fifteenth-century paneling in the Great Hall. "Jesus, Mary, and Joseph."

"Pretty much," Andie said, but Isolde was already going toward the table in the center of the room.

She put her bag on the table and looked around the hall again. "Couldn't find anyplace bigger, huh?"

"We have smaller rooms—" Andie began.

"I bet you do. Harold likes it. It'll do." She sat down at the table. "So who's in?"

"Me," Andie said, and sat down across from Isolde as Dennis and Southie took chairs on each side of her and Kelly copped the one between Southie and Isolde, saying, "This is so *exciting!*"

"Who's there?" Isolde said, nodding to the empty chair between Dennis and herself.

"That's an extra," Andie said.

"Get rid of it," Isolde said. "The last thing we want is the uninvited sitting in."

Southie got up and dragged the chair over to the wall. It was a fairly long drag.

"So light the candles," Isolde said, and Andie picked up the lighter and started on the one closest to her.

"Exactly what do the candles do?" Dennis said, trying for a neutral tone and missing.

"They make the people who put them on the table happy," Isolde said. "Me, I don't care."

Andie lit the last one and sat down again. It was growing dark now, the twilight deepening outside because of the storm, and the candlelight flickered on the ancient stone walls and made their faces seem disembodied.

"Who's he?" Isolde said, looking behind Andie, and Andie jerked around expecting to see something horrible and instead saw Bill and his camera.

"I just wanted some *footage*," Kelly said brightly.

Isolde looked at her as if she'd just crawled out from under a rock. "My fee just doubled."

"Oh." Kelly smiled again, not amused but stuck. "Well, all right."

Serves you right, you duplicitous, cheating child exploiter, Andie thought.

Isolde shook her head. "Hold hands."

"Why?" Dennis said, and Andie took his hand.

"Because people like it," Isolde said. "You gonna be doing Twenty Questions all night?"

"I'm merely trying to ascertain your methods," Dennis said, and Isolde snorted again.

"Okay," she said, as Southie took Andie's other hand. "Here's how this works. You stay quiet. If you don't believe, try to be neutral so Harold can get through. It's hard enough without a bunch of snotty nonbelievers cramping his style. He's not a happy man to begin with."

"Just who was Harold?" Dennis said, and Andie thought, *Give it a rest, Dennis, I need this.*

"Stockbroker," Isolde said. "This is his second career. You done with the questions now?"

Dennis shrugged, and Isolde took a deep breath. "You all need to relax. So deep breaths, people. In . . ." She sucked in her breath and her already thin nostrils damn near disappeared under the pressure. ". . . and out. In . . ."

"Hypnosis," Dennis whispered in Andie's ear. "She's probably got all kinds of tricks hidden under that blouse."

Andie looked at Isolde. The only thing under her blouse were her considerable breasts and her even larger shoulder pads. "I don't think so."

"Are the two of you done?" Isolde said, glaring at them again. "Because I'm trying to work here. Harold's getting fed up, and if he leaves, it's over."

"Sorry," Andie said. "Really sorry." She sucked in her breath to show that she was a team player, and Isolde went back to anesthetizing the table.

After what seemed like an eternity, Isolde said, "Harold, I'm getting old here. What have we got?"

There was a sharp knocking and the whole table except for Isolde jerked back.

"Oh, *my God*! It's the *spirits*!" Kelly said.

"It's your front door," Isolde said, her voice flat. "This keeps up, Harold's going out for a cigarette and not coming back."

"I'll get it," Andie said, and got up.

When she opened the door, she saw a tall blond man in the darkness holding out his arms to her, and her heart did a little surge for a split second until she realized it was Will.

"What are you *doing here*?" she said, annoyed.

"Andie, this is no way to end things," Will said, coming in, still trying to hug her. "I tried to call you back, and your phone is out—"

"Look, I told you *not* to come," Andie said, ducking his embrace as she closed the door behind him. "I'm *busy*."

"North's here, isn't he?"

"No. We're having a séance. You can come in, but you have to be quiet."

"A *séance*? What the—"

"I don't have time to explain this right now. Come in and don't talk, or go home." She went down the hall and heard him following her.

"So who's this?" Isolde said as they came in and Andie dragged the extra chair back to the table.

"This is Will Spenser," Andie said. "He's not invited but he'll be quiet."

Will shot her a sharp look, but he pulled the extra chair over and sat down.

"Will *Spenser*?" Kelly said, flashing her teeth at him. "The *writer*? We *must talk*."

Will looked at her politely until Andie said, "This is Kelly O'Keefe from Channel Twelve," and then he smiled back. *Good PR,* Andie thought and ignored both of them.

"Another unbeliever," Isolde said, looking at Will. "You're killing me here." She tilted her head at him. "Okay, look, Sparky, you gotta lose that anger or you're out of here. Ghosts'll grab on to that emotion like it was a porterhouse with a side of cheese fries. We want to talk to them, not feed them."

"I'm not angry," Will said.

"Right." Isolde turned back to the table. "Okay. Hold hands."

Will glared again as Dennis and Isolde took his hands, but that was his problem. Andie concentrated on Isolde and the breathing. After a shorter time, Isolde nodded.

"Okay. They're here. Two of them."

"I thought there might be three," Andie said. "Two women and a man?"

"Harold says two," Isolde said. "You want to argue?"

"No." Andie looked around, but she couldn't see anything. "Can he ask them to leave?"

"We just got them here," Isolde said.

"No, I want them out of *the house*," Andie said, and Will said, "What the hell, you *believe this stuff*?"

"Nice job, asshole," Isolde said to him. "Harold lost one of them." She closed her eyes again. "Harold, what's going on?"

There was a loud knock, and Kelly said, "What does *that* mean?"

"It means there's somebody else at your fucking door," Isolde said.

"I'll *get it*," Andie said, pushing back her chair.

She made the trek down the hall and opened the door and saw her mother, looking damp and frazzled.

"Baby!" Flo said, coming in. "What's going on? The cards are going crazy and I can't get you on the phone!" She pulled off her Ohio State bomber jacket, shook the rain off it, and handed it to Andie. "And then I almost died on that driveway. Plus the storm is *terrible*. This is just so bad."

"We're having a séance," Andie said, giving up.

"A séance!" Flo picked up speed down the hall and turned into the archway, following the candlelight. "Oh, wonderful."

"This is my mother, Flo Miller," Andie said as they reached the table. "Flo, this is Isolde Hammersmith."

"Oh, it's a pleasure," Flo said, sticking out her hand. "I've heard so much about you."

"Hello, Flo," Will said, getting up, but Flo frowned at him and said, "What are you doing here?" before she went back to smiling at Isolde.

Isolde held on to Flo's hand for a minute. "You can stay." She nodded at Will. "He has to go."

"Wait a minute," Will said, but Andie said, "Come on, Will, you can meet Carter and Alice," and he followed her out of the Great Hall and down the corridor to the library.

"Have you lost your mind?" he said. "You can't believe in this, this is crazy."

Andie gritted her teeth and kept walking. "I told you not to come and you barged in here anyway, and now you're calling me crazy without even getting my side of the story?"

Will looked taken aback. "I'm just saying . . . ghosts? That woman is a charlatan."

"Kelly? Yeah, I know."

"No, the medium. Kelly O'Keefe is a professional."

"Oh, good," Andie said as they reached the library. "You can bond with her later. For now, meet the kids. Don't upset them." She opened the library door and shoved him in.

Then she went back to the Great Hall. He could sink or swim with Alice and Carter. That's what he deserved for not listening to her.

"This one's a good one," Isolde told Andie, jerking her head at Flo as she sat down. "We can work now."

"Great," Andie said, and took Dennis's hand as Southie took her other one.

"So let's breathe," Isolde said, and they did another couple minutes of hyperventilating until she said, "Harold says they're here. Three of them. He says one of them is hot."

"So they're real?" Flo said. "How exciting!"

"There are *ghosts* here?" Kelly said, her voice too bright to be honest. "You *really believe* there are *ghosts* here?"

"There are no such things as ghosts," Dennis intoned, sounding at the limit of his patience.

"Tell them to go," Andie said to Isolde.

"Have some respect, they just got here," Isolde said to Andie.

"They're squatters. Tell them to get the hell out."

Isolde shook her head. "They've been here longer than you have."

"How long would that *be*?" Kelly said to Andie. "You know, generally speaking."

"I don't care how long they've been here," Andie said. "It's time to move on. Tell them to go toward the light."

"They're tied here," Isolde said, her voice serious now. "Harold says the man feels . . . injustice." She listened for a minute. "This is his house. To him, you're squatters."

"I'll get the paperwork and show him," Andie said, looking around for a supernatural squatter. Nothing. Damn.

Isolde listened again. "No. You don't own the house."

"No, I don't," Andie said. "But—"

"Then he doesn't care about you," Isolde said, and Andie started to say something and then stopped because Isolde was listening again. "Oh. Oh, boy."

"Now what?" Andie said.

"There's a woman. She's looking for her baby."

"Baby?" Kelly said, leaning forward. "There's a *baby*?"

"There's no baby," Andie snapped at her.

"She lost it a long time ago." Isolde was deathly serious now, all the sneer gone from her face. "There's a child here."

"Alice and Carter."

"She wants Alice," Isolde said, her face grim. "She thinks Alice is the baby she lost. She'll never give up Alice."

"Oh, *no*," Flo said, horrified.

"Fascinating," Kelly said, avid.

"It's all right," Dennis said, bored now. "None of this is real."

"The hell she won't give up Alice." Andie looked around the room. "Okay, wherever you are, you cannot have Alice. Alice is *mine*."

Something moved behind Isolde in the darkness.

"Don't do that," Isolde said sharply, and then the knocking started again. *"Damn it."*

"She can't have Alice," Andie told Isolde. "Tell her to get the hell away from my kids."

"Get the door," Isolde told her quietly. "And get control of yourself. This is very bad."

Kelly leaned forward again. "So the ghosts want the *children?*"

Andie stood up. "Just tell me how to get rid of them," she said to Isolde, and then she looked at Kelly. "I'm telling you now, if any of this ends up on television, I am kicking your ass from here to Cleveland. I know you're wiry and you probably fight dirty, but I have size and rage on my side, so don't cross me."

"Well, *really,*" Kelly said, smiling at her, all teeth. "I'm just trying to *help.*"

"Like hell," Andie said. "Also, Southie? She's cheating on you with the cameraman."

"What?" Southie said, turning to look at Bill, who said, "Hey, I was there first," and Isolde said, "This is *not helping,*" and then there was another knock and Andie went to the front door, prepared to snarl at whatever idiot was screwing up her life now.

She yanked open the door and saw Lydia Archer, standing under an umbrella and looking like avenging death.

"Is my son here?" Lydia snapped.

"Southie? Yes," Andie said.

Lydia walked in, said, "I like your teeth," shook out her umbrella and left it draining on the stone floor, and then went down the hall, following the candlelight through the stone archway in her quest for Southie.

"My teeth?" Andie said to her back and closed the door.

She picked up speed and got there just as Lydia saw Kelly.

"You!" she said, fury in her voice, and then there was a flash of lightning from the storm, and Andie saw three figures in the Great Hall that hadn't been there before: the thing in the tiered dress, a man who looked like the guy on the tower in an old-fashioned coat, and May, pirouetting with perfect grace, her dark curls flying.

Hi, she said to Andie. *You wanted to see us? We're here.*

"Oh, *my God,*" Andie said, cutting across the beginning of Lydia's tirade.

"What?" Lydia said, looking in the direction of the ghosts. *"What?"*

"Can you see them?" Isolde said to Andie.

"Yes. Tell them *to go.*"

May laughed.

It'll take more than that to get rid of them, she said. *And you need me.*

"No," Andie said to her, and then realized the whole table was watching her. "I can see her," she told them. "I can see all three of them, but two of them are . . ."

Dennis frowned in the direction she'd been staring, as if trying to see what she'd seen.

"Just energy," Isolde said. "Harold says there's not much there of two of them, just need. The other one, she's still got some life in her. Literally."

Damn straight, May said, and twirled around again, and Dennis leaned forward, squinting.

"What the hell is going on here?" Lydia snapped, and all three ghosts seemed to grow a little more defined.

"Anger," Isolde said. "Get that woman out of here or we're in trouble."

Andie stood up. "Come on, Lydia."

"Not until I've—"

There was a knocking sound, and Andie said, *"I'll get it,"* and all but shoved Lydia out of the room. "Wait here," she said when they were in the entry hall, "do *not go back in there.*"

Then she went to savage whatever idiot was screwing with her séance now, but when she opened the door, it was North, tall and strong and *calm.* She said, "Oh, thank *God,*" as he stepped in, put her arms around him, buried her face in his wet overcoat, and said, "Save me."

She heard his overnight bag hit the stone floor as his arms went around her, and he felt so good that she held on longer than was polite. He said, "That bad?" and when she looked up, he was smiling down at her, just like the old days, and she lost her breath because it was him, holding her again.

Then Lydia said, "Well, it's about time you got here," and Andie stepped back as he let go of her.

"Hello, Mother," he said, sounding annoyed.

"It's a damn good thing you came to your senses," Lydia said. "These people have all lost their minds. They're having a séance *with that O'Keefe woman in the room.*"

"A séance?" North said, looking at Andie as he took his coat off.

Andie took the coat and put it on the hall tree, trying to get her breath back while she figured out how to tell him that she believed in ghosts in front of his mother.

"It's over now," Lydia said. "I went back in and the woman who was running it said I'd brought too much anger into the room, and it was strengthening the spirits."

"They like being bullied, do they?" North said, and then Andie saw Crumb come into the entrance hall from the living room, wearing her violently orange-flowered apron and a furious expression.

Andie leaned up and whispered in the direction of North's ear, "I fired Crumb this morning. Also, remember, we're still married."

"There goes the nightly blow job," North said under his breath and crocodile-smiled past her. "Mrs. Crumb. So sorry you're leaving us."

"No we're not," Andie said.

"I heard the knocking," Crumb snapped. "We wasn't expecting *any* of you. Four people last night and now this. You need me to take care of this mess."

"You can discuss that with . . ." North looked down at Andie. "Mrs. Archer." He gestured to Lydia. "This is my mother, Mrs. Archer. The other Mrs. Archer."

"What other Mrs. Archer?" Lydia said.

"How many more are there?" Crumb said to Andie, ignoring them all.

"How many Mrs. . . . Oh, how many guests?" Andie did a fast count in her head. "Four more."

"We only got two more bedrooms. 'Course Mr. Archer will be in with you."

"What?" Lydia said, and North looked at her, and she shut up. "Fine." She looked at Andie and then at North and then went back into the Great Hall.

Okay, North's sleeping in my room, Andie thought, *no, May's room. She'll like that. It doesn't matter since I'm sleeping in the nursery with Alice.* "Of course he'll sleep in my room," she said to Crumb, and North looked interested but didn't say anything.

Crumb folded her arms. "I don't know what that is to me. I been fired."

"Good point," Andie said. "Leave."

"Well, now," Crumb began, and then Southie came into the hall, saw Crumb, and said, "For the love of God, woman, get us drinks."

Crumb looked at Andie, and Andie said, "Fine, we'll talk about it later."

The housekeeper smiled, triumphant, and said, "You're going to have to share a room, Mr. Sullivan," and went off to shift some guests.

Southie caught sight of North and came as close to a glare as Andie had ever seen from him. "How nice to see *Mother,*" he said to North.

"Don't blame me." North looked at him without sympathy. "I told you not to come here."

"The Beast of the Nightly News had him," Andie told North, trying to find her way back to sanity. There were ghosts, but North was there. It might even out, especially if she threw herself at him again, and distinct possibility given the way her mind was going south just from his sheer proximity. "Southie was helpless in her clutches. She truly is a blot on humanity."

"Excellent," North said, looking down at her with that beautiful, serious face. "Mother's been spoiling for a fight. Let her have the Blot. You take me someplace, give me a drink, and tell me what the hell is going on."

Yes, Andie thought, but she said, "I think we'd better go in with the Blot. "I'm not sure your mother can take her."

"Nonsense. A good stake through the heart and she's done." North looked at Southie. "I beg your pardon, Sullivan, I should have asked. Do you love this woman?"

"God, no," Southie said.

"Then let Mother have her." He smiled down at Andie again. "And in the meantime, you can tell me what's happening. It can't be nearly as bad as you sounded."

"It's worse," Southie said. "We—"

"Southie," North said. "Go away."

"What?" Southie blinked at him. "Oh. Right. Sure."

He went back into the Great Hall, and North looked down at her and said, "Where were we?"

"Well . . ." She stopped, knowing if she told him the truth, that there were ghosts, that he'd be calm and rational and probably have her committed.

"If it's that bad," he said as her silence lengthened, "give me the short version."

She took a deep breath and said, "There are ghosts. We're having a séance to get rid of them, but it's not working. Kelly O'Keefe is here sleeping with her cameraman and Southie at the same time and all that emotion makes the ghosts stronger. The kids won't leave because the ghosts kill anybody who tries to take them away. Your mother is furious with Kelly O'Keefe and that's making the ghosts stronger. And my mother is here, too, and you know how she and Lydia are when they get together, so we're all just *feeding* those things and I can't get the kids out and I'm so *tired* . . ."

She stopped, overcome suddenly by how awful everything was and now he was going to have her committed—

He said, "What do you want me to fix first?" and she felt all her tension go.

"Save the kids," she said. "I don't give a damn about the rest of them, but get the kids out of here."

"We can do that," he began, and then Alice screamed bloody murder in the library, and Andie took off at a run.

Andie threw open the library door and saw Alice shrieking in the middle of the room, turning blue from lack of oxygen. Her screams weren't her usual "NO NO NO," they were deeper, coming from a place of so much fear that Andie scooped her up and held her close and said, "It's okay, Alice, it's all right," as calmly as she could while Alice screamed and screamed.

"What *happened*?" she said to Carter, patting Alice frantically, and he nodded to Will. Andie turned on Will. "What did you *do*?"

He looked horrified as he stared at Alice thrashing in Andie's arms. "I told her she was going to come to Columbus to live with us."

"*Jesus,* Will! Why—"

"He told us we didn't have any choice," Carter said flatly, and Andie thought, *You fucking MORON,* but then Alice's screams deepened, her eyes rolling back into her head, and she forgot Will entirely. She turned to take her out of the room and saw North in the doorway, surveying the mess calmly, and pushed past him and into the hall, carrying Alice with her, past Southie, who looked alarmed, and Lydia, who looked confused, and a distressed Flo, and a sympathetic Dennis, and an avid, staring Kelly, up the two flights of darkened stone stairs, whispering to Alice that it was all right, that she wasn't going anywhere, that Andie was with her, but Alice was beyond that now, flailing in a place where there was only terror. Andie could hear Carter on the stairs behind her, but he was going to have to wait. She carried Alice into the nursery and sat down in the rocking chair there—*no ghosts in this one,* Andie thought—and began to rock, humming "Baby Mine" to the little girl since she couldn't hear words.

Alice's screams were guttural now, her throat raw, and Andie kept humming, her cheek on Alice's hair, rocking and rocking. Alice slowed to rasping, gasping breaths, and then as Andie hummed and patted, she quieted down even more, to shaky, moany little sighs, and Andie began to sing, and Alice listened until Andie sang, "Never to part, baby of mine."

Alice straightened, her face dirty with tearstains. "You promised."

"He was wrong, I promise I won't take you until you want to go, we're never going to be with him," Andie said, and Alice subsided into her arms again, and said, "Sing." Andie did, and Alice relaxed, sighing whenever Andie sang "baby of mine." When she'd finished the song, Alice sniffed and said in a shattered little voice, "Sing it again," and Andie did, and Alice curled into her and began to suck her thumb as they rocked.

"Again," Alice said when Andie was done, pliant now, and Andie sang again, smoothing back Alice's hair from her feverish little brow, wondering how it could be that she could hate any kind of commitment and still know she'd be with Alice forever. Because she was going to be. Nobody was going to raise Alice but her. She'd get through to Carter, too, if it took her years, he was going to feel safe and loved again. They needed her. And she needed them. This kind of love, this went so deep she'd never get out of it.

"Never to part," she sang again, more sure than ever, and Alice turned her head up. "*Never* to part," Andie said to her, looking into her eyes. "I will stay with you forever. I will never desert you. Never."

Alice took a deep shuddering breath and nodded, and then said, "Sing the other baby song," and after a moment, Andie figured out what she wanted, and began to sing "Somebody's Baby," soft and slow, and Alice put her head on Andie's arm and fell asleep, sucking her thumb.

Andie brushed the white-blond strands of hair back from Alice's clammy forehead again and kissed her. *Mine,* she thought, and then looked up and saw Carter in the doorway to the little hallway, watching them.

"She's all right now," Andie whispered to the boy, and Carter nodded and turned to go. "Carter." He turned back and she said, "That goes for you, too. All of it. I'm with you forever."

His face was in shadow and he didn't move for a long moment. Then he went down the hall to his room.

"You might have checked that with me first," Will said, exasperated, and Andie turned and saw him standing in the doorway to the gallery hall, Southie and Kelly behind him, and behind them North. Will looked annoyed, Kelly looked avid, Southie looked kind, and North looked calm. Beautifully, competently, unflappably calm.

"What do you need?" he said to her over them all, and she said, "We just need to be alone." He reached past them all and pulled the door closed, shutting them all out swiftly, and Andie stood up and carried Alice over to the bed she'd made up for her by the fireplace. She pulled the spread and sheet back and tipped Alice into bed and took off her grubby tennis shoes and looked at her narrow dirty feet. *Bath tomorrow,* she thought, comforted by the banal thought, and pulled the sheet and comforter up over her.

Then she stood and watched Alice sleep, the little girl's breath still coming in little shudders but more evenly now, her pale lashes almost invisible on her tearstained cheeks.

How had she survived the past two years? How had Carter? All that death, all that loss, all the strangers, the *ghosts*?

She leaned down to Alice's ear and whispered, "I will always be with you," and Alice smiled in her sleep.

"Oh," Andie said, and sat down on the floor beside Alice's bed and cried.

. . .

North stood in the hallway while Kelly yapped at him, ignoring her to take stock. It was one thing to hear that the little girl went crazy when they tried to take her away, another thing to see that pale little face turn blue, those wild little eyes roll back in terror. Andie was right, the first priority was to get the kids out of this house into someplace safe and normal.

"I just want to go in and *help,*" Kelly said, trying to get past him.

"Get her out of here," he told Southie, and Southie took her arm.

"Well, *really,* Sullivan," Kelly said, trying to pull away.

"We saw your newscast," North said, looking down into her greedy little face, and saw her eyes go wary.

"Newscast?" Southie said, looking at her with narrowed eyes.

"I did it for the *children,*" Kelly said, and Southie said, "Come downstairs and tell me about it," with a grimness in his voice that even Kelly heard since she let him drag her down the stairs.

"I don't care about any newscast," Will said, confronting him. "I'm going in there."

"No," North said, "you're not. That's my ward in there and you don't have my permission to interfere with her upbringing."

"Andie wants to raise the kids." Will met his eyes. "And that means I am, too. We should talk about this, since we'll probably be adopting them . . ."

North let him blather on, feeling almost kindly toward him. He was handling the situation so badly that Andie would probably break up with him before morning. Plus Andie was wearing her wedding ring again; he'd seen it on her hand as she'd cradled Alice in the rocking chair. It was probably just part of her charade, but she was wearing that cheap, pathetic ring again. His ring.

". . . so you understand why I should be in there."

"The children are not available for adoption."

Will folded his arms. "You think you'll get Andie back this way. She'll never leave those kids. They're a deal breaker for her."

"So you want to adopt them to keep Andie."

"I care about them."

"You don't even know them," North said. "If Andie decided tomorrow that she didn't want them, you'd walk away from them without a backward glance. So, no, I will not be letting you anywhere near them. Go downstairs."

"I'll go when you go," Will said, looking stubborn.

"Spenser," Southie called from the archway, and Will turned around. "Come on downstairs. I'll buy you a drink. You have to try the house brandy. I think Crumb makes it in the basement."

Will shook his head. "I—"

"You're an uninvited guest in this house," Southie said, coming to join them, still affable. "And my brother asked you to leave his wards alone. So *come down and have that drink.*"

Will got the same look on his face that Kelly had, surprise that Southie had a serious voice and wariness about what he'd do next. "I'm not leaving without Andie."

"Let me put it another way," Southie said, standing beside North. "There's two of us and one of you. And one of us is nobody to mess with. Come downstairs on your own power or we'll drag you down."

Will looked back at North, who thought, *Try me. Please,* and he must have read the look in his eyes because he gave up. "Tell Andie I need to talk to her."

"You bet," North said. *You jerk.*

Will headed for the stairs, and Southie shook his head and rolled his eyes as Will went past him and then followed him down.

Dumbass. Trying to adopt kids to keep Andie. Nobody kept Andie. And the kids deserved to be wanted for themselves, not as Andie-bait.

He leaned against the wall and stared into the echoing space above the Great Hall. They deserved a guardian who paid some attention to them, too. He'd screwed up leaving them down here, but now things would be different.

Voices rose up, two women arguing, and he looked over the rickety banister and saw his mother and Flo going at it down in the Great Hall, and another woman, sharp and odd-looking even from his angle above, watching them. No wonder Andie had been so glad to see him.

He went downstairs and into the Great Hall, and when Lydia and Flo turned to see who'd come in, he said, "Andie has enough problems without you two rehashing old arguments. Either pull together to help her or get out."

"I'm not leaving while *that woman* is here," Lydia said, but Flo nodded.

"He's right," she told Lydia. "Andie doesn't need us behaving badly, and the anger just makes the ghosts stronger."

"There are no ghosts," Lydia snapped, rounding on her.

The woman with the big hair and bigger hoop earrings said, "Oh, yeah, there are, and this one's right. You gotta calm down." She looked like a caricature of a New Jersey princess, but her voice was serious and strong.

"And I don't see why you won't leave as long as Andie's here," Flo went on, indignant. "She's been here—"

"Not Andie," Lydia said, exasperated. *"Kelly O'Keefe."*

"Oh." Flo's face changed to puzzlement. "What's she doing here? Andie didn't invite her."

"She wants Sullivan," Lydia said, her eyes practically glowing with rage, "and she's trying to ruin North using the children—"

"Well, then, we'll just get rid of her," Flo said, and Lydia shut up.

"Good idea, you work on that," North said. "She's in the sitting room right now."

"Okay." Flo turned to go and then stopped. "How's Alice?"

"She's quiet now. Andie's with her. But O'Keefe wants to talk to her—"

"Over my dead body," Lydia said.

"I say we just throw her out of the house," Flo said, and set off for the living room.

"I may have misjudged Flo," Lydia said, watching her go.

"Go help her, then," North said, and Lydia shot him a sharp look and went.

North turned back to the woman sitting at the table, watching him carefully. "I'm sorry, we haven't been introduced. I'm—"

"You're North Archer," the woman said. "You're the missing piece."

"Excuse me?"

"You're the one they're all fixated on," she went on. "Some of them are angry with you and some of them are afraid of you and some of them just want you. And I have to warn you, one of the ones who wants you is dead."

"You're the medium," North said, putting it together.

"Isolde Hammersmith." She stood up. "Things are bad here. Get these people out of here before it gets worse."

"That's my plan," North said mildly. "Do you need a ride back to town?"

"I'm staying the night." Isolde picked up her big leather bag from the stone floor. "Andie needs me."

North opened his mouth to suggest she'd be more comfortable someplace else—anyplace else—and then heard the storm pound the windows.

"Everybody's in the sitting room," he said instead. "It's probably warmer in there. Southie was going to light the fireplace."

"That's good," she said. "No ghosts. Make sure the fires are lit in the bedrooms, too. Ghosts don't like fire."

"Good to know," North said, and went out to the hall phone and checked for a dial tone. The line was working again, so he got out his address book and dialed Gabe McKenna's private number. When the answering machine picked up, he said, "I need you down here first thing tomorrow," and gave directions to the house. Whoever was playing games with Andie and the kids, Gabe would find out. And after that, he'd pack up Andie and the kids and take them home. Lydia and Southie could deal with Kelly O'Keefe and Isolde Hammersmith.

Then he picked up his overnight bag from where he'd left it by the door and went back upstairs to the nursery.

Ten

When he walked in, Andie looked up from where she was sitting on the floor beside Alice's bed, looking exhausted. "She's okay."

He sat down in the rocker. "How are you?"

Her chin went up. "I want them forever. Alice and Carter. I'm staying with them forever." She met his eyes, as if she thought he was going to argue.

"That's good."

"Who are you?" Alice mumbled, rousing a little from her sleep to blink at him.

"This is Bad Uncle, remember?" Andie said softly.

"Oh, thanks," North said.

Andie leaned closer. "But he's not taking you away. Nanny Joy got that all wrong. He won't come get you until you want to leave. He promises."

Alice turned accusing Archer blue eyes back to him, so he said, "As long as you're not in danger, you can stay here until you say,

'I want to go.' When you want to go, I will take you home to
Columbus."

Alice pushed herself up on her elbows then, her face still blotchy
with tears, an ugly doll tumbled beside her. "I'm not in danger."

"We'll see," North said.

Alice scowled, wiping her eyes with the back of her hand. "I'm
not going."

"As long as you're safe here, you don't have to," North said.

"Pinky swear?"

"Pinky swear," he said, having only a vague idea of what that
meant until she held out her hand, her little finger crooked. He
linked his little finger with hers, hoping there wasn't some kind of
ritual that he was going to screw up, and she shook his hand once
and let go.

"Okay," she said. "If you break a pinky swear, you have to cut
your finger off."

"That's the kind of thing you're supposed to tell me *before* you
make me do it," North said.

"Then you shouldn't have done it without asking," Alice said,
and since that was an argument he'd often used in court, he nodded.

"You're right. Pinky swear."

Alice lay back down again, frankly surveying him now. "You
were here before. When Daddy died. When Aunt May was here."

North nodded.

"You never came back."

"I know." All the rationales he'd used—they were in good hands
with their aunt, he didn't know anything about kids, somebody had
to run the practice—looked pretty stupid in the light of Alice's di-
rect gaze. "I was wrong. I was a Bad Uncle."

"Whoa," Andie said, and Alice looked at her. "Bad Uncle doesn't
say he's wrong very often. Well, ever."

"I've said that."

Andie looked at him, exasperated. "When?"

Right offhand, he couldn't think of an example, so he said to Alice, "I brought you something."

"Books," Alice said, and yawned again.

"No." He opened his overnight bag and pulled out the soft, furry, long-eared, pear-shaped little bunny that had felt squashy in his hands when he'd picked it up after seeing it in a store window. He'd put it on her bed in Columbus so she'd have it when she moved in and then grabbed it on his way out the door with a vague idea that there should be gifts when he arrived. Kids liked gifts. "I thought since your name was Alice that you should have a white rabbit."

"Huh?" Alice said, and then looked at the rabbit as he held it out to her.

"Alice in Wonderland?" he said and looked at Andie, who shook her head.

"She doesn't know it," she told him and then said to Alice, "There's an Alice in a book who chases a white rabbit and has ad-ventures."

Alice looked at the rabbit, and North could tell she wanted it, but something kept her from reaching out.

Andie took it instead. "My God, this is a great rabbit." She squeezed it, her strong hands holding it up in front of the little girl. "Alice, it's *squooshy.* And really soft. And it's smiling underneath its fur."

Alice stuck her chin out, clearly trying to resist but watching the bunny anyway.

"And the tag says 'Jellycat.' Do you think that's its name?"

"No. Its name is . . ." Alice frowned and then held out her hand. "Let me see."

Andie gave the bunny back to North. "It's from your uncle North."

Alice looked exasperated. North held out the bunny to her, and she took it, knocking Jessica off onto the floor as she reached for it, her eyes widening as she held it up in front of her and felt how soft it was.

"What do you say for the nice gift?" Andie said.

"Thank you, Bad," Alice said automatically, still staring at her bunny.

"You're welcome," North said, ignoring the "Bad" to watch her stare at the toy. Nobody he'd ever given a gift to had ever looked like that, all that unashamed naked wonder. Then Alice hugged the rabbit to her, and he felt his throat close in, completely blindsided by the little girl and her vulnerability. And he'd left her alone down here with a bunch of idiot nannies and some asshole who was faking ghosts to keep her there. "Bad Uncle" was exactly what he deserved.

"Good present," Andie whispered beside him, and he remembered she was there, too.

He looked back at Alice, rocking the bunny, her cheek on its head, and cleared his throat. "What's his name, Alice?"

"Her," Alice said, frowning.

"Sorry. What's her name?"

Alice pulled back to look at the bunny. "She has a pink nose. Her name is Rose Bunny."

"Not Pinky?" Andie said.

"Pinky is not a real name," Alice said sternly, and lay back down in her bed, Rose Bunny jammed under her chin.

"Good point," North said. "Rose is a fine name."

"Did you get Carter one?" Alice said, around a yawn.

"No, I got Carter something else."

"What?"

"Colored pencils. In a case. Will he like that?"

Alice's eyes closed as her lips curved in a smile that could break a heart. "Yes, he will." She snuggled deeper in her bed, looking normal now, no trace of her hysterics left except for the smudges of her tears, now mostly rubbed off on her pillow.

"Good night, Alice," Andie whispered. "Good night, Rose."

"Good night, Andie," Alice murmured back. "Good night, Bad."

"Good night, Alice," North said, and then when Andie nudged him, he added, "Good night, Rose," and watched Alice smile, half asleep.

"You did good, Bad," Andie whispered.

That's a start, North thought. "You coming downstairs?"

"I need to stay with her," Andie said, looking back at the sleeping little girl. "She's not deep asleep yet. I don't want her to wake up and be alone so soon after everything else. And there are . . . things that show up sometimes. I don't want her alone."

"Ghosts."

She stuck her chin out. "Yes."

He got up and went over and turned on the gas fireplace, checking to make sure it was safe before he turned back to her. "Your medium—"

"Isolde."

"—Isolde said that ghosts don't like fire. She said if you kept the fire going, the ghost wouldn't come in the room."

Andie shook her head. "Don't gaslight me. You don't believe in ghosts."

"No, but you do, and your expert says that this fire will keep Alice safe."

"And you think we're nuts."

"No," North said, surprised to find that he didn't. "I think something's going on here. I called Gabe and left a message for him to come down tomorrow. We're going to go over this place until we find out what's really happening."

"There really are ghosts."

"Then we'll find those, too. And when we've gotten rid of whatever the problem is, the kids will come back with us."

"With us," Andie said, doubt on her face.

"I'm not leaving without you," he told her, surprising himself and her.

Andie blinked. "Wow. You're serious. You realize that could be weeks?"

"Yes," North said, thinking, *Christ, I hope not*. "I'm going downstairs to see what fresh hell has broken loose, but I'll come back soon and check on you."

Andie turned her face up to his and smiled, and he thought, *Oh, hell,* and fought the urge to bend down and kiss her.

He turned to go and then remembered. "Will wants to talk to you."

"The hell with him," Andie said. "I told him not to come down here, he pulls this crap with Alice, and now he wants to talk to me. I don't think so."

"I'll let him know," North said, and went downstairs feeling more cheerful than he'd thought possible since he'd heard Andie say, "There are ghosts."

The party in the living room was in full swing when North walked in, although "full seethe" might have been the better term. Flo and Lydia had their heads together over in the corner, probably planning on killing Kelly O'Keefe and dumping her body in the moat. Lydia was generally sane but her sons were being threatened, and nothing North had learned about Flo in the year he'd been married to her daughter gave him any hope that she'd be a voice of reason.

Over on the couch, Southie was sitting between Isolde and an annoyed-looking middle-aged man with a jowly face. "Well, I think both ways of looking at this are good," he said, and both the jowly guy and Isolde looked at him with contempt.

Meanwhile Kelly O'Keefe had her head bent close to Will, listening to every word he said. Her cameraman lurked behind her, looking equal parts angry and fed up.

It wasn't a question of if something was going to go wrong, it was a question of which one of the time bombs gathered there was going to detonate first.

"North!" Southie called, desperation under his voice, and North went over to the couch. "You have to meet Dennis, the ghost expert I told you about."

"Right," North said, and shook Dennis's hand. "So there are ghosts."

"Of course there aren't ghosts," Dennis said, evidently pushed beyond the limits of politeness. "There is no such thing as ghosts, at least not the kind that are supposed to be here."

Isolde shrugged. "You can't see them because you don't believe."

"That's convenient," North said.

"No, she's right," Dennis said morosely. "Disbelief suppresses sensitivity."

"So you think there are ghosts," North said.

"No," Dennis said. "But if there were, I couldn't see them because I don't believe in them."

"I could use a drink," North said to Southie, and Southie reached over the back of the couch and picked up a decanter.

"You have to taste this brandy," he said, reaching for a glass, too.

"It's good?"

"No, it's odd." Southie splashed some liquor into the glass and handed it to him. "I think it's local. There's good stuff, too, I went out in the storm and stocked the bar, but that demented housekeeper decanted everything"—he jerked his head to an assortment of glass decanters on the table behind the couch—"so we're guessing what's what. But I'm positive this is the house brandy. It has quite a kick."

"Local brandy," North said, taking the glass, and then caught sight of his mother leaving the room. "Now where is she going?" he said, and put the glass down to follow her, only to be met at the door by Flo.

"I need to talk to you," she said, and he thought, *This night will never end,* and followed her into the hall.

Andie leaned against Alice's bed after North had gone, trying to be practical and failing miserably. She'd pretty much wanted him back the minute he'd come through the door, and then he'd turfed everybody out of the nursery for her, and brought Alice a rabbit, and told her he wasn't leaving until they went home with him, and if she hadn't been so tired, she'd have jumped him in the nursery except that was out of the question. Although, when she thought about it, jumping him for one night might be a good idea. Well, no it wasn't, but it *felt* like a great idea, to have his arms around her again, to let him make her crazy and forget everything for a while. What could it hurt? He was sleeping in her old bedroom next to the nursery, Isolde said that ghosts didn't like fire, she'd be right there if Alice needed her.

And God knew she needed him.

Bad idea, she thought, *bad, bad idea.*

But ten minutes of hot memories later, when the nursery door opened again, Andie looked up smiling, thinking, *Maybe,* and got Lydia instead.

"You're an idiot," Lydia said, and sat down in the rocking chair.

Wonderful, Andie thought, her hot thoughts evaporating. "Is that just a general observation, or do you have a direction you're going with it?"

"You left my son."

"Ten years ago," Andie said, incredulous. "We're over it. And you were thrilled. You probably did a dance when I left." She looked at Lydia doubtfully. "The minuet or something."

"He was happy with you," Lydia said, looking at her accusingly. "That year with you, he laughed."

"Well, I'm a funny gal," Andie said, wishing she would leave.

"You're correct, you were not what I wanted for him." Lydia lifted her chin. "I was wrong. And I'm sorry."

Andie blinked. "For what? You didn't wreck my marriage. I mean, I knew you didn't like me, but you didn't tell North to divorce me. Did you?"

"Of course not. That would have been completely inappropriate."

"Of course you wouldn't." Lydia was a bitch, but she played fair.

"He wouldn't have listened anyway," Lydia said.

Andie tried again, on the theory that if she forgave Lydia for her nonexistent sins, she'd leave, and Andie could go back to having hot thoughts about the man she wasn't going back to. "Look, North and I had problems we couldn't resolve. You have nothing to apologize for."

"I should have helped you. I should have brought you into our world, showed you how—"

"Lydia, I didn't want your world. I just wanted to love North. Then Uncle Merrill died, and all North cared about was the firm, and I couldn't stand it, and I left. I could stay with North and make us both miserable, or I could leave so he could find a woman who was crazy about his career. I was the wrong wife for him."

"That's what I thought," Lydia said. "But I was wrong. I should have been a better mother-in-law. I was delinquent in my responsibility to you."

"Lydia, I appreciate what you're saying, but you can stop. It's over, it's been over for ten years."

Lydia clamped her lips together in exasperation. "You know, Andromeda, for such an emotional woman, you are not very sensitive. It's clearly not over. My son left a major litigation to come to southern Ohio for you."

"Not for me," Andie said automatically, and Lydia closed her eyes, impatience plain on her face. "Well, it wasn't for me. You and Southie are here, there's a journalist on the loose, and we have two children—" She broke off. "He has two children he's responsible for."

"It's not over for him and it's not over for you, either, I can hear it in your voice when you talk about him." She was quiet for a moment. "I never doubted you loved him, you know. Anybody could see that you did."

"Of course I did," Andie said. "I *married* him."

"After knowing him less than a day," Lydia snapped. "The two of you were insane."

"Well, we got over it."

"That's what I'm trying to tell you," Lydia said, glaring at her. "You didn't, neither one of you. You have another chance here."

"I'm engaged," Andie lied, hoping that would get her out of the room.

"Oh, please," Lydia said.

"Why doesn't anybody take that seriously?"

"Because everybody has eyes. Listen to me." Lydia leaned forward in the rocking chair, staring into Andie's face, deadly serious. "You hurt my son terribly. He's never gotten over it. I'd want you dead for that except that you've never gotten over it, either. And now you've both changed, you're older, you could make it work this time. But if you're going back to him, you have to *stay*."

"I'm not going back," Andie said, trying not to be caught by the thought of doing it again, better this time. "And I did not hurt North. I don't think he noticed I left."

"You're an *idiot*," Lydia said, and then took a deep breath. "Look, you're very protective of that little girl." She nodded toward the sleeping Alice. "But girls are strong. We're built to withstand anything. Boys are the vulnerable ones. Alice will make it, she's got Archer steel in her spine. But Carter's bleeding inside, just the way North was bleeding when you left, and you can't see it. You don't *look*."

Andie took a breath to say that Carter was fine, and Lydia cut her off.

"I raised two boys. They feel everything and have no way to express it. They die inside, and if you're a mother, you die, too."

"Lydia—"

"If you find out what's wrong with Carter and fix it, if you bring these children to Columbus, you'll have the full force of the Archer family behind you."

"Okay," Andie said, taken aback.

"But you break my son's heart again, I'll rip out your liver and fry it for breakfast." Lydia stood up, looking down at Andie. "Don't blow it this time, Andromeda," she said, and swept from the room.

"Hey, I didn't blow it the last time," Andie said, but she was gone, and Andie was left alone in the firelight, Alice asleep behind her, Carter down in his room in terrible trouble if Lydia was right, and North downstairs as desirable as ever except that his mother was going to tear her liver out if she went for a one-night stand.

"Jesus," Andie said, and went back to thinking about the ghosts.

It was simpler.

"It's about my daughter," Flo said when North was alone with her in the Great Hall.

"She's doing a wonderful job with the children," North said politely.

Flo narrowed her eyes, so tense that every gray curl on her head bounced. "I know what you're up to, you bastard. You're trying to get her back. Or at least into bed."

Flo was crazy, North remembered, but she wasn't stupid.

"Don't even try it," Flo said. "I ran the cards. You're the Emperor."

"No I'm not," North said, confused. "I'm the King of Coins."

Flo stopped, evidently equally confused. "What?"

"Andie brought me to your house and told you we'd gotten married and you ran the cards," North said, remembering it like it was yesterday. It'd been his first clue that life with Andie was going to be seriously different.

"Oh. Yes, I did. Well, that was ten years ago."

"You told me it was forever, and that Andie I were doomed because she was the Moon. Or something."

"The Star," Flo said. "And I was right, wasn't I? It didn't last."

"You weren't right if I'm an Emperor now," North said. "Maybe you'd better run the cards again. Come back in the sitting room and I'll get you a drink—"

"Well, if you're not the Emperor, who is?" Flo said.

North started to say something soothing, and then thought, *Why am I patronizing this woman?* "Flo, I don't believe in the tarot."

"I know you don't," she said, frowning as she thought.

"Then why are you asking me about some Emperor?"

"You're a lawyer. You don't have to believe in something to argue about it." She looked up at him, still frowning. "Somebody passionate and powerful. Somebody moving all the pieces in the game. Who else would that be besides you?"

"You've got a houseful of wingnuts here," North said. "Plus ghosts. Pick one."

Flo's eyebrows went up. "The ghosts. Isolde said one of them is a man who thinks he owns the house."

"Isolde is a font of information," North said, not happy about that.

"But of course, that's it." Flo folded her arms, as if she were chilled. "That's so much worse. You'd never hurt Andie on purpose, but some awful spirit—"

"I'll keep Andie close and safe."

Flo looked up at him, scowling again. "Sea goat."

"What?"

"Sex. That's all you think about."

North looked down at her, exasperated.

Flo looked back, defiant. "Tell me you haven't been thinking about it ever since you saw Andie."

"I saw Andie for about five minutes before Alice started to scream."

"Not tonight. Since she came to your office a month ago."

She had him there. "This is the first I've seen her since then."

"You've been thinking about it," Flo said, an edge to her voice. "You're going to break her heart again. It's not fair, North, you have everything, can't you just let her go?"

"No," he said, surprising himself but not Flo, who nodded.

"It's in your stars," she said.

"I thought it was in the cards."

"There, too."

Lydia came down the stairs and into the hall. "Now what's going on?"

"Your son's going to try to seduce my daughter," Flo said. "He's a Capricorn. They do that."

"Don't you think their private lives should be private?" Lydia said, sounding virtuous.

Flo looked at her for a moment and then laughed.

"I'm going upstairs now," North said to both of them. "*Not* to seduce my ex-wife but to get some sleep. Tomorrow a private detective will be here to find out what the hell is going on, and then we'll establish that there are no ghosts, throw Kelly O'Keefe out into the storm, and take everybody back to Columbus where the two of you can continue your feud."

"We're not feuding," Flo said, glaring at Lydia.

"It's not like you to be dramatic," Lydia said to him, ignoring Flo.

"Good night," North said, and went back into the sitting room to get what he needed to seduce his ex-wife.

Andie was sitting beside Alice's bed almost asleep when North came back upstairs, carrying an ice bucket and two glasses. He put it all down on the floor next to Andie, took off his suit coat and threw it on the rocker, loosened his tie, opened his overnight bag, took out a bottle of Glenlivet, and opened it.

"Oh, good." Andie straightened to rub her back. "*My* present."

"No, I got you something else, but I'll share." North poured two generous slugs into the glasses, handed one to her. "Here's to going home to Columbus with everybody. Soon."

"I'll drink to that," Andie said and did, the smooth liquor going down like silk. "God, I needed that."

"Plenty more here." North put the bottle down beside her and sat down beside it, his back against Alice's bed, too. "Should we go into another room? Will we wake her up talking?"

"No, when she finally goes out, she's out," Andie said. "So what's my present?"

North reached over and dug into his overnight bag again. He pulled out a CD and handed it to her.

"*Clapton Unplugged*," she read with delight. "Thank you!"

"It's been out since August. I took a chance you didn't have it yet."

"No, I didn't even realize they'd recorded it. I saw it on TV . . ." She'd seen it on TV and thought of North all the way through. She smiled up at him. "Thank you. You give good gifts."

"I try. I have something else, too. Not a gifts."

He dug in the bag and pulled out a box, and she recognized her old shell box from junior high, the one she'd made from a cigar box she'd found that her mother told her had been her father's. She was pretty sure that had been a lie, but still, it was her shell box.

"Wow," she said, taking it from him. "Thank you for keeping it."

"You left some other stuff behind." He leaned back against the bed, too. "It's all in there."

"Anything important?"

"I don't know," North said. "I don't know what's important to you now. You've changed."

"In ten years? Hell, yes, I've changed." She opened the box and saw old photos and ticket stubs and, in the middle, the velvet jeweler's box from the diamond earrings he'd given her. She opened it, looked at the classic, tasteful earrings, hated them, and snapped it shut again. Of course he'd saved the damn earrings. "You haven't changed."

"You'd be surprised."

He drank again, and she felt him watching her. He was sitting close, not too close but right there on the other side of the bottle, and he looked like he always had when he'd come up to the attic after work at the beginning of their marriage, tired but alive and focused on her.

"It's been good talking to you this past month," he said. "Once we stopped fighting."

She put the box on the floor and picked up her drink, trying to ditch the memories. "Southie says we haven't been fighting, we've been bitching at each other."

"He's probably right."

"He thinks if we have one big blowup, that would clear the air."

North laughed. "And then we'd have makeup sex."

Andie grinned. "How'd you know he said that?"

"It's Southie. If it's a plan, it has a naked woman in it." He stopped smiling. "You want to have a fight? Clear the air?"

"No." Andie cradled her drink. "That was a million years ago."

"But you're still mad." North shook his head and drank again.

"I'm over it," Andie lied.

"So am I," North said.

Andie pulled back to look at him, annoyed. "What did you have to get over? I never did anything to you."

He looked at her. "You left me."

"You left me first." Andie leaned back against the bed and took another drink.

"I was right there," North said, his patience obvious.

"No you weren't, you were down in that damn office behind that damn desk."

"What did that desk ever do to you? Except support you well during sex."

"It wasn't the desk," Andie said. "It was what it stood for."

"Fine furniture?"

"The Family," Andie said dramatically and drained her glass. "Of which I was not part."

"Of course you were." His annoyance was plain now.

"No. You and Southie and Lydia were family, the family law firm. I was the woman you slept with up in the attic." Andie took the bottle and topped up her glass. "It was very Rochester of you."

"Who?"

"Jane Eyre. He kept his insane wife in the attic."

"Well, the insane part was right." North finished his drink.

"You know that fight you were talking about?" Andie said, glaring at him. "It's coming right up."

"Good. We can start by you telling me why the hell you left."

Andie let her head fall back on Alice's bed. "A million times I've said this. You left me. You stopped paying attention, hell, you stopped *seeing me.* You'd sit behind that desk eighteen hours a day and then climb into bed at one A.M. and tap me on the shoulder for sex. That got old fast."

"I thought you liked sex."

"I did. I didn't like being treated as your live-in hooker."

"Drama queen."

"Fine." Andie set her glass down so she could shift around and look him in the eye. "Tell me something we did after your uncle died that didn't involve the family business or sex."

North didn't say anything.

"I rest my case. You had two speeds at the end, 'I'm working' and 'I want sex.' Neither of them had anything to do with me."

"The sex definitely—"

"No it didn't," Andie said. "I could have been anybody."

"You were never anybody," North said with conviction. "That's why you stopped having sex with me? You thought I didn't know you were there? Because that is insane."

Andie took a deep breath. "After your uncle died, if I wanted to see you, I had to go to your office. You were always busy, but if it was six o'clock, I'd shove the papers off the desk and say, 'Remember me?', and most of the time we'd end up having sex on your desk."

"I remember that," North said over his drink.

"It was the only way I could get you to look at me," Andie said. "You were always looking down at the desk, so I'd just slide right in there so you'd see me."

"It was great. Why'd you stop doing that?"

"Because one night I came down and shoved the papers off your desk and you said, 'Damn it, Andie, I'm *busy,* I'll be up later,' and picked up the papers without even looking at me, and I thought, *Don't hurry,* and went back upstairs and that was the last time I volunteered for anything. It was humiliating enough to have to go down and remind my husband I existed, and then to get rejected . . ." She looked at his face, at the frown there, and said, "What?"

"I remember that."

"Well, I remember it, too, you jerk. I should have sued that fucking desk for alienation of affection."

"No, I remember what I was doing."

"What?"

He shook his head. "We had troubles."

"Which you never told me about."

"Family business," he said, and began to take a drink and then stopped as he realized what he'd said.

"And I wasn't part of the family," Andie said.

"*Damn* it," North said to himself.

"It's okay." Andie leaned back against the bed. "It's over."

"We were in big trouble," North said.

"It's okay, you don't—"

"Uncle Merrill took over the firm when my dad died, and he ran it for eighteen years."

"Oh," Andie said. "And he wasn't competent?"

"He was very competent," North said. "He was just crooked as all hell. Three generations of Archers established the good name of the firm and Merrill risked it all. Never got caught, either." He drank again.

"So you had to cover up for him?"

"The statute of limitations on a lot of that stuff had run out, but the big problem was that if any of it got out, the reputation of the firm was gone. My mother was grieving, Southie was too young . . ."

"So you had to do it all," Andie said. "North, even when Merrill was running the place, you did it all."

"I wasn't covering up felonies then," North said, and his voice was bitter. "I'd just found out his latest screwup and it was about to break, and it was well within the statute of limitations, and I was scrambling to find a way out, and you showed up—"

"You know, if you'd *told me*," Andie said.

"I didn't tell anybody except Southie. And I only told him when he asked."

"You should have told Lydia. She had to have known what he was like."

"She wouldn't have listened, and I didn't want to be the one to disillusion her."

"He was her brother-in-law," Andie said. "Why would she care?"

"He was her lover," North said, "and she'd care a lot."

"What?" Andie sat up straighter. "Lydia and Merrill?"

"I thought you knew."

"*How?* By telepathy?"

"From Flo." North looked genuinely surprised. "Flo never told you?"

"Flo's not one for gossip. She's a live-and-let-live kind of woman. Why would she have told me?"

"That's what started their feud." North took another drink. "Christ, you did miss a lot."

"Well, I was stuck up in that damn attic waiting for you," Andie said. "What do you mean, that's what started their feud? Flo didn't like Lydia because she was so snotty to me."

"That didn't help, but there was a catfight one day. Flo was coming down the stairs from visiting you, and I invited her to a cocktail party we were having, and Mother said, 'Yes, Flo, and bring whoever you're with that night, too.'"

"Bitch," Andie said.

"Well, Flo was pretty open-minded about who she slept with," North said.

"She still is," Andie said. "Doesn't mean Lydia gets to take shots."

"Then Flo said, 'Well, you can be sure it won't be my brother-in-law.' After that it was pretty much open warfare."

"Go, Flo," Andie said. "Although Merrill wasn't Lydia's brother-in-law anymore, your dad was dead."

North took another drink, discreetly silent.

"Oh. How far back did this affair go?"

"I think it started a year after I was born. Lydia had come through with the Archer heir, and my dad wasn't the faithful type."

Andie tried to process this new side of Lydia. "Yeah, but with his brother?"

"Merrill was the exciting one. Black sheep of the family," North said grimly.

"So they were lovers for almost thirty years." Andie thought about it, Lydia sneaking into bedrooms, or across the backyard since Merrill had the house next door. Lydia, in the middle of the night, tiptoeing through the begonias. "Wow."

"Yep," North said.

Andie squinted at him. "What else? When you get this terse, there's something else."

He hesitated.

"I know, I know, I'm not family."

"Ever notice how Southie and I don't look much alike?"

"Well, yeah, but . . . wait a minute. *You're kidding me.*"

North shook his head.

"Have you told Southie?"

"Southie told me. Uncle Merrill told him when he turned twenty-one."

"Wow." Andie sat back. "And you never told me any of this."

"Family secrets," North said. "You were right, I shut you out. I'm sorry. I was wrong."

Andie blinked at him. "You have changed."

"Yeah." North smiled at her. "Enough about the past, it's gone. Are we drinking to your engagement?"

"No, that's over." Andie sat back against the bed again. "Wow. Lydia had a son with a lover. Who was her brother-in-law. Amazing."

"Back up," North said, suddenly alert. "What do you mean, it's over?"

"I broke it off with Will two days ago. So does Lydia know that Southie knows?"

"I don't know. Are you sure you made it clear to him that it was over? Because he seems pretty sure it's not."

"He's not paying attention, then. It's a serious failing with the men in my life. What do you mean, you don't know if Lydia knows? Don't you people ever talk?"

"And say what? 'Mom, do you know that Southie knows that he's not Dad's kid?' Would you want that conversation with Lydia?"

"Oh. No."

"So to return to Will—"

"I don't want to return to Will. Will is history."

"Glad to hear it," North said.

"Why?"

"Because I'm not history," North said, and kissed her.

Eleven

It was so swift that Andie didn't have time to close her eyes first. North was just sitting there, very close, and then he was kissing her, and it hit her the way it always had, the heat slamming into her as her mind shorted out, and when he whispered, "Give me another shot, Andie," she almost said, *God, yes,* and stopped herself just in time.

"Nothing's changed," she said, but she felt the heat of his body through that crisp, white shirt, his breath on her cheek, his hand on her waist—

"Everything's changed," he said and kissed her again.

She kissed him back because it felt so good, and more than that, it felt right, but her libido had gotten her into this mess before, so she put a lid on it when he moved his hand to her breast.

"Hold it," she said against his mouth.

"My bedroom's next door," he whispered against hers.

"You should go there." She pulled away from him, from all that warmth and satisfaction. "I'm drunk, and I didn't get any sleep last night, and I'm stressed out of my mind because this place has ghosts, which you don't believe in, and I can't do this."

He was still for a moment, and then he kissed her cheek and said, "You're right, this is lousy timing. I apologize."

"You don't need to," Andie said. "I like the kissing. I like having you close like this. I just need sleep."

"Fair enough." North stood up and then held out his hand for her. "Big day tomorrow. I've got a private investigator coming down to go through the house to see what's going on here. We'll fix whatever it is and then take the kids back to Columbus with us."

Andie took his hand and let him pull her to her feet, and the alcohol and exhaustion hit her at the same time. "Do you even have a place for the kids to stay in Columbus?"

"We've got two of the bedrooms on the second floor ready for them. Mother's moving in next door with Southie—"

"Oh, poor Southie," Andie said, and then realized for the first time why Merrill had left Southie his house next door.

"It's his turn," North said, without sympathy.

"So it's going to be you and the kids in the main house? You're going to feed Alice breakfast?"

"The bedroom Mother's vacating is also on the second floor. It's yours if you want it."

"Me take over Lydia's bedroom? Living with ghosts would make me less nervous."

"She likes you."

"She called me an idiot."

"That was ten years ago."

"That was ten minutes ago."

"Oh. Sorry."

North capped the bottle of Scotch and put it in his bag, and Andie thought about that bedroom on the second floor. North was thinking she wouldn't be in that bedroom for long. And he was right.

"I can't move in," she told him. "You know what would happen and we'd end up in the same damn mess. I don't care how much you've changed, you're never going to stop working long enough to have a real relationship—"

"Oh, come on," North said. "That was *ten years ago.*"

"—and I need somebody who believes in me—"

"I believe in you."

"—not somebody who thinks I'm crazy because I want my husband with me or because I see ghosts."

"I believed in you enough to hire you for these kids."

"You did that to slow down my marriage to Will," Andie said. *Which was probably a good thing.* "It was like the alimony checks. I'd get one every month and think, 'There you are again,' and remember the good times, and then I'd remember the bad times, and then I'd have a drink. Moving in with you would be the alimony checks in 3-D."

"That makes no sense," North said.

"Well, I'm a little drunk. The smart thing to do is to stay friends. That way we don't bring our horrible screwed-up relationship into these kids' lives, we keep things calm and safe for them. Which means our only relationship is a business one."

"That," North said, "is the dumbest thing I've ever heard."

"See?" Andie said. "No respect."

"I give up." He leaned over and picked up his overnight bag and kissed her on the cheek as he straightened. "You have a good night. We'll fight this out in the morning."

"Nothing to fight about," Andie said, turning toward the other twin bed.

"I'm in here if you need me," North said, opening the door to May's bedroom.

"Yeah, yeah, yeah." Andie crawled into the twin bed, fully clothed. She just needed to lie down for a minute and then she'd get ready for bed, she was so tired . . .

That man can really kiss, she thought and fell asleep remembering the other things he could do.

Then she fell deeper into sleep, and dreamed that there were people in the room, not ghosts, people, somebody drifting dressed in orange flowers, and she shivered from the cold. Cold, that was a bad sign. She shivered. Had the fire gone out? No, this was a dream, but even in her exhaustion, she couldn't sleep, something was too wrong. She tossed and turned, and the room grew cold, and she shivered, and thought, *This is really wrong.*

And then she realized that the cold was inside her, that May was seeping through her veins, invading her muscles. She went numb, not just from the cold, although the cold was everywhere in her, needles of it easing through her, but also because May was sapping her nerves, dulling her mind, and then a wave of nausea hit her.

Nightmare, she thought. *May, stop it.*

May grew stronger inside her. *Just let go, just let go, it'll be fine—*

No! Andie thought, and woke up, and it was all real, May freezing her while she screamed, *No, no, NO,* but even then May had her, and she was rising from her bed and moving across the nursery, her world in flickering black and white as she staggered past a sleeping Alice like some monster of Frankenstein's, ice in her veins as May dragged her toward North.

NO! Andie thought and jerked away, felt warmth for a moment as May followed behind a second too late, felt her brain turn inside out as May took her back, the world flicker between color and black and white, and then May opened the door to her bedroom.

North had taken off his shirt and was holding it, staring at the sign over the bed. "This sign is not like you."

"What are you doing, honey?" May said, trying to keep her voice light as Andie battled to regain control.

"This plaque over the bed," North said, looking back at the wall. "'Always Kiss Me Goodnight.' It's kind of needy, isn't it?"

"I think it's romantic," May said, a little breathless from gritting Andie's teeth as she fought back.

"You think it's romantic?" He frowned at her, half naked, gorgeous, and Andie felt May grow warmer, distracted by her need for him, so she gathered her strength and made her move, blanketing May as she reclaimed her body, staggering as she took it back.

North said, *"What's wrong?"* and then he was there beside her, putting his arms around her as she gasped for breath, gagging from the displacement, jerking in North's arms as she fought May for control.

Then her stomach turned over from the vertigo, the whole world distorted in front of her, and May said, *Oh, for heaven's sake,* and let go of her, and she threw up on North's feet.

Andie threw up twice more in the bathroom, and then she sat on the cold tiled floor and shivered, crying hysterically while North held her. She'd been invaded, frozen out of her own body; May had betrayed her, taken away her will, used her, and the thought of it made her gag again, that cold knifing through her veins, that feeling that she was just a body to be used, that the fact of *her* meant nothing. She shivered again, couldn't stop shivering, and North finally turned the shower on and dragged her under the hot water so that the water drenched them both, his arms wrapped around her from behind, holding her up because her knees were still like rubber, letting the water course over her until she was warm again.

Then she turned in his arms and held on to him, on to the fact of him being with her again, and he kissed the top of her head and held her tight until she stopped crying.

Then he turned off the water and said, "Are you all right?" and she said, "No, but I'm getting there," and lifted her face to smile at him, to show him that everything was fine.

He was looking down at her with so much concern, so clearly seeing her and nothing else, that she burst into tears again, and he pulled her out of the shower and wrapped a towel around her, trying to keep her warm. "I'm going to call a doctor," he said, and she shook her head.

"I'm okay, I'm okay," she said, trying to stop the tears. "I just need to get these wet clothes off—"

"Are your clothes in the nursery or the bedroom?" he said, ignoring the fact that his suit pants were soaked.

"I've got a robe here," Andie said. "You go change and . . . I'll try to explain."

She stripped off her wet things, put on her robe, and combed her wet hair, and looked at herself in the mirror, trying to see May in her eyes, wanting to know that it was her, just her, nobody else in there.

Then she went to find North.

He was waiting outside in the hall, dry now in a faded T-shirt and worn sweatpants, and she began to say, "I'm sorry," but he put his arms around her before she got past "I'm—" and she leaned against him, grateful all over again for the fact of him between her and the rest of her insane life.

"Come here." He pulled her into her bedroom—May's bedroom— and sat her down on the edge of the bed, put his arm around her, and looked in her eyes. "What the hell happened?"

"I was possessed." Even saying it made her feel sick again.

His face went blank. "Possessed."

"Just listen to me," she said, exhausted and violated and hopeless. "You don't have to believe me, but just *listen*." He nodded and she went on. "There are ghosts in this house. The nanny was right. The others who left were driven away by them even if they didn't know the ghosts were here. There are three of them. Two of them came with the house, they're very old, and they're just living on . . . need. One of them wants the house and one of them wants Alice."

"Have you seen these ghosts?" North asked, his voice carefully neutral.

"Yes. But they're not the ones who possessed me. That was May, the kids' aunt, their mother's sister. I think you met her when you came down here after their dad died."

"Really young," North said. "Very friendly. Lots of dark curly hair. Looked a little bit like you."

"More beautiful than I'll ever be," Andie said, feeling sick again. "But that's her. The ghosts killed her."

North nodded again, his face a mask. "And now she walks?"

"Dances, mostly," Andie said. "She's young and she's bitter about dying and she wants her life back, she wants a do-over."

"Understandable," North said.

"And she has a crush on you. So she . . . hijacked me. I was tired and drunk and I fell asleep, and she just . . . moved in, took over, and went to you. That was May you were talking to, not me."

"I thought it was the Scotch."

"North, there are ghosts here and they're real and they're dangerous. I know you're never going to believe me, but it's true. I can't prove it to you, I can't show you anything you could take to court, but this house is haunted, and we're all in danger, and I have to do something about it, which is why we're having another séance tomorrow."

He nodded, calm as ever. "How about we all just leave? Pack up everybody right now and get the hell out of Dodge."

"Alice won't go, and if Alice won't go, Carter won't go, and if Alice and Carter won't go, I won't go. I know you told Alice she'd have to leave if she was in danger, but we can't force them, you saw what happened when Will tried. Even if we managed to get her stable after she went crazy, she'd never trust either one of us again. I'm staying until Alice says it's all right to go." North shook his head, and Andie said, "I think she's got a better grip on what's going on here than anybody else. She and Carter know things I don't. Until they trust me enough to tell me, we're not going anywhere."

"Here's my concern," North said, his voice very kind. "You believe in ghosts."

Andie closed her eyes, overwhelmed by the hopelessness of it all. He was never going to understand, he was never going to believe her. If she hadn't seen the ghosts, *she* wouldn't believe her. "I know. But they're real, and they're dangerous, and that's my big problem now. I understand if you can't help me, but that's what I've got to fix."

"I'll help you. I'll always help you. I'm just not sure how to do it." He hesitated. "There's a psychologist I work with a lot—"

"No," Andie said. "I'm not crazy and there's no room for anybody else in this house."

"Well, Lydia is evicting Kelly and her cameraman as we speak."

"She can't. It's storming like crazy outside. They'll never get that satellite truck up that drive and out onto the road without wrecking it, and they can't leave it, it's worth a fortune. They're here until the storm stops and the road dries out."

"Okay." North rubbed his forehead with his free hand, while his arm tightened around her. "Have the kids been threatened by these ghosts?"

"No."

"So whoever's doing this is focusing on you?"

"Nobody's 'doing this,'" Andie said tiredly. "There are *ghosts*." She pushed herself up off the bed, not willing to fight a useless battle. "I know you don't believe. You know I believe. We'll just have to leave it there."

He looked like he was going to say something, and when he didn't, she said, "I'm really sorry about throwing up on you. That was rude."

"It really was," he said, straight-faced.

"Well, it won't happen again. Thank you for the shower and . . . for being so kind."

"Are you trying to be funny?" North said. "Because that isn't."

"I think if your ex-wife comes to your room in the middle of the night, throws up on your feet, and tells you she's been possessed, the absolute minimum she has to say when she leaves is, 'Thank you for being so kind.' "

"I think it's what two people who care about each other should just expect."

"So if you throw up on my feet, you're not going to apologize?"

"Nope," North said, smiling at her, his shoulders broad in that ratty old T-shirt, and she wanted to say, "Let me sleep with you tonight, make this go away," but instead she said, "Well, I owe you one now anyway, so that would be fair."

"Stop keeping score, Andie." He stood up, and she tried not to look at him. "We're not married anymore but that doesn't mean we're not us."

Andie swallowed. "That's . . . good. I mean, I agree." She began to back toward the door. "I have to go now. I'm really tired and . . . Thank you." Her back hit the door and she escaped into the nursery, taking one last look at him standing tall in the lamplight, expressionless as he watched her go.

She closed the door and looked around to see if May was nearby, waiting to pounce.

The thing was at the foot of Alice's bed, and Andie sucked in her breath and then realized that the room was dark, too dark.

The fire was off. *Somebody had turned the fire off.*

She ran over and fell on her knees, feeling biting ice at her back as she turned the tap, and then the fire whooshed to life, and her back was warm again, and when she turned, there was nothing at the foot of Alice's bed, nothing in the room.

But somebody had turned the fire off.

She got up and pushed furniture against the doors to the little hall and the gallery. She hesitated before the door to May's bedroom because North was in there and she trusted him, but she didn't trust anybody else, so she shoved the worktable up against that door.

Then, barricaded in the nursery now warm from the fire, she tried to think of what to do but her mind was so addled from exhaustion . . .

She checked on Alice, who'd slept through it all, her cheek on Rose Bunny's furry head, and then she sat down on the other bed, leaned back against the wall, and thought, *I have to think, I have to think, I have to* . . .

. . . and slept.

When Andie woke, Alice was sitting on the edge of her bed, watching her.

"Good morning, baby," Andie said, yawning as she sat up.

"I can't get out," Alice said, clutching Rose Bunny to her, and Andie remembered that she'd blocked the doors to make sure nobody turned off the fire.

She got up to shove the bureau away from the door to the little hall so Alice could get to the bathroom, yawning again as she shoved. "Sorry," she said around her yawn, and then she looked at the time. It was past ten. "Oh, no," she said, waking up completely. "We overslept."

"I didn't," Alice pointed out, and then put Rose Bunny on the bed and went to get ready for the day.

Andie turned off the fire and shoved the table away from the door to May's bedroom and went in to get her clothes. North was long gone, the bed made, and she put on clean underwear and grabbed a pair of jeans and a T-shirt and then went back to the nursery to check on Alice. She was zipping up her jeans when Alice came in from the hall, dressed in leggings and her flounced skirt, and handed her the Bad Witch T-shirt she slept in.

"You can wear this, I don't want it anymore," she announced, and then went back into the hall.

Andie followed her, taking a quick look around before she went into the hall and then into Alice's room. If May decided to try another hijacking, she was going to tangle with somebody who was ready for her this time. "Alice, honey, this is your shirt—"

"No it's not," Alice said, her head in her drawer, searching for one among many black T-shirts. "It was Aunt May's. I took it after she died." She straightened, holding up a plain black T-shirt. "I don't want it anymore. You can wear it today."

Andie was pretty sure that meant something that she was missing, but she was late so she said, "Thank you," and pulled it over her head. The last thing she wanted was anything of May's, but she wasn't going to look a gift Alice in the mouth.

May had been thinner than Andie because the shirt was tight, the letters that spelled "Bad Witch" stretched out of shape across her bust, but Alice smiled and nodded, and Andie thought, *The hell with it. Most of these people think I'm crazy, might as well add slutty to the mix.* She helped Alice get her hair in her topknot, and Alice said, "Can we still do the Three O'Clock Bake this afternoon?" and she said, "Absolutely," and thought, *As long as we're done before the séance,* and took Alice downstairs for a late breakfast, keeping an eye out for May the entire time.

North had been up since seven, determined to get the mess he'd found at Archer House cleaned up and Andie and the kids back to Columbus by Sunday at the latest. Gabe McKenna must have gotten up at the crack of dawn, because he pounded on the doorknocker at eight. "I'm here," he said when North opened the door, his sharp dark eyes taking in the place without comment. "What are we looking for?"

"Ghosts," North said.

"All right then," Gabe said and walked in.

They started on the first floor since nobody was up yet. Gabe was thorough, tapping walls, looking at the stone floors, turning furniture and paintings over, and North put anything they found that didn't clearly have a purpose for where it was stored into a box. The front two rooms were empty, their walls solid stone behind the drywall, so they were done in minutes. The hallways were equally bare of furniture and decoration although the paintings that hung there took a few minutes to flip and examine. The kitchen showed the most signs of life—North saw bananas browning in a bowl on the counter and opened a cupboard and found chocolate chips and nuts, flour and sugar, and thought, *Andie's here*—but the dark little pantry off the back of the kitchen was mostly empty aside from old spices and drying herbs, half a dozen half-empty bottles of quality booze that North recognized as Southie's choices, and a jug of tea, the tea leaves sitting in a sludge at the bottom. The dining room and sitting room were pretty much storage for unused furniture. It wasn't just that there wasn't anything out of place in those rooms, it was that there wasn't anything in place: no dishes in the sideboard in the dining room, no photos on the tables in the sitting room, nothing except the furniture and the paintings on the walls.

"This place is strange," Gabe said when they headed for the library. "Nobody lives here."

"They live here," North said grimly, "but they shouldn't."

Then Gabe opened the door to the library and said, "Now we're getting somewhere."

North went in and really looked at the room for the first time. Last night, when it had been full of people and Alice screaming, he'd registered it as a library because it was lined with books, but now in the cold light of early morning, it was clear that this room was used. The window seat had books and papers tumbled in it, the big table in the middle of the room had workbooks and papers and textbooks

spread out across it, and there were more books in front of the fireplace where somebody had obviously stretched out to read.

"I think this is where Andie teaches the kids," North said, and
then he heard Kelly O'Keefe say, "Well, *hello,*" from the bottom of
the stone stairs. "We'll look here later. Avoid that woman," he said,
and Gabe nodded, waved at Kelly, who said, "Aren't you Gabe
McKenna, *the detective?*", and followed them to the basement door.

"Leave," North said, "today," and shut the basement door in her
face.

By the time Andie and Alice got to the kitchen, Flo had made
breakfast for everybody and cleaned up, so Andie got Alice her cereal and milk and took it to the library, where Carter was reading
and ignoring Kelly's efforts to talk to him.

"Get out," Andie told Kelly when she found her there. "Out of
the house, out of our lives."

"Well, *really,*" Kelly said, but she left them alone.

Andie made sure the gas fireplace was on and went to find Isolde.

"We need another séance," she told the medium when she found
her standing in the middle of the Great Hall, frowning.

"Bad idea," Isolde said. "Too many people here, too much tension."

Andie looked around. Still no May. "Could we go into a room
that has a fireplace?"

Isolde raised her eyebrows but followed her into the sitting room
where Kelly was arguing with Bill and Southie in front of the fire.

"Not here," Andie said, and took Isolde into the dining room
where Dennis had papers spread out, making notes. He looked at
them as if he wished they would leave and they ignored him, so he got
up and went into the kitchen, either passive aggressive or hungry.

Andie turned the gas fire on, and then faced the medium. "May possessed me last night, took my body. We have to stop her, all of them, get rid of them."

"Oh, fuck," Isolde said. "She took you? Are you all right?"

"Not even a little bit," Andie said. "If we ask them, will they go away?"

"No. They got a great setup here. Why should they go?"

"Can you read their minds or something? Find out how to get rid of them?"

"Two of them don't have minds," Isolde said. "The other one's still new. She's not dumb and she doesn't want to go, and no, I can't read her mind."

"Isolde, *work with me here.*"

Isolde sat down at the dining room table. "Let me think." She looked at the books and papers spread out on the table and said, "What is this?"

Andie picked up a book and looked at the marked page, which was about faked hauntings in English country houses. "It's Dennis's research." She dropped the book back on the table. "Ideas, Isolde. You're my expert here."

Isolde ignored her to look at the papers, opening the other books to scan the pages Dennis had bookmarked. "He's researching the house."

"Well, that's what he does, investigate hauntings."

Isolde nodded. "He's very methodical. This is good. He may find out something."

"Yes," Andie said patiently. "*But he doesn't believe in ghosts.* So whatever he's looking for, it's not a way to get rid of them. He and North think it's some kind of fraud, they're looking for a live person who's gaslighting me."

"It happens," Isolde said, frowning at the notes Dennis had made on a legal pad. "Not here, you've got ghosts, but people fake hauntings all the time."

"We need to get the ghosts out," Andie said. "Last night was bad, but what if they start possessing the kids?"

Isolde waved her hand. "I'm working on it. We'll do the séance at four. That gives me some time to look through this stuff and talk to Dennis—"

"What are you doing?" Dennis said stiffly from the door to the kitchen.

"Reading your notes," Isolde said without looking up from the legal pad. "Get in here, we need to talk."

"I hardly think—"

"Well, it's time you started," Isolde snapped. "Sit down here and explain this to me. They brought the contents of the house over, too?"

"The furniture," Dennis said, coming in to stand beside her. "The paintings. The accoutrements."

"That could explain how the two old ghosts got here," Isolde said to Andie. "If they'd left something behind they were tied to, and it got shoved in the back of a drawer or put behind a secret panel in a desk or something."

"Secret panel," Dennis said, barely concealing his scorn.

"Sit down and stop patronizing me, you jerk," Isolde said. "Andie needs help."

"I really do, Dennis," Andie said. "Please."

He sighed heavily and sat down beside Isolde. "What do you want to know?"

"Everything," Isolde said, and Andie said, "Thank you," and went to check on Alice and Carter in the library.

Where there was a fireplace.

On her way through the Great Hall, she ran into North and the detective he'd been friends with for years, resisting the urge to lean on North just because he was there. She really had to get over this needy phase she was going through. Once she and the kids were out of the house, she'd be independent again.

"How are you?" North said to her. "You—"

"I'm fine," she said hastily. "Good as new. Gabe, it's good to see you again. What are you doing here exactly?"

"Trying to find out who's faking your haunting," Gabe said, and Andie looked at North, thinking, *It's not a fake, damn it,* but he was looking at her T-shirt.

"Nice shirt," North said, and she looked down and saw the glowing, green "Bad Witch" stretched tight.

"Alice gave it to me," she said. "And the haunting is not a fake."

"You work on your theory, I'll work on mine," he told her. "I want you and these kids out of here, one way or another."

Andie nodded. "But there really are ghosts, so don't waste too much time." She started to go on, but then she heard "No, no, no!" coming from the library and went to find out what latest injustice had struck Alice.

She spent the rest of the day feeding people, trying to get rid of Kelly and her cameraman—the storm hadn't let up and the satellite truck wasn't going anywhere—keeping Flo and Lydia from open warfare—their allegiance against Kelly could only do so much—and maintaining as much normality as she could for the kids, which involved telling Will to leave her alone several times while she worked with them in the library, and ducking North and Gabe while they searched every inch of the house looking for something that wasn't there.

Because the house was haunted.

The only guests not giving her fits were Dennis and Isolde, who hunkered down in the dining room, forming an uneasy truce that grew less uneasy as the day passed and the level of the brandy in the decanter in front of them sank lower. Andie made sandwiches for lunch and told people to stay out of the dining room because people were working in there.

"On *what?*" Kelly said, smiling automatically even though by now she must have gotten the message that everyone loathed her.

"None of your damn business," Andie said, and went back to the library to eat with the kids.

At three, she checked in with Dennis and Isolde again, who were now sitting with their heads together over his notes.

"There's a remarkable consistency in the reports," Dennis told her. "Somebody must have written the legends down and then made sure each generation told the same story. Usually there's more randomness, more inconsistencies."

"It's the same ghosts," Isolde said. "Of course the reports are the same."

"There are no such things as ghosts," Dennis said, and this time Isolde rolled her eyes, but they were clearly on speaking terms and getting somewhere, so Andie left them alone to set up the Great Hall.

"So I'm very excited about our next séance," Kelly said, catching her as she came out of the dining room with a chair. "I'd like to interview you—"

"Go *away,*" Andie said. "Or I swear I will throw you out into the storm and you can sleep with your cameraman in the satellite truck."

"It's three o'clock," Alice said from behind her.

"What happens at *three o'clock?*" Kelly said, beaming down at her.

"We bake," Alice said, and turned her back on Kelly and went to the kitchen.

"Is it all right if I watch?" Kelly said.

"No," Andie said, "go away, forever," and went to make cookies with Alice.

By late afternoon, North and Gabe were staring defeated at the outside of the house. The rain had stopped, but the sun had given up for the day, and the house rose up over them in the gloom, crumbling and bleak. They'd left a box full of stuff they'd found in the pantry—pieces of odd-shaped metal; a length of goldish chain; a few battered, sepia-toned photographs; rusted screws and a bent screwdriver; a broken pocket watch; a woman's hair clip; and several keys that fit nothing in the house and wouldn't have helped if they had since nothing in the house was locked—but it was all junk, and North knew they were done. There wasn't anything in the house, not just nothing suspicious, but nothing. Mrs. Crumb evidently lived in the kitchen and her bedroom and ignored the rest of the house. The kids had all of their belongings in their bedrooms. Nobody had ever spread out in all of that space, nobody had lived in the house for years.

"This place has a very bad vibe," Gabe said, surveying it.

"Yes, but it's not haunted," North said, exasperated. "Somebody has Andie convinced that there are ghosts here, she's doing another séance at four. I don't know whether it's Mrs. Crumb or the kids or somebody from the outside, but there's fraud going on here."

"Why?" Gabe said. "Who would want this place?"

"I don't know. I just know it's working."

Gabe turned around to look at the grounds. "I thought somebody might be growing pot, but we've walked the whole property and there's nothing but weeds. There's no meth lab in the basement, the paintings aren't anything special, there's nothing in the walls." He kicked a clump of purple asters and watched their petals scatter. "There's something wrong here, anybody could feel that. But I'll be damned if I can find it . . ."

His voice trailed off and he stared at the asters.

"What?" North said.

Gabe bent down and picked up a dried ugly weed someone had thrown down at the edge of the garden.

"What is that?" North said.

"I need to make a phone call," Gabe said, and headed for the house with his plant.

"Here you are," Lydia said when she found Andie and Alice in the kitchen. "I wanted to talk to you about coming to Columbus."

Alice stiffened and Andie said, "Not until you say yes, Alice," and dumped the chocolate chips into the dough, keeping an eye out for May. Damn kitchen had no fireplace.

"I was hoping for banana bread," Lydia said, looking into the bowl. "I haven't had decent banana bread since you left. I put bananas on the kitchen counter at home so you could bake when we all got back."

"They have to be brown to make banana bread," Alice said severely. "The yellow ones will not do."

"That's why I left them on the counter," Lydia said. "So they'll be brown when we get there."

They'll be rotted through by the time we get there, Andie thought, *if we ever do,* and kept mixing and watching for May.

Alice reached up and turned on the radio. "We dance while we bake," she informed Lydia.

"How nice for you," Lydia said, and watched Alice pick up the beat at the end of "I'm Too Sexy" and bop around the kitchen. "Perhaps you could find a classical station?" she said to Andie.

"It's this or nothing," Andie said. "The reception here is not good. We make do." *Where the hell is May?*

"*Hello,*" Flo said, coming through the kitchen door as the music changed, beaming at them all. "Where is everybody?"

"Here!" Alice called to her. "We're dancing. Come on!"

"Dancing!" Flo said, and joined Alice to bebop around the kitchen to "Achy Breaky Heart."

They looked like a demented conga line. In Texas.

"The sooner we get these children out of here, the better," Lydia said to Andie.

The sooner we get me out of here, the better, too, Andie thought, and mixed faster.

Crumb caught North in the servants' hall as he and Gabe came in.

"There's a woman on the phone for you," she said, her voice full of scorn. "Says it's important."

North went to the entrance hall and picked up the phone. "Hello?"

"It's me," Kristin said. "Simon called from England. He said to call him as soon as you could."

"Did he find the graves?"

"He didn't say, but he found something."

"I'll call right now."

"And I found out about May Younger."

"She's buried around here?"

"She's not buried at all. She was cremated and her ashes scattered at a dance club in Grandville called . . . here it is, it's called 'The Grandville Grill.' Her friends hijacked the ashes when nobody picked them up and scattered them on the dance floor in her memory."

"Touching," North said, thinking, *At least I won't have to talk Andie out of burning her corpse.*

"Evidently she spent a lot of time there. I got the impression she had a drinking problem. The night she died, her friends had to drive her home because she was too drunk to drive. The last they saw of her, she was on the tower, waving at them."

"Good work," North said. "Thank you."

"When will you be back?" Kristin sounded a little frazzled. "People are becoming . . . demanding."

"I'm hoping by Monday. If I'm not there Monday morning, Southie will be."

"Whatever you say," Kristin said, with a lot of *this is not a good idea* in her voice. "Don't forget to call Simon."

North hung up, thinking, *May Younger got drunk and fell off the tower.* Tragic, but not supernatural. So far, so good.

He dialed England, and Simon answered on the first ring.

"It's North Archer," he said. "Did you find the graves?"

"This is a long story," Simon said, but North could tell from the sound of his voice that he was enjoying it.

"Make it shorter," North said.

"The people you were asking about were a governess and a valet who died in 1847. The governess, Mary Jessel, gave birth to a still-born baby and drowned two days later. Peter Quint the valet died from a fall after he'd been drinking and then headed home down an icy hill."

"Where are the bodies?" North asked.

"Someone dug them up and burned them in 1898. The vicar was walking through the graveyard and found the graves opened, full of bone and ash. Scandal. They closed the graves and put the head-stones back."

"Burned," North said. "Anybody know why?"

"There's a legend that if you burn a corpse, the spirit will not walk."

"Had they been walking?"

"Not that anybody remembers, although that was ninety-four years ago."

"Fine. This takes care of most of my problem anyway. Thank—"

"Not so fast. Forty years later, 1938, the next vicar walks through the graveyard and sees the graves covered in salt. He told the cur-rent vicar it looked like a snowfall."

"Salt?"

"There's a legend that ghosts can't cross salt."

"So the people in the town think the graveyard is haunted?"

"No, that's what's odd. There's no legend here of haunting, nothing about these graves except that they've been disturbed three times."

"Three?"

"Two years ago. 1990. The current vicar caught two men digging up the graves and turned them over to the police. They'd been hired by an American named Theodore Archer."

"My second cousin," North said, thinking, *Two years ago?* "What did they charge Theodore with?"

"Nothing. He died before they could contact him. In fact, he died whilst the men were digging up the graves."

Coincidence, North thought, but he didn't believe in coincidences. *Somebody who was here two years ago is faking a haunting here now.* And Theodore had investigated, and they'd killed him.

No, that was insane. Theodore had been alone in the car when he'd had a heart attack. A heart attack at forty-eight was not out of the range of the ordinary. People had seen him in the car before it went off the road and he'd been alone. He'd just died, nobody killed him.

"North?"

"Sorry, trying to think this through. Thank you. I owe you."

"Nonsense," Simon said. "You kept me out of an Ohio jail. My gratitude is limitless."

North hung up and looked at the situation from all sides.

People had been trying to put those bodies to rest for decades. Possibly even before that. So faking the haunting wasn't a new idea.

Maybe back in the beginning, in England, the haunting had been useful to keep the house private. Smuggling maybe. And somebody had believed the fake enough to dig the bodies up and burn them.

And then every ensuing generation that wanted privacy kept the tradition going, so the rumors followed the house to America. Given the kind of personality that would transport a haunted house stone by stone across an ocean, the original Archer had probably spread the legend just to make himself more interesting. "Brought myself a haunted house over from England, yes, I did." And then somebody in America believed the rumors enough to hire somebody back in England to spread salt on the grave? That was less plausible.

And then Cousin Theodore hired grave robbers and died the same night.

The clock on the kitchen wall chimed and North realized it was almost four. The séance would be starting. He headed for the Great Hall to stop it and Southie met him by the servant stairs.

"We need to stop the séance," he told Southie.

"No," Southie said, handing him a set of keys. "We need to keep the séance going as long as possible so you and Gabe can get any videotape out of the satellite truck."

North looked at the keys. "These are the keys to the truck?"

"I told Bill I'd dropped my wallet in there. He's so mad at Kelly, he'd probably just have given them to me. Don't hurt the equipment, just get the tapes. I'll keep the séance going as long as possible."

Gabe came up behind them, and said, "I know what's going on. Come with me to the pantry and I'll show you."

"We have to rob a satellite truck first," North said.

"Okay," Gabe said.

Twelve

When the cookies had come out of the oven, Andie had asked Lydia to sit with the kids in the library so Kelly couldn't get to them, and Lydia said, "No problem," with enough grimness in her voice that Andie didn't worry about the kids again. Lydia would put a stake through Kelly's heart before she'd let her near Carter and Alice.

Then she and Flo went to join the others in the Great Hall, but Will stopped her, his overnight bag in his hand.

"I'm leaving," he said, his face sulky.

"Good," Flo said, and went into the Great Hall.

Good, Andie thought at the same time. "Be careful getting out of the drive. It's really dangerous."

He nodded. But first, "I have to tell you something."

Andie looked toward the arch to the Great Hall. "Can you make it fast?"

"Sure," he snapped. "I slept with Kelly last night."

Andie swung back to him. "Really? With Kelly?"

"I was just so upset with you, with the way you handled—"

"Yeah, yeah," Andie said, "it doesn't matter, we're done, you can sleep with anybody you want, but . . . Kelly?"

"It wasn't my fault," Will said. "She came to my room. I tried to tell her no, but she said, 'Andie's in love with North, and I'm right here,' and I thought, 'She's right—'"

"Perfectly understandable," Andie said, still confused. "Best of luck in the future—"

"There's not going to be any future," Will said, sounding exasperated again. "She was weird."

"I really don't want to know," Andie began and then remembered Southie saying the same thing. "Weird how?"

"Cold. Like she wasn't really there. She wasn't like you. It wasn't like us. Andie, if you'd just be rational about this—"

"No," Andie said firmly, but she thought, *Weird?*

"So you're sure," Will said, sounding annoyed again.

"Absolutely. Be careful on the ride home," Andie said, and when she'd closed the door behind him, she headed for the Great Hall. Isolde was there, and so were Flo, Dennis, and Kelly, with Bill on camera.

"No camera," Andie began, and Isolde said, "Let her do it. Sometimes things show up on film. It can't hurt."

"It can if she shows the footage on TV," Andie said.

"It's just for *atmosphere,*" Kelly said. "I wouldn't do *anything* to make you look *bad.*"

"I wouldn't trust her an inch," Dennis said, and Andie realized he was full of brandy. So was Isolde, but she evidently could hold her cognac. Dennis, not so much.

Well, she'd dry him out later.

Southie came in and took his place and smiled at Andie. "Sorry, didn't mean to delay you. We're not in any hurry, are we?"

"Did Kelly sleep with you last night?"

Southie looked at Kelly, who said, "I *did not,*" and then at Andie.

"It's important," Andie said.

"Yeah," Southie said.

"What?" Bill the cameraman said.

"I *didn't,*" Kelly said, and she sounded honestly outraged.

"This is interesting," Dennis said owlishly.

"She slept with you, too?" Andie said to the cameraman.

"You said you were done with him," Bill said to Kelly. "I've had it with you."

"I didn't sleep with *either one of you,*" Kelly said.

"This isn't *helping,*" Isolde said to Andie. "Knock it off."

"No, it's important, she slept with Will, too," Andie said to her. "He just told me in the hall."

"I *didn't!*" Kelly's denial was clear now, outrage and anger but no guilt. "Those were *dreams.* They weren't real."

"Yeah, they were," Andie said, feeling almost sympathetic. "You were possessed. We have a nympho ghost here, and she hijacked your body and made the rounds."

Kelly stopped, her mouth open.

"Oh, crap," Isolde said.

"I don't remember anything like this in the literature," Dennis said.

"I slept with a ghost?" Southie said.

"Twice," Andie told him.

"Wish I'd known," Southie said. "I'd have paid more attention."

"That's *insane,*" Kelly said. "They were *dreams. This is crazy.*"

"Welcome to my world," Andie said.

"Can we get started?" Isolde said. "Harold's really enjoying this, but he can turn on a dime."

"Sure." Andie sat down and a visibly upset Kelly joined her.

"I *didn't* sleep with them," she said to Andie, and she sounded more distressed than angry now.

"You did, you just didn't know," Andie said. "And then when you woke up, you were freezing, and then you threw up."

Kelly's face was pale.

"There really are ghosts, May really did possess you, and it really would be better if you left before she comes back for more tonight. I'm sorry, I really am. The best thing is for you to go before she tries again."

Don't run her off, May said. *We need her.*

Andie jerked her head up and saw May, twirling in the open space beyond the table, blue and lovely and treacherous, and beyond her two shadowy forms, Miss J and the man in the old-fashioned coat.

Dennis squinted in their direction.

"Hello, May," Andie said, tamping down her anger. "We need to talk."

"What are we looking for exactly?" Gabe said when they were in the truck.

"Videotape of the kids, the house, anything." North looked at the racks of equipment. "You start at that end, I'll start down here."

Ten minutes later, they'd found tapes marked with dates, not names.

"This one's yesterday." Gabe slid it into a VCR slot and pushed play.

The tape flickered and then the camera focused on Carter, sitting in the window seat, reading.

"So you live here at *Archer House*!" Kelly's voice came from off camera.

Carter ignored her.

"What's it like living in a *haunted house*!"

Carter ignored her.

"All alone with just a *nanny*."

Carter ignored her.

"I like this kid," Gabe said.

"I do, too," North said.

Kelly evidently didn't because after three more questions, she quit. There was snow on the tape and a shot of Alice, sitting on a chair in the dining room, looking fairly depraved, her hair sliding down one side of her head, pizza stains on her shirt.

"So you live here at *Archer House!*"

"Yes," Alice said. "You have a lot of teeth. Andie says you have to brush your teeth every night or they'll rot out of your head."

"What's it like living in a *haunted house!*"

"I don't like nuts," Alice said. "But I eat them in the chocolate chip cookies and banana bread because Andie says, if you don't like nuts, don't eat the cookies."

"Andie is your *nanny,* right?"

"No. Andie is my Andie. She says you're a hag from hell." Alice smiled serenely as if she were just a cute kid, repeating what some adult had said, but North could see the glint in her eye.

"We'll edit that out," Kelly said to somebody, and then asked Alice, "Aren't you scared to live in this haunted house?"

"Guess what?" Alice said. "Andie says bananas have to be *brown* before you can bake with them."

"Alice," Kelly said, her voice stern. "Tell me about the *ghosts.*"

Alice rolled her eyes. "There aren't any such things as ghosts. I can tell you about butterflies. I have a butterfly garden. Andie says I can have a hummingbird garden, too."

"Alice, people say this house is *haunted!*"

Alice grew still, and the look in her eyes wasn't pretty. "Kelly," she said, and the pitch of her voice was so much like Andie's that North started to laugh, "people will say *anything.*"

"Forget it," Kelly said to somebody off camera, and the tape ended.

"You might as well leave that one," Gabe said. "The kids defeated her."

"No." North held out his hand and Gabe ejected the tape and gave it to him. "She'd find a way to cut it or overdub it. I want anything she filmed here."

"Fine," Gabe said and picked up the next tape.

"And we should hurry," North said, "because I don't know how long Southie can stall a séance."

"This time I want you to tell me everything that's happening," Southie said. "Like where is May standing?"

"Right there," Andie said, pointing behind him. "May, what the hell were you doing last night?"

"Can she really see them?" Flo said to Dennis, but he was frowning, squinting in May's direction.

I was taking my second chance, May said, floating closer. *It wasn't fair that I died at nineteen, I wasn't even—*

"It's not fair to steal bodies, either," Andie said. "You don't get to take our bodies because you got a bad deal. That's rape, May."

"Steal bodies?" Southie said. "Could you explain that?"

"Yes, that would be *good*," Kelly said. "Explain that *fully*. I mean, *rape*. Wow."

May drew back, scowling. *It is not rape. I can't make you do anything you wouldn't do anyway. Look at you, you wouldn't go to North no matter how hard I tried.*

"Kelly didn't—"

"What did she say?" Southie said.

"She's talking about *me*?" Kelly said. "The ghost is talking about *me*?

Kelly was going to sleep with them all anyway. She's been doing the guy with the camera to get him to bring the satellite truck down here. She's doing Southie to get her story. She went along with Will because he's famous or something and to find out about you. I was trying to seduce him and she kept asking him questions about you. She was there, Andie. She might be telling herself it's a dream, but she was there. You were there, remember?

"Does this *rape* have anything to do with *North Archer*?" Kelly said.

"It's not rape," Andie snapped. "Because May says you would have slept with all of them anyway. And since you were already doing two of them, I think she's right." She looked into the camera. "That's right, Columbus, your reporter here nailed three guys in one night, sixty percent of the adult male population of this house. Let's give the little lady a hand."

"That's not fair," Kelly said, pulling back.

"Neither is what you're doing to North." Andie turned back to May. "So she'd have done it anyway. Let's talk about me."

"Or we could talk about Kelly some more," Southie said, checking his watch. "What do you want to know?"

"*Sullivan!*" Kelly said.

"You shouldn't have gone after my brother," Southie said, before turning to the camera. "She fakes her orgasms, and she's not very good at it."

"If you were any good at it, I wouldn't *have to*," Kelly snapped.

"She fakes 'em?" Bill said from behind the camera.

"Nobody makes sounds like that naturally," Southie told him.

"Do you mind?" Andie said. "I'm trying to have a serious conversation here?"

"There's way too much emotion in this room," Isolde said quietly. "Dial it down, Andie."

Andie nodded and turned back to May. "You were out of line," she said calmly, and thought, *You body-snatching bitch.*

That was a mistake and I'm sorry. May smiled at her. *I thought you'd want to go to him. I mean, North Archer. Who wouldn't?*

"You can't ever do that again."

I don't want to, May said. *It was interesting for a night, but you're mad at me, and that Kelly was awful. At least in you I was warm. She's just cold clear through. I'm not sure there's a soul there.*

"There is, and you can't have it."

"Can't have what?" Southie said.

"Southie, *be quiet,*" Andie said.

Okay, okay. May swished again. *What's he looking at?*

"Who?" Andie followed May's eyes and saw Dennis, frowning in May's direction. "Dennis?"

"Is there something moving over there?" Dennis said. "Or am I tipsy?"

"Yes," Isolde said. "There's something moving and you're drunk." She turned back to the table. "Harold, find out what the hell is going on."

Oh, hell, not Harold, May said. *He keeps hitting on me. I don't know what the hell he thinks we can do. We're both fucking dead.*

He thinks you can do dead fucking, Andie thought. "You have to go."

Where? I'm tied to this place, I can't leave. You think I'd stay here if I could haunt someplace else? My best friend scattered my ashes at the Grand-ville Grill, but do I get to haunt there? No. I'm stuck here with Crumb.

"Ashes," Andie said with a sinking heart. If May had been cremated . . .

"Harold says she says she was cremated," Isolde told Andie. "What about the others, Harold?"

I don't know about the others, May said. *Harold, get the fuck off my leg, I am not interested in you. Jesus, men. They don't listen.*

"I know," Andie said. "May, you have to move on. To the other side."

May stopped dancing. *You mean, DIE?*

"You're dead," Andie said. "It's over. Move on."

It's not over, May snapped. *I'm here. I'm staying.*

"Harold says you're making her mad," Isolde said to Andie.

"Yeah, well, she pissed me off first," Andie said.

"I can see two people," Dennis said, a little pompously. "Early nineteenth-century dress. I don't think they belong here."

He's loaded, May said, not judgmentally.

"Harold says their names are Peter and Miss J," Isolde said. "But they're not communicating much else."

"Tell me how to get rid of the other two," Andie said to May. "Okay, you can stay"—*The hell you can*—"but you must know how to get rid of them."

I don't know anything about them, May said. *Keep the fires going and you'll be fine.*

"I had a fire going in the nursery. Somebody turned it off."

May stopped dancing. *I made Crumb do it. I just wanted to be with North Archer. He liked me when he came down that first time. He was so beautiful and expensive, and he liked me, he told me he really appreciated everything I was doing with the kids, like I was doing him a favor . . .*

That was North, Andie thought. All that cool charm, and there was nineteen-year-old May—

. . . and I thought he'd come back and then he'd love me, and I waited but he never did.

"May," Andie said.

So I wrote him and asked for things, but I always got his secretary, and that's when I decided it was time to take the kids to live with him. We'd all live with him. She swished her skirt again. *And once I was there, he'd love me. I'm lovable.*

"Yeah, you probably were," Andie said.

I'm lovable NOW, May said, her face contorting for a moment, and Andie saw the empty eyes she'd seen that first night, the skull beneath the phantom skin May clung to.

"All right," Andie said.

And then that bitch KILLED ME.

"Harold says things are not good," Isolde said. "I'm ending this."

"She killed you," Andie said, talking fast, "so let's return the favor. Let's get rid of her. How do we do it?"

May hesitated.

"She stole your life," Andie said. "For no reason, she took your life. Let's end hers. *Tell me something that will get rid of them.*"

There might be one thing, May said.

. . .

"Somebody's been doping people here with salvia," Gabe told North when they'd locked the satellite truck and were in the pantry with the tapes.

"Salvia." North shook his head. "Red flowers?"

"Wrong branch of the family. I called Chloe and had her look it all up to make sure, but I remember this stuff. We caught Riley growing it out behind the agency once a couple of years ago. You know teenagers."

"I will very shortly. Carter's twelve. What's salvia?"

"*Salvia divinorum.* Very old natural high, not dangerous, produces visions."

"Hallucinations," North said, everything dropping into place.

"Yep. It's not illegal, it's not addictive, and it doesn't hurt anybody. It's not a crime to grow it. I still kicked Riley's ass, though."

"So how—"

Gabe pulled the jug of tea out of the lineup of decanters. "I tasted this. It's not tea." He jerked his thumb at what North had thought was a bundle of dried herbs. "Somebody's drying *Salvia divinorum,* steeping the dried leaves and, I will bet you anything, spiking your booze with it."

"Andie told me she drinks tea with a shot of Amaretto at night to sleep," North said.

"Which somebody spiked." Gabe leaned back against the counter. "I don't know what's going on here, but I know why people see ghosts. They've been doped."

"You are a good man," North said, more relieved than he thought possible. "Let's go tell Andie."

But when they got to the doorway to the Great Hall and saw the séance in progress, Gabe stopped him.

"It'd be smarter to watch this," he told North in a low voice. "See who's benefiting from people believing."

"It has to be Crumb," North said. "She's the one who's been here with Andie and the kids the whole time."

"Yeah, but what if somebody is paying her to do it?"

North looked at the people around the séance table, watching Andie talk to empty air. Southie wouldn't drug Andie, but the rest . . .

Isolde, whose reputation rested on ghosts being real.

Dennis, who'd told him the night before that he could get a book sold if he ever really saw a ghost.

And Kelly, who needed the fraud for her big comeback.

"Okay," he told Gabe. "Let's watch."

There's a piece of each of them someplace in the house, May said. *I don't know where, I'd tell you if I did, but there's a piece from each of them. Find that and burn it. I think that'll do it.*

"It didn't do it for you," Andie said. "You were cremated."

Part of me is here, too, May said. *You said I could stay. But not them. That bitch killed me and I want her gone.*

"Okay, a piece of each of them. Like what? What are we looking for?"

But May had turned and was looking at the thing that Alice called Miss J. *Get rid of her. Burn her out. I HATE HER.*

The thing moved toward her, its empty eyes trained on her, and May laughed and went for it, and Isolde stood up and said, *"End it, Harold, get them out of here,"* and then they were gone, and the Great Hall was empty, and Andie sat back and thought, *Something in the house.*

"I have no idea what just happened here," Southie said. "Was any of that tape usable, Kelly?"

"Yes," Kelly said, all the animation in her voice gone when she looked at Southie. "Good, give it to me," Southie said. "So Isolde and Andie can see it."

"I'll make a copy of it for you." Kelly stood up.

"No, I'll take the tape now."

"No, it's the property of the station."

"But you didn't have permission to tape here."

"Of course I did," Kelly said, outraged. "Isolde and Andie—"

"Don't own the house and aren't the guardians of the children." Southie held out his hand to Bill. "You don't really want to go to court for taping this, do you?"

"No," Bill said and handed the tape over.

"Bill!"

"Three of us," Bill said, disgusted, and Kelly grabbed him by the arm and dragged him over to the window and began spitting words at him, too low for the others to hear.

"Well, this has been a nightmare," Isolde said to Andie.

"May says we need to find something in the house that belonged to them," she told Isolde. "There's something of theirs here."

"We need to get the hell out of here," Isolde said. "Harold says he doesn't like it. He's thinking about going back to Florida. And he hated Florida."

"I couldn't see anything," Flo said, sounding disappointed.

"I couldn't, either," Southie said, cheerful again now that he had the tape. "It's like listening to somebody else have a phone conversation. So explain to me again how I slept with a ghost?"

Dennis got up and left the table and went back into the dining room.

"Was it something I said?" Southie said.

"Of course, Harold hates Ohio, too," Isolde said. "The big thing is, Harold's getting cold feet."

"He's a ghost," Southie said. "He always has cold feet."

Isolde glared at him and he shut up. "It's too dangerous, Andie," she said, serious as death. "No more séances, I won't do any more."

"I just have to find out what it is that's holding them here," Andie told her. "I just need to know that."

"No. More. Séances," Isolde said.

"Then I'll find out without you," Andie said, and went to check on the kids before she searched the house.

North watched her go, and said, "So what did you learn from that?" and Gabe shook his head.

"I got nothing," he said. "They're all crazy."

North saw him to the front door and then went to look for Andie, finding her in the library with the kids. "I need to talk to you," he told her, and when she came out, he tried to take her into the sitting room, but Isolde was in there by the fire, looking exhausted, so he took her into the dining room, but Dennis was there, making notes— "The brandy's gone," he said—and North nodded and moved on to the kitchen.

"It's almost five," Andie said. "Talk to me while I make dinner."

"Sit down," North said, and Andie looked surprised, but she sat down. "You've been drugged."

Andie blinked at him.

"Mrs. Crumb has been putting a hallucinogen called salvia in the liquor," North said, "and in God knows what else. You've been systematically drugged since you got here." *And I let it happen.*

"No," Andie said.

"I should have been here," North said, the guilt that had been pressing him down since he'd heard about the salvia finally breaking. "I sent you down here alone. I left you alone again."

"North—"

"Salvia looks like a weed. Crumb grows it in Alice's butterfly garden, then she makes it into tea and cuts the liquor with it. That's why she decants it. Anybody who's had a drink here has been doped."

Andie started up from the table, and North said, "Gabe took samples of it and we dumped the rest down the sink. I've already talked to Mrs. Crumb and there's a car coming from town to take her out of here. She's packing now. She swears she didn't do it—"

"She didn't," Andie said. "Crumb's not the type to garden. It was May. The butterfly garden was May's."

"There is no May," North said gently. "May died."

"May possessed Crumb to do it," Andie said, sounding calm even though what she was saying was insane. "You don't understand, the ghosts are *real.*"

North nodded, trying to think of a way to reach her through the hallucinations. They had to have felt very real, especially since she was down here alone, nobody to talk to. "Have the ghosts ever told you anything you didn't already know?"

"Yes," Andie said. "May told me about earrings her boyfriend gave her. She told me how she died. She——"

"Those aren't facts," North said. "They're things you could have made up in a hallucination."

"No," Andie said.

North shook his head. "Honey, you were drugged. I don't know why Alice and Carter won't leave, we'll find that out now, but it's not because of ghosts. There are no ghosts. Ghosts aren't real."

He watched her face as she struggled with the idea, her brain so soaked in salvia by now that it probably couldn't separate fantasy and reality.

And he'd been in Columbus the whole time. Keeping in touch by phone. A real help.

"God, I'm sorry, Andie," he said. "I'll never leave you again, I swear."

"They're not real?" she said, looking distressed and confused. "They have to be real."

"Imagine if they're not," he said, trying to break through. "Imagine if this has all been hallucinations. Maybe the conversations you had with May were things you had to work out for yourself. Maybe it was like talking to yourself and she'd say the things you couldn't say."

Something in that got to her.

"What?" he said gently.

"The first night we talked," Andie said, looking almost sad, "she told me she was my younger self. She asked me who I loved and I said Will and then she said, no, who do you really love, and it was you." She looked him in the eyes then. "We always talked about you. She had such a crush on you. She so wanted you to love her."

"She wasn't real," North said. "And I love you."

Andie took a deep breath. "I love you, too."

He closed his eyes for a moment just from sheer relief. "I'll never let you down again. I will never let you down again."

"It was all a hallucination," Andie said. "Which means I've been driving the kids crazy because I thought there were ghosts." She stopped. "They're so *real*, North."

"Hallucinations always seem real," he told her. "And the kids are fine. We'll talk everything out with them, and they'll be fine, and we'll take them back to Columbus and start a new life."

"I'm not sure—"

"Whatever you want," he told her. "We'll do whatever you want. Just accept that the place isn't haunted. We'll work the rest out from there." She hesitated and he said, "Andie, this is reality. There are no ghosts in reality. You're a levelheaded woman, use your common sense. You know there aren't ghosts here. You were drugged. None of it was real."

She bit her lip and nodded, and he got up and went around the table to her, and she rose up out of her chair to meet him.

"It's going to be all right," he told her, and she put her arms around him, and he thought, *Because this time I am not going to fuck this up.*

Then Alice came through the kitchen door and said, "I'm hungry *now,* I'm *starving,* what are you doing?" and Andie let go of him to make dinner.

"Were you hugging Andie?" Alice demanded.

"Yes," North said. "I'm going to be doing it a lot, so get used to it."

"We'll see," Alice said darkly, and he left her to help Andie with dinner—"No broccoli!"—so he could sort out the rest of the wing-nuts in the house.

Andie walked her way through cooking and serving dinner like an automaton, trying to find her way through the I-was-drugged and There-are-ghosts paradox. She believed North, North would never lie to her, but she believed May, too.

Except that everything that May had said about wanting North, that was her, too. She'd been isolated and sexually frustrated and she had wanted North, she was pretty sure she'd taken the job so she could stay in touch with him, and that was May all over. That girl with the curly hair like hers had been in love with North the way she'd been in love ten years before. May danced all the time the way she had danced ten years ago, the way she'd started dancing with Alice in the kitchen again. Maybe the hallucinations were just her way of getting back to the reality that she loved North. Maybe seeing May was seeing herself, the way she was supposed to be, carefree and dancing and unashamedly in love with North Archer.

If that was true, everything was good. May hadn't possessed her, she'd just been so drugged on brandy that her subconscious had tried to drag her into that bedroom while her conscious mind fought it because it was such a bad idea, like a nightmare while she was awake.

Maybe Kelly hadn't been possessed, maybe she'd just made the rounds to solidify her career and then lied about it.

Maybe everything was all right. Maybe all she had to do was get her grip on reality again. Common sense told her there were no ghosts. The salvia had convinced her otherwise, but that was over. There were no ghosts.

"Are you okay?" Flo said to her anxiously in the sitting room when dinner was over. "You haven't said a word."

"Yeah," Andie said, trying a smile. "I think everything's okay."

"Well, I could use a *drink*," Kelly said. "Where's the brandy?"

"Gone," Southie said. "But there's a case of beer in the car. Every bottle sealed with its own little cap."

"Aren't they always that way?" Kelly said, confused, and Andie left them all and went into the kitchen to think.

She turned on the radio, pulled out her baking stuff, and began on the six bananas she had that were sufficiently brown to make bread.

North had to be right. It had all been a hallucination. Because, rationally, ghosts did not exist.

She let out her breath. It was okay. Everything was okay. Reality was back.

Once she accepted it, the relief was overwhelming. So was the anger—if North hadn't turfed Crumb, she'd have strangled her with her apron—but there weren't ghosts, she'd just been drugged, everything was fine . . .

The radio blared, "And now here's Kathy Troccoli, going out to Steve from Jen . . . 'Everything Changes'!"

"*Yes,*" Andie said to herself, and picked up her bowl full of bananas and bopped around the kitchen, mashing as she went.

May had been right. No, she had been right. Dancing made you know you were alive. Life was good. Life was *normal*. If she hadn't lost her grip on reality, if she hadn't lost her common sense, she wouldn't have been so crazy the past month. And now she wasn't crazy anymore. Thanks to North, she wasn't crazy at all.

"I'll never be the same," she sang, as she dumped in egg and vanilla and butter and then mixed them as she danced. Fifteen minutes and four song dedications later, two loaves of banana bread were in the oven, and when the DJ said, "And here's an oldie, going out from Joe to Brenda . . ." Andie belted out "Hurt So Good" using her pepper mill as a microphone as she danced around the kitchen because that's what normal people did when they sang to the radio.

Then she looked up and saw North, leaning in the doorway, holding a longneck beer bottle and grinning at her, and she thought, *That's normal, too,* and kept dancing and singing, happier than she'd been in years.

Ten years.

The music stopped, and North said, "Southie sent me in here. He didn't tell me it was a concert," but he was smiling at her in that old way that said, *I don't care what you do, I just want to be next to you when you do it.*

"I'm *happy,*" Andie said, smiling back as she put down the pepper mill. "I've decided you're right, it was all just a hallucination because I was here all alone, and from now on I'm not going to be crazy, I'm not going to lose my grip on reality, I am going to be smart and sensible."

"Okay," North said, looking not sure about it. "You got all of that from finding out there aren't ghosts?"

"I really believed there were. I talked to the kids as if there really were ghosts. They must have thought I was nuts. And then you saved me." She beamed at him. "Plus, you saved Alice and Carter from Crazy Andie, which means extra points for you."

"What do I get for extra points?" North said, his eyes steady on her, and she felt her blood heat from relief and happiness, but mostly from looking at him, strong and tall and beautiful in the doorway, feeling the way she'd used to before everything had gone wrong.

Which didn't mean it would go wrong again.

"Listen," she said sensibly. "We can't go back to where we were. We've changed too much, there's too much at stake with the kids—"

"I don't want to go back to where we were," he said, and she

thought, *Oh,* and felt depressed. Then he said, "I want to start something new," and she said, "Oh," and thought, *Don't lose your grip here.*

"Well," she began, trying to be rational about the whole thing,
and then the DJ on the radio said, "This one goes out to Andie, from
North. North of what, I don't know. Okay, then, here you go,
Andie . . ." and the first bars of Clapton's acoustic "Layla" began.

North looked as surprised as she did. "Not me."

"Southie sent you in here, right? Southie called that in." Clapton's guitar distracted her with that low, swinging rhythm, and
she took a deep breath. *Sexiest song ever.* "Why 'Layla'?" she asked
him, trying to get her mind back to reality.

He grinned, and she said, "Tell me," and he shook his head and
crooked two of his fingers at her.

Like I'd just come because you called, she thought, but he was moving toward her, and she met him halfway without even thinking
about it.

It's just dancing, she thought as he reached for her. *Nothing crazy
about this.*

"I've missed you," he said as he slid his arm around her waist, and
she shivered and said, "I've missed you, too," and he pulled her close
and rocked her to that perfect rhythm, pulling her hips to his as her
blood heated, and she didn't miss a beat. Ten years went away and
they were dancing in the attic again, everything was the way it
was . . .

No it's not, she thought, but he was there, and she was glad, she
never wanted to stop dancing with him, never wanted to lose his
hands sliding over her, never wanted to leave him . . .

"Andie," he whispered, and she knew the question without him
asking.

"No," she whispered back. "The place is full of people, we'd get
caught."

He smiled down at her, rocking her to the beat, and she thought,
If it wouldn't be so insane, I'd say yes, I would, I would.

"Andie," he said, and she put her forehead on his chest.

"No," she said, "we're in the real world now, we have to think about the consequences," but his breath was warm on her neck as he kissed her there, his hands hot on her as he pulled her hips against his, and she thought, *Don't lose your grip on reality, that never works for you.*

The song ended and there was some advertising blather but she couldn't hear because North said, "Andie," as he gently pressed her back against the counter, and she breathed deep and realized that reality was losing its grip on her.

"Okay, somebody's going to walk in on us," Andie said breathlessly.

"I like this T-shirt," he said in her ear, making her shiver. Then he drew his finger slowly across the "Bad Witch" lettering, and made her shudder.

"Don't do that," she whispered, but his hand had already moved to cup her breast, and he was bending down to her, and she tried to think, but all she wanted was his mouth on hers, her hips tilting to meet his.

He kissed her softly, going deeper as she relaxed against him, his hands moving under her T-shirt now as he slipped his tongue in her mouth, and she forgot everything else, kissing him back, wanting him more than she ever had before.

"Okay, but upstairs," she breathed as he pushed her T-shirt up. "We have to be practical here. Come on."

She tried to slide away from him, but he held her trapped against the counter.

"Here," he said, his eyes dark, the old, hot, demanding North back, unsnapping her bra with one hand and unzipping her jeans with the other.

"No, no, this is crazy, I'm not crazy anymore," she said, fumbling to block his hands. "You were right. Reality, common sense, *come upstairs.*"

"Here," North said, his voice low, going right into her spine, and she shivered, and then he stripped her shirt and bra over her head and tossed them behind him.

"Wait!" she said, grabbing for them and missing, and then closed her eyes as she felt his lips on her skin. "Crazy," she whispered. "We should—"

"Here." He bent his head down and kissed her neck, and then she felt his mouth on her breast, and common sense evaporated along with sanity and all the other buzzkills, and she said, "Yes."

Thirteen

Someone rapped on the kitchen door, and Andie jerked back as Southie said loudly from the hall, "I think we should stay out of the kitchen. It's really Andie's turf."

"Stop," Andie whispered to North, and then she heard Lydia say, "Sullivan, I don't know what your problem is, but I want a drink and I'm going in there," and North pulled Andie down the counter and into the pantry, her jeans sliding off her hips on the way.

He kicked the door closed, and they were in the dark, and she thought about Lydia finding her bra and Bad Witch shirt on the floor, and then he touched her again, and she didn't give a damn. She yanked his shirt up, wanting his skin on hers, wanting all of him, and he pulled the shirt off as she shoved her jeans the rest of the way down, tangling her ankles and almost knocking herself over in Crumb's hallucinogenic pantry. He caught her the way he always did and boosted her up onto the pantry counter, and she wrapped herself around him, around all that muscle and heat and power and safety and sense, everything she'd lost ten years before, all of it focused on her, his hands and mouth urgent on her, teasing her, heating her, making her insane.

"What happened to sanity?" she said, gasping. "You were such a fan."

"I saw you again," he said in her ear as he slid his hand between her legs. "And I went crazy."

"Oh," she said, and then his fingers moved inside her and she said, *"Oh,"* and bit him hard on the shoulder, raking her hands down his back, and he grew rougher, too, making her moan and gasp, until she couldn't stand it, until she banged her head on his shoulder and said, *"Now,"* and he pulled her hips to him and slid hot inside her, and she cried out because he felt so damn good after so damn long.

He moved with the old, familiar, deliberate rhythm that always made her mindless, touching her everywhere as she touched him, blanketing her mind with heat until she moaned, sliding against him, tasting the salt of his skin and feeling his breath on her neck, hearing him whisper low to her that she was beautiful, that she was everything, that she was his. His rhythm built inside her until she was sobbing from the tension, until it was too much and she arched up and bit down, her eyes closed tight, and felt it coming, now, now, *now,* and then he moved hard against her and she broke just as hard, crying out as he held her tight and the spasms took her. And when she was quiet and gasping, she felt him shudder, too, and held him as tightly as she could, leaning back to take his weight as he lost his mind.

After a while, he took a deep breath and eased out of her, and she said, exhausted and exhilarated, "Tell me again about common sense."

"Fuck common sense," he said, his voice husky, and then he got rid of the condom, and she thought, *Where the hell did he get a condom?* and realized he must have brought them with him. *Pretty sure of yourself, weren't you?* she thought, but she didn't care, and that wasn't it, anyway. He'd have brought them just in case, to protect her. Because he was North and that was practical.

He cupped her face in his hands and said softly, "You okay?" and she kissed him, long and slow and deep, mindless with love again, and he said, "You're okay," and put his hands on her waist to help her down.

She stood next to him, breathing deep, her arms around his waist, her head on his chest, practicality coming back with sanity, knowing she should tell him that she didn't want to make the same mistake all over again, that they were going to have to have a serious talk about the reality of their situation, that they were going to have to deal with the ghost of their old marriage, but all she wanted was to go upstairs with him and do that again, slower and longer this time.

We won't even have to light the fire, she thought. *May was a hallucination. We're safe.*

North kissed the top of her head and said, "Do you want me to get your clothes?"

"I can get them," she said, lifting her face to his. "On my way upstairs. To the bedroom."

"That's it," North said. "Play hard to get."

He kissed her again, and she thought, *I'm yours,* and then she stopped thinking again and just loved him.

It wasn't that simple, of course. She had to put Alice and Carter to bed, Alice protesting, Carter picking up a comic book without a word, and then she had to be polite to the guests in the sitting room, which she did on autopilot because all she could see was North, smiling at her. Southie pulled her aside and whispered, "You're a little obvious there, tone it down some," but she didn't care. There weren't any ghosts and she was back with North, even if it was just for tonight, she was back with North, so at the earliest possible moment, she said brightly, "Well, I should go check on the kids. You all have a good night," and left to run up the stone stairs to the kids' rooms, really meaning to check on them until she heard North's step behind her.

"You should have waited fifteen minutes," she whispered over the railing to him. "People are going to notice."

"People already noticed," North said, gaining on her. "Also, I don't care."

She picked up speed, but when she got to the landing, she heard music coming from the nursery.

"Damn it," Andie said as North hit the last stair, and went into the nursery to see Alice dancing to "Make a Move on Me" in the light of the gas fire.

"What are you doing, young lady?"

"I woke up," Alice said, bopping around the room. "There were noises. So I turned on the music!" She flung her arms over her head and danced wildly, a little savage in her nightgown.

"Noises?" Andie looked around but there was nobody there except for North, standing in the doorway. Waiting. *Not for long,* Andie thought and said to Alice, "Back in bed, it's way too late for you to be up."

Olivia Newton-John sang, "I'm the one you want," and North laughed in the doorway.

"What's so funny?" Alice said, annoyed.

"I just recognized the song," he told her. "Andie and I danced to this once."

"Really?" Alice said, as Andie pulled back her covers.

"Get into bed," Andie said to Alice, and Alice climbed in. "We'll be right in the next room."

"You and Bad danced to this?"

"Not that I remember," Andie said, pulling the covers up.

"Arts Ball," North said, his voice lazy with satisfaction. "The band was awful, and Southie got his boom box out of the car and set it up in the hall because the girl he was with—"

"Oh, *yes,*" Andie said, remembering the hall, and Southie, and North laughing with her, and how happy she'd been. "The little ballerina. The one who was so damn flexible."

North laughed again. "That was her. Bridget?"

"No," Andie said, thinking hard. "Brin. Short for Brinda." She laughed, too. "Brinda. My God."

"Right. And Southie said she must have had a dyslexic mother. And she got mad, and he got the boom box, and she wanted this song . . ."

"I remember now. I was wearing the skirt you got me, the green-blue one with the sequins. Alice loves that skirt."

"I love that skirt," Alice said solemnly.

"And I dragged you out—"

"And then you danced me down that hall," Andie said, smiling as she remembered. "All those mirrors. We stayed out there for the rest of the ball. Remember, Southie went and got champagne . . ."

"And we sat on the floor while he fed Brin caviar," North said. "Charmed the socks right off her."

"Southie can charm the socks off anybody. That was a good time."

"I should have been there," Alice said from her bed.

"You weren't *born* yet, monkey," Andie said, and then the music changed to Jackson Browne, and the memories came pounding back.

"What's wrong?" Alice said.

"Nothing," North said, smiling at the little girl now. "This is our song, Andie's and mine."

"Why is it yours?" Alice scowled at him. "I like it, too."

"When people fall in love, they get a song." North didn't look at Andie, just smiled at Alice. "This is the song that was playing when we met."

"Did you dance?" Alice said.

"Oh, yeah," North said.

"Show me," Alice said, and North walked into the room and held out his hand to Andie, and she let him pull her against him because her days of saying no to him were gone.

He held her close and began to move, and she moved with him and the music, full of the memory of him and the reality of him, blanketed by all the satisfaction he'd released in her, feeling again the incredible, irresistible erotic pull he had on her, every cell expanding at his touch, back from the long, cold dead. He twirled her away from him and back to him, catching her the way he always had, holding her tight until the music slowed and then he stood, smiling down at her, heat in his eyes again, always.

"Hey," Alice said, and North reached over and turned off the tape deck.

"Bedtime," he said, and she grumped, but she slid back under her covers.

Andie let go of him to kiss Alice good night. "I love you, baby," she said, "sleep tight," and pulled the covers up over her.

"Good night, Bad," Alice called.

"Good night, Alice," North said.

"Tomorrow, you have to dance with me," she said.

"Whatever you want, kid," North said, and Alice nodded as if that was the way she thought things should be, too, and rolled over.

North took Andie's hand and tugged her toward her open bedroom door. "Come here," he said, and his voice went to her spine.

She followed him through the door, taking one last backward glance at Alice as he closed it, and when she turned back, he bent and kissed her, and it hit hard again, and she clung to him, shaking, drinking in that kiss as if she were dying.

"So," he whispered when she pulled back, his voice husky, "I think we should take it slower this time—"

She pushed him back onto the bed and climbed on top of him, straddling him.

"Or not," he said, and May said, *You've got troubles,* and Andie pushed North away and rolled off him to scoot back on the bed, saying, "No, *no!*"

"What?" North said, sitting up. "What's wrong?"

May floated in the room in front of them and Andie realized they hadn't put the fire on. Because ghosts weren't real. "You're not real."

That Kelly woman is doing something down in the Great Hall. Sneaking around. I can possess her and stop her if you want. May smiled, helpful and eager to please. *I don't think she has a soul, so it wouldn't matter.*

"I'm hallucinating." Andie slid off the far side of the bed. "Crumb fed us all salvia, and you are a hallucination."

"Andie?" North said, alarmed, reaching for her.

Fine, May said, swishing her skirt and scowling. *But you might want to look downstairs anyway because she's got that camera guy and they're filming. And I think Carter's got trouble, too. Although he's used to it.*

"Carter?" Andie said. "What's wrong with Carter?"

May swished her skirt again. *That was good stuff you did down in the pantry, but it's stirred things up. You better go look.*

"Andie," North said, putting his hand on her arm. "It's okay. I'm here. Maybe it'll take a while until the salvia's out of your system, but whatever you're seeing isn't real."

May swished her skirt again and said, *I may not be real, but you'd better go look anyway.*

"She's not real," Andie said to herself out loud.

"Right," North said, trying to pull her back to bed. "Come on, you just need to sleep it off—"

I'm real, Andie, May said, and Andie knew it was true.

She pulled her hand free from North's grasp. "Kelly's filming in the Great Hall," she said as she headed for the door. "And Carter's in trouble. You go stop Kelly, and I'll help Carter."

She went through the nursery, where Alice was still sleeping, and out into the gallery, thinking, *She's not real, she's not real.*

Then she saw a flickering light from Carter's room and ran.

North left the bedroom, trying to get some blood back to his brain. He almost followed Andie to Carter's room, but he saw a glow from downstairs and looked over the railing to see lights and Bill the cameraman pointing his camera at something under the gallery.

Kelly O'Keefe really was filming again.

He hit the back stairs at a run.

"A *little girl,*" Kelly was saying into her microphone when he ran into the Great Hall, "in tears, *terror-stricken,* while her guardian *ignores* her and her nanny *talks to ghosts,*" and then North pulled the plug on Bill's extension cord and flipped on the big chandelier overhead. "What the hell?" Kelly snapped at Bill, who nodded toward North.

Kelly turned on him angrily and then saw who it was. Her smile flashed back on. "North! We were just—"

"Finished," North held out his hand to Bill. "Give me the tape."

"That's the property of the station," Kelly said righteously.

"Give me the tape or I'll take it," North said, really wanting to hit something.

Bill pulled the tape out and handed it over.

"*Bill!*" Kelly snapped and then she turned to North. "You're violating my First Amendment rights!"

"I hope it was as good for you as it was for me," North said. "You're out of here. Now. If you're still here in the morning, I'll call the police and have you arrested for trespassing."

Bill nodded and began to break down equipment.

"You'll be hearing from our lawyers," Kelly snapped.

"That'll be fun," North said and waited until they were out of the house. Then he took the tape upstairs with him, trying to figure out how the hell Andie had known Kelly was at work again.

"What's going on?" Lydia said, meeting him in the back hall on the second floor as he headed for the third. "I heard something."

"Kelly and her cameraman are leaving. Andie's checking on Carter. Alice is asleep. I'm going back to bed."

"So everything's all right?" Lydia said.

"Yes," North said, and went upstairs to talk Andie down from her ghost fixation again.

Andie stopped in Carter's doorway.

The boy was sitting cross-legged on the bed, staring at the door, looking thin in his flannel pajamas, his wrists dangling over his knees, his head lowered so that his eyes were dark and shadowed under his brows.

He had candles burning on tables on both sides of his bed, a dozen of them at least.

"Carter? What the *hell* are you doing?"

He ignored her, and she felt a chill rise as she saw that he was shaking. Whatever was going on, he was concentrating hard on not being terrified, and not doing very well at it.

She walked over to the bed and sat down beside him. "Carter?" she said softly, and reached for his hand.

"Get out," he said, staring at the door. *"Get out."*

"What—why?"

His breathing quickened and his eyes widened, staring at something beyond her, and Andie felt cold air on her back.

When she turned, an icy blue fog was taking shape in the open door.

"Smoke?" she said, her heart kicking up, but she knew it wasn't, the cold in the room was growing, crystallizing the night air on the windows, chilling her through and through.

Carter shivered beside her in his pajamas, and the fog rose up clumsily and took the rough shape of the man in the old-fashioned coat, stronger, more solid than ever before, his face a blur with holes for eyes.

He leaned forward and his face became sharper, grinning at them, blocking the door.

"*No!*" Andie said, scrambling onto the bed in front of Carter.

"*Get out,*" Carter whispered to her. "He comes for me. *Get out.*"

"*No.*" She knelt on the bed between the thing and Carter, facing it down over the foot of the bed. "Go *away. You can't have him.*"

The thing moved closer, losing definition as it moved, re-forming into the man as it came closer, giving her vertigo again.

Andie scooted back against Carter, spreading out her arms to shield him. "*No.* This kid is off limits. Go haunt somebody your own age, you pervert. *No.*"

The thing arched over them, and Andie felt the cold in her bones, and then something went sailing over her shoulder and another and another, and she realized that Carter was throwing lit candles, the old singed carpet igniting again, flames shooting up. She swung her arm through the thing, tearing through its definition yelling, "*This kid is mine!*" her arm searing with cold. She grabbed Carter by the back of his pajama collar and dragged him around the icy mist that was re-forming above the flames, through the door and the halls to the nursery where she slammed the door behind them both.

She shoved the boy in front of the fireplace. "*You stay here.*"

Then she grabbed the small fire extinguisher from the mantel and ran back down the gallery and into Carter's bedroom, terrified that the flames would have ignited the bed by now, but the fire was out and the room was empty and cold, cold beyond anything natural, so she slammed the door and ran back to the nursery.

Carter was shaking so hard his teeth were chattering.

"Oh, baby." She sank down next to him on the hearth and pulled him into her arms. "I'm so sorry. I should have been there."

He was rigid in her arms, unyielding the way Alice used to be, but Carter didn't scream, he just endured.

"I'll take care of it," Andie told him, holding him tightly. "I'll get rid of them. I'll get you out of here—"

"What's wrong?" Alice said, from her bed, sitting up, groggy with sleep.

"There was a ghost in Carter's room," Andie said.

Alice slid off the bed. "Is he okay? Was it Peter?"

"Peter," Andie said, thinking, *Fucking hallucination, my ass.*

"The ghost who wants the house," Carter said.

"Why didn't you keep your fireplace lit?" Andie said. He was still so cold in her arms, and she rocked him a little bit, just because she was so guilt-stricken about leaving him to handle his ghost alone.

"It doesn't work," Carter said.

"Jesus Christ," Andie said, thinking, *Why didn't you tell me?*, thinking, *Crumb knew that fireplace didn't work and still put him in there*, thinking, *I let him down so badly.* "I'm so sorry, Carter, I'm so sorry."

"You didn't do anything," he said, still stiff in her arms.

"That's why I'm sorry."

He pulled away from her, and she let go, almost in tears because she'd done so badly by him.

"I'm okay," he said. "It's okay."

She nodded. "We'll move your stuff in from your room later. You're never going back there."

"I'm okay," he said again, that flat look back in his eyes.

She grabbed his arms, as if she could shake some response into him. "Carter, it's going to be different, I swear. I'm going to get you out of here. I know Miss J killed May because she was trying to take you away—"

"That wasn't why," Carter said.

Andie waited.

He swallowed and then he started to talk and it was as if once he started, he couldn't stop. "Alice was screaming in the hall by the bathroom because we'd been alone all night while Aunt May was out, and Alice was scared. Aunt May came home and went up on the tower and yelled at her friends, and then she came down and said, 'Shut up, Alice,' but Alice couldn't stop crying. Aunt May put on her prom dress and swished around and said, 'See, Alice? See how pretty?' but Alice couldn't stop, and Aunt May was drunk, and I tried to get Alice to stop, but she couldn't, and Aunt May slapped her . . .'"

He took a deep shuddering breath, his eyes bleak, and Andie thought, *Fucking May.*

"I grabbed Alice, and Aunt May said she was sorry. She said she was just so lonely, she talked about some guy who wouldn't pay attention to her. She said she was doing a good job, but he wouldn't come back, he wouldn't love her, and I didn't care." His voice hardened. "She'd slapped Alice."

"Right," Andie said. "You were right."

"Then she started to cry and went out into the gallery, and Alice followed her, crying, telling her not to cry, and I heard them both scream." He swallowed hard. "When I got out there, Alice was by the gallery rail, screaming, and the railing was broken, and Aunt May was . . . down in the hall." He looked sick for a minute. "I looked over the edge and she was all . . . Her neck was wrong and there was blood . . . under her head. A lot of it. Alice said it was Miss J, that Miss J had come up out of the carpet, but then Crumb came out and saw me. She told me to shut Alice up and to keep my mouth shut and go back to bed."

Andie put her arm around him again and pulled him close, and this time he leaned against her. "Crumb's gone, your uncle North threw her out of the house this afternoon. And you're not alone anymore. I'm here, I know there are ghosts, and I'm not leaving you. You never have to go through that again."

He looked at her with eyes as flat as ever, a twelve-year-old who'd seen too much. "The police said Aunt May fell into the moat, but Crumb dragged her body there and then washed up the blood. After that, the nannies came."

Andie nodded. "And that's when Alice started to scream all the time."

"She's afraid somebody else will die. That's why we get rid of the nannies. The ghosts aren't going to kill Crumb, she's been here forever. It's the new people who try to change things . . ." He lifted his chin. "You should get out of here."

"Not without you."

"They'll never let us go," Carter said.

"The hell they won't," Andie said, and then North came in.

"I just threw Kelly O'Keefe and her cameraman into the storm," he began and then he stopped. "What happened?"

"They're not hallucinations, they're ghosts," Andie said.

"Andie," he began, and she shook her head, slowly.

"Do not fuck with me on this one," she said. "There are ghosts."

Andie asked North to sit with the kids while she went to find Isolde, so he stayed, watching Alice fall back asleep and Carter stare into the fire.

Carter looked like Southie at twelve, the same flop of brown hair, the same blue eyes, the same gangly, growing-in-all-directions body. The difference was that Southie had laughed all the time when he was twelve. Carter looked like he'd never laughed in his life.

"I don't believe in ghosts," North told him.

Carter nodded, evidently not surprised.

"But I believe something bad is going on here, and I believe you've been handling it on your own for too long."

"Andie's good," Carter said, and then when North didn't say anything, he added, "It's been better with her here."

"I'm here now, too."

Carter nodded, not impressed.

North studied the boy's face, the circles under his eyes, the exhaustion that wasn't just from this night, the kind of tiredness that came from never letting down your guard. "My dad died when I was twelve."

Carter gave him a "so what?" look.

"My mom had a hard time with it. She felt guilty about a lot of things. So I covered for her. I had to. I had a little brother, and he was really scared. But I got really tired of handling it."

Carter nodded.

"And then about six months after my dad died, my uncle Merrill came back from this long trip he'd been on, and bought the house next door, and took over the family, and everything got better. Not back to normal because my dad was still dead, but . . . better. Because somebody had my back."

Carter sat very still, and North remembered how it had been, how he'd just stared at his uncle when he'd finally said, "Sorry, boy, I let you down. I'll take care of things now." Even though Merrill had screwed up the firm, he'd taken damn good care of the family. You could forgive a lot if somebody was there to take care of things until you grew up.

"I've got your back now," North said. "The ghost thing, I don't believe in that. But you are not the only one taking care of your sister now. It's not just Andie taking care of Alice and you. From now on, I'll be here."

"Here," Carter said.

"I'll stay here with you until I can get you out of here," North said, having no idea how the hell he was going to do that and keep up with his cases. "And then you'll come to Columbus and live with us. Your rooms are ready now. I'll be there for you. I will be there for you as long as you need me. And I'm sorry as hell that I didn't say this two years ago."

"Wouldn't have done any good," Carter said. "We can't leave."

The boy sounded hopeless, not obstinate.

"Why?"

"People die when we try to leave."

"Who?"

"My dad. Aunt May. The last governess almost. They want us here."

"The ghosts?"

Carter nodded. "I know you think we're crazy, but we see them. Andie does, too. I didn't think she did, I thought she was just trying to make us feel better, but she yelled at Peter, she saw him. And she talks to Aunt May."

"She thinks she does, anyway. Look, we can protect—"

"No." Carter shook his head. "It was bad enough before Andie, when Aunt May died. Alice is scared to death that Miss J will kill somebody else. And it's not just that." He stopped and looked over at his little sister, sleeping like a ghost under her sequined comforter. "Alice loves Andie. Aunt May, we liked her fine, but Andie . . . If Andie dies, Alice really will go crazy. We can't leave."

"Andie's not going to die," North said, chilled by the resignation in the boy's voice.

"You can't stop them," Carter said. "You don't even believe in them."

"If I take you to Columbus, will you be all right?" North said, grasping for something logical. "Will they follow you? These ghosts?"

"I don't know. Miss J kills people to keep Alice from leaving, so I don't think she can go. But they'll never let us go. You don't get it. We can't leave."

"You're right, I don't get it," North said. "But I'll figure it out. I know a lot more than I did when I got here, and I'll figure out the rest. And then I'll end it, and I'll take you home to Columbus. Your life will be normal again, Carter. I'll see to it."

Carter looked back at the fire again. He wasn't shaking anymore, he was warm again, but he didn't believe anybody was going to save him.

I couldn't have screwed this up more if I'd worked at it, North thought.

Carter looked up. "Thanks."

"What?" North said.

"For trying to help." He hesitated a minute and then he said, formally, "We appreciate it." Then he climbed up into the other twin bed and settled in, his back to North.

"You're welcome," North said and thought, *I'm getting you out of here, kid,* and began to think things through, methodically and thoroughly, wishing he had a legal pad and his pen.

"There are ghosts upstairs," Andie said to Dennis when she found him still working in the dining room.

"Which one?" Dennis said.

"Peter. They're getting stronger. Where's Isolde?"

"She went to bed," Dennis said, shuffling through his notes. "Peter. Right. A man named Peter was murdered here. The official report was that he was found on a path, but gossip at the time was that it happened in this house, which is why he walks here."

"Other people knew he was here?"

"I can't find much," Dennis said, pulling a very old book toward him. "But this was in the library here. It's a journal from a governess who was here then. She admires him, but she says he's very proprietary about the house. I'm assuming now that he's dead, he still thinks he owns the place."

"Wait a minute," Andie said. "You believe in ghosts?"

"I saw them," Dennis said.

Andie sat down beside him. "What did you see?"

"A beautiful woman." His face lit up as he spoke. "Lots of curly dark hair, big eyes, beautiful smile."

"That's May," Andie said. "She's the kids' aunt."

"Another woman. And a man. Is this them?"

He pulled out three more papers, rough amateur sketches, but Andie recognized May in all her curly-headed glory, Miss J in her flounced skirt and hollow eyes, and Peter in his coat, standing with his hands on his hips, looking like he did own the place. Dennis had drawn them not with great skill but in great detail.

"That's them, all of them."

"I've seen ghosts," Dennis said, wonder in his voice. "I was so afraid I was just hallucinating."

"Well, there's a chance," Andie began and then looked at the drawings again. Lots of detail.

"These are really the ghosts?" he said. "Does May have those earrings, does the other woman have that locket, the man with that coat, that watch? I got the details right?"

"Yeah. You saw ghosts."

Dennis closed his eyes, smiling. "All my life I wanted to see ghosts. This is wonderful!"

"No, this is awful. They're dangerous, Dennis, they want the kids and the house and they kill people who get in their way." She looked at the sketches again. "They might not be happy about this. I think you'd better leave first thing tomorrow."

"Leave *ghosts*?" Dennis said, incredulous. "No, I'm here to help you. In fact, I might stay and study them after you're gone, if that's all right."

"The housekeeper's gone," Andie said. "And it's *dangerous*."

"I don't need a housekeeper," Dennis said. "I can be the housekeeper, I'll take care of the place for you, just let me study them. Can we have another séance tomorrow? I know Isolde is against it, but if I can just talk to them this time, like you do— "

"No," Andie said, standing up. "If you see Isolde before I do tomorrow, tell her I need to talk to her before she leaves."

"She can't leave," Dennis said. "There really are ghosts here." He sounded as if he were saying, "The circus really is here!" with all the happiness and wonder of a little kid.

"Good night, Dennis," Andie said, and went back upstairs to North.

"The kids are asleep in the nursery," he said when she went into the bedroom where the gas fire was now burning. "I put the fire on in here, too."

"I know you don't believe, but the ghosts are real," Andie said. "Dennis saw them, too."

"Dennis was drunk on doped brandy," North said.

"They're real." Andie sat down on the edge of the bed, too tired to be open-minded.

North pulled back the covers, and she fell back against the pillows as he climbed in bed beside her. "Let's just get the kids out of here," he said, putting his arms around her.

She curled against him, grateful he was there, even if he was clueless about what they were facing. "Yeah. Let's do that. Do you have a plan?"

"I'll have a plan tomorrow." North kissed her forehead. "Go to sleep. You've had a rough day."

"Tomorrow," Andie said, wondering what the hell she was going to do tomorrow that was going to make any difference as she fell asleep in his arms.

The next morning, Andie met Isolde at the bottom of the stairs on her way to make breakfast.

"Dennis saw the ghosts," she told the medium.

"I know, he told me," Isolde said. "Fucking amateurs."

"He wants another séance."

"Over my dead body."

"Don't say that here," Andie said. "Just help me exorcise the dead we already have."

"I've been thinking about that," Isolde said. "Did you see Dennis's drawings? The woman had a locket."

"Yeah," Andie said, trying to remember.

"I think it's the locket Alice is wearing."

Andie stopped at the foot of the stairs. "She told me it was a treasure. Maybe that means she found it. Are you sure it's the same one?"

"Dennis has the drawing."

Andie picked up speed and went into the dining room where all Dennis's work was still spread out. She sorted through the papers until she found the drawing of Miss J.

The drawing wasn't great, but that was Alice's locket.

"It's the same one," she said to Isolde and then realized Isolde wasn't with her. "Isolde?"

She went out into the Great Hall and Isolde came out of the sitting room to join her, pale as death.

"What's wrong?" Andie said.

"We have to call the police," Isolde said, and Andie thought, *Oh God, no, something really bad has happened this time,* and tried to go into the sitting room.

Isolde stopped her.

"It's Dennis," she said. "He's dead."

Fourteen

Andie had gone into the sitting room while Isolde called 911. Dennis was sitting there on the green-striped couch, leaning against one of the green-striped bolsters by the arms, staring straight ahead, looking not that different from when he was alive except that he wasn't blinking, but Andie knew instantly because there was no heh heh, no asthmatic cough, no lame jokes, nothing. So when she sat with him, and took his cold hand, and said, "Dennis, I'm so, so, sorry," she knew he wasn't there. She just didn't know what else to do.

North came in and said, "Isolde just came to get me. Andie, I'm so sorry," and she knew how he felt, impotent to help her, because she felt the same way for Dennis. Then the EMTs arrived, and Andie stood back and let them work, letting North answer their questions, helping him when he didn't know the answers, part of her still believing Dennis would wake up, that he'd come walking in from the kitchen later with some banana bread, saying, "This is really extraordinary," and ask for a brandy. Then she went up to the nursery and found the kids sitting together in front of the fire, Carter's arm around Alice, Alice's arms around his waist, waiting for her to tell them why there'd been sirens outside.

"What happened?" Carter said.

"Dennis died," Andie said, and Alice's face crumpled.

Andie went over to the window seat and sat down, putting her arms around both of them. Alice reached out as she wept and wound her fist into Andie's sweater, pulling her closer to Carter, huddling between them.

"They killed him," Alice sobbed. "And he was *nice!*"

"He was good man," Andie said, holding her close. "He died very quickly of a heart attack, and he didn't suffer. I don't think the ghosts killed him, Alice. I think he was really happy when he died because he'd seen the ghosts in the séance. He'd always wanted to, you know."

"They killed him, *they killed him,*" Alice wailed.

"No," Andie said, holding her close. "He wasn't trying to take you away. Why would they hurt him?" Unless he'd found out something else about them . . .

"Why did he have a heart attack?" Carter said, no emotion in his voice at all.

"He'd been drinking a lot and the séance really excited him." *Plus he was doped to the gills on salvia.* "Maybe he just had a weak heart."

Carter had that stubborn look on his face. "He didn't look sick. One of the teachers at my school had a heart condition and he was really pale all the time. Dennis looked healthy."

"It can happen like that. Sometimes hearts just blow out."

"Do you think he'll come back?" Carter said, and then the emotion was there, guilt and worry and a need for comfort. "Like Aunt May did?"

"No." Andie smoothed his hair back and for once he didn't flinch. "I think he'd done everything right in his life, and I don't think he had any unfinished business. I think the only thing he really wanted to do, even though he wouldn't admit it, was see a ghost. And he saw a ghost."

"Which one?" Carter said, tense again.

"All of them," Andie said. "He talked about how beautiful your aunt May was."

"Which one did he see when he died?" Carter said.

"I don't think any. I was in the dining room with him before he died, and he was definitely excited, but the room was warm and I didn't see anybody in there." Carter relaxed, and then she said, "I'm pretty sure he was alone when he died."

"You weren't with him?" Carter said, tense again.

"I went to bed." *I left him alone.* "Isolde found him in the sitting room this morning."

"You weren't with him when he died."

"No," Andie said.

Carter looked down at Alice who had stopped crying now.

"What?" Andie said.

"The ghosts killed him," Carter said, and Alice nodded sadly.

"Ghosts can't kill people," Andie said. "They can't touch—"

"There was a big black cloud and Aunt May screamed," Alice said. "It was Miss J. I bet she killed Dennis the same way."

"Listen," Andie said. "We have to talk about you leaving. It's too dangerous to stay here, the ghosts are too strong now. So we have to figure out a way to do this."

"We can't," Alice said, starting to cry again.

"We can do anything," Andie said. "Don't cry, *think.*"

"I just miss Dennis," Alice wailed.

"I'll think," Carter said, and Andie held Alice and said, "We'll all think."

By ten, North had talked to the ambulance crew and the police, discovered Dennis had no next of kin, left a message with his university, waved the police and the ambulance down the drive as they left with Dennis's body, and refused Southie's offer of a beer.

Instead he went into the Great Hall where Isolde sat at the round table there, staring out the big mullioned windows on the front of the house.

"Can I get you anything?" he said gently, and she shook her head.

He waited a moment, studying her. She was a caricature of a woman dangerously out of touch with fashion, all dark eye makeup, big hair, and shoulder pads, but the emotion she was feeling was real, and he couldn't leave her alone in that icy barn of a hall, especially since she really believed the place was haunted.

"The sitting room is warmer," he told her before he remembered that the sitting room was where Dennis had died.

She shook her head.

He sat down across from her.

"It wasn't your fault," he told her.

"I know that," she said, all of her former snap gone.

North nodded. "Can you tell me why you don't want to move someplace warmer?"

She looked at him with interest then. "It's cold because of the ghosts. They're feeding on the emotion here. I don't know what they're doing or who they are because Harold is gone, but they're still here in this room. That's why it's cold."

I don't believe in ghosts, North thought, but she clearly did. Whatever Isolde Hammersmith was, she wasn't a faker or a con artist. "Harold is gone?"

"He went to the other side. He said he'd had enough of humanity, living and dead." Isolde took a deep breath. "Which is pretty rich considering he killed himself because he'd gotten caught fleecing humanity. He liked them just fine when he was taking their money."

"Fleecing?"

"He was Harold Rich, the guy who ran the big Ponzi scheme out of Florida."

"Oh," North said, taken aback. If she was going to make up a spirit guide, Harold Rich was an interesting choice.

"Not a nice person," Isolde said, "but very good at reading people. And ghosts. I was down there doing a reading and he was wandering around, bitching and moaning, so I took him on. He was
really pissed when I brought him back to Ohio, but then nothing
was ever good enough for Harold. Damn good spirit guide, though.
Good with investments, too. Harold helped me a lot, so I put up
with his lousy personality."

"So that must be hard, losing Harold," North said, trying to
stick to the key points. "I'm sorry. But I really think you should
come into the sitting room. It's too cold in here."

"If the room gets warmer, it means the ghosts have gone somewhere else. Which would be bad because I think they have a plan.
So I want to know where they are." She smiled at him, a tight little
smile that he was pretty sure wasn't natural to her.

"I can get my brother to come monitor the temperature in here.
He thinks a lot of you. I'm sure he'd want you someplace warm—"

"Southie," Isolde said, with some of her old spirit. "There's a
great guy."

"Yes, he is," North said. "Let me get him—"

"Dennis was a good guy, too," Isolde said, and North shut up. If
she wanted to talk, he could sit in an ice-cold hall and listen for a
few minutes. "He didn't believe, you know, and he wanted to. He
wanted to see ghosts in spite of not believing. Then he saw them
during the séance. Did a complete one-eighty. He was so excited."

"You think he died because of that? His excitement gave him the
heart attack?"

Isolde smiled at him kindly, as if he weren't quite bright. "No, I
think one of the ghosts killed him."

North sat back. "Isolde—"

"I think one of the ghosts went in there when he was weakened
and scared him to death. I think they have a plan, and he knew too
much about ghosts, and he was getting in their way. His information

was very good, you know. He didn't believe, but he did his home-work."

North nodded, trying to think of a way to make her suspicion normal. Maybe somebody in the house, the housekeeper, had done something to keep the fantasy of the ghosts alive and frightened Dennis to death accidentally. Except Dennis wouldn't have been scared to death by a human being. He'd investigated the best and lived to tell about it.

"I know you don't believe," Isolde said. "That's all right, most people don't. But the danger is real. They want your children and they want your wife."

North stiffened, but Isolde went on.

"I don't know why they want them. Harold didn't think two of them were even sane. But the danger is real. So I'm sitting here try-ing to . . . sense them. To see if they'll come to me. I think—"

She stopped and stiffened, as if she were listening.

"Isolde?" North said.

"It's getting warmer in here," she said, and he realized she was right.

"They're moving," she said and stood up.

"Where are you going?" North said, as she walked toward the big stone arch.

"To find the cold spots," she said, and even though he didn't be-lieve, he followed her.

Andie made sure the gas fire was burning brightly in the nursery, told Alice and Carter to stay put, and went downstairs to get them lunch. The police and the EMTs were gone, even Isolde was gone from the Great Hall, so she went into the sitting room and sat down on the green-striped sofa. Dennis's sofa. He had been alive right here and then he was dead right here and—

North came to the doorway between the sitting room and the dining room.

"I'm going through the house with Isolde," he said. "She's upset and I don't want to leave her alone. Do you need me to sit with you?"

The idea of North sitting with anybody for comfort was so ludicrous that she laughed, and then she burst into tears.

He came over and sat down beside her and put his arms around her.

"I only knew him two days," Andie said, trying to stop the tears as she cried into his chest. "But he was a good man. And he didn't believe in ghosts but he tried to help us anyway, and then he did believe and he was so happy and one of them killed him . . ."

"Isolde thinks they killed him, too," North said. "She's going through the house looking for cold spots."

"It had to be Peter," Andie said. "Murderous son of a bitch. Dennis never had a chance. You can't fight something you don't believe in." She drew a long breath and sat up, pulling back from North. "You know what? This is the first time I've really thought about death. I mean, Dennis is *gone*. I'm surrounded by ghosts but this is the first time I really understood what it meant. And Dennis did the right thing, he went on, he didn't stay around preying on the living . . ." She stopped, realizing that was a slap at May who could be lurking anywhere. "It's not natural for them to stay," she said finally.

"There I agree," North said. "Southie and Mother are in the kitchen with Flo, putting together some kind of lunch. I'll find Isolde. You go eat something."

Andie shook her head. "I just want to sit here alone for a while and think about Dennis."

North rubbed her shoulder. "Okay. I'll go find Isolde."

Andie nodded, and North left, closing the door behind him, and she let the tears come then, quietly dripping while she thought about poor Dennis who'd died just as he'd opened a new chapter in his life. Well, she thought, trying to get a grip, he was opening a new chapter now. Whatever came next, she hoped it was wonderful for him. She straightened the bolsters on the couch and found something soft behind one of them, and when she shook it out, she realized it was Dennis's godawful green argyle sweater, the one she'd gotten the pizza sauce out of the first night. He'd been so grateful. God, it was so sad, such a dweebish piece of clothing, but it was so Dennis, and Dennis had been so . . .

The tears came back with a vengeance this time, and she put her face in the sweater and cried hard for the poor sweet parapsychologist who'd just wanted to see a ghost and had finally seen one right before he died.

It's all right, Andie.

Andie sniffed the tears back and looked toward the door, expecting to see North, but it was still closed. "North?" She put the cardigan down in her lap and wiped her eyes. "Hello?" she called.

That's my cardigan. It's okay, I don't need it, but—

"Dennis?" Andie jerked her head around. "Dennis, is that you? I can't see you."

I'm dead, the voice said reasonably.

"And yet, that's not a problem with those other people from hell who keep showing up." Andie clutched the sweater to her. "Dennis, is it really you? How do I know it's you?"

I don't know. We really didn't have time to get to know one another well, although I do think a bond was formed under stress. That's often common in wartime. And of course, you've become attuned to supernatural elements because of your concern for Alice, which strengthened the telepathic connection, although Alice isn't here now, so I'm going to have to look at that hypothesis again—

"Okay, it's you." Andie looked around the room, still trying to catch of glimmer of *something* to talk to. "Oh, Dennis, *how are you?*"

Dead.

"I *know,*" Andie said, feeling horrible again. "I'm so sorry. Is it awful?"

No. I don't think it's something I'd choose, given the choice, which of course I wasn't . . .

Andie clutched his cardigan, trying hard not to cry. "Dennis, are you suffering?"

Oh, no. In fact, in many ways it's wonderful. Andie, there really are ghosts!

Annoyance replaced pity. "Yes, Dennis, we talked about that."

Something moved out of the corner of her eye, and Andie turned, but there was nothing there.

But now I know. It's amazing.

"What's it like? Tell me it's not awful."

There's no feeling at all. Well, no physical feeling. There are emotions, of course.

"Emotions," Andie said. "Are you sad?"

No. In fact, I'm rather jubilant. There are ghosts, they're real!

"I don't see that as the upside here."

Yes, but I didn't believe you. I couldn't talk to them. And now . . .

"You can?" Andie held his sweater closer. "Can you tell them to go away?"

They can't.

Andie felt a chill to her left, a draft, probably, but she turned that way, just in case.

They're tied to something in the house. They have to stay here.

"Okay, how do we evict them? A séance?"

Another one? It's getting pretty crowded here on this side already, I don't think you want to take out another civilian.

"Four of you now."

Yes, and some of us aren't quite top drawer.

"How upsetting for you." She waited a minute and then said, "Dennis? Did one of them kill you?"

I think so.

"Which one?"

I don't know. I was sitting on the couch talking to May—she's lovely, Andie—and then she left, and all of a sudden this thing rose up out of the carpet like a dark, screaming cloud, and I died.

"It scared you to death?"

I wouldn't think so. But I'm dead, so it's a reasonable hypothesis.

Andie looked at the carpet. "It's just a carpet, Dennis."

Well, something came out of it and here we are.

She got down on her hands and knees to see what she could find—*ectoplasm in the broadloom?*—and when she got up, her hands were dirty, covered in a fine, dark dust. "What's this stuff?"

I don't know. I'd wash it off. It might be deadly.

"I think it's just dirt." She dusted her hand off. "Okay, we have to get rid of the ghosts. It was probably Peter who killed you. You weren't threatening Alice in any way so Miss J wouldn't go after you, and May was sitting with you, right?"

It's a moot point now. It's not like we can bring them to justice. I think the best course is for us all to leave.

"Yes, that had occurred to all of us, too." Andie tried to pull her thoughts together and a new wrinkle popped up. "Wait a minute. I can hear you but I can't see you. Oh, hell, Dennis, you're a crisis apparition!"

I wish all my students paid attention the way you do, Andie. That's very astute.

"But that means this is it." Andie looked around wildly for him. "You're going to . . . go toward the light or something. I mean, that's good, you should do that, but we don't have much time."

Well, the light is definitely here. Annoying, too. It's really a blessing I don't need sleep now, because that light would make it impossible.

"So what have you come to tell me?" Andie said. "I mean, the message you have to deliver before you go. Was it to leave the house? Because I'm on it."

I'm not going. I'm not leaving you and May to deal with those mad discarnate entities.

"That's sweet, Dennis. But really—"

May has a beautiful soul. You should see it.

"I've seen it. It's been in me. Not that beautiful."

No, no, she has a voluptuous soul.

"Dennis, are you leering?"

The ghostly laughter ended in asthmatic coughing, which was a comfort.

"You okay there?"

Yes. You'd think now that I don't have lungs—

"Dennis, if you're a crisis apparition, we don't have time for this. If you have any advice on how to get rid of those things, now's the time to share."

Well, of course, they'd be weaker if everybody would just stay calm.

"Crumb and Kelly and her cameraman are gone."

That's a help, Dennis said.

"Who are you talking to?" North said, and Andie turned to see him in the doorway.

"Get in here and shut the door," Andie said, standing up. "We have a new . . . wrinkle."

North came in and shut the door. "I don't want a wrinkle."

Andie turned back to where she thought Dennis was. "Can he hear you?"

I don't know, Dennis said. *You're the only one who's heard me so far. Besides May, of course. She has a—*

"Voluptuous soul, I know." Andie looked at North. "Did you hear that?"

"Voluptuous soul?" North said, looking confused.

"Okay, here's the short version. Dennis is here. I think he's a crisis apparition, which means he can't stay long and shouldn't stay long because he's got to go toward the light—"

I really think that's an option.

"—because we don't want him to miss the bus to Paradise. But he's staying because he's worried about the ghosts and because he's attracted to May—"

I wouldn't say "attracted." We have mutual interests.

"—and so he's dragging his feet," Andie finished. She turned back in the direction of Dennis. "Maybe you could take the rest of the ghosts with you. Get them a seat on the bus, too   "

I'm not going.

"Dennis, this is the *afterlife* we're talking about here."

Yes, and it's my afterlife. I'm staying here. I'd like to go to Cincinnati and give that fraud Boston Ulrich the scare of his life, but I can't seem to leave—

"Andie?" North said, concern in his voice.

Andie turned back to him. "I swear to God, he's here, North. I am not crazy, Dennis is here."

"Well, this is where he died," North said reasonably. "On the other hand, I would remind you that you're grieving and he's dead."

"That's what I'm trying to tell him," Andie said, exasperated. "Go toward the light. But now that he's dating May—"

Andie!

"Andie, I know you liked Dennis a lot, but he's dead."

You told him you liked me a lot?

"Not *now*, Dennis. He's here, North. I don't care whether you believe me or not, he's here. What are you doing?"

He sat down next to her on the couch and put his arm around her. "I was thinking—"

If you're going to neck, you should probably do it somewhere else, Dennis said. *I can't seem to leave this couch.*

"The couch?" Andie said. "You're tied to the couch?"

North looked around. "Who's tied to the couch?"

"*Dennis,*" Andie said to him, exasperated.

I can't seem to move away from it, Dennis said. *I'm hoping that's temporary. I don't want to be a supernatural couch potato. Heh heh heh.* He coughed then, asthmatic wheezing from beyond the grave, and Andie gave up.

"I have to take the kids lunch," she said, standing up. "If I don't see you again, it was a pleasure knowing you."

"Andie, Dennis is dead," North said, gently but firmly.

I'm not going anywhere, Dennis said, and Andie gave up on both of them and went to the kitchen.

Andie carried the lunch tray up to the nursery. Both kids were in bed, Alice with her Walkman and Rose Bunny, and Carter with a comic book.

"So," Andie said. "About Dennis."

"He came back?" Carter said.

"Yes. How'd you know?"

"Did he say who'd killed him?"

"No. He said it was just this thing that came out of the carpet."

"Black cloud," Alice said, and picked up her sandwich.

"Okay," Carter said and went back to his comic book.

"Can I go talk to him?" Alice said, and Andie was tempted to let her, but with any luck Dennis would have found his way to the light by now, and Alice would have one fewer person on her chatting-with-the-dead list.

"Maybe later," Andie said. "Eat your lunch."

She went out onto the gallery and heard voices below, so she looked over the railing to see North below, talking to Southie, and went around the corner of the gallery and through the stone archway to the stairs so she could join them.

Something surged up out of the carpet, black and stinging, swirling into a solid mass of staring death's-head, and she screamed and turned blindly to run only to see May rushing toward her, her face a skull as she screamed like a banshee, and Andie turned, screaming again, caught between the two horrors, and fell, hitting the rickety rail around the gallery with her shoulder, feeling it give way, reaching out and grasping only air, and then somebody caught her arm and dragged her back and the ghosts were gone and she was gasping on the carpet, looking at the gaping hole in the gallery railing, with Isolde bending over her, still holding on to her arm.

"Bastards," Isolde said calmly.

"Yeah," Andie said, shaking as she tried to sit up.

"What stopped you from going over?"

"You," Andie said, thinking, *JESUS CHRIST, WHAT WAS THAT??*

"Nope, I got here at the end and caught your arm, but before that you were headed straight for that railing and then you turned away."

"May." Andie tried to calm down enough to think. "May was there."

"Who was the other one?"

"I don't know. This *stuff* just came out of the carpet. That's what Dennis said. He said this thing came out of the carpet . . ."

Isolde reached down and picked up some of the black particles. "It's dirt. Whatever it was just pulled up all the dirt in the carpets and threw it at you."

"It was more than that, it was a *shape, a skull,*" Andie said, and then North ran through the arch and said, *"What the hell?"*

"They tried to kill her," Isolde said as North pulled Andie up into his arms.

"What happened?" North said, looking into Andie's eyes. "Are you all right?"

"Isolde grabbed me before I went through the rail," Andie said, trying to sound normal, but wanting to hold on to him, just the same. "It's the way May died. The ghosts killed May and now they're coming after us. We have to get rid of them, North." She looked at Isolde. "I want another séance. I want to pull them in so we can look at them, find out—"

"Harold's gone," Isolde said. "I can't work without a spirit guide."

"Well, give it a shot," Andie said. "We'll put Flo in the nursery with the kids—"

"Lydia," Isolde said. "I need Flo. I need believers."

"Okay, Lydia, and we'll make it work this time."

It's never worked before.

Andie turned and saw May floating in front of the broken railing. "Thank you. I know you saved me."

If there'd been someone there for me, I wouldn't have died.

"I'm sorry, I really am, May, you got such a raw deal on this. But thank you for stopping me."

Yeah, you owe me, May said, and then smiled her beautiful smile. *You're welcome.*

"Can you be Isolde's spirit guide at the séance?" Andie said.

"Wait a minute," Isolde said.

You should ask Dennis, May said. *He'd love that. He's very career-minded.*

"Dennis," Andie said to Isolde. "Unless he's left us."

"I could do Dennis," Isolde said, and Andie went downstairs to see if he'd gone toward the light yet.

Half an hour later, Lydia was upstairs hearing the Princess Alice story, and Andie, Isolde, Flo, Southie, and a reluctant North were at the table they'd dragged in from the Great Hall and put in front of Dennis's couch which Dennis was refusing to leave.

"I have a bad feeling about this," Isolde said as she sat down across from the couch, looking even paler than usual.

It's a little late for that, isn't it? Dennis said.

"What?" Isolde said, looking around.

"That's Dennis," Andie said. "Are you sure you can do this?"

"Yes?" Isolde pushed her narrow glasses up the narrow bridge of her nose.

"Maybe they'll be feeling guilty for killing Dennis," Southie said.

They don't give a rat's ass, Dennis said.

"Watch the language," Isolde said.

"What language?" Southie said.

"Dennis is grumpy," Andie said.

"Do you want a permanent job, Dennis?" Isolde said.

No.

"He's going toward the light as soon as we're done here," Andie said firmly.

No I'm not.

"Don't be hasty about turning me down," Isolde said. "It's interesting work."

I have a job. I'm researching ghosts.

"Well, you'll meet a lot more with me," Isolde said. "Think about it."

It's a moot point. I can't leave this couch.

"Oh, suck it up, Dennis," Isolde said. "You're too old for a security blanket."

I believe I would know if it were possible for me to establish a wider range.

"You've been a ghost for six hours, but you're an expert," Isolde snorted.

I was an expert before I was a ghost, Dennis snapped.

"Not that I don't find this fascinating," Andie said, "but we need to find out what it is that the ghosts left behind that's keeping them here. Since Dennis had dibs on the couch, it's not that, so let's just leave the furniture out of it for now. We have to be looking for something smaller, a lock of hair maybe, the Victorians did a lot of mourning jewelry. Or . . . a finger or something."

"A finger?" Southie said.

"Probably not. We need to find out what's holding them here so we can burn it and send them on to . . . wherever."

"Are they here?" Isolde said. "It doesn't feel like they're here."

No, Dennis said. *I'm the only one here.*

"Then we'll have to call them. Just remember, they're killers. If things start getting dicey, I'm calling it quits for good on this one."

"Now that is a sane idea," North said.

"Sit down," Isolde said, and he did. "Join hands. Breathe."

The thing about those long slow breaths was that they were very peaceful. Andie relaxed into her chair a little more, but she watched for any movement in the air, any clue that there might—

This again? May said. *You know, you could just ask me.*

"Not you," Andie said. *"Them."*

What do you want?

"Is there something tying them here, some souvenir with a lock of hair or something that would keep them from being evicted?"

It would have had to have come with the house, May said. *That was years and years ago. Something really old. Our family wouldn't have anything that old.*

"Old," Andie said. "Something from the early 1800s."

"Pocket watch," North said.

Andie jerked around, distracted. "What?"

"We found a pocket watch when we searched the house. I'll go get it."

North left the table, clearly glad to be able to do so.

"Good," Isolde said. "With him gone, I can see a lot clearer. What do you think, Dennis?"

I think it's all a crock.

"My God," Andie said. "You're dead and you still don't believe in ghosts?"

I don't believe in the burning of the pocket watch. Victorian mourning jewelry was rings and lockets.

"Lockets," Andie said. "The locket you drew on Miss J is around Alice's neck. I'll be right back." She turned and ran for the stairs, double-timing it up to the nursery, only to see Lydia standing in front of Alice's bed, snarling, *"Get out"* at North, and when Andie said, "What the hell?" he turned around.

North's eyes were empty and black, cruel and evil, and then she saw the pocket watch in his hand and realized she was looking into Peter's white face of damnation. North was gone.

Fifteen

"Get *out of him,*" she said, as he advanced on her. "That's not your body, give it back."

She took a step back, keeping her eyes on the watch in his hand. "We have to burn that watch, Lydia," she called out as her back hit the door. "It's—"

He grabbed for her, and she ducked and tried to knock the watch from his hand, but he got her by the throat, lifting her up off her feet as she choked, her eyes level with his, staring into the empty evil horror that was there. "North," she choked out, but the room began to spin, there was a rushing in her ears, and then suddenly he dropped to the floor and she went with him, and Carter was standing over them with the small fire extinguisher from the mantel.

"I hit him," Carter said, anguished, and North began to struggle to his feet, the back of his head bleeding, and then Miss J was there, too, and Andie felt ice in her veins.

"*No!*" she screamed and grabbed the watch from the floor, triggering the catch so that it opened as she flung it into the fire. She heard Miss J shriek like nothing on God's earth, and then the ice in her blood was gone, but North was reaching for Alice, and Carter and Lydia and Andie all dragged him back while he fought them, and Alice shrank back against the wall, terrified, screaming, *"Bad!"*, as her necklaces swung forward—

Andie lunged over North, still struggling on the floor, and screamed, *"Give me the locket!"*, and Alice ripped it off without question and threw it to her.

North surged up from the floor, Carter and Andie hanging on to him, and Andie flung the locket into the flames.

The locket blackened in the fire, but Peter fought on in North's body, rage distorting his face.

"It didn't work," Andie yelled, grabbing North around the neck and holding on to him while the others fought to keep him down.

"It didn't open," Carter yelled back, and reached into the flames and pulled it out, his face twisting as the fire burned him, and then he stamped on the locket and broke it open, exposing a brown curl of hair inside.

Peter screamed, and Carter threw the curl into the fire where it crackled and then turned to ash, and North collapsed on the floor, unconscious.

Lydia bent over him. *"What the hell was that thing?"*

"A ghost." Andie grabbed the pitcher of ice water from the lunch tray and plunged Carter's hand into it. "That was incredibly brave," she told him. "Keep your hand cold."

"Jesus Christ," Lydia said. *"That was evil."*

Andie left Carter and bent over North, looking at the back of his head as he came to. Carter had really smacked him, there was blood back there, but with any luck he hadn't cracked his skull.

"North?" she said. "North? Honey?"

His eyelids fluttered, and then he said, "Ouch," his voice wobbly, and sat up, wincing, dizzy enough that he leaned on her. "What was that?"

"You were possessed," Andie said. "Didn't you know? Didn't you feel it?"

North put his hand on the back of his head and then pulled it back to look at the blood on it. "I blacked out. What the hell happened?"

"You were possessed and tried to choke me and Carter hit you with a fire extinguisher to save me."

North's eyes widened, and Carter said, "Sorry."

"I'm not," Andie said.

May came to the door and stopped, barred by the fire. *What happened?*

Then Southie was there, staring through May, saying, "What the hell?" and Flo looked at them all from behind him and said, "Oh, no," and went to Carter, and Isolde stood in the doorway next to May and stared.

"So," Lydia said. "Ghosts are real and they can do that?"

It was the pocket watch? May said. *And the locket? Because Miss J and Peter are gone. Really, they're gone. I felt them go. Ask Dennis if you don't believe me. He's down on the couch.*

"We burned the watch but he kept going," Andie said to May.

That makes sense. It was his watch, so he'd put a lock of her hair in there. And she'd put his in her locket.

"They're both gone," Alice said, and sat back, an odd look on her face.

Carter nodded, holding his hand in the ice water, and Flo said, "You've burned yourself, let me take care of that," and Lydia and Southie helped North to his feet.

North turned green and bolted for the bathroom.

"What's wrong?" Lydia said, starting to follow him, and Andie said, "You do that after you've been possessed," and turned back to Alice.

"Are you okay?" she said.

"Yes," Alice said. "You're here."

"So you got rid of them," Isolde said.

Not all of them, May said. *I'm still here.*

Andie looked up at her. "And we're going to talk about that now."

Andie went out into the hall with May. "Remember when you told me that the others had had their humanity burned away? I think you're going that way. You possessed me, and then when I was too strong for you, you possessed Kelly. That's evil, May. That's wrong. From the way the kids have talked about you, that's not who you were."

Well, I wasn't DEAD before.

"It's more than that. You know it's more than that."

I saved your life.

"I know. But what you're doing, staying here, it's wrong. This is not the way it works. You know it's wrong."

May pulled back, doing that shifting thing that always made Andie's stomach turn. *I didn't know my life would be over so fast. It's not my fault. That insane bitch killed me before I had a chance. Everybody deserves a second chance. That's all I want, a second chance.*

"I know," Andie said miserably. "I know all of that, but that's not the way it played out. And the way you're living now . . . You're not living, May. You're just a shadow."

I can't give up. But it's okay, I have a plan.

"May—"

Take me to Columbus, and I'll take Kelly.

"No!"

Andie, I've been inside her and there's nothing there, it's just all this greed and need, and you know how she was after the kids, she's a miserable bitch—

"You can't hijack somebody else's life, May."

—and it's not like I'm getting a great deal there, she must be pushing forty. I'm nineteen, Andie. I had my whole life ahead of me.

"And now it's gone," Andie said, making it sound as final as she could. "You got screwed over, no doubt about it, you deserved so much more, but it's done. It's over."

No!

"Look, maybe there's something wonderful if you move ahead. Maybe if you go toward the light—"

Maybe there's nothing there. Maybe if I go into the light, I really do die.

"You're already dead."

No. No, this is ME. I'm here.

"May. I don't know how to help you. But you can't stay here trying to steal other people's lives."

Don't leave me here.

Andie stared at the girl helplessly. "May, I'm not even sure you can leave here. I think you're tied to the house."

No. No, there's a lock of my hair in my old jewelry box. My mother braided mine and April's together.

"Who's April?"

My sister. Carter and Alice's mother.

Andie looked around. "Is she here, too?"

No, I don't think she stayed after she died. I think she just snuffed out like a candle. I was alive then so I don't know. I didn't even know this existed.

"Maybe she knew what she was doing."

Maybe she just gave up. I'm not giving up.

Andie took a deep breath. "Think this through. If you're tied to that lock of hair, you're stuck wherever the hair is. I can take you to school with me once I start another job, but then you're going to be hanging out listening to high school kids murder Shakespeare. You can stay in the house and watch the kids grow up, but somehow, that doesn't seem like it's enough for you."

It's SOMETHING.

May sounded frantic, which was natural considering what she was facing, but there was an edge there that hadn't been there before, a savagery under the complaint.

"You sound different."

I'm scared. I'm angry. What do you expect?

Andie bit her lip. "What if you're losing your humanity? The others did, they became monsters. You don't want to become a monster—"

They hung around for two hundred years. You'll be dead before I start to lose it. Then we can really talk.

"We don't know that," Andie said. "We don't—"

So you're saying no.

"I'm saying you're not where you're supposed to be. You're not supposed to be stuck between two planes living a shadow life. This is wrong for you. It's wrong for everybody. And if we don't fix it, if you don't move on, I think things could get really bad."

May was silent, and even worse, Andie couldn't see her moving. It was as if May had finally stopped dancing. Maybe because she was starting to think.

"May?"

I don't want to move on.

"Okay." Andie got up. "It's your choice. But I can't take you to Columbus. It's just wrong, May. You'll have to stay here."

I hate it here. I've been stuck here in this stupid town and then this stupid house all my life.

"And when your life ended, you should have been free."

You're taking Dennis back.

"Not necessarily," Andie said, exasperated, "I'm trying to talk him toward the light, too. You're both being stubborn. But if he insists, I'll take him back to his home in Cleveland. He doesn't belong here, he was just visiting. But first I'm going to try to talk him into going."

Would you go?

"Yes."

How can you know?

"Because I wouldn't ever want to be stuck watching somebody

else live. Because if there's a new adventure ahead of me, I want to go toward it. Because living like a shadow would make me insane."

So you'd just let go.

"It's what people who die are supposed to do. Not hang on to the past. Go toward the future."

What if there isn't any future?

"I think there's something in the light. And I think because it's light, it's probably good. Or at least interesting and not eternal damnation in some sadist's idea of an afterlife. That is just something somebody dreamed up to keep other people in line."

You don't think there's a hell.

"I don't see how a hell makes sense. What's the point of tormenting souls forever? Where's the poetry in that, what use is it? If there is a guiding intelligence that created this world, which is amazing, why would it design eternal pain and torment for the next one? It's just a stupid concept."

To punish the bad people.

"Forever?" Andie said, getting impatient. "What good is that? That's just vengeance, it doesn't accomplish anything. The whole hell thing annoys me, it's such a power play."

May was quiet for a long while, and finally Andie said, "May?"

All right.

Andie hesitated, and when May didn't say anything else, she went to check on Dennis. She'd have to be insane to take May back to Columbus with her. Even thinking about taking Dennis was crazy but at least he belonged up north. Well, no he didn't. He belonged on the other side. Wherever that was.

"Dennis?" she said at the door of the sitting room.

You got rid of them. Good for you.

"You can tell they're gone."

Yes. They're gone. It's much better here now.

"It's still Hell House, Dennis. Now, about you."

Don't worry about me, Dennis said. *I can stay. I'm not going to kill anybody.*

"Right," Andie said and went back upstairs to the kids, meeting Flo on the first flight of stairs as she went to get bandages for Carter; and Lydia on the second flight, carrying the lunch tray down.

"North's throwing up in the bathroom," Lydia said.

"Well, it's his turn," Andie said and went up to the nursery.

When she opened the nursery door, the fire was off, and May was there with Alice and Carter.

"Hey!" Andie said, but May said, *All right.*

"All right what?"

I'll move on. Alice has the lock of hair.

Alice held out a thick, dark curl, her face sober.

"Did you tell them what it means?" Andie said.

They know. I just need one favor from you.

"All right," Andie said cautiously.

I want to hug them good-bye.

"Okay. Go ahead."

No, really hug them. I want to borrow your body.

"No!" Andie took a step back. "No. You did it before and it was horrible. No."

Andie, I'm never going to see them again. This is the end for us. You don't have anything to worry about. I'll go. Even if I didn't, you're stronger than I am. You can get rid of me any time you want.

Andie looked back at the kids, standing silent and miserable. They'd never had a chance to say good-bye, she was their last close family member, maybe it would help them—

I just want to hug them.

Andie swallowed. "All right."

Thank you, May said. *Just relax.*

"That's not happening," Andie said, and felt the cold in her bones again, felt May fill her as she shivered, saw everything go black and white, and then May was lifting her arms over her head, stretching to feel her muscles.

"A body," May said. "You don't know how awful it is not to have a body!"

Yes, I do, Andie said. *Make this fast. This is horrible.*

May turned toward the kids and Andie went with her, feeling her body follow somebody else's command, the nausea rising again from the sheer wrongness of it. May bent down and hugged Alice, and the little girl hugged her back.

"Keep your promise," she whispered in Andie's ear, and May said, "I will."

Then May straightened and held out Andie's arms to Carter. "Come say good-bye, Carter!"

Carter turned and walked away.

"Carter!" May called. "It's me. It's not Andie, it's *me.*"

He turned back at the door. "I'd hug Andie," he said and walked out.

"He's just upset," May said to Alice.

"You promised," Alice said.

Promised what? Andie said. *What's going on?*

"That I wouldn't keep your body," May said, and let go, and Andie slumped from the relief of it, the cold leaving her as May went.

She was weak and nauseous but she was the only one in her head again.

Thank you, May said, and then Carter came back in.

"You okay?" he said to Andie.

"Yes," Andie began, and Carter took the curl from Alice and put it in the fire. May took one sorrowful look back and vanished, and Andie said, "Wait! May! I'm sorry. Good luck . . . May?"

The curl turned to ash, and there was nothing there.

"Oh," she said, looking at the kids. "She's gone. Are you all right?"

Carter turned and left.

"We're okay," Alice said, and followed him.

"Wait a minute," Andie said, but they'd just lost their aunt, really lost her this time, and if they wanted to talk about it, they'd tell her. *Hell, I want to talk about it,* she thought, but the only person she really wanted to talk to was North and he was throwing up with a concussion.

So she got boxes and went through the nursery cupboards, packing up everything she found that was theirs, and when the kids came back half an hour later, she said, "I'm packing. We can go to Columbus now, right?"

Carter nodded, and she took a deep breath, just from the relief of it all.

"It'll be okay now," she told Carter, but his face was a mask again. "You'll like Columbus," she told Alice.

Alice nodded and held Rose Bunny closer.

Andie kissed her cheek, and Alice suddenly wrapped her arms around Andie's neck and pulled her down.

"I love you, Andie," she said.

"I love you, too, baby," Andie said, blinking back tears. "It'll all be all right now, I swear."

Alice nodded and said, "Can I have a box? I'll pack my clothes."

"There's more in the hall," Andie told her, thinking, *It's safe to go into the hall because the ghosts are gone.*

When she turned, Carter was watching them, his jaw set.

"I love you, too," she told him. "I know you don't believe me, but I'll make it all right for you, I swear."

"I believe you," he said, and went out to the hall and picked up two boxes, even as Flo came up and said, "Oh, honey, be careful of your hand."

It was going to be all right. They were packing. It was over.

And May was gone forever, all that gaiety and passion burned away in an instant.

I'm sorry, May, Andie thought, and went to pack her own things.

By eight, the kids were packed, fed, and put to bed, ready to leave the next morning.

"I can't believe we're really going," Andie said to North when she went into May's bedroom. "How's your head?"

"Bashed in," North said, sitting up in bed. "But I've stopped throwing up. Tell me again why Carter hit me with a fire extinguisher?"

"Just get some sleep. You have a lot of stuff to move tomorrow."

"Are the kids okay?"

Andie nodded. "I think they're relieved, but it's hard to tell. They had a rough day."

"They're good kids," North said. "We'll take them home and keep them safe, and in a while, they'll be—"

"Normal? Not a chance." Andie climbed into bed beside him and stretched. "God, I'm tired."

She reached over and turned out the light and settled in beside him. There was a long silence and then he said, "You're coming back, too, right? You're moving in with us?"

"Yes," she said.

"Good."

She lay in the darkness next to him, and thought about the future. She'd been concentrating so long on getting the kids out of the house, and now they were going to be out of the house and she had to look at the next problem. No matter what North said, he was going to get caught up in work again, she had to accept that. He was a hard worker, that was one of the things she loved about him. She could make him eat with the kids every night, she could force him to remember them, but she was going to have to live with him spending more time with his desk than he did with her. *This has to be enough,* she thought, and decided it was. Even if it all happened the way it did the last time, this time she could stand it. She was different now.

North's voice came out of the dark. "You all right?"

"I'm just fine." She rolled to face him and felt his hand slide under her waist. "I'm just thinking about the future."

"It'll be different this time," he said. "I swear, I won't make the same mistakes."

"Me, either. We'll make different ones, though. But it doesn't matter, I'll stick this time. We were just too young and we got married too fast. And I was unrealistic. I wanted to be adored, and that's just not your style. Which I would have known if I'd gotten to know you first. I was just . . . immature." She sighed. "And then I got the guy who adored me with Will and I didn't like that, either. I don't know what I want. Besides you. I want you. I know I want you."

He was quiet for so long that she thought he'd fallen asleep, and then he said, "I lost your scent first. I kept your pillowcase unwashed for three weeks and then Lydia sent in the cleaners and it was gone. It's hard to remember scent. I dated a woman for a month once, Lydia and Southie despised her, and I didn't like her much, but I couldn't let go until Southie pointed out that she used the same shampoo you did. Sense memory. She smelled like you."

"Oh," Andie said.

"I kept your voice longer. At least a year. And after that I got a tape, you'd done that morning show for the school, remember? I got the tape so I could hear your voice. Close my eyes and think you were in the same room. But it was a tape and it didn't sound quite right and I lost your voice."

"North—"

"I never lost your face."

Andie went up on one elbow to face him, not sure what was going on. "It's okay."

"I adored you," North said. "I just didn't tell you. You were the most amazing thing that had ever happened to me. Nothing else like you in my world before or since. I was crazy about you. I still am. Ten years later you walk into my office and I see you and it's like the first time, I can't think, I can't talk, I just need you *with me*. It makes me crazy, but now that I've got you back . . . You're everything, Andie. I should have told you that before."

"Oh," Andie said, swallowing back tears. "I still have your T-shirt. The one I bought you at the Jackson Browne concert. You used to sleep in it and when I left, I took it because I wanted something of yours. I've never washed it. I keep finding it every time I unpack and I think, 'I should throw that out,' but I can't. And I still have the ring." She held up her hand, knowing he couldn't see it in the dark but wanting to show him anyway.

"It's a terrible ring," North said, his voice thick.

"I love this ring," Andie said, her throat thick, too. "I love you. I loved you then, too, so much. That's why it hurt so much when you left me, I loved you so much and I thought you didn't love me, but I've never stopped loving you, North, never even for a moment, I—"

He pulled her to him and kissed her hard, and she clung to him.

"This time we'll do it right," he said to her. "We won't do it over, we'll do it new. This time, we'll make it."

"Yes, please," she said, and believed it.

"I swear," he said and kissed her again, and she moved against him, wanting him again.

"How bad does your head feel?" she whispered to him.

"It feels fine," he said and pulled her down to him and loved her.

Andie got downstairs early the next morning in time to catch Isolde before she left. "Call me when you get to Columbus," she said, handing Andie her card. "If you ever need help. Or make banana bread and want company."

"I will do that," Andie said, and meant it.

Then she went back into the house, passing North and Southie and Carter carrying boxes to the cars, and stopped in the sitting room to deal with her last loose end.

She said, "Dennis?," prepared to convince him to embrace the afterlife.

Good morning.

"Dennis, we're leaving."

Yes, I know.

Andie smiled at where she thought he was. "I'm thinking maybe you should, too."

With you?

"No, I was thinking more of the next plane of existence for you. The kids and I are going to Columbus. It's not the same thing."

I might like Columbus.

Andie sat down. "I'm worried about you not going toward the light. I'm afraid you're going to miss it."

It's not a bus, Andie, it's the afterlife.

"Yes, but isn't Somebody going to get pissed if you keep rejecting the invitation?"

I don't think so. Dennis sounded thoughtful. *I think I was taken before my time, so I have some leeway. It's not like it was a natural death.*

"Stop rationalizing, Dennis. I'm pretty sure death doesn't have a no-fair clause." If it had, May would have used it.

I want to go to Columbus with Alice and Carter and you.

"Dennis, be reasonable."

I'm dead. I don't have to be reasonable. The fact of my continued existence is in itself unreasonable.

"Okay. Let me think." Really, it was pretty much a choice between Columbus and the afterlife. Unless . . . "How about this: Harold's gone, so Isolde needs a spirit guide. If you'd . . . attach to her in some way, you could stay with her. She left already, but she said she'd keep in touch. Maybe—"

I'm not sure about spending the rest of my life with Isolde.

"The rest of your life is over," Andie said. "And I don't think she'd hold you captive. Harold was there willingly."

Harold ran like a rabbit the first chance he got.

"Fine. You have any ideas on how we can pack you up and take you with us?"

I'm tied to this couch.

"Isolde says you aren't. She said you're using it as a security blanket."

And this is the woman you want me to spend eternity with.

"She has a point. I don't see any other ghosts tied to furniture."

Just lockets and pocket watches.

"Which were portable," Andie pointed out. "And also contained parts of their . . . bodies. You didn't cut your nails on the couch, did you?"

The silence stretched out.

"Okay, fine, be snitty," Andie said. "But I don't think we can tie this thing to the top of Lydia's Lexus."

"I'm packing up the bedroom next," North said, coming in from the flagstoned yard. "Did you want that plaque over the bed, the 'Always Kiss Me Good Night' thing?"

"God, no," Andie said.

"Good. What can't you tie to the top of Lydia's Lexus?"

"What? Oh. This couch. Dennis won't go toward the light, won't go with Isolde, and won't leave the couch."

"Uh huh," North said, and went through the dining room into the kitchen.

Andie looked back in the general direction of Dennis. "I keep forgetting he doesn't believe in ghosts."

He never will. He's too rational. He's going to miss a lot that way.

"Says the guy who didn't believe in them when he was alive."

I've learned. I've grown. I'm a better person now.

"Dennis, you're not a person. And I am seriously worried about your afterlife. May told me that the longer a ghost hangs around, the less humanity it has. That's why she went willingly. She didn't want to turn into a monster."

That's not going to happen to me.

"Really. Why not?"

I have no passion.

That was so true that Andie felt suddenly sad for him, which was ridiculous because he was dead.

The others turned because the reason they stayed was their passion. It was the tie holding them to this plane, so when everything else evaporated, that's all that was left.

"Uh huh," Andie said, considering this. "So what's tying you here?"

Intellectual curiosity.

"I see. So when your humanity burns away . . ."

You'll have a supernatural encyclopedia on your couch.

"Oh, Dennis," Andie said, laughing in spite of herself. "Look, we—"

North came through on his way to the outside. "New Essex has a rental place with a van available. Southie and I will go get it. We'll put Dennis and his couch in there. Southie came down in Kelly's car, so he'll drive my car back and I'll take the van. If there's anything else you want from here, now's the time to mention it. We'll stick that in the van, too."

"Uh, make sure you put the bolsters in, too, I think they're part of the couch," Andie said, stunned, and then North was gone. She turned back to Dennis. "Do you believe that? He got you a van."

No, he got you a van. He doesn't believe in me, but he believes in you. And you need a van.

"Damn," Andie said. "You're right."

I'm always right.

"Fine." Andie turned for the door and then stopped. "I'm really glad you're coming with us. I think it would be better for you if you went on to the next plane or whatever, but selfishly, I'm glad we're going to have you around."

Thank you, Dennis said, sounding touched.

"But work on separating yourself from the couch, will you? It would make everything so much easier," Andie said and went to look for Alice and Carter.

Andie climbed the stairs and found Alice in her room, Rose Bunny under one arm, and her comforter under the other. There was more comforter than there was Alice, so Andie said, "I'll carry that," and Alice handed it over.

"Your suitcase is in my car," Andie told her. "And your box of toys. The rest of your stuff is in Grandma Flo's car. Grandmother Lydia has Carter's things. And Bad and Southie are putting Dennis and the couch in the rental van now. They've even got the bolsters, everything's out there. We're ready to go." She waited for Alice to say something, but the little girl just looked around. "Are you ready to go, Alice?"

Alice was quiet for a moment and then she nodded. Andie held out her hand and Alice took it, and they walked down the wide stone staircase for what Andie sincerely hoped was the last time ever.

"Columbus will be better," she told Alice quietly, not sure why she was keeping her voice low.

"Will there be butterflies?" Alice said.

"Yes," Andie said. "In the spring, there'll be butterflies, just like here. And a butterfly garden, just like here." *Except for the salvia.*

Alice nodded.

When they went out the back door, Lydia was putting on her gloves by the driver's side door. "Carter's going to ride with North in the van," she said to Andie.

"Okay," Andie said and opened the door to her Mustang. "Alice, are you ready to go?"

Alice looked around again, as if she were listening for something, and then Carter got out of the van and came toward her. She lifted up her face as he came up to her. "It's okay. Get in the car."

Don't back out now, baby, Andie prayed, and Alice crawled into the front seat.

"What's wrong?" she said to Alice, and the little girl looked at her for a long minute and then shook her head.

"You're okay with us all leaving here," Andie said.

Alice nodded.

"Then let's go."

Andie waved to North who waved back and got in the driver's seat of the van. Carter went around to the other side of the van and Andie heard the door slam. Southie came out of the house with a last box, put it in the back of the van, slammed the doors and then smacked the side, and North began to pull out onto the bridge.

There's something wrong, Andie thought. The kids were too quiet. Everything was too quiet. She looked around but there was nothing, no Miss J, no Peter, no May. They were gone. They really were.

"I don't get it," she said, and Southie heard her and came over.

"What's wrong?"

"Something," she said. "But I don't know what."

"Is it something you can deal with in Columbus?" Southie said, genial as ever.

"If it isn't, we'll find out when we try to leave."

"Then let's leave and find out."

North had slowed the van just before it went into the trees, and Carter leaned out and yelled, "Come *on!*"

"Follow me out," Southie told his mother, and Andie got in the car with Alice, made sure her seat belt was on, and belted herself in. Through the window she saw Southie get in North's car and start up the drive toward the van, and then Flo got in her car and followed, and Lydia followed behind her. Andie said, "You ready to go, Alice?" and Alice said, "Yes," and Andie started the car, and thought, *We're not going to get out of here. Something will stop us.*

The line of cars wound down through the trees and then up to the road, each one gunning its motor to make it up the insane incline, and then Andie gunned the motor and the Mustang shot forward and they were actually out of the drive. She braced herself for what was to come, some supernatural gatekeeper swooping down to snatch Alice away from her, but the only things that swooped were the crows in the trees, circling and cawing at them as they drone away.

She looked over at the little girl. Alice had pulled her comforter over her, up to her chin, and was looking quiet and tense, only her pale little face showing above the blue chiffon.

"I was afraid we wouldn't get out," she told Alice.

"It's okay," Alice said. "We can go to Columbus."

"You'll like it," Andie told her. "They painted your bedroom blue."

Alice nodded, and Andie looked in her rearview mirror.

There was nothing back there, just an empty stretch of road.

Did I imagine all of that? she thought, and kept an eye on the rearview until she turned onto the main highway and the idea of ghosts coming after them seemed ridiculous.

So it's over, Andie thought and leaned back, trying to get all the foreboding out of her brain.

"It'll be okay," Alice said from beside her.

She knows something, Andie thought. *That's why she keeps saying that.* "How do you know?"

"I just know," Alice said and closed her eyes and went to sleep.

Sixteen

By the time Andie pulled up in front of the Victorian, North and Carter were already carrying in the couch with its bolsters, past shrieking kids in their Halloween costumes.

"It's Halloween," Andie said to Alice as she helped her with her seat belt. "Next year, we'll dress up, too. And see? Dennis is even here. Carter's helping to carry the couch in."

Alice nodded and slipped out of her seat, still clutching Rose Bunny.

"I'll get your comforter," Andie called to her, and Alice nodded and walked toward the house.

Andie got out and met Lydia on the walk.

"Is she all right?" Lydia said, watching Alice's straight, sturdy little back. "She seems quiet."

"It might just be the change," Andie said, watching Alice go up the steps to the porch. "Kids aren't good with change. I don't know."

"Well, she's safe now," Lydia said briskly, and went toward the house.

Flo went past carrying a box for Carter and said, in passing, "I still think there's an Emperor in this somewhere."

"I'm sure there is," Andie said, and then Southie said, "How's Alice?", and Andie turned and saw him carrying Carter's box of art supplies toward her.

"Very quiet," Andie said.

Southie shook his head. "That's not our Alice. North said Carter was quiet, too, but he's always quiet."

"Maybe not this quiet," Andie said, and followed him into the house.

She found Alice standing at the bottom of the stairs, looking around.

"You okay, honey?" she said.

"I like this wallpaper," Alice said solemnly.

Since the wallpaper was a faded red Victorian nightmare of a pattern, Andie said, "Oh, good. Your room is upstairs."

Alice went up the first two treads and then stopped to look into the reception room.

Andie craned her neck to look, too. They must have moved the old couch out because Dennis's green striped settee was in its place, its bolsters snugged against its arms.

"Good night, Dennis," Alice called.

Good night, Alice. Welcome to Columbus.

Alice nodded and went up the stairs, and Andie followed.

"Here's your room," Lydia said, opening a door, and Alice stopped on the threshold.

Andie looked past her to see pale blue walls and ceiling painted with clouds, and a white four-poster bed draped in a blue-sequined chiffon canopy.

"Do you like it?" Lydia said, and Andie thought she was actually anxious about it.

"It's bee-you-tee-ful," Alice said, sincerity in every syllable, and then she crossed the room and sat down on the bed and bounced a little. "I love it."

Lydia smiled, and Andie walked across the hall to the other open door.

Carter sat on a solid wood bed, his striped comforter already thrown across it, but he was staring at the wall on the other side of the door, so Andie stepped in to see what he was looking at.

A huge drawing table with an adjustable lamp was in the center of the wall, flanked by floor-to-ceiling shelves filled with art supplies and books.

"North had a local art store do it," Lydia said from behind her. "I thought it was overdone, but evidently not."

"You okay, Carter?" Andie said.

He looked at her, his face drawn. "It's great."

"What's wrong?" she said, and he shook his head.

"This is really great," he said, and he sounded sincere.

"Give him some time to settle in," Lydia said.

"Sure," Andie said, and gave him one more anxious look before she went to help unpack the cars.

They'll be okay, she told herself, *everything's fine, the nightmare's over, they'll be okay.*

When they were unpacked, they ordered pizza in, and then Alice said, "We should play Go Fish, I will teach you," and Southie said, "What are we, amateurs?" and they played Go Fish for an hour, North bringing gravity to the game, shaking his head solemnly at Alice because he had no eights.

I'm happy, Andie thought, *it's all right now,* and when the kids were ready for bed, she stood in the hall between their rooms and said, "Really, it's all right now."

Carter went into his room, but Alice said, "Okay," and hugged her.

"Love you, Andie," she said when Andie tucked her in, and Andie said, "Love you, too, baby," and went downstairs to the reception room.

"Dennis?"

Yes?

"Are you feeling all right?"

I can't feel anything. I'm dead.

"Right, sorry. I just wanted to make sure—"

A light in the office caught her eye and she took a couple of steps so she could see through the doorway.

North was in there, sorting through papers, but when he looked up and saw her, he dropped them. "How are the kids?" he said, as he came around the desk to meet her.

"Weird. Also, from now on you are out of here every night at five o'clock, no exceptions. Dinner with me and the kids every night."

She braced herself for the argument to come, but he said, "How about six? I meet you and the kids in the dining room for dinner, we help them with their homework and play Go Fish until eight, the kids go to bed, and then it's you and me."

She lost her breath for a moment. "I thought you'd argue."

"Am I stupid?" He put his arms around her. "That was a long, cold ten years you were gone, Andromeda."

She held on to him, amazed all over again that she had him back. "Yes, it was. What about the practice?"

"Southie's got a law degree. It's time he used it. We can cut our client list. Beyond that, I don't care. I'm done living for the firm."

"God, I love you," Andie said, stretching up for his kiss, and then she heard Dennis cough out in the reception hall and say, *It would be good if I had something to read.*

"Dennis is out there," Andie said to North as he leaned down to kiss her.

"Right. Dennis is on the couch," North said, clearly not buying that Dennis was on the couch. Being possessed hadn't done a thing for him.

"You don't have to believe it, just accept it."

"I accept it," North said, letting go of her. "Look, I have to go through this stuff to get caught up on what I've missed. Are you going to take it personally if I do that now?"

"Nope," Andie said. "Lydia left bananas for me, so I am going to go make banana bread in my kitchen. I missed that kitchen."

"So if I meet you upstairs in an hour, I get hot banana bread and sex?"

"The bread definitely," Andie said. "The sex, I don't know. I might not be in the mood. You know me." *If you're there, I'm in the mood.*

"I know you," North said and kissed her, and she cuddled close and thought, *It really is okay. It really is,* and kissed him back.

I'm right here, Dennis said. *At least give me something to read and close the door.*

"Dennis needs some attention," she told North and went out into the reception room. "Books would be useless, Dennis, you can't turn pages."

Maybe a computer screen.

"You can't scroll."

Fine, I'll just sit here in the dark.

"Don't be passive aggressive, Dennis, it's unattractive. I will work something out for you, I swear. For tonight, just . . . explore your options. Maybe you have hidden talents."

Unlikely.

"Good *night,* Dennis," Andie said, and looked back through the office door.

North said, "One hour. You upstairs, naked with banana bread."

"You're on," Andie said, and went down the hall to the kitchen she'd left ten years before.

Everything was going to be different this time. Except her banana bread.

The kitchen was just as she'd remembered it, and Lydia's bananas were exactly the right amount of brown. She got out her mixing bowl and reached for the radio, a good station this time, she thought, since they were back in Columbus—

The cold knifed through her, and she gasped, and May was everywhere, flowing through her veins, staring out from behind her eyes, filling her, blotting her out.

Stop! Andie said, but no words came out because May had taken her tongue.

May stretched Andie's body to feel it move. "*God,* this is good."

Get out, get out, get out NOW! She gave a frantic shake for air and light, but May smothered her, held her.

"Oh, please. I gave you every chance. I told you I wouldn't quit, and you really thought I'd just give up?"

Andie pushed back frantically, trying to push May out, and May laughed as she expanded her hold, and Andie's world went black and white, full of icy cold filling her like the taste of poison.

"You really think you evicted me that night at the house with North? I quit because you threw up, you idiot. You have no idea what I can do. You think Crumb put the salvia in your tea? Half the time you were talking to her, it wasn't her at all, *it was me!*"

NO, Andie screamed, but she was blocked everywhere she turned, her own thoughts drowning in May's—

"Andie?" Alice said, and May turned around to see the little girl in her nightgown.

Run, Andie thought, but Alice couldn't hear her.

"I want to make banana bread, too," Alice said, pulling a chair over to the counter.

"We can't, honey," May said brightly. "See? The bananas are all brown."

Alice froze climbing onto the chair.

"We'll get new yellow ones tomorrow," May went on, but Alice was backing away. "What's wrong?"

Run, Andie screamed at her.

"Nothing," Alice said. "I'm just very tired. We'll make banana bread tomorrow."

She walked out of the kitchen calmly, and then Andie heard her on the stairs. Running.

"I blew that one," May said. "What'd I do wrong?"

Get out of my body! Andie screamed at her.

"You have two choices here," May said. "You can share this body with me, or you can fight me and I'll smother you and take it all for myself. Which, frankly, is what I'd like. I know it's mean, but a girl has to live."

Stay away from Alice! Stay away from my kids!

"Hey, they were my kids first. I love those kids. I'll take good care of them. And I'll be better to North than you ever were. I'll *like* the things he wants to give me, I'll *like* being his wife."

NO, this is MY LIFE, Andie raged, but she could feel the sound echo as her body felt farther away, and her view of the world became scratchier, like a battered old black-and-white film.

"You weren't even using it. Don't be a dog in the manger." May smiled at her reflection in the dark window over the kitchen sink. "It'll be all right. In a little while, you won't even know. I held on to Crumb too long once and she almost stroked out. I think the part that's you will just . . . fade away. You said you'd rather die than be a shadow."

You're not going to do this, I'll stop you—

"You can't. This is one thing you can't fix. So just go toward the light, honey. I have it on very good authority that there's something wonderful over there."

"Who are you talking to?" North said from the doorway.

May whirled around. "Nobody! Just myself. You know what a flake I am!"

"I never thought of you as a flake."

He came into the kitchen and May went to him and put her arms—*My arms,* Andie thought—around him.

Andie thought, *He'll know,* but she knew he wouldn't, there was no way he could know, he didn't believe in ghosts, and May had been studying her for a month, watching the two of them together for four days, and she was smart. May wouldn't make mistakes.

"Boy, are you cold," North said and rubbed her arms.

"Make me warm then," May said and kissed him, pressing her— *MY!*—body against him.

North kissed her back, the deep, longing kiss that always made Andie's knees weak, and she could feel May respond, feel her own body respond, but it wasn't her. *NO, it's not me, it's not me, STOP!,* but when he pulled back, he looked deep into her eyes, and she thought, *He can't see me. He couldn't see me when it was me, he'll never see me now.*

North pushed against her with his hips, trapping her against the counter, his body hard on hers, and Andie thought, *She's winning,* she was drowning in black and white, the cold immobilizing her, as if she were trapped in May's cold, dead body . . .

"Tell me what you remember," he said to her.

"What?" May said, and he kissed her again, and she smiled.

"Tell me what you remember about us," he said, "tell me what you've missed."

You don't remember anything, Andie taunted her. *You don't know him. You don't know us.*

"I missed this," May said, grinding her hips against his. "I missed you, lover."

"Tell me something we did that you want to do again, something just for us." He smiled into her eyes.

"Uh, dancing. I love dancing with you. And . . . baking. And . . ."

You don't know, Andie said, and grew a little warmer, not warm, but not quite so freezing cold, as May began to panic.

"I don't care about the past, make love to me," May whispered to North, sliding her hand down his chest. "You know you want to."

North caught her hand. "Not even when you were alive," he said and held her as she jerked away. "I want Andie back. *Now.*"

Oh, thank God!

Andie could feel May's grip loosen more from the shock. *He knows,* Andie taunted her, trying to find her way back. *He knows you're not me. He doesn't love you*—May's grip loosened more—*He'll never love you*—Almost, almost—*He loves me!*

"North, are you *crazy?*" May said, fighting back. "This is *me.* This is *Andie. I love you!*"

"You don't know a damn thing about love," North said, colder than Andie had ever seen him.

"I could learn," May said, pressing against him now. "You could teach me. I could love you—"

He loves me, Andie whispered inside May's head. *He loves me. It's me he wants to kiss good night.*

"You're not my wife," North said, gripping her harder.

"It's her *body,*" May was saying desperately. "It's all you need. I'm more fun. I have her body—"

"You're not her," North said, his face grim as he held her, "and I will send you to hell to get her back."

May tried to yank away, and Andie felt the cold grow again. "Well, you can't. There's nothing you can do. I'm *Andie*—"

"You're Aunt May," Carter said from behind them, and North turned so that Andie could see him coming toward them, his lighter in his hand, Alice crying behind him.

"I'm sorry, Andie," Alice said. *"I'm sorry."*

Look what you're doing to Alice! Andie said, trying to find whatever humanity was left in May.

Carter's face was stolid. "She made us hide a piece of her hair in Alice's Walkman before we burned the rest of it."

Look what you're doing to Carter!

"Shut up!" May screamed.

"I'm sorry," Alice cried. "Andie, Andie, *I'm sorry.*"

You're torturing Alice, Andie whispered to May.

"I'm Andie," May said, desperate now. *"I'm Andie."*

"You *promised,*" Alice sobbed. "You promised you wouldn't do this, you *promised!*"

She doesn't love you, Andie whispered. *You betrayed her, you lost her love, you've lost everything now. Nobody loves you, you're a monster, nobody loves you—*

"No!" May said, but she was weakening, Andie could feel warmth again, and color flickered in front of her now.

North said to Carter, "What do we have to do?" and Carter held out his hand to Alice.

Alice hesitated, then put her Walkman on the table and unsnapped the blue leatherette cover.

"No," May said, lunging for it, but North held her, and Andie took back more of herself as they struggled, surrounded by people who loved her.

They love me, she whispered. *They want me. Who do you love? Nobody. Who kisses you good night? NOBODY.*

"Carter." May reached for him, but North grabbed her arm. "Carter, *please,* I deserve to have this. I *love you.*"

"So does Andie," he said, cold as ice. "And she's alive. Let go. Or . . ." He clicked his lighter and the flame spurted high.

"No!" May said.

"Do it," North said to Carter, and Carter took the curl, and May screamed, *"NO!"* and slammed her elbow into North's stomach, shoving him back, falling as she ripped the lighter from Carter's hand. Carter caught her, held her, wrapping his arms around Andie's body and saying, "Andie! *Andie!*" as May struggled to reach the curl. Andie held on to the sound of Carter's voice, and clawed her way back into her body, fighting May now with everything she had, and then she saw Alice holding the curl, weeping, little Alice, tears streaming down her face as she looked at them, and then Carter said, *"There!"* nodding at the lighter, and she picked it up from the floor, and flicked it open, and the flame shot up.

"*Alice, no!*" May howled, like the cry of a creature hurled over an abyss, and then Alice put the curl into the flame and held it while it seared her fingers, staring at Andie, and Andie felt the flame everywhere, blue and red, and then she was back in her body, clinging to Carter as the world swung around, and she screamed at May, "*Go toward the light, damn it!*" and May cried out, "*There is no light!*"

And then May was gone, heat rushing back, color and sound, and Andie was free again.

"Andie?" Carter said, and she put her head on his shoulder, exhausted and dispossessed, and said, "It's me," and saw North boosting Alice up on the counter and running cold water over her burned fingers.

"Andie?" Alice said, her voice full of tears.

"You saved me," Andie said to her, her voice shaky as she held on to Carter and fought the nausea that was swamping her. "You and Carter. You were so brave, and you saved me."

"She's gone," Carter said stolidly. "Right?"

"Yes," Andie said. "It's over." She took a deep breath. "And now I'm going to throw up."

She shoved herself up off the floor and bolted for the powder room, and behind her she heard North say, "Good job, Carter," while he cooled the burn on Alice's fingers.

After throwing up everything she'd eaten all day and then standing under a hot shower in the attic bathroom for twenty minutes, Andie pulled herself together, toweled off, brushed her teeth, put on her pajamas, and came out to face North who was sitting on the edge of the bed waiting for her in the quiet night.

"You okay?"

"I will be." She went over and sat down beside him, and he put his arm around her.

"Well, the good news is, now I believe in ghosts."

"You knew it wasn't me," she said, and felt the tears press against the back of her eyes again.

"Of course I knew," he said, sounding insulted. "I asked the questions just to make sure, but I could see it wasn't you from your eyes. It was obvious."

"She looked just like me. She *was* me."

He moved his arm against her neck and pulled her over to him and kissed her on the top of the head. "She wasn't anything like you. Should we get you a doctor? Did she strain your heart?"

Andie looked up at him, tears in her eyes. "Whatever she did to my heart, you fixed it."

"You sure?"

"I'm positive," Andie said, and he kissed her again, solid and sure, and she thought, *He knows me,* and kissed him back.

"Get into bed," he said finally. "You need rest."

"I need you," she told him. "But I need to see Alice and Carter first."

"I talked to them. I told them what they did was brave and that they saved you." He tightened his arms around her. "They really are amazing kids."

"You have no idea," Andie said.

"Well, I'm going to. I'll have years with them to find out." He stood up. "Want me to go with you?"

Andie shook her head and stood up, too. "I'll just be a minute. Don't wait up. Make the bed warm for me." She tried a smile, and he bent and kissed her again, and she thought, *Oh, thank God, he knows me,* and then she went downstairs to the kids' rooms.

"Carter?" she said, knocking softly on his door, and he said, "Come in."

He was sitting on his bed, holding his bandaged hand, looking exhausted, but finally at peace.

"That was really brave," she began, and he shook his head.

"I should have stopped it." He sounded older, serious, and Andie got a glimpse of the adult he'd become. "I knew she wasn't gone, but—"

"She was your aunt," Andie said, coming to sit on the side of his bed. "She was the last family you had left."

"She was dead," Carter said. "And she wasn't the last. We have you. And North." He tried to make the last two words casual, but there was respect there.

"Yes, you do," Andie said, vowing not to cry. "And Southie."

"And Lydia," Carter said, not sounding as sure, and Andie laughed and then he did, too. "No, she's cool."

"She's a good person to have on your side," Andie said. "Like you're a good person to have on mine. I'll never forget this, Carter." She leaned forward and kissed his cheek. "Never. Now go to sleep. You're starting school next week."

"*Already?*" he said, appalled, and she laughed again and ruffled his hair and made him duck away.

"Sleep tight," she said, and went to talk to Alice.

Alice's room was empty.

Andie felt a clutch of panic and then got a grip. Alice would not run away, Alice would not leave the house, Alice would never leave Carter, Alice—

She heard voices from below and went to the head of the stairs. There was light in the hallway, as if from another room, and she went down to the ground floor and into the law office's reception room.

She's in the office, Dennis said.

"Did she tell you—"

About May? Yes. Sorry, I never saw her. I was in the van with North and Carter. She must have been in the car with you. And then she didn't come in here—

"She wasn't stupid. What's Alice doing?"

Talking to Merry.

"Who the hell is Merry?"

I don't know. They're in the office. I'm stuck to the couch, remember?

"Right." Andie went to the door of North's office, trying not to panic. She was really too damn tired to panic.

Alice was sitting in the chair across from North's desk, talking to North's desk chair. "I'm not going to remember all of that," she said. "I'm *eight*."

"Remember what?" Andie said, and Alice turned around and smiled, all her tension gone, and Andie thought, *She's all right, she smiled.*

"Merry has a lot of stuff he wants me to tell Bad."

"Merry who?" Andie said, keeping a wary eye on the empty desk chair. "Nobody named Merry . . ."

Something moved in the desk chair and she saw, in flickers, the patterned waistcoat, the cigar, and heard a fat under-the-breath laugh that she hadn't heard in over ten years. *"Uncle Merrill?"*

Alice looked across the desk and then back at Andie. "He says you're looking good, Andie."

Andie looked at the desk chair, trying to organize the shifting shadows there. "You've been there for *ten years*?"

Alice listened and nodded. "He has a lot of stuff he wants to say."

"Yeah, well, North has a few things he'd like to say to you, too. And also, I know about Southie. What the hell were you thinking?"

Alice listened and then said, "He says not to be such a prune. Why are you a prune?"

"Prude," Andie said. "Merrill, you should meet Dennis, he's out in Reception. I doubt if you'll bond, he's a good guy, but later on, I'll kill a deck of cards and you can play gin. Don't cheat. For now, Alice goes to bed."

Alice got up. "It was very nice meeting you, Merry," she said, and then walked over and took Andie's hand. "I'm very sorry," she said, looking up at Andie, but she seemed confident now that she was loved.

"You did the right thing," Andie said, knowing she meant May. "And it's okay now. From now on everything's going to be . . ." She looked back at North's desk chair that was swiveling gently, and then in the other direction, into Reception at Dennis's couch. ". . . normal."

"That's good," Alice said and went up the stairs with her, and when Andie tucked her into bed, she said, "I like this room. Can I draw on the walls?"

"You'll have to negotiate that with Lydia."

"Oh, hell," Alice said and scooted under the covers with Rose Bunny.

Two minutes later, Andie crawled into North's warm bed and sighed in relief.

North slid his arm under her shoulders and pulled her closer. "Everything okay?"

"Everything is perfect," she said, cuddling against him. "Well, almost. Your uncle Merrill has been haunting your office for ten years."

"Joke?"

"No, for real. I can't see him, but Alice can. He has a lot to tell you, Alice says."

"Yeah, well, I have a lot to tell that old bastard, too," North said. "I suppose this means he's been watching everything I've done since he died."

"Including all the sex we had on that desk. Knowing Merrill, he'll probably be critiquing your style and my thighs."

"There is nothing wrong with my style," North said, running his hand down her side. When he reached her hip, he said, "And there's definitely nothing wrong with your thighs."

She laughed and he kissed her, and she thought, *Thank God I found my way back to him,* and then he held her tighter, and she said, "North?"

"I didn't have a damn clue how to save you," he said. "If the kids hadn't been here, she could have—"

"We'd have found a way," Andie said. "She wasn't just up against us, she was up against Fate. We're supposed to be together. Will you marry me again?"

His hand tightened on her hip, and when she went up on one elbow to meet his eyes without blinking, saying, "I'm sure, I really am," he said, "Yes."

"Good," Andie said, snuggling down into the covers he'd made warm for her. "We should have the wedding here. Small ceremony, just family. That way Merrill and Dennis can come, too."

"Wonderful," North said, and turned out the light.

"You going to sleep?" Andie said, putting her hand on his chest.

"You had a rough night," he said and kissed her on the forehead.

"Not that rough," Andie said, and pulled his mouth down to hers, kissing him hard.

"Now we're back to normal," North said, and Andie wrapped herself around him and thought, *Now I'm home,* and made love with her husband in the attic, while her family slept below.

It was close to midnight, the clock ticking loudly in the dark kitchen, the game of solitaire on the big table lit only by one steadily burning candle, when Mrs. Crumb lifted her head to listen.

"You're back, are you?" She gathered up the cards and began to shuffle them.

How the hell did I get back here?

Mrs. Crumb stopped shuffling long enough to hold up the old church envelope that had been on the bulletin board by the phone. "I cut an extra lock of hair from your head that night you fell through the railing. You died bad. I thought I might need it if you walked."

Jesus Christ—

"You know I don't like that kind of language."

Fuck you. You don't even belong here. They threw you out.

Mrs. Crumb shrugged. "They're never coming back. They'll never see this place again. I got my social security to live on."

So now I'm trapped with you? Goddammit!

Mrs. Crumb pushed the envelope toward the other side of the table. "You don't like it, take me and make me burn it."

The silence stretched out.

"That's what I thought. From now on, you just remember, any time I want to, I can snuff you out like a candle."

After a moment, the candle on the table flickered as if somebody had passed behind it.

Mrs. Crumb nodded. "That's what I thought." She leaned back and got the card rack from the drawer behind her and put it in front of the chair across from her.

"It's my deal," she said, and began to pass out the cards.